Praise for *The Couple Next Door*

"Where did that baby go! It's hard not to read to the end to find out, and the twists waiting there are gratifyingly clever."
—*USA Today*

"The twists come as fast as you can turn the pages."
— *People*

""Shari Lapena has written a stunning debut thriller. Turn on the night lights and lock all your doors and windows. *The Couple Next Door* grabs you with each twist and shocks you with every betrayal."
—Linda Fairstein, *New York Times* bestselling author of *Killer Look*

"Expertly paced and finely crafted, *The Couple Next Door* is a gripping thriller of the highest order. I couldn't put it down."
—A. J. Banner, bestselling author of *The Good Neighbor*

"Gripped me from the very beginning to the very end!"
—Becky Masterman, author of *Rage Against the Dying*

"Brilliant! This utterly riveting psychological thriller hurtles along at breakneck speed, never giving you the opportunity to catch your breath. Twisty, turny, and unputdownable."
—C. L. Taylor, bestselling author of *The Lie*

THE COUPLE NEXT DOOR

Shari Lapena worked as a lawyer and as an English teacher before turning to writing fiction. Her suspense debut, *The Couple Next Door*, as well as her second novel, *A Stranger in the House*, were *New York Times* and international bestsellers. Lapena's next book, *An Unwanted Guest*, is forthcoming in summer 2018.

THE
COUPLE
NEXT
DOOR

SHARI LAPENA

SEAL BOOKS

SEAL BOOKS, 2018

Copyright © 2016 1742145 Ontario Limited

Seal Books with colophon is a registered trademark of
Penguin Random House Canada.

THE COUPLE NEXT DOOR
Seal Books/published by arrangement with Penguin Random House Canada
Doubleday Canada edition published 2016

Library and Archives Canada Cataloguing in Publication available
upon request

ISBN 978-1-4000-2688-3

Cover design by Roseanne Serra
Cover image © Yulia Tsernant / Eyeem / Getty Images
Text design by Alissa Rose Theodor

Printed and bound in the USA

Seal Books are published by Penguin Random House Canada.
"Seal Books" and the portrayal of a seal are the property of
Penguin Random House Canada.

www.penguinrandomhouse.ca

2 4 6 8 9 7 5 3

Penguin
Random House
SEAL BOOKS

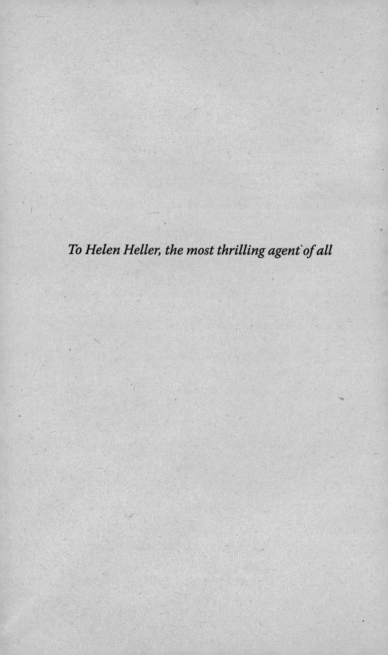

To Helen Heller, the most thrilling agent of all

Acknowledgments

I owe thanks to so many. To Helen Heller, agent extraordinaire—thank you for everything. Heartfelt thanks also to everyone at the Marsh Agency for their superb representation worldwide.

Huge thanks to Brian Tart, Pamela Dorman, and all the people at Viking Penguin (U.S.). Huge thanks also to Larry Finlay and Frankie Gray at Transworld U.K. and the fabulous team there. Thanks also to Kristin Cochrane, Amy Black, Bhavna Chauhan, and the supportive team at Doubleday Canada. I have the great good fortune to have wonderful marketing and publicity teams on both sides of the Atlantic.

Thanks to Ilsa Brink for Web site design.

I'm also very grateful to my first readers—Leslie Mutic, Sandra Ostler, and Cathie Colombo.

And of course, I couldn't have written the book at all without the support of my family.

THE
COUPLE
NEXT
DOOR

ONE

Anne can feel the acid churning in her stomach and creeping up her throat; her head is swimming. She's had too much to drink. Cynthia has been topping her up all night. Anne had meant to keep herself to a limit, but she'd let things slide—she didn't know how else she was supposed to get through the evening. Now she has no idea how much wine she's drunk over the course of this interminable dinner party. She'll have to pump and dump her breast milk in the morning.

Anne wilts in the heat of the summer night and watches her hostess with narrowed eyes. Cynthia is flirting openly with Anne's husband, Marco. Why does Anne put up with it? Why does Cynthia's husband, Graham, allow it? Anne is angry but powerless; she doesn't know how to put a stop to it without looking pathetic and ridiculous. They are all a little tanked. So she ignores it, quietly seething, and sips at the chilled wine. Anne wasn't brought up to create a scene, isn't one to draw attention to herself.

Cynthia, on the other hand . . .

All three of them—Anne, Marco, and Cynthia's mild-mannered husband, Graham—are watching her, as if fascinated. Marco in particular can't seem to take his eyes off Cynthia. She leans in a little too close to Marco as she bends over and fills his glass, her clingy top cut so low that Marco's practically rubbing his nose in her cleavage.

Anne reminds herself that Cynthia flirts with everyone. Cynthia has such outrageous good looks that she can't seem to help herself.

But the longer Anne watches, the more she wonders if there could actually be something going on between Marco and Cynthia. Anne has never had such suspicions before. Perhaps the alcohol is making her paranoid.

No, she decides—they wouldn't be carrying on like this if they had anything to hide. Cynthia is flirting more than Marco is; he is the flattered recipient of her attentions. Marco is almost too good-looking himself—with his tousled dark hair, hazel eyes, and charming smile, he's always attracted attention. They make a striking couple, Cynthia and Marco. Anne tells herself to stop it. Tells herself that of course Marco is faithful to her. She knows he is completely committed to his family. She and the baby are everything to him. He will stand by her no matter what—she takes another gulp of wine—no matter how bad things get.

But watching Cynthia drape herself over Marco, Anne is becoming more and more anxious and upset. She is still more than twenty pounds overweight from her pregnancy, six months after having the baby. She thought she'd be back to her pre-pregnancy figure by now, but apparently it takes at least a year. She must stop looking at the tabloids at the grocery-store checkout and comparing herself to all those celebrity moms with their personal trainers who look terrific after mere weeks.

But even at her best, Anne could never compete with the likes of Cynthia, her taller, shapelier neighbor—with her long legs, nipped-in waist, and big breasts, her porcelain skin and tumbling jet-black hair. And Cynthia always dressed to kill, in high heels and sexy clothes—even for a dinner party at home with one other couple.

Anne can't focus on the conversation around her. She tunes it out and stares at the carved marble fireplace, exactly like the one in her own living-dining room, on the other side of the common wall that Anne and Marco share with Cynthia and Graham; they live in attached brick row houses, typical of this city in upstate New York, solidly built in the late nineteenth century. All the houses in the row are similar—Italianate, restored, expensive—except that Anne and Marco's is at the end of the row and each reflects slight differences in decoration and taste; each one is a small masterpiece.

Anne reaches clumsily for her cell phone on the dining table and checks the time. It is almost one o'clock in the morning. She'd checked on the baby at midnight. Marco had gone to check on her at twelve thirty. Then he'd gone out for a cigarette on the back patio with Cynthia, while Anne and Graham sat rather awkwardly at the littered dining table, making stilted conversation. She should have gone out to the backyard with them; there might have been a breeze. But she hadn't, because Graham didn't like to be around cigarette smoke, and it would have been rude, or at least inconsiderate, to leave Graham there all alone at his own dinner party. So for reasons of propriety, she had stayed. Graham, a WASP like herself, is impeccably polite. Why he married a tart like Cynthia is a mystery. Cynthia and Marco had come back in from the patio a few minutes ago, and Anne desperately wants to leave, even if everyone else is still having fun.

She glances at the baby monitor sitting at the end of the table, its small red light glowing like the tip of a cigarette. The video screen is smashed—she'd dropped it a couple of days ago and Marco hadn't gotten around to replacing it yet—but the audio is still working. Suddenly she has doubts, feels the wrongness of it all. Who goes to a dinner party next door and leaves her baby alone in the house? What kind of mother does such a thing? She feels the familiar agony set in—*she is not a good mother.*

So what if the sitter canceled? They should have brought Cora with them, put her in her portable playpen. But Cynthia had said no children. It was to be an adult evening, for Graham's birthday. Which is another reason Anne has come to dislike Cynthia, who was once a good friend—Cynthia is not baby-friendly. Who says that a six-month-old baby isn't welcome at a dinner party? How had Anne ever let Marco persuade her that it was okay? It was irresponsible. She wonders what the other mothers in her moms' group would think if she ever told them. *We left our six-month-old baby home alone and went to a party next door.* She imagines all their jaws dropping in shock, the uncomfortable silence. But she will never tell them. She'd be shunned.

She and Marco had argued about it before the party. When the sitter called and canceled, Anne had offered to stay home with the baby—she hadn't wanted to go to the dinner anyway. But Marco was having none of it.

"You can't just stay home," he insisted when they argued about it in their kitchen.

"I'm fine staying home," she said, her voice lowered. She didn't want Cynthia to hear them through the shared wall, arguing about going to her party.

"It will be good for you to get out," Marco countered, lowering his own voice. And then he'd added, "You know what the doctor said."

All night long she's been trying to decide whether that last comment was mean-spirited or self-interested or whether he was simply trying to help. Finally she'd given in. Marco persuaded her that with the monitor on next door they could hear the baby anytime she stirred or woke. They would check on her every half hour. Nothing bad would happen.

It is one o'clock. Should she check on Cora now or just try to get Marco to leave? She wants to go home to bed. She wants this night to end.

She pulls her husband's arm. "Marco," she urges, "we should leave. It's one o'clock."

"Oh, don't go yet," Cynthia says. "It's not that late!" She obviously doesn't want the party to be over. She doesn't want Marco to leave. She wouldn't mind at all if Anne left, though, Anne is pretty sure.

"Maybe not for you," Anne says, and she manages to sound a little stiff, even though she's drunk, "but I have to be up early to feed the baby."

"Poor you," Cynthia says, and for some reason this infuriates Anne. Cynthia has no children, nor has she ever wanted any. She and Graham are childless by choice.

Getting Marco to leave the party is difficult. He seems determined to stay. He's having too much fun, but Anne is growing anxious.

"Just one more," Marco says to Cynthia, holding up his glass, avoiding his wife's eyes.

He is in a strangely boisterous mood tonight—it seems almost forced. Anne wonders why. He's been quiet lately, at home. Distracted, even moody. But tonight, with Cynthia, he's the life of the party. For some time now, Anne has sensed that something is wrong, if only he would tell her what it is. He isn't telling her much of anything these days. He's shutting her out. Or maybe he's withdrawing from her because of her depression, her "baby blues." He's disappointed in her. Who isn't? Tonight he clearly prefers the beautiful, bubbly, sparkly Cynthia.

Anne notices the time and loses all patience. "I'm going to go. I was supposed to check on the baby at one." She looks at Marco. "You stay as late as you like," she adds, her voice tight. Marco looks sharply at her, his eyes glittering. Suddenly Anne thinks he doesn't seem that drunk at all, but she feels dizzy. Are they going to argue about this? In front of the neighbors? Really? Anne begins to glance around for her purse, gathers up the baby monitor, realizes then that it's plugged into the wall, and bends over to unplug it, aware of everyone at the table silently staring at her fat ass. Well, let them. She feels like they're ganging up on her, seeing her as a spoilsport. Tears start to burn, and she fights them back. She does not want to burst into tears in front of everyone. Cynthia and Graham don't know about her postpartum depression. They wouldn't understand. Anne and Marco haven't told anyone, with the exception of Anne's mother. Anne has recently confided in her. She knows that her mother won't tell anyone, not even her father. Anne doesn't want anyone else to know, and she suspects Marco doesn't either, although he hasn't said as much. But pretending all the time is exhausting.

While her back is turned, she hears Marco's change of heart in the tone of his voice.

"You're right. It's late, we should go," he says. She hears him set his wineglass on the table behind her.

Anne turns around, brushing the hair out of her eyes with the back of her hand. She desperately needs a haircut. She gives a fake smile and says, "Next time it's our turn to host." And adds silently, *You can come to our house, where our child lives with us, and I hope she cries all night and spoils your evening. I'll be sure to invite you when she's teething.*

They leave quickly after that. They have no baby gear to gather up, just themselves, Anne's purse, and the baby monitor, which she shoves into it. Cynthia looks annoyed at their swift departure—Graham is neutral—and they make their way out the impressively heavy front door and down the steps. Anne grabs hold of the elaborately carved handrail to help her keep her balance. It is just a few short paces along the sidewalk until they are at their own front stairs, with a similar handrail and an equally impressive front door. Anne is walking slightly ahead of Marco, not speaking. She may not speak to him for the rest of the night. She marches up the steps and stops dead.

"What?" Marco says, coming up behind her, his voice tense.

Anne is staring. The front door is ajar; it is open about three inches.

"I know I locked it!" Anne says, her voice shrill.

Marco says tersely, "Maybe you forgot. You've had a lot to drink."

But Anne isn't listening. She's inside and running up the staircase and down the hall to the baby's room, with Marco right at her heels.

When she gets to the baby's room and sees the empty crib, she screams.

Two

Anne feels her scream inside her own head and reverberating off the walls—her scream is everywhere. Then she falls silent and stands in front of the empty crib, rigid, her hand to her mouth. Marco fumbles with the light switch. They both stare at the empty crib where their baby should be. It is impossible that she not be there. There is no way Cora could have gotten out of the crib by herself. She is barely six months old.

"Call the police," Anne whispers, then throws up, the vomit cascading over her fingers and onto the hardwood floor as she bends over. The baby's room, painted a soft butter yellow with stencils of baby lambs frolicking on the walls, immediately fills with the smell of bile and panic.

Marco doesn't move. Anne looks up at him. He is paralyzed, in shock, staring at the empty crib, as if he can't believe it. Anne sees the fear and guilt in his eyes and starts to wail—a horrible, keening sound, like an animal in pain.

Marco still doesn't budge. Anne bolts across the

hall to their bedroom, grabs the phone off the bed-side table, and dials 911, her hands shaking, getting vomit all over the phone. Marco finally snaps out of it. She can hear him walking rapidly around the second floor of the house while she stares across the hall at the empty crib. He checks the bathroom, at the top of the stairs, then passes quickly by her on his way to search the spare bedroom and then the last room down the hall, the one they have turned into an office. But even as he does, Anne wonders in a detached way why he is looking there. It's as if part of her mind has split off and is thinking logically. It's not like their baby is mobile on her own. She is not in the bathroom, or the spare bedroom, or the office.

Someone has taken her.

When the emergency operator answers, Anne cries, "Someone has taken our baby!" She is barely able to calm herself enough to answer the operator's questions.

"I understand, ma'am. Try to stay calm. The police are on their way," the operator assures her.

Anne hangs up the phone. Her whole body is trembling. She feels like she is going to be sick again. It occurs to her how it will look. They'd left the baby alone in the house. Was that illegal? It must be. How will they explain it?

Marco appears at the bedroom door, pale and sick-looking.

"This is your fault!" Anne screams, wild-eyed, and pushes past him. She rushes into the bathroom at the top of the stairs and throws up again, this time into the pedestal sink, then washes the mess from her shaking hands and rinses her mouth. She catches a glimpse of herself in the mirror. Marco is standing right behind her. Their eyes meet in the mirror.

"I'm sorry," he whispers. "I'm so sorry. It's my fault."

And he is sorry, she can tell. Even so, Anne brings her hand up and smashes at the reflection of his face in the mirror. The mirror shatters, and she breaks down, sobbing. He tries to take her in his arms, but she pushes him away and runs downstairs. Her hand is bleeding, leaving a trail of blood along the banister.

An air of unreality permeates everything that happens next. Anne and Marco's comfortable home immediately becomes a crime scene.

Anne is sitting on the sofa in the living room. Someone has placed a blanket around her shoulders, but she's still trembling. She is in shock. Police cars are parked on the street outside the house, their red lights flashing, pulsing through the front window and circling the pale walls. Anne sits immobile on the sofa and stares ahead as if hypnotized by them.

Marco, his voice breaking, has given the police a quick description of the baby—six months old, blond, blue eyes, about sixteen pounds, wearing a disposable diaper and a plain, pale pink onesie. A light summer baby blanket, solid white, is also missing from the crib.

The house is swarming with uniformed police officers. They fan out and methodically begin to search the house. Some of them wear latex gloves and carry evidence kits. Anne and Marco's fast, frantic race through the house in the short minutes before the police arrived had turned up nothing. The forensic team is moving slowly. Clearly they are not looking for Cora; they are looking for evidence. The baby is already gone.

Marco sits down on the sofa next to Anne and puts his arm around her, holds her close. She wants to pull away, but she doesn't. She lets his arm stay there. How would it look if she pulled away? She can smell that he's been drinking.

Anne now blames herself. It's her fault. She wants to blame Marco, but she agreed to leave the baby alone. She should have stayed home. No—she should have brought Cora with them next door, to hell with Cynthia. She doubts Cynthia would have actually thrown them out and had no party for Graham at all. This realization comes too late.

They will be judged, by the police and by everybody else. Serves them right, leaving their baby alone. She would think that, too, if it had happened to someone else. She knows how judgmental mothers are, how good it feels to sit in judgment of someone else. She thinks of her own mothers' group, meeting with their babies once a week in one another's homes for coffee and gossip, what they will say about her.

Someone else has arrived—a composed man in a well-cut dark suit. The uniformed officers treat him with deference. Anne looks up, meets his piercing blue eyes, and wonders who he is.

He approaches and sits down in one of the armchairs

across from Anne and Marco and introduces himself as Detective Rasbach. Then he leans forward. "Tell me what happened."

Anne immediately forgets the detective's name, or rather it hasn't registered at all. She only catches "Detective." She looks at him, encouraged by the frank intelligence behind his eyes. He will help them. He will help them get Cora back. She tries to think. But she can't think. She is frantic and numb at the same time. She simply stares into the detective's sharp eyes and lets Marco do the talking.

"We were next door," Marco begins, clearly agitated. "At the neighbors'." Then he stops.

"Yes?" the detective says.

Marco hesitates.

"Where was the baby?" the detective asks.

Marco doesn't answer. He doesn't want to say.

Anne, pulling herself together, answers for him, the tears spilling down her face. "We left her here, in her crib, with the monitor on." She watches the detective for his reaction—*What awful parents*—but he betrays nothing. "We had the monitor on over there, and we checked on her constantly. Every half hour." She glances at Marco. "We never thought . . ." but she can't finish. Her hand goes to her mouth, her fingers press against her lips.

"When was the last time you checked on her?" the detective asks, taking a small notebook from the inside pocket of his suit jacket.

"I checked on her at midnight," Anne says. "I remember the time. We were checking on her every half hour, and it was my turn. She was fine. She was sleeping."

"I checked on her again at twelve thirty," Marco says.

"You're absolutely certain of the time?" the detective asks. Marco nods; he is staring at his feet. "And that was the last time anyone checked on her, before you came home?"

"Yes," Marco says, looking up at the detective, running a nervous hand through his dark hair. "I went to check on her at twelve thirty. It was my turn. We were keeping to a schedule."

Anne nods.

"How much have you had to drink tonight?" the detective asks Marco.

Marco flushes. "They were having a small dinner party, next door. I had a few," he admits.

The detective turns to Anne. "Have you had anything to drink tonight, Mrs. Conti?"

Her face burns. Nursing mothers aren't supposed to drink. She wants to lie. "I had some wine, with dinner. I don't know how much exactly," she says. "It was a dinner party." She wonders how drunk she looks, what this detective must think of her. She feels like he can see right through her. She remembers the vomit upstairs in the baby's room. Can he smell drink on her the way she can smell it on Marco? She remembers the shattered mirror in the upstairs bathroom, her bloodied hand, now wrapped in a clean dish towel. She's ashamed of how they must look to him, drunken parents who abandoned their six-month-old daughter. She wonders if they will be charged with anything.

"How is that even relevant?" Marco says to the detective.

"It might affect the reliability of your observations," the detective says evenly. He is not judgmental. He is merely after the facts, it seems. "What time did you leave the party?" he asks.

"It was almost one thirty," Anne answers. "I kept checking the time on my cell. I wanted to go. I . . . I should have checked on her at one—it was my turn—but I thought we'd be leaving any minute, and I was trying to get Marco to hurry up." She feels agonizingly guilty. If she had checked on her daughter at one o'clock, would she be gone now? But then there were so many ways this could have been prevented.

"You placed the call to 911 at one twenty-seven," the detective says.

"The front door was open," Anne says, remembering.

"The front door was open?" the detective repeats.

"It was open three or four inches. I'm sure I locked it behind me when I checked on her at midnight," Anne says.

"How sure?"

Anne thinks about it. *Was* she sure? She had been positive, when she saw the open front door, that she'd locked it. But now, with what had happened, how can she be sure of anything? She turns to her husband. "Are you sure you didn't leave the door open?"

"I'm sure," he says curtly. "I never used the front

door. I was going through the back to check on her, remember?"

"You used the back door," the detective repeats.

"I may not have locked it every time," Marco admits, and covers his face with his hands.

Detective Rasbach observes the couple closely. A baby is missing. Taken from her crib—if the parents, Marco and Anne Conti, are to be believed—between approximately 12:30 a.m. and 1:27 a.m., by a person or persons unknown, while the parents were at a party next door. The front door had been found partly open. The back door might have been left unlocked by the father—it had in fact been found closed but unlocked when the police arrived. There is no denying the distress of the mother. And of the father, who looks ~~badly~~ shaken. But the whole situation doesn't feel right. Rasbach wonders what is really going on.

Detective Jennings waves him over silently. "Excuse me," Detective Rasbach says, and leaves the stricken parents for a moment.

"What is it?" Rasbach asks quietly.

Jennings holds up a small vial of pills. "Found these in the bathroom cabinet," he says.

Rasbach takes the clear plastic container from Jennings and studies the label: ANNE CONTI, SERTRALINE, 50 MG. Sertraline, Rasbach knows, is a powerful antidepressant.

"The bathroom mirror upstairs is smashed," Jennings tells him.

Rasbach nods. He hasn't been upstairs yet. "Anything else?"

Jennings shakes his head. "Nothing so far. House looks clean. Nothing else taken, apparently. We'll know more from forensics in a few hours."

"Okay," Rasbach says, handing the vial of pills back to Jennings.

He returns to the couple on the sofa and resumes his questioning. He looks at the husband. "Marco—is it okay if I call you Marco?—what did you do after you checked on the baby at twelve thirty?"

"I went back to the party," Marco says. "I had a cigarette in the neighbors' backyard."

"Were you alone when you had your cigarette?"

"No. Cynthia came out with me." Marco flushes; Rasbach notices. "She's the neighbor who had us over for dinner."

Rasbach turns his attention to the wife. She's an attractive woman, with fine features and glossy brown hair, but right now she looks colorless. "You don't smoke, Mrs. Conti?"

"No, I don't. But Cynthia does," Anne says. "I was sitting at the dining-room table with Graham, her husband. He hates cigarette smoke, and it was his birthday, and I thought it would be rude to leave him alone inside." And then, inexplicably, she volunteers, "Cynthia had been flirting with Marco all evening, and I felt bad for Graham."

"I see," Rasbach says. He studies the husband, who looks utterly miserable. He also looks nervous and guilty. Rasbach turns to him. "So you were outside in the backyard next door shortly after twelve thirty. Any idea how long you were out there?"

Marco shakes his head helplessly. "Maybe fifteen minutes, give or take?"

"Did you see anything or hear anything?"

"What do you mean?" The husband seems to be in some kind of shock. He is slurring his words slightly. Rasbach wonders just how much alcohol he's had.

Rasbach spells it out for him. "Someone apparently took your baby sometime between twelve thirty and one twenty-seven. You were outside in the backyard next door for a few minutes shortly after twelve thirty." He watches the husband, waits for him to put it together. "To my mind it's unlikely that anyone would carry a baby out your front door in the middle of the night."

"But the front door was open," Anne says.

"I didn't see anything," Marco says.

"There's a lane running behind the houses on this side of the street," Detective Rasbach says. Marco nods. "Did you notice anyone using the lane at that time? Did you hear anything, a car?"

"I . . . I don't think so," Marco says. "I'm sorry, I didn't see or hear anything." He covers his face with his hands again. "I wasn't paying attention."

Detective Rasbach had already checked out the area quickly before coming inside and interviewing the parents. He thinks it unlikely—but not impossible—that a stranger would carry a sleeping child out the front door of a house on a street like this one and risk being seen. The houses are attached row houses set close to the sidewalk. The street is well lit, and there is a fair bit of vehicular and foot traffic, even late at night. So it is odd—perhaps he's being deliberately misled?—that the front door was open. The forensics team is dusting it for fingerprints now, but somehow Rasbach doesn't think they'll find anything.

The back holds more potential. Most of the houses, including the Contis', have a single detached garage opening onto the lane—behind the house. The backyards are long and narrow, fenced in between, and most, including the Contis', have trees and shrubs and gardens. It is relatively dark back there; there are no streetlights as there are in the front. It's a dark night, with no moon. Whoever has taken the child, if he had come out the Contis' back door, would only have had to walk across the backyard to the garage, with access from there to the lane. The chances of being seen carrying an abducted child out the back door to a waiting vehicle are much less than the chances of being seen carrying an abducted child out the front door.

The house, yard, and garage are being thoroughly searched by Rasbach's team. So far they have found no sign of the missing baby. The Contis' garage is empty, and the garage door has been left wide open to the lane. It's possible that even if someone had been sitting out back on the patio next door, he or she might not have noticed anything. But not likely. Which narrows the window of the abduction to between approximately 12:45 and 1:27 a.m.

"Are you aware that your motion detector isn't working?" Rasbach asks.

"What?" the husband says, startled.

"You have a motion detector on your back door, a light that should go on when someone approaches it. Are you aware that it isn't working?"

"No," the wife whispers.

The husband shakes his head vigorously. "No, I . . . it was working when I checked on her. What's wrong with it?"

"The bulb has been loosened." Detective Rasbach watches the parents carefully. He pauses. "It leads me to believe that the child was taken out the back, to the garage, and away, probably in a vehicle, via the lane." He waits, but neither the husband nor the wife says anything. The wife is shaking, he notices.

"Where is your car?" Rasbach asks, leaning forward.

"Our car?" Anne echoes.

THREE

Rasbach waits for their answer.

She answers first. "It's on the street."

"You park on the street when you've got a garage in back?" Rasbach asks.

"Everybody does that," Anne answers. "It's easier than going through the lane, especially in the winter. Most people get a parking permit and just park on the street."

"I see," Rasbach says.

"Why?" the wife asks. "What does it matter?"

Rasbach explains. "It probably made it easier for the kidnapper. If the garage was empty and the garage door was left open, it would be relatively easy for someone to back a car in and put the baby in the car while the car was in the garage, out of sight. It would obviously be more difficult—certainly riskier—if the garage already had a car in it. The kidnapper would run the risk of being seen in the lane with the baby."

Rasbach notices that the husband has turned another shade paler, if that is even possible. His pallor is quite striking.

"We're hoping we will get some shoe prints or tire tracks from the garage," Rasbach adds.

"You make it sound like this was planned," the mother says.

"Do you think it wasn't?" Rasbach asks her.

"I . . . I don't know. I guess I thought Cora was taken because we left her alone in the house, that it was a crime of opportunity. Like if someone had snatched her from the park when I wasn't looking."

Rasbach nods, as if trying to understand it from her point of view. "I see what you mean," he says. "For example, a mother leaves her child playing in the park while she fetches an ice cream from the ice-cream truck. The child is snatched while her back is turned. It happens." He pauses. "But surely you realize the difference here."

She looks back at him blankly. He has to remember that she is probably in shock. But he sees this sort of thing all the time; it is his job. He is analytical, not at all sentimental. He must be, if he is to be effective. He will find this child, dead or alive, and he will find whoever took her.

He tells the mother, his voice matter-of-fact, "The difference is, whoever took your baby probably knew she was alone in the house."

The parents look at each other.

"But nobody knew," the mother whispers.

"Of course," Rasbach adds, "it is possible that she might have been taken even if you were sound asleep in your own bedroom. We don't know for sure."

The parents would like to believe that it isn't their fault after all, for leaving their baby alone. That this might have happened anyway.

Rasbach asks, "Do you always leave the garage door open like that?"

The husband answers. "Sometimes."

"Wouldn't you close the garage door at night? To prevent theft?"

"We don't keep anything valuable in the garage," the husband says. "If the car's in there, we generally lock the door, but we don't keep much in there otherwise. All my tools are in the basement. This is a nice neighborhood, but people break into garages here all the time, so what's the point of locking it?"

Rasbach nods. Then he asks, "What kind of car do you have?"

"It's an Audi," Marco says. "Why?"

"I'd like to have a look. May I have the keys?" Rasbach asks.

Marco and Anne regard each other in confusion. Then Marco gets up and goes to a side table near the front door and grabs a set of keys from a bowl. He hands them over to the detective silently and sits back down.

"Thank you," Rasbach says. Then he leans forward and says deliberately, "We will find out who did this."

They stare back at him, meeting his eyes, the mother's entire face swollen from crying, the father's eyes puffy and bloodshot with distress and drink, his face pasty.

Rasbach nods to Jennings, and together they leave the house to check the car. The couple sit on the sofa silently and watch them go.

Anne doesn't know what to make of the detective. All this about their car—he seems to be insinuating something. She knows that when a wife goes missing, the husband is usually the prime suspect, and probably vice versa. But when a child goes missing, are the parents usually the prime suspects? Surely not. Who could harm their own child? Besides, they both have solid alibis. They can be accounted for, by Cynthia and Graham. There is obviously no way they could have taken and hidden their own daughter. And why would they?

She is aware that the neighborhood is being searched, that there are police officers going up and down the streets knocking on doors, interviewing people roused from their beds. Marco has provided the police with a recent photo of Cora, taken just a few days ago. The photo shows a happy blond baby girl with big blue eyes smiling up at the camera.

Anne is angry at Marco—she wants to scream at him, pummel him with her fists—but their house is full of police officers, so she doesn't dare. And when she looks at his pale, bleak face, she sees that he is already blaming himself. She knows she can't survive this on her own. She turns to him and collapses into his chest, sobbing. His arms come up around her, and he hugs her tightly. She can feel him shaking, can feel the painful thumping of his heart. She tells herself that together they will get through this. The police will find Cora. They will get their daughter back.

And if they don't, she will never forgive him.

Detective Rasbach, in his lightweight summer suit, steps out the front door of the Contis' house and down the steps into the hot summer night, closely followed by Detective Jennings. They have worked together before. They have each seen some things that they would like to be able to forget.

Together they walk toward the opposite side of the street, lined with cars parked bumper-to-bumper. Rasbach presses a button, and the headlights of the Audi flash briefly. Already the neighbors are out on their front steps, in their pajamas and summer bathrobes. Now they watch as Rasbach and Jennings walk toward the Contis' car.

Rasbach hopes that someone on this street might know something, might have seen something, and will come forward.

Jennings says, his voice low, "What's your take?"

Rasbach answers quietly, "I'm not optimistic."

Rasbach pulls on a pair of latex gloves that Jennings hands him and opens the door on the driver's side. He looks briefly inside and then silently walks to the back of the car. Jennings follows.

Rasbach pops open the trunk. The two detectives look inside. It's empty. And very clean. The car is just over a year old. It still looks new.

"Love that new-car smell," Jennings says.

Clearly the child isn't there. That doesn't mean she hadn't been there, however briefly. Perhaps forensic investigation will reveal fibers from a pink onesie, DNA from the baby—a hair, a trace of drool, or maybe blood. Without a body they will have a tough case to make. But no parents ever put their baby in the trunk with good intentions. If they find any trace of the missing child in the trunk, he will see that the parents rot in hell. Because if there's anything Rasbach has learned in his years on the job, it is that people are capable of almost anything.

Rasbach is aware that the baby could have gone missing at any time before the dinner party. He has yet to question the parents in detail about the previous day, has yet to determine who, other than the parents, last saw the child alive. But he will find out. Perhaps there is a mother's helper who comes in, or a cleaning lady, or a neighbor—someone who saw the baby, alive and well, earlier that day. He will establish when the baby was last known to be alive and work forward from there. This leaving the monitor on, checking every half hour while they dined next door, the disabled motion detector, the open front door, it could all simply be an elaborate fiction, a carefully constructed fabrication of the parents, to provide them with an alibi, to throw the authorities off the scent. They might have killed the baby at any time earlier that day—either deliberately or by accident—and put her in the trunk and disposed of the body before going to the party next door. Or, if they were still thinking clearly, they might not have put her in the trunk at all but in the car seat. A dead baby might not look that different from a sleeping baby. Depending on how they killed her.

Rasbach knows that he's a cynic. He hadn't started out that way.

He says to Jennings, "Bring in the cadaver dogs."

Four

Rasbach returns to the house, while Jennings checks in with the officers on the street. Rasbach sees Anne sobbing on the end of the sofa, a woman police officer sitting beside her with her arm across Anne's shoulders. Marco is not with her.

Drawn by the smell of fresh coffee, Rasbach makes his way to the kitchen at the back of the long, narrow house. The kitchen has obviously been remodeled, and fairly recently; it is all very high-end, from the white cabinetry to the expensive appliances and granite counters. Marco is in the kitchen, standing by the coffeemaker with his head down, waiting for it to finish brewing. He looks up when Rasbach comes in, then turns away, perhaps embarrassed by such an obvious attempt to sober up.

There is an awkward silence. Then Marco asks quietly, without taking his eyes off the coffeemaker, "What do you think has happened to her?"

Rasbach says, "I don't know yet. But I'll find out."

Marco lifts the coffeepot and pours coffee into three china mugs on the spotless stone counter. Rasbach notices that Marco's hand trembles as he pours. Marco offers the detective one of the mugs, which Rasbach accepts gratefully.

Marco leaves the kitchen and returns to the living room with the other two mugs.

Rasbach watches him go, steeling himself for what is ahead. Child-abduction cases are always difficult. They create a media circus, for one thing. And they almost never end well.

He knows he will have to apply pressure to this couple. It's part of the job.

Each time Rasbach is called out on a case, he never knows what to expect. Nonetheless, each time he unravels the puzzle, he is never surprised. His capacity for surprise seems to have evaporated. But he is always curious. He always wants to *know*.

Rasbach helps himself to the milk and sugar that Marco has left out for him and then pauses in the doorway of the kitchen with his coffee mug in his hand. From where he stands, he can see the dining table and the sideboard near the kitchen, both obviously antiques. Beyond that he can see the sofa, upholstered in dark green velvet, and the backs of Anne and Marco Conti's heads. To the right of them is a marble fireplace, and above the mantelpiece hangs a large oil painting. Rasbach doesn't know what it is a painting of, exactly. The sofa faces the front window, but more immediately in front of the sofa there is a coffee table and, across from that, two deep, comfortable armchairs.

Rasbach makes his way into the living room and resumes his previous seat across from the couple, in the armchair nearest the fireplace. He notes how Marco's hands still shake as he brings the mug to his mouth. Anne simply holds the cup in her hands on her lap, as if she doesn't realize it's there. She has stopped crying, for the moment.

The lurid lights of the police cars parked outside still play across the walls. The forensic team goes about its tasks in the house quietly, efficiently. The atmosphere inside the house is busy but subdued, grim.

Rasbach has a delicate task before him. He must convey to this couple that he is working for them, doing everything possible to find their missing baby—which he is, along with the rest of the police force—even while he knows that in most cases when a child goes missing like this, it is the parents who are responsible. And there are factors here that certainly make him suspicious. But he will keep an open mind.

"I'm very sorry," Rasbach begins. "I can't even imagine how hard this is for you."

Anne looks up at him. The sympathy makes her eyes instantly well up with more tears. "Who would take our baby?" she asks plaintively.

"That's what we have to find out," Rasbach says, setting his mug on the coffee table and taking out his notebook. "This may seem too obvious a question to ask, but do you have any idea who might have taken her?"

They both stare at him; such an idea is preposterous. And yet here they are.

"Have you noticed anyone hanging around lately, anyone showing interest in your baby?"

They both shake their heads.

"Do you have any idea, any idea at all, who might want to do you harm?" He looks from Anne to Marco.

The two parents shake their heads again, equally at a loss.

"Please, give it some thought," Rasbach says. "Take your time. There has to be a reason. There's always a reason—we just have to find out what it is."

Marco looks like he's about to speak, then thinks better of it.

"What is it?" Rasbach asks. "This is no time to hold back."

"Your parents," Marco says finally, turning to his wife.

"What about my parents?" she says, clearly surprised.

"They have money."

"So?" She doesn't seem to understand what he's getting at.

"They have a *lot* of money," Marco says.

Here we go, Rasbach thinks.

Anne looks at her husband as if dumbfounded. She is, possibly, an excellent actress. "What do you mean?" she says. "You don't think someone took her for . . ." Rasbach watches the two of them carefully. The expression on her face changes. "That would be good," she says, looking up at him, "wouldn't it? If all they want is money, I could get my baby back? They won't hurt her?"

The hope in her voice is heartbreaking. Rasbach is almost convinced that she has nothing to do with this.

"She must be so scared," she says, and then she falls completely apart, sobbing uncontrollably.

Rasbach wants to ask her about her parents. Time is of the essence in kidnapping cases. Instead he turns to Marco. "Who are her parents?" Rasbach asks.

"Alice and Richard Dries," Marco tells him. "Richard is her stepfather."

Rasbach writes it down in his notebook.

Anne regains control over herself and says again, "My parents have a lot of money."

"How much money?" Rasbach asks.

"I don't know exactly," Anne says. "Millions."

"Can you be a little more precise?" Rasbach asks.

"I think they're worth somewhere around fifteen million," Anne says. "But it's not like anybody knows that."

Rasbach looks at Marco. His face is completely blank.

"I want to call my mother," Anne says. She glances at the clock on the mantelpiece, and Rasbach follows her gaze. It's two fifteen in the morning.

Anne has a complicated relationship with her parents. When Marco and Anne are having issues with them, which is frequently the case, Marco tells her that her relationship with them is fucked up. Maybe it is, but they are the only parents she has. She needs them. She makes things work the best she can, but it isn't easy.

Marco comes from an entirely different kind of background. His family is large and squabbling. They yell good-naturedly when they see one another, which isn't often. His parents emigrated from Italy to New York before Marco was born and own a dry-cleaning and tailoring business. They have no money to speak of, but they get by. They are not overly involved in Marco's life, as Anne's wealthy parents are in hers. Marco and his four siblings have had to fend for themselves from a young age, pushed out of the nest. Marco has been living his life on his own—and on his own terms—since he was eighteen. He put himself through school. He sees his parents occasionally, but they are not a big part of his life. He isn't exactly from the wrong side of the tracks in anybody's book, except for Anne's parents' and their well-heeled friends at the Grandview Golf and Country Club. Marco comes from a middle-class, law-abiding family of hardworking people, who have done well enough but no better than that. None of Anne's friends from college or from her job at the art gallery think Marco is from the wrong side of the tracks.

It is only old money that would see him that way. And Anne's mother is from old money. Anne's father, Richard Dries—actually her stepfather; her own father died tragically when she was four years old—is a successful businessman, but her mother, Alice, has millions.

Her wealthy parents enjoy their money, their rich friends. The house in one of the finest parts of the city, the membership at the Grandview Golf and

Country Club, the luxury cars and five-star vacations. Sending Anne to a private girls' school, then to a good university. The older her father gets, the more he likes to pretend that he's earned all that money, but it isn't true. It's gone to his head. He's become quite full of himself.

When Anne "took up" with Marco, her parents acted as if the world were coming to an end. Marco looked like the quintessential bad boy. He was dangerously attractive—fair-skinned for an Italian—with dark hair, brooding eyes, and a bit of a rebellious look, especially when he hadn't shaved. But his eyes lit up warmly when he saw Anne, and he had that million-dollar smile. And the way he called her "baby"—she couldn't resist him. The first time he showed up at her parents' house, to pick her up for a date, was one of the defining moments of Anne's young adulthood. She was twenty-two. Her mother had been telling her about a nice young man, a lawyer, the son of a friend, who was interested in meeting her. Anne had explained, impatiently, that she was already seeing Marco.

"Yes, but . . . ," her mother said.

"But what?" Anne said, folding her arms across her chest.

"You can't be serious about him," her mother said.

Anne can still remember the expression on her mother's face. Dismay, embarrassment. She was thinking about how it would look. Thinking about how she would explain to her friends that her daughter was dating a young man who came from nothing, who worked as a bartender in the Italian part of the city and rode a motorcycle. Her mother would forget about the business degree Marco had earned at the same university that was considered good enough for their daughter. They wouldn't see how his working his way through school at night was admirable. Maybe nobody would ever be good enough for her parents' little girl.

And then—it was perfect—Marco had roared up on his Ducati, and Anne had flown out of her parents' house and straight into Marco's arms, her mother watching from behind the curtains. He kissed her hard, still straddling the bike, and handed her his spare helmet. She climbed on, and they roared away, manicured gravel spitting up in their wake. That was the moment she'd decided she was in love.

But you aren't twenty-two forever. You grow up. Things change.

"I want to call my mother," Anne repeats now. So much has happened—has it been less than an hour since they returned home to an empty crib?

Marco grabs the phone and hands it to her, then sits back down on the sofa with his arms crossed in front of him, looking tense.

Anne dials the phone. She starts to cry again before she's even finished dialing the number. The phone rings, and her mother answers.

"Mom," Anne says, dissolving into incoherent sobbing.

"Anne? What's wrong?"

Anne finally gets the words out. "Someone has taken Cora."

"Oh my God," her mother says.

"The police are here," Anne tells her. "Can you come?"

"We'll be right there, Anne," her mother says. "You hold on. Your father and I are coming."

Anne hangs up the phone and cries. Her parents will come. They have always helped her, even when they're angry at her. They will be angry now, at her and Marco, but especially at Marco. They love Cora, their only grandchild. What will they think when they hear what she and Marco have done?

"They're on their way," Anne says to Marco and the detective. She looks at Marco, then looks away.

FIVE

Marco feels like an outcast; it's a feeling he often gets when Anne's parents are in the room. Even now, with Cora missing, he is ignored, while the three of them—his distraught wife, her always-composed mother, and her overbearing father—slip into their familiar three-person alliance. Sometimes their exclusion of him is subtle, sometimes not. But then again, he knew what he was getting into when he married her. He thought it was a deal he could live with.

He stands at the side of the living room, useless, and watches Anne. She's seated in the middle of the sofa, her mother at her side, pulling Anne into her for comfort. Her father is more aloof, sitting up straight, patting his daughter on the shoulder. No one looks at Marco. No one offers *him* comfort. Marco feels out of place in his own home.

But worse than that, he feels sick, horrified. All he wants is his little Cora back in her crib; he wants all of this never to have happened.

He feels the detective's eyes on him. He alone is

paying attention to Marco. Marco deliberately ignores him, even though he knows he probably shouldn't. Marco knows he is a suspect. The detective has been insinuating as much ever since he got here. Marco has overheard the officers in the house whispering about bringing in the cadaver dogs. He isn't stupid. They would only do that if they thought Cora was dead before she left the house. The police obviously must think he and Anne killed their own baby.

Let them bring in the dogs—he's not afraid. Maybe this is the kind of thing the police deal with on a regular basis, parents who kill their children, but he could *never* hurt his baby. Cora means everything to him. She has been the one bright light in his life, the one reliable, constant source of joy, especially these last few months as things have fallen steadily apart and as Anne has become increasingly lost and depressed. He hardly knows his wife anymore. What happened to the beautiful, engaging woman he married? Everything has been going to shit. But he and Cora have had a happy little bond of their own, the two of them, waiting it out, waiting for Mommy to return to normal.

Anne's parents will hold him in more contempt than ever now. They will forgive Anne quickly. They will forgive her almost anything—even abandoning their baby to a predator, even this. But they will never forgive him. They will be stoic in the face of this adversity; they are always stoic, unlike their emotional daughter. Perhaps they will even rescue Anne and Marco from their own mistakes. That is what they like to do best. Even now he can see Anne's father looking off over the heads of Anne and her mother, his brow furrowed, concentrating on the problem—the problem Marco created—and on how he might solve it. Thinking about how he can rise to this challenge and come out triumphant. Maybe he can show Marco up, one more time, when it really counts.

Marco despises his father-in-law. It's mutual.

But the important thing now is to get Cora back. That's all that matters. They're a complicated, screwed-up family in Marco's view, but they all love Cora. He blinks back a fresh surge of tears.

Detective Rasbach notes the coolness between Anne's parents and their son-in-law. In most cases a crisis like this dissolves such barriers, if only for a short time. But this is not an ordinary crisis. This is a situation where the parents ostensibly left their baby alone in the house and she was taken. Watching the family huddled on the sofa, he can see at once that the adored daughter will be absolved from any blame by her parents. The husband is a handy scapegoat—he alone will be blamed, whether it's fair or not. And it looks as if he knows it.

Anne's father gets up from the sofa and approaches Rasbach. He is tall and broad-shouldered, with short, steel gray hair. There is a confidence about him that is almost aggressive.

"Detective?"

"Detective Rasbach," he supplies.

"Richard Dries," the other man says, offering his hand. "Tell me what you're doing to find my granddaughter." The man speaks in a low voice but with authority; he is used to being in charge.

Rasbach tells him. "We have officers searching the area, interviewing everyone, looking for witnesses. We have a forensics team going through the house and the surrounding area. We have the baby's description out locally and nationally. The public will soon be informed by the media coverage. We may get lucky and catch something on CCTV cameras somewhere." He pauses. "We hope to get some leads quickly." *We are doing everything we can. But it probably won't be enough to save your granddaughter,* Rasbach thinks. He knows from experience that investigations generally move slowly, unless there is an early, significant break. The little girl doesn't have much time, if she's even still alive.

Dries moves closer to him, close enough that Rasbach can smell his aftershave. Dries glances over his shoulder at his daughter and says more quietly, "You checking out all the perverts?"

Rasbach regards the larger man. He is the only one who has put the unthinkable into words. "We are checking out all the ones we know about, but there are always those we don't know about."

"This is going to kill my daughter," Richard Dries says to the detective under his breath, looking at her.

Rasbach wonders how much the father knows about his daughter's postpartum depression. Perhaps this is not the time to ask. Instead he waits a moment and then says, "Your daughter has mentioned that you have considerable wealth. Is that right?"

Dries nods. "You could say that." He looks over at Marco, who is not looking his way but staring at Anne.

Rasbach asks, "Do you think this could be a financially motivated crime?"

The man seems surprised but then considers it. "I don't know. Do *you* think that's what it is?"

Rasbach gives a slight shake of his head. "We don't know yet. It's certainly possible." He lets Dries ponder that for a minute. "Is there anyone you can think of, in your business dealings perhaps, who might have a grudge against you?"

"You're suggesting that someone took my granddaughter to settle a grudge against me?" The man is clearly shocked.

"I'm just asking."

Richard Dries doesn't dismiss the idea at once. Either his ego is large enough, Rasbach thinks, or he's made sufficient enemies over the years that he considers that it might just be possible. Finally Dries shakes his head. "No, I can't think of anybody who would do that. I don't have any enemies—that I know of."

"It's not likely," Rasbach agrees, "but stranger things have happened." He asks casually, "What kind of business are you in, Mr. Dries?"

"Packaging and labeling." He turns his eyes to meet Rasbach's. "We have to find Cora, Detective. She's my only grandchild." He claps a hand on Rasbach's shoulder and says, "Keep me in the loop, will you?" He produces his business card and then turns away. "Call me, anytime. I'd like to know what's going on."

A moment later Jennings comes up to Rasbach and speaks low in his ear. "The dogs are here."

Rasbach nods and leaves the stricken family behind him in the living room.

He goes out to the street to meet with the dog handler. A K-9 Unit truck is parked outside the house. He recognizes the handler, a cop named Temple. He's worked with him before. He's a good man, competent.

"What do we have?" Temple asks.

"Baby reported missing from her crib sometime after midnight," Rasbach says.

Temple nods, serious. Nobody likes missing-children cases.

"Only six months old, so not mobile." This is not the case of a toddler who woke up in the middle of the night, wandered off down the street, got tired, and hid in a garden shed somewhere. If that were the case, they would use tracking dogs to follow the child's scent. This baby was carried out of the house by someone.

Rasbach has asked for the cadaver dogs to see if they can determine whether the child was already dead inside the house or the car. Well-trained cadaver dogs can detect death—on surfaces, on clothing—as little as two or three hours after it has occurred. Body chemistry changes quickly upon death, but not instantly. If the baby was killed and moved immediately, the dogs won't pick it up, but if she was killed and not moved right away—it's worth a shot. Rasbach knows that the information that may be gained via the dogs is useless from an evidentiary standpoint without corroborating evidence, like a body. But he is desperate to get any information he can. Rasbach is one who will avail himself of every possible investigative tool. He is relentless in his pursuit of the truth. He must know what happened.

Temple nods. "Let's get started."

He goes to the back of the truck, opens the hatch. Two dogs jump down, matching black-and-white English springer spaniels. Temple uses his hands and voice to direct the dogs. They don't wear leashes.

"Let's start with the car," Rasbach says. He leads them to the Contis' Audi. The dogs heel by Temple's side, perfectly obedient. The forensics team is already there. Seeing the dogs, they step silently back.

"Are we good here? Can I let the dogs have a look?" Rasbach asks.

"Yeah, we're done. Go ahead," the forensics officer says.

"Go," Temple tells the two dogs.

The dogs go to work. They circle the car, sniffing intently. They jump into the trunk, into the backseat, then the front seat, and quickly jump out again. They come and sit by their handler and look up. He hands them a treat, shakes his head. "Nothing here."

"Let's try inside," Rasbach says, relieved. He hopes that the missing baby is still alive. He wants to be wrong about her parents. He wants to find her. Then he reminds himself not to be hopeful. He must remain objective. He can't afford to become emotionally invested in his cases. He would never survive.

The dogs test the air all the way up the front steps and enter the house. Once inside, the handler takes them upstairs and they start in the child's bedroom.

Six

Anne stirs when the dogs come in, shrugs out from underneath her mother's arm, and stands up unsteadily. She watches the handler go upstairs with the two dogs without a word.

She feels Marco come up beside her. "They've brought in tracking dogs," she says. "Thank God. Now maybe we'll get somewhere." She feels him reach for her arm, but she shrugs him off, too. "I want to see."

Detective Rasbach holds up a hand in front of her. "Better that you stay down here and let the dogs do their work," he tells her gently.

"Do you want me to get some of her clothing?" Anne asks. "Something that she wore recently, that hasn't been washed yet? I can get something out of the laundry downstairs."

"They're not tracking dogs," Marco says.

"What?" Anne says, turning to Marco.

"They're not tracking dogs. They're cadaver dogs," Marco says.

And then she gets it. She turns back to the detective, her face white. "You think we killed her!"

Her outburst stuns everyone. They are all frozen in shock. Anne sees her mother put her hand to her mouth. Her father's face looks stormy.

"That's preposterous," Richard Dries blurts out, his face a rough brick red. "You can't honestly suspect my daughter would harm her own child!"

The detective says nothing.

Anne looks back at her father. He has always stood up for her, for as long as she can remember. But there isn't much he can do to help her now. Someone has taken Cora. It is the first time in her life, Anne realizes, looking at him, that she has ever seen her father afraid. Is he afraid for Cora? Or is he afraid for her? Do the police really think she killed her own child? She does not dare look at her mother.

"You need to do your job and find my granddaughter!" her father says to the detective, his belligerence a transparent attempt to mask his fear.

For a long moment, no one says anything. The moment is so strange that no one can think of anything to say. They listen to the sound of the dogs' toenails clicking on the hardwood floor as they move around overhead.

Rasbach says, "We are doing everything in our power to find your granddaughter."

Anne is unbearably tense. She wants her baby back. She wants Cora back unharmed. She can't bear the thought of her baby suffering, being hurt. Anne feels she might faint and sinks down again into the sofa. Immediately her mother puts a protective arm around her. Anne's mother refuses to look at the detective anymore.

The dogs come scampering down the stairs. Anne looks up and turns her head to watch them descend. The handler shakes his head. The dogs move into the living room, and Anne, Marco, and Richard and Alice Dries all hold perfectly still, as if not to draw their attention. Anne sits petrified on the sofa while the two dogs, noses testing the air and running along the area carpets, investigate the living room. Then they approach and sniff her. There is a police officer standing behind her to see what the dogs will do, perhaps waiting to arrest her and Marco on the spot. *What if the dogs start to bark?* Anne thinks, dizzy with fear.

Everything is tilting sideways. Anne knows that she and Marco did not kill their baby. But she is powerless and afraid, and she knows that dogs can smell fear.

She remembers that now, as she looks into their almost-human eyes. The dogs sniff her and her clothes—she can feel their panting breath on her, warm and rank, and recoils. She tries not to breathe. Then they leave her and go to her parents, and then to Marco, who is standing by himself, near the fireplace. Anne shrinks back into the sofa, relieved when the dogs seem to draw a blank in the living room and dining room and then move toward the kitchen. She can hear their claws scuttling across the kitchen tile, and then they are loping down the back stairs and into the basement. Rasbach leaves the room to follow them.

The family sits in the living room waiting for this part to be over. Anne doesn't want to look at anyone, so she stares at the clock on the mantelpiece. With every minute that goes by, she feels more hopeless. She feels her baby moving farther and farther away from her.

Anne hears the back door in the kitchen open. She imagines the dogs going through the backyard, the garden, the garage, and the lane. Her eyes are staring at the clock on the mantelpiece; what she sees is the dogs in the garage, rooting around the broken clay pots and rusted rakes. She sits rigid, waiting, listening for barking. She waits and worries. She thinks about the disabled motion detector.

Finally Rasbach returns. "The dogs drew a blank," he says. "That's good news."

Anne can sense her mother's relief beside her.

"So can we now get serious about finding her?" Richard Dries says.

The detective says, "We are serious about finding her, believe me."

"So," Marco says, with a touch of bitterness, "what happens next? What can we do?"

Rasbach says, "We will have to ask you both a lot of questions. You may know something you don't realize you know, something that will be helpful."

Anne looks doubtfully at Marco. *What can they know?*

Rasbach adds, "And we need you to talk to the media. Someone might have seen something, or someone might see something tomorrow or the next day, and unless this is in front of them, they won't put it together."

"Fine," Anne says tersely. She will do anything to get her baby back, even though she is terrified of meeting with the media. Marco also nods but looks nervous. Anne thinks briefly of her stringy hair, her face bloated from crying. Marco reaches for her hand and clasps it, hard.

"What about a reward?" Anne's father suggests. "We could offer a reward for information. I'll put up the funds. If somebody saw something and doesn't want to come forward, they might think twice about not speaking up if the money's right."

"Thank you," Marco says.

Anne merely nods.

Rasbach's cell phone rings. It is Detective Jennings, who has been going door-to-door in the neighborhood. "We might have something," he says.

Rasbach feels a familiar tension in his gut—they are desperate for a lead. He walks briskly from the Contis' home and within minutes arrives at a house on the street behind them, on the other side of the lane.

Jennings is waiting for him on the front step. Jennings taps the front door again, and it is immediately opened by a woman who looks to be in her fifties. She has obviously been roused from her bed. She is wearing a bathrobe, and her hair is held back with bobby pins. Jennings introduces her as Paula Dempsey.

"I'm Detective Rasbach," the detective says, showing the woman his badge. She invites them into the living room, where her now wide-awake husband is sitting in an armchair, wearing pajama bottoms, his hair mussed.

"Mrs. Dempsey saw something that might be important," Jennings says. When they are seated, he says, "Tell Detective Rasbach what you told me. What you saw."

"Right," she says. She licks her lips. "I was in the upstairs bathroom. I got up to take an aspirin, because my legs were aching from gardening earlier in the day."

Rasbach nods encouragingly.

"It's such a hot night, so we had the bathroom window all the way up to let the breeze in. The window looks out over the back lane. The Contis' house is behind this one, a couple houses over."

Rasbach nods again; he's noted the placement of her house in relation to the Contis'. He listens carefully.

"I happened to look out the window. I have a good view of the lane from the window. I could see pretty well, because I hadn't turned the bathroom light on."

"And what did you see?" Rasbach asks.

"A car. I saw a car coming down the lane."

"Where was the car, exactly? What direction was it going?"

"It was coming down the lane toward my house, after the Contis' house. It might have been coming from their garage, or from any of the houses farther down."

"What kind of car was it?" Rasbach asked, taking out his notebook.

"I don't know. I don't know much about cars. I wish my husband had seen it—he would have been more help." She glances toward her husband, who shrugs helplessly. "But of course I didn't think anything of it at the time."

"Can you describe it?"

"It was smallish, and I think a dark color. But it didn't have its headlights on—that's why I noticed it. I thought it was odd that the headlights weren't on."

"Could you see the driver?"

"No."

"Could you tell if there was anyone in the passenger seat?"

"I don't think there was anyone in the passenger seat, but I can't be sure. I couldn't see much. I think it might have been an electric car, or a hybrid, because it was very quiet."

"Are you sure?"

"No, I'm not sure. But sound carries up from the lane, and the car was very quiet, although maybe that's because it was just creeping along."

"And what time was this, do you know?"

"I looked at the time when I got up. I have a digital alarm clock on my bedside table. It was twelve thirty-five a.m."

"Are you absolutely sure of the time?"

"Yes." She adds, "I'm positive."

"Can you remember any more detail about the car, anything at all?" Rasbach asks. "Was it a two-door? Or a four-door?"

"I'm sorry," she says. "I can't remember. I didn't notice. It was small, though."

"I'd like to take a look from the bathroom window, if you don't mind," Rasbach says.

"Of course."

She leads them up the stairs to the bathroom at the back of the house. Rasbach looks out the open window. The view is good—he can see clearly into the lane. He can see the Contis' garage to the left, the yellow police tape surrounding it. He can tell that the garage door is still open. How unfortunate that she was not just a couple of minutes earlier. She might have seen the car without headlights coming out of the Contis' garage, if in fact it had. If only he had a witness who could put a car in the Contis' garage, or coming out of their garage, at 12:35 a.m. But this car might have been coming from anywhere farther down the lane.

Rasbach thanks Paula and her husband, hands her his card, and then he and Jennings depart the house together. They stop on the sidewalk in front of the house. The sky is beginning to lighten.

"What do you make of that?" Jennings asks.

"Interesting," Rasbach says. "The timing. And the fact that the car's headlights were off." The other detective nods. Marco had checked on the baby at twelve thirty. The car was driving away from the direction of the Contis' garage at 12:35 a.m. with its headlights off. A possible accomplice.

The parents have just become his prime suspects.

"Get a couple of officers to talk to everybody who has garage access to that lane. I want to know who was driving a car down that lane at twelve thirty-five a.m.," Rasbach says. "And have them go up and down both streets again and try to find out specifically if anybody else was looking out a window at the lane at that time and if they saw anything."

Jennings nods. "Right."

Anne holds Marco's hand tightly. She is almost hyperventilating before meeting the press. She has had to sit down and put her head between her knees. It is seven in the morning, only a few hours since Cora was taken. A dozen journalists and photographers are out on the street waiting. Anne is a private person; this kind of media exposure is awful to her. She has never been one to seek attention. But Anne and Marco need the media to take an interest. They need Cora's face plastered all over the newspapers, the TV, the Internet. You can't just take a baby out of someone else's house in the middle of the night and have no one notice. It's a busy neighborhood. Surely someone will come forward with information. Anne and Marco must do this, even though they know that they'll be the target of some nasty press once it all comes out. They are the parents who abandoned their baby, left her home alone, an infant. And now someone has her. They are a Movie of the Week.

They have agreed on a prepared statement, have crafted it at the coffee table with Detective Rasbach's help. The statement does not mention the fact that the baby was alone in the house at the time of the kidnapping, but Anne has no doubt whatsoever that that fact will get out. She has the feeling that once the media invade their lives, there will be no end to it. Nothing will be private. She and Marco will be notorious, their own faces on the pages of supermarket tabloids. She is frightened and ashamed.

Anne and Marco walk out their front door and onto the front step. Detective Rasbach is at Anne's side, and Detective Jennings stands beside Marco. Anne hangs on to her husband's arm for support, as if she might fall. They have agreed that Marco is to read the statement—Anne is simply not up to it. She looks as though a stiff breeze will knock her over. Marco gazes into the crowd of reporters, seems to shrink, then lowers his eyes to the piece of paper shaking visibly in his hands. The cameras flash repeatedly.

Anne looks up, stunned. The street is full of reporters, vans, TV cameras, technicians, equipment and wires, people holding microphones to their heavily made-up faces. She has seen this on TV, has watched this very thing. But now she is front and center. It feels unreal, like it's not actually happening to her but to someone else. She feels strange and disembodied, as if she is both standing on the front step looking out and also watching the scene from above and a little to the left.

Marco holds up a hand to indicate that he wishes to speak. The crowd quiets suddenly.

"I'd like to read a statement," he mumbles.

"Louder!" someone shouts from the sidewalk.

"I'm going to read a statement," Marco says, more loudly and clearly. Then he reads, his voice growing stronger. "Early this morning, sometime between twelve thirty and one thirty, our beautiful baby girl,

Cora, was taken from her crib by a person or persons unknown." He stops for a moment to collect himself. No one makes a sound. "She is six months old. She has blond hair and blue eyes and weighs about sixteen pounds. She was wearing a disposable diaper and a plain, pale pink onesie. There is a white blanket also missing from her crib.

"We love Cora more than anything. We want her back. We say to whoever has her, please, *please* bring her back to us, unharmed." Marco looks up from the page. He is crying now and has to stop and wipe away the tears to continue reading. Anne sobs quietly at his side, looking out at the sea of faces.

"We have no idea who would steal our beautiful, innocent little girl. We are asking for your help. If you know anything, or saw anything, please call the police. We are able to offer a substantial reward for information leading to the recovery of our baby. Thank you."

Marco turns to Anne, and they collapse in each other's arms as more bulbs flash.

"How much of a reward?" someone calls out.

SEVEN

No one understands how it could have been missed, but shortly after the press conference outside the Contis' front door, an officer approaches Detective Rasbach in the living room holding a pale pink onesie between two gloved fingers. The eyes of every person in the room—Detective Rasbach, Marco, Anne, and Anne's parents, Alice and Richard, are instantly fixed on the piece of clothing.

Rasbach starts. "Where did you find that?" he asks curtly.

"Oh!" Anne blurts out.

Everyone turns from the officer holding the pink onesie to look at Anne. All the color has drained from her face.

"Was that in the laundry hamper in the baby's room?" Anne asks, getting up.

"No," the officer holding the article of clothing says. "It was underneath the pad on the changing table. We missed it the first time."

Rasbach is intensely annoyed. How could it have been missed?

Anne colors, seems confused. "I'm sorry. I must have forgotten. Cora was wearing that earlier in the evening. I changed her outfit after her last feeding. She spit up on that one. I'll show you." Anne moves toward the officer and reaches for the onesie, but the officer moves back, out of her reach.

"Please don't touch it," he says.

Anne turns to Rasbach. "I changed her out of that one and put her into another one. I thought I put that onesie in the laundry hamper by the changing table."

"So the description we have is inaccurate?" Rasbach says.

"Yes," Anne admits, looking confused.

"What *was* she wearing, then?" Rasbach asks. When Anne hesitates, he repeats, "What was she wearing?"

"I . . . I'm not sure," Anne says.

"What do you mean, you're not sure?" the detective persists. His voice is sharp.

"I don't know. I'd had a bit to drink. I was tired. It was dark. I nurse her in the dark for her last feeding, so she won't wake up completely. She spit up on her onesie, and when I changed her diaper, I changed her outfit, too, in the dark. I threw the pink one in the laundry—I thought I did—and I took another one out of the drawer. She has a lot of them. I don't know what color." Anne feels guilty. But clearly this man has never changed a baby in the middle of the night.

"Do you know?" Rasbach asks, turning to Marco.

Marco looks like a deer caught in headlights. He shakes his head. "I didn't notice that she'd changed her outfit. I didn't turn the lights on when I checked on her."

"Maybe I can look through her drawer and figure out which one she has on," Anne offers, filled with shame.

"Yes, do that," Rasbach agrees. "We need an accurate description."

Anne runs upstairs and pulls open the drawer to the baby's dresser where she keeps all the onesies and sleepers, the little T-shirts and tights. Flowers and polka dots and bees and bunnies.

The detective and Marco have followed her and watch as she kneels on the floor, pulling everything out, sobbing. But she can't remember, and she can't figure it out. Which one is missing? What is her daughter wearing?

She turns around to Marco. "Maybe get the laundry from downstairs."

Marco turns and goes downstairs to do her bidding. He soon returns with a hamper of dirty clothes. He dumps them on the floor in the baby's room. Someone has cleaned up the vomit from the floor. The baby's dirty clothes are mixed in with their own clothes, but Anne seizes on all the little baby articles and puts them aside.

Finally she says, "It's the mint green one, with the bunny embroidered on the front."

"Are you sure?" Rasbach asks.

"It has to be," Anne says miserably. "It's the only one that's not here."

Forensic study of Anne and Marco's home has revealed little in the hours since Cora was taken. The police have found no evidence that anyone unaccounted for has been in Cora's room or in the Contis' house, none at all. There is not one shred of evidence—not one fingerprint, not one fiber—inside the house that cannot be innocently explained. It appears that no one has been inside their home, other than themselves, Anne's parents, and their cleaning lady. They have all had to submit to the indignity of being fingerprinted. No one seriously considers the cleaning lady, an older Filipino woman, to be a possible kidnapper. Nonetheless, both she and her extended family are being carefully checked out.

Outside the house, however, they have found something. There are prints of tire tracks in the garage that on investigation do not match the tires on the Contis' Audi. Rasbach has not yet shared this information with the parents of the missing baby. This, in combination with the witness who saw a car going down the lane at 12:35, is the only solid lead in the investigation so far.

"They probably wore gloves," Marco says when Detective Rasbach tells them about the lack of any physical evidence of an intruder in the house.

It is now midmorning. Anne and Marco look exhausted. Marco looks like he might still be hungover as well. But they won't even try to rest. Anne's parents have been asked to go to the kitchen and have coffee while the detective questions Anne and Marco further. He must constantly reassure them that they are doing everything possible to recover their baby, that he is not simply wasting their time.

"Very likely," the detective says, agreeing with Marco's guess about the gloves. But then he points out, "Still, we would expect to see some footprints or impressions inside the house—and certainly outside, or in the garage—that don't match yours."

"Unless he went out the front," Anne says. She remembers what she saw: the front door was open. She is clearer on that now, now that she is completely sober. It is her belief that the kidnapper took the baby out the front door and down the front steps to the sidewalk, and that is why they have found no strange footprints.

"Even then," Rasbach says, "we would expect to find something." He looks pointedly at them both. "We have interviewed everyone we possibly can. No one admits to seeing anybody carrying a baby out your front door."

"That doesn't mean it didn't happen," Marco says, his frustration showing.

"You haven't found anyone who saw her being carried through the back door either," Anne points out sharply. "You haven't found a damn thing."

"There is the bulb that was loosened in the motion detector," Detective Rasbach reminds them. He pauses, then adds, "We have also found evidence of tire tracks in your garage that don't match your car." He waits for the information to sink in. "Has anyone used your garage lately, that you know of? Do you let anyone park there?"

Marco looks at the detective and then quickly looks away. "No, not that I know of," he says.

Anne shakes her head.

Anne and Marco are clearly stressed. It is not surprising, as Rasbach has just implied that in the absence of any physical evidence of anyone else carrying their baby out of the house—specifically across the backyard to the garage—it must have been one of them who removed her from the home.

"I'm sorry, but I must ask you about the medication in your bathroom cabinet," Rasbach says, turning to Anne. "The sertraline."

"What about it?" Anne asks.

"Can you tell me what it is for?" Rasbach asks gently.

"I have mild depression," Anne says defensively. "It was prescribed by my doctor."

"Your family doctor?"

She hesitates. She looks at Marco, as if not sure of what to do, but then she answers. "By my psychiatrist," she admits.

"I see." Rasbach adds, "Can you tell me the name of your psychiatrist?"

Anne looks at Marco again and says, "Dr. Leslie Lumsden."

"Thank you," Rasbach murmurs, making a note in his little book.

"Lots of mothers get postpartum depression, Detective," Anne says defensively. "It's quite common."

Rasbach nods noncommittally. "And the mirror in the bathroom? Can you tell me what happened to it?"

Anne flushes and looks uneasily at the detective. "I did that," she admits. "When we came home and found Cora missing, I smashed the mirror with my hand." She holds up her bandaged hand. The hand her mother had bathed and disinfected and bandaged for her. "I was upset."

Rasbach nods again, makes another note.

According to what the parents had told Rasbach earlier, the last time anyone other than one of them saw the child alive was at about two in the afternoon on the day of the kidnapping, when Anne had grabbed a coffee at the Starbucks on the corner. According to Anne, the baby had been awake in her stroller and smiling and sucking her fingers, and the barista had waved at the little girl.

Rasbach had been to the Starbucks earlier that morning and had spoken to the same barista, who fortunately had already been at work by then. She remembered Anne and the baby in the stroller. But it looks as if no one else will be able to confirm that the baby was alive after 2:00 p.m. on Friday, the day she disappeared.

"What did you do after you stopped at Starbucks yesterday?" Rasbach asks now.

"I came home. Cora was fussy—she's usually fussy in the afternoon—so I was walking around the house holding her a lot," Anne says. "I tried to put her down for a nap, but she wouldn't sleep. So I picked her up again, walked her around the house, the backyard."

"Then what?"

"I did that until Marco got home."

"What time was that?" Rasbach asks.

Marco says, "I got home about five. I knocked off a bit early, because it was Friday and we were going out."

"And then?"

"I took Cora from Anne and sent Anne upstairs for a nap." Marco leans against the back of the sofa and rubs his hands up and down his thighs. Then he starts to jiggle one of his legs. He is restless.

"Do you have kids, Detective?" Anne asks.

"No."

"Then you don't know how exhausting they can be."

"No." He shifts his own position in the chair. They are all getting tired. "What time did you go next door to the party?" Rasbach asks.

"About seven," Marco answers.

"So what did you do between five and seven o'clock?"

"Why are you asking us this?" Anne says sharply. "Isn't this a waste of time? I thought you were going to help us!"

"I have to know everything that happened. Please just answer as best you can," Rasbach says calmly.

Marco reaches out and puts a hand on his wife's thigh, as if to settle her down. He says, "I played with Cora while Anne slept. I fed her some cereal. Anne woke up around six."

Anne takes a deep breath. "And then we had an argument about going to the party."

Marco stiffens visibly beside her.

"Why did you argue?" Rasbach asks, looking Anne in the eyes.

"The babysitter canceled," Anne says. "If she hadn't canceled, none of this ever would have happened," she says, as if realizing it for the first time.

This was new. Rasbach hadn't known there was to be a babysitter. Why are they just telling him this now? "Why didn't you say this before?"

"Didn't we?" Anne says, surprised.

"Who was the babysitter?" Rasbach asks.

Marco says, "A girl named Katerina. She's our regular babysitter. She's a twelfth-grader. She lives about a block from here."

"Did you talk to her?"

"What?" Marco says. He doesn't appear to be paying attention. Perhaps his exhaustion is catching up with him, Rasbach thinks.

"When did she cancel?" Rasbach asks.

"She called about six o'clock. By then it was too late to get another sitter," Marco says.

"Who spoke to her?" Rasbach is writing a note in his book.

"I did," Marco says.

"We could have *tried* to get another sitter," Anne says bitterly.

"At the time I didn't think it was necessary. Of course, now . . ." Marco trails off, looking at the floor.

"Can I have her address?" Rasbach asks.

"I'll get it," Anne says, and goes to the kitchen to retrieve it. While they wait, Rasbach hears murmured voices coming from the kitchen; Anne's parents want to know what's going on.

"What was the argument about, exactly?" Rasbach asks after Anne has returned and handed him a piece of paper with the name and address of the babysitter scribbled on it.

"I didn't want to leave Cora home by herself," Anne says bluntly. "I said I'd stay home with her. Cynthia didn't want us to bring the baby because she fusses a lot. Cynthia wanted an adults-only party—that's why we called the sitter. But then, once she canceled, Marco thought it would be rude to bring the baby when we'd said we wouldn't, and I didn't want to leave her home alone, so we argued about it."

Rasbach turns to Marco, who nods miserably.

"Marco thought if we had the monitor on next door and checked her every half hour, it would be fine. Nothing bad would happen, you said," Anne says, turning with sudden venom on her husband.

"I was wrong!" Marco says, turning to his wife. "I'm sorry! It's all my fault! How many times do I have to say it?"

Detective Rasbach watches the chinks in the couple's relationship widen. The tension he had picked up on immediately after their daughter was reported missing has already blossomed into something more— *blame*. The united front they had shown in the first minutes and hours of the investigation is starting to erode. How could it not? Their daughter is missing. They are under intense pressure. The police are in their home, the press is pounding at their front door. Rasbach knows that if there is anything here to find, he will find it.

EIGHT

D etective Rasbach leaves the Contis' house and
sets off to interview the babysitter at her home
to confirm their story. It is late morning, and
as he walks the short distance down the leafy streets,
he turns the case over in his mind. There is no evidence that an intruder was in the house or yard. But
there are fresh tire tracks on the cement floor of the
garage. He is suspicious of the parents, but now there
is this news about the babysitter.

When he arrives at the address Anne provided, a
distraught-looking woman answers the door. She has
obviously been crying. He shows her his badge.

"I understand Katerina Stavros lives here." The
woman nods. "She's your daughter?"

"Yes," the girl's mother says, finding her voice.
"I'm sorry. This isn't a good time," she says, "but I
know why you're here. Please come in."

Rasbach steps into the house. The doorway opens
into a living room that appears to be full of women
crying. Three middle-aged women and a teenage girl

are sitting around a coffee table covered with plates of food.

"Our mother died yesterday," Mrs. Stavros says. "My sisters and I are trying to make arrangements."

"I'm very sorry to bother you," Detective Rasbach says. "I'm afraid it's important. Is your daughter here?" But he's already spotted her on the sofa with her aunts—a chubby sixteen-year-old, her hand hovering over a plate of brownies as she lifts her eyes and sees the detective enter the living room.

"Katerina, there's a policeman here to see you."

Katerina and all the girl's aunts turn to stare at the detective.

The girl starts spouting fresh, genuine tears and says, "About Cora?"

Rasbach nods.

"I can't believe someone would take her," the girl says, putting her hands back in her lap, forgetting about the brownies. "I feel so bad. My grandma died, and I had to cancel."

Immediately all the aunts hover around the girl while her mother perches on the arm of the sofa beside her.

"What time did you call the Contis' house?" Rasbach asks kindly. "Do you remember?"

The girl begins to weep. "I don't know."

Her mother turns to Detective Rasbach. "It was about six. We had a call from the hospital around then, asking us to come, because it was the end. I told Katerina to call and cancel and come to the hospital with us." She puts a hand on her daughter's shoulder. "We feel terrible about Cora. Katerina is very fond of her. But this is not Katerina's fault." The mother wants everyone to be very clear on this point.

"Of course not," Rasbach says emphatically.

"I can't believe they left her alone in the house," the woman says. "What kind of parents would do that?"

Her sisters shake their heads in disapproval.

"I hope you find her," the girl's mother says, looking worriedly at her own daughter, "and that she's okay."

"We will do everything we can," Rasbach says, and turns to go. "Thank you for your time."

The Contis' story has checked out. The baby was almost certainly still alive at 6:00 p.m., or how would the parents have dealt with the expected sitter? Rasbach realizes that if the parents had killed or hidden the baby, it had to have happened after that six o'clock call. And either before seven, when they went over to the neighbors', or sometime during the party. Which means they probably wouldn't have had enough time to dispose of the body.

Maybe, Rasbach thinks, *they're telling the truth.*

With the detective out of the house, Anne feels she can breathe a little more easily. It's like he's watching them, waiting for them to make a misstep, to make a mistake. But what mistake can he possibly be waiting for? They don't have Cora. If they had found some physical evidence of an intruder, she thinks, he wouldn't be zeroing in, wrongly, on them. But whoever has taken Cora has obviously been very careful.

Perhaps the police are incompetent, Anne thinks.

She is worried that they will bungle everything. The investigation is moving too slowly. Every hour that goes by ratchets her panic up another notch.

"Who could have taken her?" Anne whispers to Marco when they're alone. Anne has sent her parents home for the time being, even though they'd wanted to settle themselves in the spare room upstairs. But Anne, as much as she relies on her parents, especially in times of stress and trouble, finds they make her anxious, too, and she is anxious enough. Plus, having them around always makes things more difficult with Marco, and he already looks like he's about to snap. His hair is a mess, and he hasn't shaved. They've been up all night, and the day is half gone. Anne is exhausted and knows she must look as bad as Marco does, but she doesn't care. Sleep is impossible.

"We have to think, Marco! Who would take her?"

"I have no idea," Marco says helplessly.

She gets up and starts pacing back and forth in the living room. "I don't understand why they haven't found any evidence of an intruder. It doesn't make sense. Does that make sense to you?" She stops pacing and adds, "Except for the loosened lightbulb in the motion detector. That's obviously evidence that there was an intruder."

Marco looks up at her. "They think we loosened the lightbulb ourselves."

She stares at him. "That's ridiculous!" There is a note of hysteria in her voice.

"It wasn't us. We know that," Marco says fiercely. He runs his hands nervously up and down his thighs on his jeans, a new habit. "The detective is right about one thing—it looks planned. Somebody didn't just walk by, see the door open, and go in and take her. But if she was taken for ransom, why wouldn't the kidnapper have left a note? Shouldn't we have heard from them by now?" He checks his watch. "It's almost three o'clock! She's been gone over twelve hours already," he says, his voice breaking.

That's what Anne thinks, too. Surely they should have heard from someone by now. What was normal in cases of kidnapping? When she'd asked Detective Rasbach, he'd said, "There is no normal in a kidnapping. They're all unique. If ransom is demanded, it can be within hours—or days. But generally kidnappers don't want to be holding on to the victim for any longer than they have to. The risks go up over time."

The police have put a wiretap on their phone to record any potential conversations with the kidnapper. But so far no one claiming to have Cora has called.

"What if it's someone who knows your parents?" Marco suggests. "Maybe one of your parents' acquaintances?"

"You'd like to blame this on them, wouldn't you?" Anne snaps, walking back and forth in front of him with her arms crossed.

"Hang on," Marco says. "I'm not blaming this on them, but think about it for a minute! The only ones with real money around here are your parents. So it has to be somebody who knows them and knows they've got money. We don't have the kind of money a kidnapper would be after, obviously."

"Maybe they should be monitoring my parents' calls," Anne says.

Marco looks up at her and says, "Maybe we need to be more creative with the reward."

"What do you mean? We already offered a reward. Fifty thousand dollars."

"Yes, but fifty thousand dollars for information leading to our getting Cora back—how much is that going to help if nobody saw anything? If anybody actually saw something, don't you think they would have told the police by now?" He waits while Anne considers this. "We have to get things moving," Marco says urgently. "The longer they have Cora, the greater the chance they'll harm her."

"They think I did it," Anne says suddenly. "They think I killed her." Her eyes are wild. "I can tell from the way that detective looks at me that he's already made his mind up about me. He's probably just trying to decide how much *you* had to do with it!"

Marco jumps up off the sofa and tries to embrace her. "Shhhh," he says. "They don't think that." But he's worried that that is exactly what they think. The postpartum depression, the antidepressants, the psychiatrist. He doesn't know what to say to her to soothe her. He can feel her agitation building and wants to prevent a crisis.

"What if they go see Dr. Lumsden?" Anne says.

Of course they'll go see Dr. Lumsden, Marco thinks. How could she imagine for a moment that they wouldn't visit her psychiatrist?

"They probably will," Marco says, his voice deliberately calm, even matter-of-fact. "But so what? Because you had nothing to do with Cora's disappearance, and we both know it."

"But she'll tell them things," Anne says, clearly frightened.

"No she won't," Marco says. "She's a doctor. She can't tell them anything you told her. Doctor-patient privilege. There's no way they can get your doctor to tell them anything you talked to her about."

Anne starts to pace up and down the living room again, wringing her hands. Then she stops and says, "Right. You're right." She takes some deep breaths. And then she remembers. "Dr. Lumsden's away. She's gone to Europe for a couple of weeks."

"That's right," Marco says. "You told me."

He places his hands on both her shoulders and presses down on her firmly, anchors her with his eyes. "Anne, I don't want you to worry about that," he says resolutely. "You have nothing to be afraid of. Nothing to hide. So they find out you've had some problems with depression even before the baby so what? Half the people out there are probably depressed. That fucking detective is probably depressed himself."

He fixes her with his eyes until her breathing returns to normal and she nods.

Marco drops his arms. "We need to focus on getting Cora back." He flops down on the sofa, exhausted.

"But how?" Anne says. She is wringing her hands again.

Marco says, "What I was starting to say before,

about the reward. Maybe we're going about this the wrong way. Maybe we should try to deal directly with whoever has her—maybe we offer a lot of money for her and see if he calls us."

Anne thinks for a minute. "But if a kidnapper has her, why hasn't he made a ransom demand?"

"I don't know! Maybe he panicked. Which scares the hell out of me, because then maybe he'll kill Cora and dump her somewhere!"

Anne asks, "How do we start negotiating with the kidnapper if he's not even in touch with us?"

Marco looks up. "Through the media."

Anne nods, thinking. "How much do you think it would take, to get her back?"

Marco shakes his head in despair. "I have no idea. But we only get one shot at this, so we have to make it worthwhile. Maybe two or three million?"

Anne doesn't even flinch. "My parents adore Cora. I'm sure they'll pay. Let's get them back here, and Detective Rasbach, too."

Rasbach returns hurriedly to the Contis' house, summoned by Marco on his cell phone.

Both Marco and Anne are standing in the living room. They have freshly tearstained faces, but they look resolved. For a brief moment, Rasbach thinks they are about to confess.

Anne is watching for her parents at the front window. At that moment Richard and Alice arrive and come swiftly up the steps past the reporters, somehow maintaining their dignity in spite of the flash of cameras around them. Anne lets them in, careful to remain unseen behind the door.

"What's happened?" Richard says, alarmed, looking at his daughter, at the detective. "Did you find her?"

Alice's sharp eyes try to take everything in at once. She seems both hopeful and frightened.

"No," Anne says. "But we need your help."

Rasbach watches all of them closely. Marco says nothing.

Anne speaks. "Marco and I think we should offer money directly to the kidnapper. A significant amount. Whoever's got her, maybe if we offer enough money and promise not to prosecute, he'll give her back." She turns to her parents. Marco stands beside her. "We have to do something," she says piteously. "We can't just sit here and wait for him to kill her!" Her eyes desperately search her parents' faces. "We need your help."

Alice and Richard regard each other very briefly. Then Alice says, "Of course, Anne. We'll do anything to get Cora back."

"Of course," Richard agrees, nodding emphatically.

"How much do you need?" Alice asks.

"What do you think?" Anne says, turning to Detective Rasbach. "How much would be enough to get someone to give her up?"

Rasbach considers the question carefully before answering. If you're innocent, it would be natural to want to throw money, any amount of money, at the person who has your child. And this family appears to have almost unlimited funds. It's certainly worth a try. The parents may not be involved at all. And time is running out.

"What were you thinking, in terms of amount?" Rasbach asks.

Anne looks uncomfortable, as if she's embarrassed to put a price tag on her child. She has no idea, really. How much is too much? How much is too little? "Marco and I were thinking maybe a couple million, maybe more?" Her uncertainty is obvious. She looks at her mother and father uneasily. Is she asking too much of them?

"Of course, Anne," Alice says. "Whatever you need."

"We'll need some time to get it," Richard says, "but we'll do anything for Cora. And for you, too, Anne. You know that."

Anne nods tearfully. She hugs her mother first, then goes over and puts her arms around her father, who hugs her back. He holds her while her shoulders shake with sobs.

For a brief moment, Rasbach thinks about how much easier life is for the wealthy.

Rasbach watches Richard look over his daughter's head at his son-in-law, who says nothing at all.

NINE

T hey settle on three million dollars. It's a lot of money, but it won't ruin Richard and Alice Dries. The couple has millions more. They can afford it.

Less than twenty-four hours after they first reported their baby missing, early Saturday evening, Anne and Marco face the media again. They have not spoken to the press since seven o'clock that morning. Once again they have carefully crafted a message at their coffee table with the help of Detective Rasbach and then gone out onto the front steps to give a statement.

This time Anne has changed into a simple but chic black dress. No jewelry, save pearl earrings. She has showered, washed her hair, even applied a small amount of makeup, trying to put on a brave face. Marco has also showered and shaved and changed into a white shirt and clean jeans. They look like an attractive, professional couple in their thirties, blindsided by tragedy.

When they step out onto the small porch, just

before the six o'clock newscasts, the cameras flash as before. Interest in the case has built throughout the day. Marco waits for the hubbub to die down and then addresses the reporters. "We would like to make another statement," he says loudly, but he is immediately interrupted before he can begin.

"How do you explain the mix-up in what the baby was wearing?" someone asks from the sidewalk below them.

"How could you make a mistake like that?" another voice demands.

Marco glances at Rasbach and then answers, not bothering to hide his annoyance. "I believe the police already issued a statement about that earlier, but I'll tell you again." He takes a deep breath. "We put Cora down earlier in the evening in the pink onesie. When my wife fed her at eleven o'clock, the baby spit up on her sleeper. My wife changed her into a different one, a mint green onesie, in the dark, but then in all the distress of her being taken we simply forgot that." Marco's manner is cold.

The crowd of reporters is silent at this, digesting it. Suspicious.

Marco takes advantage of the silence and reads from his prepared text. "Anne and I love Cora. We will do anything to get her back. We beg whoever took her to return her to us. We are able to offer the sum of three million dollars." There is a gasp from the crowd, and Marco waits. "We are able to offer three million dollars to whoever has our baby. I'm speaking to you, to whoever has Cora—call us and we will talk. I know you are probably watching. Please contact us, and we will find a way to get the money to you in exchange for our daughter's safe return."

Then Marco lifts his head and says directly to the cameras, "I say to the person who has her, I promise you there will be no charges. We just want her back."

He has gone off the prepared script with this last bit, and Detective Rasbach's right eyebrow rises slightly.

"That's all."

The bulbs flash furiously as Marco lowers the piece of paper in his hand. The reporters pepper him with questions, but he turns his back on them and helps Anne into the house. Detectives Rasbach and Jennings follow them inside.

Rasbach knows that regardless of Marco's message, the kidnapper, whoever he or she is, will not be immune from prosecution. The parents don't get to make that call. The kidnapper no doubt knows it as well. If this is in fact a kidnapping for ransom, the trick is to get the money into the hands of the person who has the baby and get the baby back unharmed without anybody panicking and doing something stupid. But the crime of kidnapping is a serious one, so for a kidnapper, if things go south, the temptation to kill the victim and dump the body to avoid being caught is strong.

Back inside the house, Rasbach says, "Now we wait."

Marco is finally able to persuade Anne to go upstairs and try to get some rest. She's had some soup and crackers—all she's had to eat all day. She's had to pump her breast milk periodically, retreating to the baby's room to do this in privacy. But pumping is not as effective as nursing a suckling baby, and now she is engorged, her breasts swollen, hot to the touch, and sore.

Before she tries to nap, she must pump again. She sits in her nursing chair and is overwhelmed with tears. How is it possible that she is sitting in this chair and instead of looking down at her baby girl at her breast—opening and closing her little fists and staring up at her mother with those big round blue eyes, those long lashes—she is pumping out her milk by hand into a plastic container to be dumped down the bathroom drain? It takes a long time. First one breast, then the other.

How is it that she can't remember changing the baby out of the pink onesie? What else can she not remember about that night? It's shock, she's sure. That's all it is.

Finally she is done. She rearranges her clothing and gets up out of the nursing chair and makes her way to the bathroom at the top of the stairs. As she dumps the breast milk into the sink, she stares at herself in the fractured mirror.

Rasbach walks a few blocks from the Contis' home to a street of fashionable shops, galleries, and restaurants.

It is another hot, humid summer evening. He stops for a quick meal and reviews what he knows. The babysitter unexpectedly canceled at 6:00 p.m.—he has to assume the baby was alive at that time. The Contis were at the neighbors' by seven o'clock, probably giving them insufficient time to kill and dispose of the baby between the call from the babysitter and going next door. Also, no one appears to have seen either of them leave the house between 6:00 and 7:00 p.m. the day before, with or without the baby.

Both Marco and Anne say that Marco had checked on the baby—using their back door—at twelve thirty. Marco claims that the motion detector was working at that time. Forensics has found fresh tire tracks in the garage that don't match the Contis' car. Paula Dempsey witnessed a car without headlights going quietly down the lane away from the Contis' house at 12:35 a.m. The lightbulb in the motion detector had obviously been loosened.

Which means either the kidnapper struck after twelve thirty—sometime between when Marco checked on the baby and when the couple returned home—and the car Paula Dempsey saw was irrelevant, or Marco was lying and had disabled the light himself and taken the baby out to the waiting car. The baby didn't fly to the garage. Someone carried her, and the only footprints in the yard belong to Marco and Anne. The driver, or accomplice, if there had been one, likely never got out of the car. Then Marco returned to the party and sat casually smoking cigarettes in the neighbors' backyard and flirting with the neighbor's wife.

There's one problem: the babysitter. Marco could not have known that the babysitter would cancel. The fact that there was supposed to be a babysitter in the home argues against this being a carefully planned kidnapping for ransom.

But—he might be looking at something more spontaneous.

Had the husband or wife killed the baby accidentally, in a fit of anger perhaps, either between six and seven—perhaps the baby was harmed during their argument—or at some time when they were checking on her through the night? If something like that had happened, had they then hurriedly arranged for someone to help them dispose of the baby in the early hours of the morning?

It bothers him, the pink onesie. The mother says she tossed it in the laundry hamper beside the changing table. But it was found hidden underneath the pad of the changing table. Why? Perhaps she was sufficiently drunk that she hadn't stuffed the soiled sleeper into the laundry hamper but instead shoved it underneath the pad. If she was drunk enough to think she'd put the onesie in the hamper when she hadn't, was she drunk enough to drop the baby? Maybe she dropped her, and the baby struck her head and died. Maybe the mother smothered her. If that's what happened, how had the parents arranged so quickly for someone to take the baby away? Who would they call?

He has to find the possible accomplice. He will get the Contis' home- and cell-phone records and find out whether either of them called anyone between six and twelve thirty on the night in question.

If the baby hadn't been killed, either accidentally or deliberately by either one of the parents, would they stage a kidnapping?

Rasbach can guess why they might. There's three million dollars to be had. Possibly more. Motivation enough for almost anybody. The ease with which the child's grandparents offered the money to the distressed parents was telling.

Rasbach will soon know as much as it is possible to know about Anne and Marco Conti.

Now it's time to interview the neighbors.

TEN

Rasbach stops by the Contis' house and picks up Jennings. When the detectives arrive, watched by reporters, at the neighbors' door, they find that the husband, Graham Stillwell, is not at home.

Rasbach had already met the couple, briefly, in the middle of the previous night, when the child had first been reported missing. Cynthia and Graham Stillwell had been shocked into speechlessness by the abduction of the baby next door. At that time Rasbach had focused his attention on the backyard, the fence, and the passageway between the two houses. But now he wants to talk to Cynthia, the hostess of the dinner party, to see what light, if any, she can shed on the couple next door.

She is a beautiful woman. Early thirties, long black hair, large blue eyes. She has the kind of figure that stops traffic. She is also fully aware of her own attractiveness, and she makes it difficult for anyone else not to be aware of it, too. She is wearing a blouse, deeply unbuttoned, flattering linen trousers, and high-heeled sandals. She is perfectly made up, even though someone stole her guests' baby while they were at her house late the night before. But beneath the perfect makeup, she is obviously tired, as if she has slept poorly, or not at all.

"Have you found out anything?" Cynthia Stillwell asks once she's invited them in. Rasbach is struck by the similarities with the house next door. The layout is the same, and the carved wooden staircase curving to the upper floor, the marble fireplace, and the front window are identical. But each home has the unmistakable stamp of its own occupants. The Contis' home is done in subdued colors and filled with antiques and art; the Stillwells' has more modern leather furniture—white—glass-and-chrome tables, and punches of bright color.

Cynthia takes the chair in front of the fireplace and elegantly crosses one leg over the other, dangling a sandaled foot featuring perfectly painted scarlet toenails.

As he and Jennings seat themselves on the sleek leather sofa, Rasbach smiles regretfully and says, "I'm afraid we're not at liberty to discuss details." The woman across from him seems nervous. He wishes to put her at ease. "What do you do, Mrs. Stillwell?" he asks.

"I'm a professional photographer," she says. "Freelance, mostly."

"I see," he says, flicking his eyes to the walls, which display several nicely framed black-and-white photos. "Yours?"

"Yes, actually." She gives a small smile.

"It's a terrible thing, the baby being taken," Rasbach says. "It must be very unsettling for you."

"I can't stop thinking about it," she says, in evident distress. She furrows her brow. "I mean, they were here when it was happening. Here we all were, having a good time, oblivious. I feel awful." She licks her lips.

"Can you tell me about the evening?" Rasbach asks. "Just tell me about it in your own words."

"Okay." She takes a deep breath. "I had planned a party for Graham's fortieth birthday. He just wanted something small. So I invited Marco and Anne for dinner because we sometimes have dinner together and we're all good friends. We used to have dinner together a lot before the baby, not so much after. We hadn't seen much of them for a while."

"Did you suggest that they leave the baby at home?" Rasbach asks.

She flushes. "I didn't know they couldn't get a sitter."

"My understanding is that they *had* a sitter but she canceled at the last minute."

She nods. "Right. But I would never have said they couldn't bring the baby, if they didn't have a sitter. They showed up with the baby monitor and said the sitter had canceled and they would just plug the monitor in and check on her a lot."

"And what did you think of that?"

"What did *I* think of it?" she asks, raising her eyebrows in surprise. Rasbach nods and waits. "I didn't think anything of it. I'm not a parent. I assumed they knew what they were doing. They seemed fine with it.

I was too busy getting the dinner prepared to give it much thought." She adds, "To be honest, with one of them leaving every half hour to check on her, it would probably have been less disruptive just to have the baby here." Cynthia pauses. "On the other hand, she's a pretty fussy baby."

"And Anne and Marco—you say they went next door to check on the baby every half hour?"

"Oh, yes. They were rigid about it. The perfect parents."

"How long would they be gone when they checked on her?" Rasbach asks.

"It varied."

"How do you mean?"

She tosses her black hair over her shoulder and straightens her back. "Well, when Marco went, he'd be pretty quick. Like five minutes or less. But Anne would stay away longer. I remember I joked with Marco at one point that maybe she wasn't coming back."

"When was this?" Rasbach leans forward slightly, fastening his eyes on hers.

"I think around eleven. She was gone a long time. When she did come back, I asked her if everything was all right. She said everything was fine, she'd just had to feed the baby." Cynthia nodded firmly. "That's right, it was eleven, because she said she always feeds the baby at eleven, and then the baby sleeps through till about five." Cynthia suddenly looks uncertain and adds, "When she came back after the eleven o'clock feeding, it looked like she'd been crying."

"Crying? Are you sure?"

"That's how it looked to me. She'd washed her face after, I think. Marco looked at her like he was worried. I remember thinking it must be a bore having to worry about Anne all the time."

"Why do you think Marco was concerned?"

Cynthia shrugs. "Anne can be moody. I think she's finding motherhood harder than she expected." She flushes, realizing the awkwardness of what she's just said, given the circumstances. "I mean, motherhood has changed her."

"Changed her how?"

Cynthia takes a deep breath and settles more into her chair. "Anne and I used to be better friends. We used to have coffee, go shopping, talk. We actually had a lot in common. I'm a photographer, and she worked in an art gallery downtown. She's mad about abstract art—at least she used to be. She was damn good at that gallery—a good curator, good at sales. She has an eye for quality and for what will sell." She pauses, remembering.

"Yes?" Rasbach prompts.

Cynthia continues. "Then she got pregnant, and it seemed like all she could think about was babies. She only wanted to shop for baby things." Cynthia gives a little laugh. "Sorry, but I found it a bit tedious after a while. I think she was hurt that I wasn't that interested in her pregnancy. We had less in common. Then, when the baby was born, it took up all her time. I understand that—she was exhausted—but she became less interesting, if you know what I mean." Cynthia pauses and crosses her long legs. "I think she should have gone back to work after the baby was a few months old, but she didn't want to. I think she felt she had to be the perfect mother."

"Has Marco changed much since the baby came?" Rasbach asks.

She tilts her head, thinking about it. "Not really, no, but then we haven't seen much of him. He seems the same to me, but I think Anne's been bringing him down a bit. He still likes to have fun."

Rasbach asks, "Did Anne and Marco speak privately after she returned from checking the baby?"

"What do you mean?"

"Did you and your husband go into the kitchen to clean up or anything and leave them alone together at all during the evening? Did they sit together in a corner or anything?"

"I don't know. I don't think so. Marco was mostly hanging out with me, because you could tell that Anne wasn't in too cheerful a mood."

"So you don't remember them conferring together throughout the evening?"

She shakes her head. "No, why?"

Rasbach ignores her question. "Describe how the rest of the evening went, if you don't mind."

"We were sitting around in the dining room mostly, because it's air-conditioned, and it was such a hot night. Marco and I were doing most of the talking. My husband is generally pretty quiet, sort of an intellectual. He and Anne are alike that way. They get along."

"And you and Marco get along?"

"Marco and I are more extroverted, for sure. I liven up my husband, and Marco livens up Anne. Opposites attract, I guess."

Rasbach waits, letting silence fill the room. Then he asks, "When Anne came back after the eleven o'clock feeding, besides looking like she might have been crying, did she seem different in any way?"

"Not that I noticed. She just seemed tired—but that's the way she is these days."

"Who checked on the baby next?"

Cynthia thinks. "Well, Anne got back around eleven thirty, I think, so Marco didn't go. He was going on the half hour, and she was going on the hour—that's the arrangement they had. So Anne went again at midnight, and then Marco went at twelve thirty."

"How long was Anne gone when she went to check the baby at midnight?" Rasbach asks.

"Oh, not long, a couple of minutes."

"And then Marco went at twelve thirty."

"Yes. I was in the kitchen, clearing up a bit. He slipped out the back door saying he was going to pop out and check the baby and he'd be right back. He winked at me."

"He winked at you?"

"Yes. He'd been drinking quite a lot. We all had."

"And how long was he gone?" Rasbach asks.

"Not long, two or three minutes. Maybe five."

Cynthia shifts in her seat, recrosses her legs. "When he got back, we went outside to the patio for a cigarette."

"Just the two of you?"

"Yes."

"What did you two talk about?" Rasbach asks. He remembers the way Marco flushed when he mentioned having the cigarette with Cynthia, remembers how angry Anne had been about her husband flirting with the woman sitting across from him.

Cynthia says, "Not much. He lit me a cigarette." Rasbach waits, saying nothing. "He began stroking my legs. I was wearing a dress with a slit up the side." She looks uncomfortable. "I don't think any of this is relevant, do you? What does this have to do with the baby being kidnapped?"

"Just tell us what happened, if you don't mind."

"He was stroking my legs. And then he got all hot and pulled me onto his lap. He kissed me."

"Go on," Rasbach says.

"Well . . . he got pretty excited. We both got a little carried away. It was dark, we were drunk."

"How long did this go on?" Rasbach asks.

"I don't know, a few minutes."

"Were you not worried about your husband or Anne coming out and finding you and Marco . . . embracing?"

"To be honest, I don't think we were thinking too clearly. As I said, we'd had a lot to drink."

"So nobody came and found you."

"No. I eventually pushed him off me, but I was nice about it. It wasn't easy, because he was all over me. Persistent."

"Are you and Marco having an affair?" Rasbach asks bluntly.

"What? No. We're not having an affair. I thought it was just a harmless flirtation. He's never touched me before. We'd had too much to drink."

"After you pushed him away, then what happened?"

"We straightened ourselves out and went back inside."

"What time was it then?"

"It was almost one, I think. Anne wanted to leave. She didn't like that Marco had been with me out on the back patio."

I bet, Rasbach thinks. "Were you out on the patio anytime earlier in the evening?"

She shakes her head. "No. Why?"

"I'm wondering if you had an opportunity to notice whether the motion-detector light went on when Marco went into the house anytime earlier in the evening?"

"Oh. I don't know. I didn't see him go over there."

"Other than you and your husband—and Marco and Anne, of course—do you know if anyone else knew that the baby was alone next door?"

"Not that I'm aware of." She shrugs her elegant shoulders. "I mean, who else would know?"

"Is there anything you can add, Mrs. Stillwell?"

She shakes her head. "Sorry, I'm afraid not. It seemed like a normal night to me. How could anyone imagine something like this happening? I wish they'd just brought the baby with them."

"Thank you for your time," Rasbach says, and rises to go. Jennings stands up beside him. Rasbach hands her his card. "If you remember anything else, anything at all, please give me a call."

"Of course," she says.

Rasbach looks out the front window. The reporters are milling around, waiting for them to emerge. "Do you mind if we slip out the back?" he says.

"Not at all," Cynthia says. "The garage is open."

The detectives slip out the sliding glass doors in the kitchen and make their way across the backyard and through the Stillwells' garage. They stand in the lane, unseen from the street.

Jennings looks sidelong at Rasbach and raises his eyebrows.

"Do you believe her?" Rasbach asks him.

"About what, exactly?" the other man asks. The two detectives speak in low voices.

"About the hanky-panky in the backyard."

"I don't know. Why would she lie? And she *is* pretty hot."

"People lie all the time, in my experience," Rasbach says.

"Do you think she was lying?"

"No. But something about her is off, and I don't know what it is. She seemed nervous, like she was holding something back or hiding something," Rasbach says. "The question is, assuming she's telling the truth, why was Marco making a pass at her shortly after twelve thirty? Was he able to do that because he had no idea that his baby was being taken at roughly that time, or did he do it because he'd just handed the baby off to an accomplice and had to look like he didn't have a care in the world?"

"Or maybe he's a sociopath," Jennings offers. "Maybe he handed the baby off to an accomplice and it didn't bother him at all."

Rasbach shakes his head. "I don't think so." Virtually all the sociopaths Rasbach has come across—and after decades on the force he's come across a few—have had an air of confidence, even grandiosity, about them.

Marco looks like he's about to crack under the strain.

ELEVEN

A nne and Marco wait in the living room by the phone. If the kidnapper calls, Rasbach— or if Rasbach isn't there, someone else from the police—will be present to coach Marco through the call. But there is no call from the kidnapper. Family and friends have called, reporters, cranks, but no one claiming to be the kidnapper.

Marco is the one answering the phone. If the kidnapper does call, Marco will do the talking. Anne doesn't think she can hold it together; nobody thinks Anne can hold it together. The police don't trust Anne to keep a cool head and follow instructions. She is too emotional; she has moments approaching hysteria. Marco is more rational, but he is certainly jumpy.

Around 10:00 p.m. the phone rings. Marco reaches for it. Everyone can see that his hand is shaking. "Hello?" he says.

There is nothing on the other end but breathing.

"Hello," Marco says, more loudly, his eyes shifting quickly to Rasbach. "Who is this?"

The caller hangs up.

"What did I do wrong?" Marco says, panicked.

Rasbach is by his side instantly. "You didn't do anything wrong."

Marco gets up and starts pacing the living room.

"If that was the kidnapper, he'll call back," Rasbach says evenly. "He's nervous, too."

Detective Rasbach watches Marco closely. Marco is clearly agitated, which is understandable. He is under a lot of pressure. If this is all an act, Rasbach thinks, he is a very good actor. Anne is crying quietly on the sofa, periodically wiping her eyes with a tissue.

Careful police work has determined that nobody with a garage opening onto the lane was driving down the lane at 12:35 a.m. the night before. Of course, the lane is also used by others, not just those with garages there—it opens out to side streets at each end, and drivers use it to get around the problem of the one-way streets. The police are trying desperately hard to find the driver of that vehicle. Paula Dempsey is the only one they've found who saw the car at that time.

If there is a kidnapper, Rasbach thinks, they would probably have heard from him by now. Perhaps there will never be any call from a kidnapper. Maybe the parents killed the baby and got help disposing of the body and this is all an elaborate charade to divert suspicion of murder from them. The problem is, Rasbach has pulled their cell-phone records and their home-phone records, and there were no calls made

by either of them to anyone after six o'clock the previous night, except the emergency call to 911.

Which means that if they did it, it might not have
been spontaneous. Perhaps it was planned all along
and they prearranged to have somebody waiting in
the garage. Or maybe one of them has an untraceable, prepaid cell phone that was used. The police
haven't found one, but that doesn't mean it didn't
exist. If they got help disposing of the body, they must
have called someone.

The phone rings several more times. They have
been told that they are murderers and to stop fucking
the police around. They have been told to pray. They
have been offered psychic services—for a fee. But no
one claiming to be the kidnapper has called.

Finally Anne and Marco go upstairs to bed. Neither of them has slept in the last twenty-four hours,
and for the day before that. Anne has tried to lie
down, but she's been unable to sleep. Instead she sees
Cora in her mind's eye and can't believe that she is
unable to touch her, that she doesn't know where her
baby is or if she's okay.

Anne and Marco lie down on the bed together in
their clothes, ready to jump up if the phone rings.
They hold each other and whisper.

"I wish I could see Dr. Lumsden," Anne says.

Marco pulls her close. He doesn't know what to
say. Dr. Lumsden is away in Europe somewhere, for
the next couple of weeks. Anne's appointments have
been canceled. "I know," Marco whispers.

Anne whispers back, "She said I could see the doctor who's covering for her if I needed to. Maybe I should."

Marco considers. He's worried about her. He worries that if this goes on too long, it will truly damage her. She has always been fragile when stressed. "I don't know, baby," Marco says. "With all those reporters out there, how would you go to the doctor's?"

"I don't know," Anne whispers bleakly. She doesn't want the reporters following her to a psychiatrist's office either. She is worried about the press learning of her postpartum depression. She saw what they were like about the mistake with the onesie. So far the only ones who know about her depression are Marco and her mother, her doctor and her pharmacist. And the police, of course, who went through their house right after the baby was taken and found her medication.

If she hadn't been in treatment by a psychiatrist, would the police be circling them now like wolves? Maybe not. It's her fault they're under suspicion. The police have no reason to suspect them otherwise. Unless it's because they left the baby in the house alone. That was Marco's fault. So they're both to blame.

Anne lies in bed remembering what it felt like to hold her baby against her own body, to feel the warmth of her pudgy little infant daughter in her arms, wearing only a diaper, her skin smelling of baby and bath time. She remembers Cora's beautiful smile and the curl in the middle of her forehead—like the little girl in the nursery rhyme. She and Marco have often joked about it.

There was a little girl, and she had a little curl,
Right in the middle of her forehead.
And when she was good, she was very, very good,
And when she was bad, she was horrid.

As broken as she feels—*what kind of mother feels depressed after the gift of a perfect baby?*—Anne loves her daughter desperately.

But the exhaustion had been overwhelming. Cora was a fussy, colicky baby, more demanding than most. When Marco had gone back to work, the days had begun to feel unbearably long. Anne filled the hours as best she could, but it was lonely. All the days began to seem the same. She couldn't imagine them ever being any different. In her fog of sleep deprivation, she couldn't remember the woman she used to be when she worked at the art gallery—could hardly remember how it felt to help clients add pieces to their collections or the thrill of finding a promising new artist. In fact, she could hardly remember what she was like before she'd had the baby and stayed home to care for her.

Anne didn't like to ask her mother to come and help—she was busy with her friends and the country club and her charities. None of Anne's own friends were staying home with babies at the same time. Anne struggled. She felt ashamed that she wasn't coping well. Marco suggested hiring someone to help, but that made her feel inadequate.

The only relief was her moms' group, which met for three hours once a week, on Wednesday mornings. But she hadn't really connected with any of the other moms sufficiently to share her feelings. They all seemed genuinely happy, and more competent at motherhood than she was, even though it was the first baby for each of them.

And there was the one session a week in the early evening with Dr. Lumsden, while Marco watched Cora.

All Anne wants now is to go back twenty-four hours. She looks at the digital clock on her bedside table—11:31. Twenty-four hours ago, she was just leaving Cora in her crib to return to the party. None of this had happened; everything was fine. If only she could turn the clock back. If she could have her baby back, she would be so grateful, she would be so happy, she didn't think she would ever be depressed again. She would cherish every minute with her daughter. She would never complain about anything, ever again.

Lying in bed, Anne makes a private deal with God, even though she does not believe in God, and weeps into her pillow.

Eventually Anne falls asleep, but Marco lies awake beside her for a long time. He cannot stop the buzzing in his brain.

He looks over at his wife, sleeping restlessly on her side, her back to him. It is her first sleep in more than thirty-six hours. He knows she needs to sleep if she is to cope with this.

He stares at her back and thinks about how much she has changed since the baby was born. It was entirely unexpected. They'd looked forward to the baby so much together—decorating the nursery, shopping for baby things, attending the birth-preparation classes, feeling the baby kick in her tummy. They had been some of the happiest months of his life. It had never occurred to him that it would be hard afterward. He hadn't seen it coming.

Her labor had been long and difficult; they hadn't been prepared for that either. Nobody ever tells you about that in birthing classes—everything that can go wrong. In the end Cora had been born by emergency C-section, but she was fine. She was perfect. Mother and baby were both fine, and they came home from the hospital to a new life.

The recovery, too, had taken longer and been more difficult for Anne because of the C-section. She seemed disappointed that she hadn't had a normal birth. Marco had tried to talk her out of it. It wasn't what he'd imagined, either, but it hadn't seemed like a big deal to him. Cora was perfect, Anne was healthy, and that was all that mattered.

Anne had trouble breast-feeding in the beginning, getting the baby to latch on. They'd had to get professional help. Anne's own mother had been of no use—she'd bottle-fed her baby.

Marco wants to reach out and lightly stroke Anne's back, but he's afraid of waking her. She has always been emotional, sensitive. She is one of the most refined women he's ever met. He used to love dropping in on her at the gallery. Sometimes he would surprise her there at lunchtime, or after work, just because he wanted to see her. He got a kick out of watching her with clients, the way she lit up when talking about a painting or a new artist. He'd think, *I can't believe she's mine.*

Whenever there was an opening for a new show, she would invite him; there would be champagne and hors d'oeuvres, women in smart dresses and men in well-cut suits. Anne would circulate around the room, stopping to talk with the people clustered in front of the paintings—wild, abstract splashes of color or more somber, tonal works. Marco didn't understand any of it. The most beautiful, the most arresting thing in the room, for him, would always be Anne. He would stay out of her way, stand over by the bar eating cheese, or off to the side, and watch her do her thing. She had been trained for it, getting her degree in art history and modern art, but more than that, she had an instinct for it, a passion. Marco had not grown up with art, but it was part of her life, and he loved her for it.

For their wedding he'd bought her a painting in the gallery that she fervently desired but that she said they could never afford—a very large, moody abstract work by an up-and-coming painter she greatly admired. It hangs over their mantelpiece in the living room. But she no longer even looks at it.

Marco rolls onto his back and stares at the ceiling,

his eyes burning. He needs her to keep it together. He can't have the police suspecting her, suspecting them, any more than they do already. What she said about Dr. Lumsden disturbed him. The fear in her eyes. Had she said something to the doctor about wishing to harm the baby? That's what women with postpartum depression sometimes thought about.

Jesus. Jesus. Fuck.

His computer at the office. He'd Googled "postpartum depression" and followed the links to "postpartum psychosis," read those horrible stories about women who'd murdered their babies. The woman who had smothered her two kids. The woman who'd drowned her five children in the bathtub. The one who had driven her kids into a lake. Jesus fucking Christi. If the police look at his computer at the office, they'll find all that.

Marco starts to sweat just lying in bed. He feels clammy, sick. What would the police make of that if they found it? Do they already think that Anne killed Cora? Do they think he helped her cover it up? If they saw his browser history, would they think he'd been worried for weeks about Anne?

He lies there flat on his back, eyes wide open. Should he tell the police about it, before they find it themselves? He doesn't want to look like he's hiding anything. They'll wonder why he researched it at work, instead of using his home computer.

His heart is racing now, as he gets up. He makes his way downstairs in the dark, leaving Anne snoring lightly behind him. Detective Rasbach is in the chair in their living room that he seems to have chosen as his favorite, doing something on his laptop. Marco wonders if the detective ever sleeps, wonders when he's going to leave their house. He and Anne can't exactly kick him out, although they would both like to.

Detective Rasbach looks up as Marco comes into the room.

"I can't sleep," Marco mumbles. He sits down on the sofa, tries to think of how to begin. He can feel the detective's eyes on him. Should he tell or not? Have they been to his office yet? Have they looked at his computer? Have they found out the mess his business is in? Do they know that he's at risk of losing his company? If they don't yet, they soon will. He knows they're suspicious of him, that they're looking into his background. But having financial problems doesn't make you a criminal.

"There's something I'd like to tell you," Marco says nervously.

Rasbach looks at him calmly and puts his laptop aside.

"I don't want you to misconstrue this," Marco says.

"Okay," Detective Rasbach says.

Marco takes a deep breath before he begins. "When Anne was diagnosed with postpartum depression a few months ago, it really kind of freaked me out."

Rasbach nods. "That's understandable."

"I mean, I had no experience with this kind of thing. She was getting very depressed, you know, crying a lot. She seemed listless. I was worried about her, but I thought she was just exhausted, that it was temporary. I thought she'd get over it when the baby started sleeping through the night. I even suggested that maybe she should go back to work part-time, because she loved her job at the gallery and I thought it would give her a break. But she didn't want to do that. She looked at me like I thought she was a failure as a mother." Marco shakes his head. "Of course I didn't think that! I suggested she get a bit of help during the day, maybe get a girl in so she could nap, but she wouldn't hear of it."

Rasbach nods again, listening intently.

Marco continues, feels himself getting more nervous. "When she told me her doctor said she had postpartum depression, I didn't want to make it into a big deal, you know? I wanted to be supportive. But I was worried, and she wasn't telling me much." He starts rubbing his hands on his thighs. "So I looked it up online, but not here at home, because I didn't want her to know I was worried. So I used my computer at the office." He feels himself flushing. This is coming out all wrong. He sounds as if he suspects Anne, as if he doesn't trust her. It sounds like they're keeping secrets from each other.

Rasbach stares back at him, inscrutable. Marco can't make out what the detective is thinking. It's unnerving.

"So I just wanted you to know, if you check my computer at work, why I was looking at those sites about postpartum depression. I was trying to understand what she was going through. I wanted to help."

"I see." Rasbach nods as if he completely understands. But Marco can't tell what he's really thinking.

"Why do you want to tell me that you were researching postpartum depression at your office? It seems a natural enough thing to do, in your situation," Rasbach says.

Marco feels a chill. Has he just made things worse? Has he just made them want to examine his office computer? Should he explain further about following the links to the murders or just leave things as is? For a moment he panics, unsure of what to do. He decides he has already screwed up enough. "I just thought I should tell you, that's all," Marco says gruffly, and gets up to go, angry with himself.

"Wait," the detective says. "Do you mind if I ask you something?"

Marco sits back down. "Go ahead." He crosses his arms in front of him.

"It's about last night, when you went back to the neighbors' house after checking on the baby at twelve thirty."

"What about it?"

"What were you and Cynthia talking about out there?"

The question makes Marco feel uncomfortable. What *had* they talked about? Why is he asking? "Why do you want to know what we were talking about?"

"Do you remember?" Rasbach asks.

Marco can't remember. He doesn't remember talking much at all.

"I don't know. Just trivial stuff. Chitchat. Nothing important."

"She's a very attractive woman, wouldn't you agree?"

Marco is silent.

"Wouldn't you agree?" Rasbach repeats.

"I guess," Marco says.

"You say that you don't remember seeing or hearing anything when you were out back last night between shortly after twelve thirty and just before one a.m., when the two of you returned inside."

Marco hangs his head, doesn't look at the detective. He knows where this is going. He starts to sweat.

"You said"—and here the detective flips back through his notebook for a bit—"you said you 'weren't paying attention.' Why were you not paying attention?"

What the hell should he do here? He knows what the detective is getting at. Like a coward, Marco says nothing. But he feels the pulse in the vein at his temple, wonders if the detective notices.

"Cynthia says that you came on to her, that you made sexual advances to her out on the patio."

"What? No I didn't." Marco lifts his head sharply and looks at the detective.

The detective consults his notes again, flips some pages. "She says you ran your hand up her legs, that you kissed her, pulled her onto your lap. She says you were quite persistent, that you got carried away."

"That's not true!"

"It's not true? You didn't kiss her? And get carried away?"

"No! I mean—I didn't come on to her, *she* came on to *me*." Marco can feel himself blush deeply and is furious with himself. The detective says nothing. Marco fumbles over the words in his haste to defend himself, all the while thinking, *That lying bitch.*

"That's not how it happened," Marco insists. "*She* started it." He cringes at how that sounds, how juvenile. He takes a steadying breath. "She came on to me. I remember, she came and sat on my lap. I told her she shouldn't be on my lap and tried to nudge her off. But she took my hand and placed it inside her skirt. She was wearing this long dress with a slit up the side." Marco is really sweating now, thinking how this must sound. He tries to relax. Tells himself no matter how much of a heel the detective must think him, there's no reason for him to think this has anything to do with Cora. "*She* kissed *me*." Marco stops, colors again. He can tell that Rasbach doesn't believe a word of it. "I kept protesting, and telling her we shouldn't, but she wouldn't get off my lap. She got my fly down. I was afraid someone would see us."

Rasbach says, "You had a lot to drink. How reliable is your memory of what happened?"

"I was drunk, but I wasn't *that* drunk. I know what happened. I didn't start anything with her. She practically threw herself at me."

"Why would she lie?" Rasbach asks simply.

Why would she lie? Marco is asking himself the same question. Why would Cynthia screw him over like this? Was she pissed that he told her no? "Maybe she's mad because I turned her down."

The detective purses his lips as he looks at Marco.

Desperately, Marco says, "She's lying."

"Well, one of you is lying," Rasbach says.

"Why would I lie about something like that?" Marco says stupidly. "You can't arrest me for kissing another woman."

"No," the detective says. He waits a moment or two and says, "Tell me the truth, Marco. Are you and Cynthia having an affair?"

"No! Absolutely not. I love my wife. I wouldn't do that, I swear." Marco glares at the detective. "Is that what Cynthia says? Did she tell you we're having an affair? That's absolute bullshit."

"No, she didn't say that."

Anne, sitting in the dark at the top of the stairs, hears it all. She goes cold all over. She now knows that last night, when their baby was being taken, her husband was kissing and fondling Cynthia next door. She doesn't know who started it—from what she'd observed the night before, it could have been either one of them. They were both guilty. She feels sick to her stomach, betrayed.

"Are we done here?" Marco says.

"Yeah, sure," the detective answers.

Anne scrambles quickly to her feet at the top of the stairs and, barefoot, pads quickly back to their bedroom. She's shaking. She climbs into the bed under the duvet and pretends to sleep but fears that her ragged breathing will give her away.

Marco comes into the bedroom, his footsteps heavy. He sits down on the edge of the bed, facing away from her, looks at the wall. She opens her eyes slightly and stares at his back. She pictures him making out with Cynthia on the patio chair while she was bored out of her mind with Graham in the dining room. And while he had his hand in Cynthia's panties and Anne was pretending to listen to Graham, someone was taking Cora.

She will never be able to trust him again. Never. She turns over and pulls the covers higher, while silent tears roll down her face and pool around her neck.

Cynthia and Graham are in their bedroom next door, having a heated argument. Even so, they are careful to keep their voices quiet. They don't want to be overheard. There is a laptop open on their queen-size bed.

"No," Graham says. "We should just go to the police."

"And say what?" Cynthia asks. "A little late for that, don't you think? They were already over here, questioning me, while you were out."

"It's not that late," Graham counters. "We tell them we had a camera on the backyard. We don't have to say any more than that. They don't have to know why we put it up there."

"Right. And how do we explain, exactly, why we haven't mentioned it up till this point?"

"We can say we forgot about it." Graham is leaning up against the headboard, looking worried.

Cynthia laughs, but there's no humor in it. "Really. The police were swarming all over the place because a baby has been kidnapped, and we *forgot* that we have a pinhole camera trained on our backyard." She gets up and starts taking off her earrings. "They're never going to believe that."

"Why not? We can say that we never check it, or that we thought it was broken, or that the battery was dead. We can say we thought it didn't work and it was just for show."

"Just for show—to scare thieves away. When it's so well hidden that the police didn't even see it." She drops an earring into a mirrored jewelry box on her dressing table. She shoots him an annoyed look and mutters, "You and your fucking cameras."

"You enjoy watching the films, too," Graham says.

Cynthia doesn't correct him. Yes, she enjoys watching the films, too. She enjoys watching herself having sex with other men. She likes the way it turns her husband on to see her with them. But what she enjoys even more is that it gives her permission to flirt with and have sex with other men. Men more attractive and more exciting than her husband, who has proved to be a bit of a disappointment lately. But she didn't get very far with Marco. Graham had hoped she would be able to give Marco a proper blow job, or that he would lift up her skirt and fuck her from behind. Cynthia knew exactly how the camera was positioned to get the best angle.

Graham's job was to keep the wife occupied. That was always his job. It was tedious for him, but it was worth it.

Except now they have a problem.

TWELVE

It is Sunday afternoon. There have been no new leads. No one has called claiming to have Cora. The case appears to be at an impasse, but Cora is still out there somewhere. *Where is she?*

Anne walks over to the living-room window. The curtains are drawn shut for privacy, filtering the room's light. She stands to the side and holds the curtain open a little to peek out. There are a lot of reporters on the sidewalk, spilling over onto the street.

She is living in a fishbowl, everyone tapping on the glass.

Already there are indications that the Contis aren't turning out to be the media darlings the press had hoped for. Anne and Marco haven't welcomed the media; they clearly see the reporters as an intrusion, a necessary evil. They are not particularly photogenic either, even though Marco is handsome and Anne was pretty enough, before. But it's not enough to be handsome—one should preferably have charisma, or at least warmth. There is nothing charismatic about Marco now. He looks like a shattered ghost. They both look guilty, beaten down by shame. Marco has been cold in his interactions with the media; Anne has said nothing at all. They have not been warm to the press, and so the press has not warmed to them. This is, Anne realizes, probably a tactical mistake, one they may live to regret.

The problem is that they had not been home. It has come out that they were next door when Cora was taken from her crib. Anne was horrified when she saw that morning's headlines: COUPLE NOT HOME WHEN BABY TAKEN, STOLEN BABY WAS LEFT ALONE. If they'd been sound asleep in their own house while their child was kidnapped from her room, there would have been a much greater outpouring of sympathy, from the press and from the public. The fact that they were attending a party next door has scalded them. And of course the postpartum depression has also been made public. Anne doesn't know how these things happen. She certainly didn't tell the press. She suspects Cynthia might have been the source of the leak about their leaving the baby alone in the house, but she doesn't know how the media found out about her depression. Surely the police would not have leaked her private medical information. She has even asked them, and they say it didn't come from them. But Anne doesn't trust the police. Whoever is responsible for the leaks, they have only damaged Anne further in the eyes of everyone—the public, the press, her parents, her friends, everyone. She has been publicly shamed.

Anne turns to look at the steadily increasing pile

of toys and other colorful debris collecting on the sidewalk at the bottom of their front steps. There are bouquets of wilted flowers, stuffed animals of all colors and sizes—she can see teddy bears, even an outsize giraffe—with notes and cards stuck on them. A mountain of cliché. Such an outpouring of sympathy. And of hate.

Earlier that day Marco had gone out and brought an armful of the toys and notes in to her, to cheer her up. That was a mistake he won't make again. Many of the notes were venomous, even shocking. She read a few of them, gasped, balled them up, and threw them to the floor.

She twitches the curtains with her fingers and looks out again. This time a thrill of horror slides down her back. She recognizes the women coming single file down the sidewalk toward the house, pushing their baby strollers: it is three—no—four women from her moms' group. The reporters fall away to let them through, sensing impending drama. Anne watches in disbelief. Surely, she thinks, they have not come to visit her *with their babies.*

She sees the one in front, Amalia—mother of cute, brown-eyed Theo—reach beneath her stroller and grab what looks like a large container of prepared food. The other women behind her do the same thing, applying the brakes to their strollers, reaching for covered dishes in the baskets beneath the seats.

Such kindness, and such thoughtless cruelty. She can't bear it. A sob escapes Anne as she turns abruptly from the window.

"What is it?" Marco says, alarmed, coming up to her.

He pushes the curtain aside and looks out the window at the sidewalk.

"Get rid of them!" Anne whispers. *"Please."*

On Monday morning at nine o'clock, Detective Rasbach requests that Marco and Anne come to the police station for formal questioning. "You are not under arrest," he assures them as they stare back at him, dumbstruck. "We would like to take a statement from each of you and ask a few more questions."

"Why can't you do that here?" Anne asks, in obvious distress. "Like you've *been* doing?"

"Why do we have to go to the station?" Marco echoes, looking appalled.

"It's standard procedure," Rasbach says. "Would you like some time to freshen up first?" he suggests.

Anne shakes her head, as if she doesn't care what she looks like.

Marco does nothing at all, just stares at his feet.

"Okay, then, let's go," Rasbach says, and leads the way.

When he opens the front door, there is a flurry of activity. The reporters cluster around the front steps, cameras flashing. "Are they under arrest?" someone calls out.

Rasbach answers no questions and remains stonily silent as he steers Marco and Anne through the crush to the police cruiser parked in front of the house. He opens the rear door, and Anne goes in first and slides across the backseat. Marco steps in after her. No one speaks, except the reporters, who clamor after them with their questions. Rasbach climbs into the passenger seat, and the car pulls away. The photographers run after them, taking pictures.

Anne stares out the window. Marco tries to hold her hand, but she pulls it away. She watches the familiar city pass by the window—the produce stand on the corner, the park where she and Cora sit on a blanket in the shade and watch children splash in the wading pool. They cross the city—now they are not far from the art gallery where she used to work, close to the river. Then they are going past the Art Deco building where Marco has his office, and then suddenly they are out of downtown. It all looks very different from the back of a police cruiser, on the way to be questioned in the disappearance of your own child.

When they arrive at the police station, a modern building of concrete and glass, the cruiser stops at the front doors and Rasbach shepherds them in. There are no reporters here—there had been no advance warning that Anne and Marco would be taken in for questioning.

When they walk into the station, a uniformed officer at a circular front desk glances up with interest. Rasbach hands Anne over to a female officer. "Take her to Interview Room Three," Rasbach tells her.

Anne looks at Marco in alarm. "Wait. I want to be with Marco. Can't we be together?" Anne asks. "Why are you separating us?"

Marco says, "It's okay, Anne. Don't worry. Everything's going to be okay. We haven't done anything.

They just want to ask us some questions, and then they're going to let us go, isn't that right?" he says to Rasbach, a hint of challenge in his voice.

"That's right," the detective says smoothly. "As I said, you are not under arrest. You are here voluntarily. You are free to leave at any time."

Marco stands still and watches Anne go down the hall with the female officer. She turns and looks back at him. She's terrified.

"Come with me," Rasbach says. He takes Marco into an interview room at the end of the hall. Detective Jennings is already there. The room contains a metal table with a single chair on one side and two chairs on the other side for the detectives.

Marco doesn't trust himself to make any sense, to keep things straight. He can feel the exhaustion hitting him. He tells himself to talk slowly, to think before he answers.

Rasbach is wearing a clean suit and a fresh shirt and tie. He is newly shaven. Jennings is, too. Marco is wearing old jeans and a wrinkled T-shirt that he hauled out of his drawer that morning. He hadn't known he was going to be brought down to the station. He realizes now that he should have taken advantage of the detective's offer to shower, shave, change clothes. He would have felt more alert, more in control. And he would have looked less like a criminal on the permanent recording of this interview; he has just realized that he is probably going to be videotaped.

Marco sits down and nervously watches the two detectives standing across the table from him. It's different being here, instead of in his own home. It's frightening. He feels the shift of control.

"If it's okay with you, we're going to videotape this interview," Rasbach says. He gestures to a camera positioned just below the ceiling, pointing toward them at the table.

Marco has no idea if he really has a choice. He hesitates for a fraction of a second, then says, "Yeah, sure, no problem."

"Would you like some coffee?" Rasbach offers.

"Yeah, sure, thanks," Marco says. He tries to relax. He reminds himself he is here to help the police find out who has taken his child.

Rasbach and Jennings go out to get coffee, leaving Marco alone to fret.

When the two detectives return, Rasbach places Marco's paper cup on the table in front of him. Marco sees that he has brought him two sugars and one cream—Rasbach has remembered how Marco takes his coffee. As Marco fumbles with the sugar packets, his hands are trembling. They all notice.

"Please state your name and today's date," Rasbach says, and they begin.

The detective leads him through a series of straightforward questions that establish Marco's version of what happened on the night of the kidnapping. It is a rehash of what has gone before, nothing new. Marco can feel himself relaxing as the interview progresses.

Finally he thinks they're finished, that they're about to let him go. His relief is enormous, although he's careful not to show it. He has time then to wonder how it's going in the other room, with Anne.

"Good, thank you," Rasbach says when they've taken his statement. "Now, if you don't mind, I just have a few more questions."

Marco, who had started to rise out of his metal chair, sits back down.

"Tell us about your company, Conti Software Design."

"Why?" Marco asks. "What has my company got to do with anything?" He stares at Rasbach, trying to hide his dismay. But he knows what they're getting at. They've been looking into him; of course they have.

"You started your company about five years ago?" Rasbach prompts.

"Yes," Marco says. "I have degrees in business and computer science. I'd always wanted to go into business for myself. I saw an opportunity in software design—specifically, in designing user interfaces for medical software. So I started my own company. I've got some key clients. A small staff of software-design professionals, all working remotely. Mostly we visit clients on site, so I travel a fair bit on business. I keep an office downtown myself. We've been quite successful."

"Yes, you *have* done very well," Rasbach agrees. "Impressive. It can't have been easy. Is it expensive? To start a company like that?"

"It depends. I started out very small, just me and a couple of clients. I was the only designer in the beginning—I worked from home and put in very long hours. My plan was to build the business gradually."

"Go on," Rasbach says.

"The company became very successful, very quickly. It grew fast. I needed to hire more designers to keep up with demand, and to take the business to the next level. So I expanded. The time was right. There were bigger costs then. Equipment, staff, office space. You need money to grow."

"And where did that money come from, to expand your business?" the detective asks.

Marco looks at him, annoyed. "I don't see why it matters to you, but I got a loan from my in-laws, Anne's parents."

"I see."

"What do you see?" Marco says irritably. He has to remain calm. He can't afford to get ruffled. Rasbach is probably doing this just to piss him off.

"I didn't mean anything by it," the detective says mildly. "How much money did you get from your wife's parents?"

"Are you asking me, or do you know already?" Marco says.

"I *don't* know. I'm asking."

"Five hundred thousand," Marco says.

"That's a lot of money."

"Yes, it is," Marco agrees. Rasbach is baiting him. He can't rise to it.

"And has the business been profitable?"

"For the most part. We have good years and not-so-good years, like anybody else."

"What about this year? Would you say it's been a good year or a not-so-good year?"

"It's been a rather shitty year, since you ask," Marco says.

"I'm sorry to hear that," Rasbach says. And waits.

"We've had some setbacks," Marco says finally. "But I'm confident things will get on track. Business is always up and down. You can't just throw in the towel when you have a bad year. You have to tough it out."

Rasbach nods thoughtfully. "How would you describe your relationship with your wife's parents?"

Marco knows that the detective has seen him and his father-in-law in the same room. There is no point in lying.

"We don't like each other."

"And yet they still loaned you five hundred thousand dollars?" The detective's eyebrows have gone up.

"Her mother and father together loaned it to us. They have the money. They love their daughter. They want her to have a good life. My business plan was sound. It was a solid business investment for them. And an investment in their daughter's future. It's been a satisfactory arrangement for all concerned."

"But isn't it the case that your business desperately needs a cash infusion?" Rasbach asks.

"Every business these days could use a cash infusion," Marco says, almost bitterly.

"Are you on the verge of losing the company you've worked so hard to build?" Rasbach says, leaning forward slightly.

"I don't think so, no," Marco says. He is not going to let himself be intimidated.

"You don't think so?"

"No."

Marco wonders where the detective has gotten his information. His business *is* in trouble. But as far as he knows, they didn't have a warrant to go through his business or bank records. Is Rasbach guessing? Who has he spoken to?

"Does your wife know about your business troubles?"

"Not entirely." Marco squirms in his seat.

"What do you mean?" the detective asks.

"She knows that business hasn't been great lately," Marco admits. "I haven't burdened her with the details."

"Why's that?"

"We have a new baby, for Christ's sake!" Marco snaps, raising his voice. "She's been depressed, as you know. Why would I tell her the business is in trouble?" He runs his hand through his hair, which falls back haphazardly into his eyes.

"I understand," Rasbach says. "Have you approached your in-laws for help?"

Marco sidesteps the question. "I think things will turn around."

Rasbach lets it go. "Let's talk about your wife for a moment," he says. "You say that she's been depressed. You told me earlier that she was diagnosed with postpartum depression by her doctor. Her psychiatrist. A doctor . . ." He consults his notes. "Lumsden." He lifts his eyes. "Who is currently away."

"Yes, you know that," Marco says. "How many times do we have to go over this?"

"Can you describe her symptoms for me?"

Marco moves restlessly in the uncomfortable metal chair. He feels like a worm pinned to a board. "As I've told you before, she was sad, crying a lot, listless. She seemed overwhelmed at times. She wasn't getting enough sleep. Cora's a pretty fussy baby." When he says this, he remembers that she is gone and has to pause a moment to regain his self-control. "I suggested she get someone to help her with the baby, so that she could take a nap during the day, but she wouldn't. I think she felt she should be able to manage on her own, without help."

"Your wife has a history of mental illness?"

Marco looks up, startled. "What? No. She has a bit of a history of depression, like a million other people." His voice is firm. "Mental illness, no." Marco doesn't like what the detective is suggesting. He braces himself for what's coming next.

"Postpartum depression is considered a mental illness, but let's not quibble." Rasbach leans back in his chair and looks at Marco as if to say, *Can we speak frankly?* "Did you ever worry that Anne might harm the baby? Or harm herself?"

"No, never."

"Even though you looked up postpartum psychosis on the Internet?"

So they *have* been through his computer. They've

seen what he's looked at, the stories about women murdering their children. Marco can feel the sweat break out in tiny beads on his forehead. He moves around in his chair. "No. I told you about that. . . . When Anne was diagnosed, I wanted to know more about it, so I did some searches on postpartum depression. You know what it's like on the Internet, one thing leads to another. You follow the links. I was just curious. I didn't read those stories about women who went crazy and killed their kids because I was worried about Anne. No way."

Rasbach stares at him without saying anything.

"Look, if I was worried that Anne might harm our baby, I wouldn't have left her home alone with the baby all day, would I?"

"I don't know. Would you?"

The gloves have come off. Rasbach looks at him, waiting.

Marco glares back. "Are you going to charge us with something?" Marco asks.

"No, not at this time," the detective says. "You're free to go."

Marco stands up slowly, pushing his chair back. He wants to run the hell out of there, but he's going to take his time, he's going to look like he's in control, even if it isn't true.

"Just one more thing," Rasbach says. "Do you know anyone with an electric car, or possibly a hybrid?"

Marco hesitates. "I don't think so," he says.

"That's all," the detective says, rising from his chair. "Thanks for coming in."

Marco wants to get right in Rasbach's face and snarl, *Why don't you do your goddamned job and find our baby?* But instead he strides, too quickly, out of the room. Once outside the door, he realizes he doesn't know where Anne is. He cannot leave without her. Rasbach comes up behind him.

"If you'd like to wait for your wife, we shouldn't be too long," he says, and goes down the corridor and opens a door into another room, where, Marco presumes, his wife sits waiting.

THIRTEEN

Anne sits in the cool interview room and shivers. She is wearing jeans and only a thin T-shirt. The room is over-air-conditioned. The woman officer stands by the door, discreetly watching her. They told Anne that she's here voluntarily, that she's free to go at any time, but it feels like she's a prisoner.

Anne wonders what is going on in the other room, where they're interviewing Marco. It is a stratagem, to separate them. It makes her nervous and unsure of herself. The police obviously suspect them. They are going to try to set Anne and Marco against each other.

Anne needs to prepare herself for what's coming, but she doesn't know how.

She considers telling them that she wants to speak to a lawyer but fears that will make her look guilty. Her parents could afford to get her the best criminal lawyer in the city, but she's afraid to ask them. What would they think if she asked them to get her a lawyer? And what about Marco? Do they each need a separate lawyer? It infuriates her, because she knows they did not harm their baby; the police are wasting their time. And meanwhile Cora is alone somewhere, terrified, abused, or— Anne feels like she's going to be sick.

To stop herself from throwing up, she thinks instead about Marco. But then she sees it again in her mind, him kissing Cynthia, his hands on her body— the body that is so much more desirable than her own. She tells herself that he was drunk, that Cynthia probably came on to him, just like he said, rather than the other way around. She'd watched Cynthia come on to Marco all night. Still, Marco went out back with her for a cigarette. He was just as much to blame. They both denied they were having an affair, but she doesn't know what to believe.

The door opens, making her jump in her seat. Detective Rasbach enters, followed by Detective Jennings.

"Where's Marco?" Anne asks, her voice shaky.

"He's waiting for you in the lobby," Rasbach says, and smiles briefly. "We won't be long," he says gently. "Please relax."

She smiles weakly back at him.

Rasbach points to a camera mounted near the ceiling. "We'll be videotaping this interview."

Anne glances at the camera, dismayed. "Do we have to do this on camera?" she asks. Then she looks nervously at the two detectives.

"We record all our interviews," Rasbach tells her. "It's to protect everyone concerned."

Anne straightens her hair nervously, tries to sit up taller in her chair. The woman officer remains stationed at the door, as if they're afraid she'll make a run for it.

"Can I get you anything?" Rasbach asks. "Coffee? Water?"

"No, thank you."

Rasbach says, "Okay, then, let's get started. Please state your name and today's date." The detective leads her carefully through the events of the night the baby went missing. "When you saw that she wasn't in the crib, what did you do?" Rasbach asks. His voice is kind, encouraging.

"I told you. I think I screamed. I threw up. Then I called 911."

Rasbach nods. "What did your husband do?"

"He looked around the upstairs while I was calling 911."

Rasbach looks more sharply at her, his eyes on hers. "How did he seem?"

"He seemed shocked, horrified, like me."

"You found nothing out of place, nothing disturbed, other than that the baby was gone?"

"That's right. We searched the house before the police arrived, but we didn't notice anything. The only thing different or odd—other than that she wasn't there and that her blanket was gone—was that the front door was open."

"What did you think when you found the crib empty?"

"I thought someone had taken her," Anne whispers, looking down at the table.

"You told us that you smashed the bathroom mirror after finding the baby gone, before the police arrived. Why did you smash the bathroom mirror?" Rasbach asks.

Anne takes a deep breath before answering. "I was angry. I was angry because we had left her at home alone. It was our fault." Her voice is dry; her lower lip trembles. "Actually, could I have some water?" she asks, looking up.

"I'll get it," Jennings offers, and he leaves the room, soon returning with a bottle of water that he places on the table in front of Anne.

Gratefully, she twists off the cap and takes a drink.

Rasbach resumes his questioning. "You said you'd had some wine. You're also on antidepressant medication, the effects of which are increased with the use of alcohol. Do you think your memories of what happened that night are reliable?"

"Yes." Her voice is firm. The water seems to have revived her.

"You are certain of your version of events?" Rasbach asks.

"I'm certain," she says.

"How do you explain the pink onesie that was found underneath the pad on the changing table?" Rasbach's voice is not so gentle now.

Anne feels her composure deserting her. "I . . . I thought I put it in the hamper, but I was very tired. It must have gotten shoved under there somehow."

"But you can't explain how?"

Anne knows what he's driving at. How much can he trust her version of events when she can't explain something as simple as how the onesie, which she said she remembered putting into the laundry hamper, was underneath the pad on the changing table?

"No. I don't know." She begins to wring her hands in her lap beneath the table.

"Is there any possibility that you might have dropped the baby?"

"What?" Her eyes snap up to meet the detective's. His eyes are unnerving; she feels they can see right through her.

"Is there any possibility that you might have accidentally dropped the baby, that she was harmed in some way?"

"No. Absolutely not. I would remember that."

Rasbach is not so friendly now. He leans back in his chair and cocks his head at her, as if he doesn't believe her. "Perhaps you dropped her earlier in the evening and she hit her head, or perhaps you shook her and when you came back to see her, she wasn't breathing?"

"No! That didn't happen," Anne says desperately. "She was fine when I left her at midnight. She was fine when Marco checked her at twelve thirty."

"You don't actually know if she was fine when Marco checked on her at twelve thirty. You weren't there, in the baby's room. You only have your husband's word for it," Rasbach points out.

"He wouldn't lie," Anne says anxiously, continuing to wring her hands.

Rasbach lets silence fill the room. Then, leaning forward, he says, "How much do you trust your husband, Mrs. Conti?"

"I trust him. He wouldn't lie about that."

"No? What if he went to check on the baby and found she wasn't breathing? What if he thought you had harmed her—hurt her by accident or held a pillow over her face? And he arranged for someone to take the body away because he was trying to protect you?"

"No! What are you saying? That I killed her? Is that what you really think?" She looks from Rasbach to Jennings to the woman officer at the door, then back at the detective.

"Your neighbor, Cynthia, says that when you returned to the party after you fed the baby at eleven, you looked like you'd been crying and that you'd washed your face."

Anne colors. This is a detail she'd forgotten. She *had* cried. She'd fed Cora in her chair in the dark at eleven with tears running down her face. Because she was depressed, because she was fat and unattractive, because Cynthia was tempting her husband in a way that she could no longer tempt him, and she felt useless and hopeless and overwhelmed. Trust Cynthia to notice—and to tell the police.

"You are under the care of a psychiatrist, you said. A Dr. Lumsden?" Rasbach sits up straight now and picks up a file from the table. Opens it and looks inside.

"I already told you about Dr. Lumsden," Anne says, wondering what he's looking at. "I am seeing her for mild postpartum depression, as you know. She prescribed an antidepressant that's safe while breast-feeding. I have never thought about harming my child. I didn't shake her or smother her or hurt her in any way. I didn't drop her by accident either. I wasn't that drunk. I was crying when I fed her because I was sad about being fat and unattractive, and Cynthia—who is supposed to be a friend—had been flirting with my husband all evening." Anne draws strength from the anger she feels, remembering this. She sits up straighter and looks the detective in the eye. "Maybe you should become a little better informed about postpartum depression, Detective. Postpartum depression is not the same thing as postpartum psychosis. I am clearly not psychotic, Detective."

"Fair enough," Rasbach says. He pauses, puts down the file and asks, "Would you describe your marriage as a happy one?"

"Yes," Anne says. "We have some issues, like most couples, but we work them out."

"What kinds of issues?"

"Is this really relevant? How is this helping to find Cora?" She moves restlessly in her chair.

Detective Rasbach says, "We have every available person working on finding Cora. We are doing everything we can to find her." Then he adds, "Maybe you can help us."

She slumps, discouraged. "I don't see how."

"What sorts of issues come up in your marriage? Money? That's a big one for most couples."

"No," Anne says tiredly. "We don't fight about money. The only thing we ever fight about is my parents."

"Your parents?"

"They don't like one another, my parents and Marco. My parents never approved of him. They think he's not good enough for me. But he is. He's perfect for me. They can't see any good in him because they don't want to. That's just the way they are. They never liked anyone I dated. No one was ever good enough. But they hate him because I fell in love with him and married him."

"Surely they don't hate him," Rasbach says.

"It seems that way sometimes," Anne says. She looks down at the table. "My mother doesn't think he's good enough for me, basically because he's not from a wealthy family, but my father really seems to hate him. He baits him all the time. I can't understand why."

"They have no particular reason to dislike him?"

"No, not at all. Marco's never done anything wrong." She sighs unhappily. "My parents are very hard to please, and they're very controlling. They gave us money when we were starting out, and now they think they own us."

"They gave you money?"

"For the house." She flushes.

"You mean, as a gift?"

She nods. "Yes, it was a wedding gift, so we could buy a house. We couldn't afford one on our own, without help. Houses are so expensive, at least nice ones in good neighborhoods are."

"I see."

"I love the house," Anne admits. "But Marco hates feeling beholden to them. He didn't want to accept the wedding gift. He would rather have made it all on his own—he's proud that way. He let them help us for me. He knew I wanted the house. He would have been happy to start out in a crappy little apartment. Sometimes I think I made a mistake." She's wringing her hands in her lap. "Maybe we should have refused their wedding gift, started out in some shabby place, like most couples. We might still be there, but we might be happier." She starts to cry. "And now they think it's his fault that Cora's gone, because it was his idea to leave her at home alone. They won't stop reminding me about it."

Rasbach slides the tissue box on the table to within Anne's reach. Anne takes a tissue and dabs her eyes. "And really, what can I say? I try to defend him to them, but it *was* his idea to leave her at home. I didn't like it. I still can't believe I agreed to it. I'll never forgive myself."

"What do *you* suspect happened to Cora, Anne?" Detective Rasbach asks.

She looks away from him and stares at the wall, unseeing. "I don't know. I keep thinking about it and thinking about it. I was hoping that someone took her for ransom, because my parents are rich, but no one has been in touch with us, so . . . I don't know, it's hard to stay positive. That's what Marco thought at first. But he's losing hope, too." She looks back at him, her face bleak. "What if she's dead? What if our baby is already dead?" She breaks down and sobs. "What if we never find her?"

Fourteen

Rasbach had gone through Marco's office computer. No wonder Marco was worried about that. While it was understandable that a man in Marco's position might Google postpartum depression, his browser history showed that he'd strayed quite far into postpartum psychosis. He'd read about the woman found guilty of drowning her five children in a bathtub in Texas. He'd read about the mother who'd killed her children by driving her car into a lake, the woman in England who had strangled her two young children in a closet. He'd read about other women who had drowned, stabbed, smothered, and throttled their own children. Which meant, to the detective's mind, that either Marco was afraid his wife might become psychotic or he was interested in that information for some other reason. It occurs to Rasbach that Marco may be setting his wife up to take a big fall. The baby might just be collateral damage. Does he simply want out?

But this isn't his favorite theory. As Anne pointed out, she is not psychotic. These women who killed their babies were clearly in the throes of psychosis. If she killed the baby, it was probably accidentally.

No, his favorite theory is that Marco arranged the kidnapping to get the badly needed ransom money—despite what Marco said about things turning around, his business is clearly in serious trouble.

They haven't been able to account for the car. No one has come forward to acknowledge driving down the lane at 12:35 on the night of the kidnapping. The police have sought the public's help in the matter of the mystery car. If anyone in the area had been driving innocently down the lane at the relevant time, given all the newspaper and TV coverage, that person would in all likelihood have come forward. But no one had come forward—probably because whoever it was was an accomplice to the crime. Detective Rasbach believes that the person in that car took the baby away.

Rasbach thinks the child was either killed accidentally by the parents and the body taken away by an accomplice or that this is a staged kidnapping and the baby was handed off by Marco to someone who has lost his nerve and hasn't made the expected arrangements to receive the ransom money and return the baby. If so, the wife may or may not be in on it; Rasbach needs to look closely at her. If what Rasbach suspects is true, Marco must be going out of his mind.

But the babysitter is troubling him. Would Marco have staged a kidnapping if there was going to be a babysitter in the house?

Rasbach sees no point in having a police officer sitting around the Contis' house waiting for a ransom call that will probably never come. He makes a strategic decision. They will retreat; he will get the police out of the house and see what happens when the two of them are alone. If he is right, and something has gone wrong, if he is to find out what it is, he must take a step back and give Marco enough rope to hang himself.

And the baby? Rasbach wonders if even Marco knows whether the missing child is still alive. Rasbach remembers the famous Lindbergh kidnapping case, where it looked as if the baby died accidentally, either during or soon after the kidnapping. Maybe that's what happened here. He can almost feel sorry for Marco. Almost.

It is Tuesday morning, the fourth day since Cora went missing. Now the last police officer is leaving. Anne can't believe that they are to be left all alone. "But what if the kidnapper calls?" she protests to Rasbach in disbelief.

Marco says nothing. It seems obvious to him that the kidnapper is not going to call. It seems equally obvious to him that the police don't believe there *is* a kidnapper.

Rasbach says, "You'll be fine. Marco can handle it." She gives him a doubtful look. "Maybe our being here is scaring him off—maybe if we leave, he'll call." He turns to Marco. "If anyone claiming to have Cora calls, remain calm, try to get instructions, and keep him talking as much as possible. The more you can get him to reveal, the better. We still have the wiretap on, so it will be taped. But it is very unlikely that we would be able to trace the call. Everyone these days uses untraceable prepaid cell phones. Makes our job much harder."

Then Rasbach leaves. Marco, for one, is glad to see him go.

Now Anne and Marco are alone in the house. The number of reporters outside on the street has dwindled as well. With no developments the media have little to report—they are losing enthusiasm. The pile of wilted flowers and teddy bears is not growing any larger.

"They think I killed her," Anne says, "and that you covered it up."

"They can't think that," Marco says, trying to reassure her. There isn't much else he can say. What's he going to tell her? *Either that or they think I took her and faked the kidnapping for the ransom money.* But he doesn't want her to know how bad their financial situation really is.

Marco goes upstairs to lie down. He is exhausted. His grief and distress are such that he can hardly bear to look at his wife.

Anne putters around the house, somewhat relieved to be rid of the police after all, tidying up. She moves in a sleep-deprived fog, putting things away, washing coffee cups. The kitchen phone rings, and she stops. She looks at the caller ID. It's her mother. Anne hesitates, not sure she wants to speak to her. Finally, on the third ring, she picks up the phone.

"Anne," her mother says. Anne immediately feels her heart sink. Why did she answer? She can't deal with her mother right now. She sees Marco coming quickly down the stairs, his eyes alert. She mouths *My mother* at him and waves him away. He turns and goes back upstairs.

"Hi, Mother."

"I'm so worried about you, Anne. How are you doing?"

"How do you think?" Anne holds the phone to her ear, walks to the rear of the kitchen, and looks out the window to the backyard.

Her mother is quiet for a moment. "I just want to help."

"I know, Mom."

"I can't imagine what you're going through. Your father and I are hurting, too, but it must be nothing compared to what you're feeling."

Anne starts to cry, the tears rolling silently down her cheeks.

Her mother says, "Your father is still very upset about the police taking you in for questioning yesterday."

"I know, you told me that yesterday," Anne says wearily.

"I know, but he won't stop talking about it. He says they should be focusing on finding Cora, not harassing you."

"They say they're just doing their job."

"I don't like that detective," her mother says uneasily. Anne sinks into one of the kitchen chairs. Her mother says, "I think I should come over and you and I should have some tea and a private talk. Just the two of us, without your father. Is Marco home?"

"No, Mom," Anne says. Anxiety rises in her throat. "I can't today. I'm too tired."

Her mother sighs. "You know your father is very protective of you," she says. She pauses, then adds tentatively, "Sometimes I wonder if it was right for us to keep things from him when you were younger."

Anne freezes. Then she says, "I have to go," and hangs up the phone.

She stands by the window looking out at the backyard, trembling, for a long time.

Detectives Rasbach and Jennings are in a police cruiser, Jennings behind the wheel. It is hot in the cruiser, and Rasbach adjusts the air-conditioning. They soon arrive at St. Mildred's School, an exclusive private school in the northwest part of the city for girls from kindergarten to twelfth grade. Anne Conti spent her entire academic life here before college, so they ought to know something about her.

Unfortunately for the detectives, it is the middle of the summer holidays, but Rasbach called beforehand and made an appointment with a Ms. Beck, the headmistress, who apparently has plenty of work to do, even in the summer.

Jennings parks in the empty lot. The school is a

lovely old stone building that looks a bit like a castle, surrounded by greenery. The place oozes money. Rasbach imagines all the luxury cars driving up and disgorging privileged girls in uniform at the front doors. But at the moment it is dead quiet, except for the sound of a man on a riding mower cutting the grass.

Rasbach and Jennings walk up the shallow stone steps and press the buzzer to get in. The glass door opens with a loud click, and the two detectives enter and follow the signs down a wide hall to the main office, their shoes squeaking on the glossy floors. Rasbach can smell wax and polish.

"I don't miss school, do you?" Jennings says.

"Not a bit."

They arrive at the office, where Ms. Beck greets them. Rasbach is immediately disappointed to see that she is relatively young, in her early forties. The chances of her having been at St. Mildred's during Anne Conti's years there are remote. But Rasbach is hoping there might still be some staff around who'd remember her.

"How can I help you, Detectives?" Ms. Beck asks as she conducts them into her spacious inner office.

Rasbach and Jennings sit in the comfortable chairs in front of her desk as she positions herself behind it.

"We're interested in one of your former students," Rasbach says.

"Who is that?" she asks.

"Anne Conti. But when she was a student here, her name would have been Anne Dries."

Ms. Beck pauses, then gives a small nod. "I see."

"I imagine you weren't here yourself when she was a student here," Rasbach says.

"No, that would have been before my time, I'm afraid. The poor woman. I saw her on TV. How old is she?"

"Thirty-two," Rasbach says. "She was at St. Mildred's from kindergarten to twelfth grade, apparently."

Ms. Beck smiles. "Many of our girls start here in kindergarten and don't leave until they attend a good college. We have an excellent retention rate."

Rasbach smiles back at her. "We'd like to look through her file, ideally speak to some people who knew her while she was here."

"Let me see what I can do," Ms. Beck says, and exits the room.

She returns a few minutes later holding a buff-colored file. "She was here, as you say, from K to twelve. She was an excellent student. Went on to Cornell."

Most of the woman's job is PR, Rasbach imagines as he reaches for the file. Jennings leans in to look at it with him. Rasbach is sure that she wishes the now possibly notorious Anne Conti had never graced the halls of St. Mildred's.

He and Jennings review the file silently while Ms. Beck fidgets at her desk. There is not much there except solidly excellent report cards. Certainly nothing leaps out at them.

"Do any of her former teachers still teach here?" Rasbach asks.

Ms. Beck considers. Finally she says, "Most of them have moved on, but Ms. Bleeker just retired last year. I saw in the file that she was Anne's English teacher for several years in the later grades. You could talk to her. She lives not too far from here." She writes down the name and address on a piece of paper.

Rasbach takes the paper and says, "Thank you for your time."

He and Jennings get back into the sweltering car. Rasbach says, "Let's go see Bleeker. We'll grab a sandwich on the way."

"What do you expect to find out?" Jennings asks.

"Never expect, Jennings."

FIFTEEN

When they arrive at the retired teacher's house, they are met by a woman with a straight back and sharp eyes. She looks just the way a retired English teacher from a private girls' school would look, Rasbach thinks.

Ms. Bleeker studies their badges closely and then sizes up the two detectives themselves before she opens her door. "You can't be too careful," she says.

Jennings gives Rasbach a look as she leads them down a narrow hall and into her front room. "Please be seated," she says.

Rasbach and Jennings promptly take seats in two upholstered armchairs. She settles down slowly on the couch opposite. There's a thick novel—a Penguin Classics edition of Trollope's *Barchester Towers*—on the coffee table and an iPad beside it.

"What can I do for you gentlemen?" she asks, and then adds, "Although I think I can guess why you're here."

Rasbach gives her his most disarming smile. "Why do you think we're here, Ms. Bleeker?"

"You want to talk about Anne. I recognized her. She's all over the news." Rasbach and Jennings exchange a quick glance. "She was Anne Dries when I taught her."

"Yes," Rasbach says, "we want to talk to you about Anne."

"It's a terrible thing. I was very sad when I saw it on TV." She sighs deeply. "I don't know what I can tell you about what happened back then, because I don't know anything. I tried to find out, but nobody would tell me anything."

Rasbach feels excitement prickle at his neck. "Why don't you start at the beginning," he says patiently.

She nods. "I liked Anne. She was a good English student. Not inspired, but hardworking. Serious. She was pretty quiet. It was difficult to know what was going on in her head. She liked to draw. I knew that the other girls were picking on her. I tried to put a stop to it."

"Picking on her how?"

"The usual spoiled-rich-girl stuff. Kids with more money than brains. They told her she was fat. She wasn't, of course. The other girls were rail thin. Unhealthy."

"When was this?"

"Probably when she was in about tenth or eleventh grade. There were three girls—thought they were God's gift. The three prettiest girls in school found one another and formed a private club that no one else could join."

"Do you remember their names?

"Of course. Debbie Renzetti, Janice Foegle, and Susan Givens." Jennings writes the names in his notebook. "I won't forget those three."

"And what happened?"

"I don't know. One day the three pretty girls were hassling Anne, as usual, and the next thing you know, one was in the hospital and the other two were giving Anne a very wide berth. Susan missed school for a couple of weeks. The story was that she fell off her bike and got a concussion."

Rasbach leans forward slightly. "But you don't believe the story, do you? What do you think actually happened?"

"I don't know, exactly. There were some closed-door meetings with the parents. It was all hushed up. But I'm betting Anne had had enough."

Back at the station, Rasbach and Jennings do some digging and learn that two of the girls mentioned by the retired English teacher, Debbie Renzetti and Susan Givens, had moved away with their families by the end of high school. Janice Foegle, as luck would have it, still lives in the city. When Rasbach calls her, his luck holds—she's home and she's willing to come in to the station and talk to them that afternoon.

Rasbach is called to the front desk when Janice Foegle arrives, right on time. He goes out to meet her. He knows what to expect, but still, she is a striking woman.

What must it have been like, Rasbach wonders, to possess that kind of beauty in high school, when most of the other kids are struggling to come to terms with their own unsatisfactory appearance? He wonders how it has shaped her. He is reminded, fleetingly, of Cynthia Stillwell.

"Ms. Foegle," Rasbach says. "I'm Detective Rasbach. This is Detective Jennings. Thank you for coming in. We have a few questions for you, if you wouldn't mind."

She gives him a resigned frown. "To be honest, I've been expecting someone to call me," she says.

They take her to one of the interview rooms. She looks tense when they mention the video camera, but she doesn't complain.

"You knew Anne Conti in high school—she was Anne Dries then—when you were at St. Mildred's," Rasbach begins, once the preliminaries are out of the way.

"Yes." Her voice is quiet.

"What was she like?"

Janice pauses, as if unsure of what to say. "She was nice."

"Nice?" Rasbach waits for more.

Suddenly her face crumples and she begins to cry. Rasbach gently pushes the tissue box within her reach and waits. "The truth is, she was a nice girl and I was a total bitch. Me and Susan and Debbie, we were awful girls. I'm ashamed of it now. I look back at what I was like and I just can't believe it. We were so mean to her, for no reason."

"Mean to her how?"

Janice looks away and blows her nose delicately. Then she looks up at the ceiling and tries to compose herself. "We teased her. About her looks, about her clothes. We thought we were above her—above everyone, really." She gives him a wry look. "We were fifteen. Not that that excuses anything."

"So what happened?"

"This went on for months, and she just took it. She was always nice back to us and pretended it didn't bother her, but we thought she was just pathetic. Actually, I thought it was a kind of strength, being able to pretend you're not bothered, day after day, when she obviously was, but I kept that to myself."

Rasbach nods, encouraging her to continue.

She looks down at the tissue in her hands, sighs heavily, and looks back up at Rasbach. "One day she just lost it. The three of us—Debbie, Susan, and I— we'd stayed late after school for some reason. We were in the girls' bathroom, and Anne walked in. She saw us and froze. Then she said hi and gave a little wave and went into one of the stalls to pee. That took a certain amount of guts, I have to admit." She pauses, then continues. "Anyway, we started saying some things." She stops.

"What kinds of things?" Rasbach asks.

"I'm ashamed to say. Things like 'How is your diet coming along? Because you look like you've gained weight'—things like that. We were pretty awful to her. She came out of the stall and went right for Susan. None of us were expecting it. Anne grabbed her by the throat and slammed her against the wall. It was one of those cement walls, painted a glossy cream, and Susan hit it hard with her head. She just kind of slid down. There was a big smear of blood all down the wall." Janice's face twists, as if she is back in that school bathroom seeing her friend crumpled on the floor, the blood smeared on the wall. "I thought Anne had killed her."

"Go on," Rasbach encourages.

"Debbie and I were screaming, but Anne was completely silent. Debbie was closer to the door, so she ran for help. I was terrified to be left alone with Anne, but she was between me and the door and I was too scared to move. Anne looked at me, but her eyes were blank. Like she wasn't really there. I didn't know if she was even seeing me. It was creepy. Finally one of the teachers came, and then the headmistress. They called an ambulance." Janice falls silent.

"Did anyone call the police?"

"Are you kidding?" She looks at him in surprise. "That's not the way things are done in private schools. The headmistress was all damage control. I know they worked something out. Anne's mother came in, and our parents, and it was all just . . . *handled*. You see, we had it coming, and everybody knew it."

Rasbach says gently, "What happened after they called the ambulance?"

"When it arrived, they put Susan on a stretcher and took her down to the ambulance. Debbie and I and the other teacher followed Susan. Debbie and I were crying, hysterical. The headmistress took Anne to her office to wait for her mother. The ambulance took Susan away, and Debbie and I waited in the parking lot with the other teacher for our parents to come."

"Do you remember anything else?" Rasbach asks.

She nods. "Before the headmistress took Anne away, Anne looked at me, like she was completely normal, and said, 'What happened?'"

Rasbach says, "What did you think when she said that?"

"I thought she was crazy."

The mailman is outside the front door trying to push the volumes of mail through the slot in the door. Anne stands in the kitchen and watches. She could open the door and take it from him, to make his job easier, but she doesn't want to. She knows all that hate mail is for her. He looks up then, through the window, and sees her. Their eyes meet for just a second, and then he looks down and works on pushing more envelopes through the slot. She and this same mailman used to exchange pleasantries, less than a week ago. But everything is different now. The letters have dropped onto the floor by the door in a jumbled pile. He's struggling to push a large, thick envelope through the slot, but it won't go. He pushes it halfway in and then turns and goes back down the walk and on to the next house.

Anne stands staring at the pile on the floor, at the package stuffed in the slot. The package is holding the slot open. She goes to the door and tries to pull it through. It's one of those bubble envelopes. It's stuck, and she can't unwedge it. She will have to open the door and grab it from the outside. She peers through the window to see if anyone is out there. The reporters who were there earlier in the morning while the police were packing up have cleared off. Anne opens the door and yanks the package out of the slot, quickly slips back inside, closes the door, and relocks it.

Without thinking, she opens the package.

There's a mint green onesie inside.

Sixteen

Anne screams.

Marco hears her scream and bolts downstairs from the bedroom. He sees her standing by the front door, a pile of unopened mail at her feet, a package in her hand. He can see the green onesie peeking out of the package.

She turns to him, her face white. "This just came in the mail," she says, her voice strange and hollow.

Marco approaches her, and she holds the package out to him. They look down at it together, almost afraid to touch it. What if it's a prank? What if someone thought it would be funny to send a mint green onesie to the awful couple who left their baby home alone?

Marco takes the package from Anne and gently opens it further. He draws out the onesie. It looks right. He turns it over. There's the embroidered bunny on the front.

"Oh, God," Anne gasps, and bursts into tears, her hands up to her face.

"It's hers," Marco says, his voice harsh. "It's Cora's."

Anne nods but can't speak.

There's a note pinned to the inside of the little outfit. It's typewritten, in a small font.

The baby is fine. Ransom is five million dollars. Do NOT tell the police. Bring the money on Thursday at 2 pm. Any sign of police you will never see her again.

There is a detailed map at the bottom of the note.

"We're going to get her back, Anne!" Marco cries.

Anne feels as though she might faint. After all they've been through, it seems too good to be true. She takes the onesie from him and holds it to her face and breathes in. She can smell her baby. *She can smell her.* It is overwhelming. She breathes in again, and her knees weaken.

"We'll do exactly what it says," Marco says.

"Shouldn't we tell the police?"

"No! It says *not* to tell them. We can't risk screwing this up. Don't you see? It's too risky to involve the police. If he thinks he's going to get caught, he might just kill Cora and get rid of her! We have to do it his way. No police."

Anne nods. It scares her, doing this on their own. But Marco is right. What have the police done for them? Nothing. All the police have done is suspect them. The police are not their friends. They will have to get Cora back on their own.

"Five million," Marco says, his voice tense. He looks up at her, suddenly worried. "Do you think your parents will be okay with five million?"

"I don't know." She bites her lip anxiously. "They have to be."

"We don't have a lot of time. Two days," Marco says. "We have to ask your parents. They have to start getting the money together."

"I'll call them." She moves toward the phone in the kitchen.

"Use your cell phone. And, Anne, tell them right up front—no police. No one can know."

She nods and reaches for her cell.

They sit on the sofa in the living room, Anne and Marco, side by side. Anne's mother perches elegantly on the edge of the armchair while Anne's father paces the floor of the living room between the front window and the sofa. They all watch him.

"You're sure that's the right outfit?" he says again, pausing in his pacing.

"Yes," Anne says sharply. "Why don't you believe me?"

"We just need to be sure. Five million dollars is a lot of money." He sounds petulant. "We have to be sure we're dealing with the person who actually has Cora. This has been all over the papers. Somebody could take advantage."

"It's Cora's sleeper," Marco says firmly. "We recognize it."

"Can you get us the money or not?" Anne asks, her voice strident. She looks anxiously at her mother. Just when she was getting her hopes up again, this might all fall apart. How could her father be doing this to her?

"Of course we can get the money," her mother says firmly.

"I didn't say we couldn't get the money," her father answers. "I said it might be difficult. But if I have to move mountains, then I'll move mountains."

Marco watches his father-in-law, trying to keep his dislike from showing itself on his face. They all know it's mostly Anne's mother's money, but he has to act like it's all his. Like he earned it all himself. What a jerk.

"Two days isn't much time to raise that much money. We'll have to cash in some investments," Richard says self-importantly.

"That's not a problem," Anne's mother says. She looks at her daughter. "Don't worry about the money, Anne."

"Can you do it quietly, without anyone knowing?" Marco asks.

Richard Dries exhales loudly, thinking. "We'll talk to our lawyer about how to handle it. We'll figure it out."

"Thank God," Anne says in relief.

"How exactly is this going to work?" Richard asks.

Marco says, "Just like the note says. No police. I'll go, with the money. I give them the money, and they give me Cora."

"Maybe I should come with you, so you don't screw it up," Anne's father says.

Marco regards him with open malice. "No." He adds, "If they see someone else, they might not go through with it."

They stare at each other. "I'm the one with the big checkbook," Richard says.

"Actually, *I'm* the one with the big checkbook," Alice says sharply.

"Dad, *please*," Anne says, terrified that her father is going to ruin everything. Her glance darts anxiously from him to her mother.

"We have no proof that Cora is even alive," Richard says. "It could be a trick."

"If Cora isn't there, I won't leave the money," Marco says, watching Richard continue to pace in front of the window.

"I don't like it," Richard says. "We should tell the police."

"No!" Marco says. The two men glare at each other. Richard looks away first.

"What choice do we have?" Anne asks, her voice shrill.

"I still don't like it," Richard says.

"We will do exactly what the note says," Anne's mother says firmly, giving her husband a sharp glance.

Anne's father looks at her and says, "I'm sorry, Anne. You're right. We don't have a choice. Your mother and I had better get started on the money."

Marco watches his father- and mother-in-law get into their Mercedes and drive off. He's barely eaten since this all started. His jeans hang loose on his body.

It was an awful moment when Richard was being difficult about raising the money. But he'd just been grandstanding. He had to make sure everybody knew what a great guy he was. Had to make sure everybody appreciated how important he was.

"I knew they would come through for us," Anne says, suddenly beside Marco.

How did she always manage to say exactly the wrong thing? At least when it came to her parents. How could she not see her father for what he was? Couldn't she see how manipulative he was? But Marco is silent.

"It's going to be okay," Anne says, taking Marco's hand in hers. "We're going to get her back. And then everyone will see that we were the victims here." She squeezes his hand. "And then we should make the damn police apologize."

"Your father will never let us forget that they bailed us out."

"He won't see it that way! He'll see it as saving Cora, I'm sure of it! They won't hold it over us."

His wife can be so naïve. Marco gives her hand a squeeze back. "Why don't you lie down and try to get some rest? I'm going to go out for a bit."

"I doubt I'll be able to sleep, but I'll try. Where are you going?"

"I'm going to pop into the office and check on a few things. I haven't been there since . . . since Cora was taken."

"Okay."

Marco puts his arms around Anne and gives her a hug. "I can't wait to see her again, Anne," he whispers.

She nods against his shoulder. He lets her go.

Marco watches her walk up the stairs. Then he grabs his car keys from the bowl on the table in the front hall and heads out.

Anne intends to lie down. She's too keyed up, though—almost daring to hope she might get her baby back soon, yet still terrified that it might all go horribly wrong. As her father said, they have no proof that Cora is even still alive.

But she refuses to believe that Cora is dead.

She carries the green onesie with her, holding it to her face and breathing in the scent of her baby. She misses her so much it physically hurts. Her breasts ache. In the upstairs hall, she stops, leans against the wall, and slides down to the floor outside the baby's room. If she closes her eyes and presses the onesie to her face, she can pretend that Cora is still here, in the house, just across the hall. For a few moments, she lets herself pretend. But then she opens her eyes.

Whoever sent them the onesie has demanded five million dollars. Whoever it is knows that their little girl is worth five million dollars to them and obviously has a pretty good idea that Anne and Marco can get the money.

Perhaps it is someone they know, if only slightly. She gets to her feet slowly, pauses on her way into their bedroom. Perhaps it is even someone they know fairly well, someone who knows they have access to money.

When this is all over, she thinks, after they get Cora back, she will devote her life to her child—and to finding the person who took her. Maybe she will never stop looking at people they know, wondering if that person is the one who took their baby—or knows who did.

She suddenly realizes she probably shouldn't be handling the onesie like this. If it all goes wrong and they don't get Cora back, they will have to turn the onesie—and the note—over to the police, as evidence and to convince them of their innocence. Surely the police will no longer suspect them now. But any evidence that the outfit might have offered up has probably been ruined by the way she has been touching it and breathing on it and even wiping her tears with it. She puts it down on her dresser in the bedroom and lays it flat. She looks at it, forlorn, on the dresser. She leaves it there, with the note pinned to it containing their instructions. They cannot afford to make a mistake.

It's the first time she's been alone in the house, she realizes, since midnight on the night Cora was taken. If only she could go back in time. The last few days have been a blur, of fear and grief and horror and despair—and betrayal. She told the police that she trusted Marco, but she lied. She doesn't trust him with Cynthia. She thinks that he might have other secrets from her. After all, she has secrets from him.

She wanders from her dresser over to Marco's and pulls open the top drawer. Aimlessly, she rummages through his socks and underwear. When she has finished with the top drawer, she opens the second. She doesn't know what she's looking for, but she'll know when she finds it.

SEVENTEEN

Marco gets into the Audi and drives. But not to the office. Instead he takes the nearest exit and drives out of the city. He weaves in and around traffic; the Audi is responsive to his touch. After about twenty minutes, he turns off onto a smaller highway. Soon he reaches a familiar dirt road that leads to a fairly secluded lake.

He pulls in to a graveled parking area in front of the lake. There is a small, stony beach with some old, weathered picnic tables, which he has rarely seen anyone use. A long dock projects out into the lake, but no one launches boats from here anymore. Marco has been coming here for years. He comes here alone, whenever he needs to think.

He parks the car under the shade of a tree, facing the lake, and gets out. It's hot and sunny, but there's a breeze coming off the lake. He sits on the hood of the car and looks out at the water. There is no one else here; the place is deserted.

He tells himself that everything will be all right. Cora is fine; she has to be. Anne's parents will get the money. His father-in-law would never pass up an opportunity to be a hero or a big shot, even if it cost him a small fortune. Especially if it looks like he's bailing Marco out. They won't even miss the money, Marco thinks.

He takes a deep breath of the lake air and expels it, trying to calm himself. He can smell dead fish, but no matter. He has to get air into his lungs. The last few days have been a living hell. Marco isn't made for this. His nerves are shot.

He has regrets now, but it will all be worth it. When he gets Cora back and he has the money, everything will be okay. They'll have their daughter. And he'll have two and a half million dollars to get his business on track again. The thought of taking money from his father-in-law makes Marco smile. He hates the bastard.

With this money he'll be able to sort out his cash-flow problems and take his business to the next level. It will have to be funneled into the business through a silent, anonymous investor, by way of Bermuda. No one will ever know. His accomplice, Bruce Neeland, will get his half share, go away, and keep his mouth shut.

Marco almost hadn't gone through with it. When the babysitter canceled at the last minute, he'd panicked. He'd almost called the whole thing off. He knew Katerina always fell asleep with her earbuds in when she was babysitting. Twice they'd come home before midnight and surprised her dead to the world on the living-room sofa. She wasn't that easy to wake up either. Anne didn't like it. She thought Katerina wasn't a very good babysitter, but it was hard to get a sitter at all, since there were so many young children in the neighborhood.

The plan had been for Marco to go out for a smoke at twelve thirty, let himself into the house quietly, grab the sleeping baby, and take her out through the back while Katerina slept. If she'd woken up and seen him come in, he would have told her he'd come to check on the baby, since they were just next door. If she'd woken up and seen him carrying the baby out, he would have told her he was going to take Cora next door for a minute to show her off. In either case he would have aborted the whole thing.

If he'd pulled it off, the story would have been about a child abducted from her bedroom while the babysitter was downstairs.

But then she canceled. Marco was desperate, so he'd had to improvise. He persuaded Anne to leave Cora at home with the proviso that they'd check on her every half hour. It wouldn't have been possible if the video on the baby monitor had still been working, but with just the audio, he thought it would be all right. He would take Cora out the back to the waiting car when he checked on her. He knew it would make him and Anne look bad, leaving the baby home alone, but he thought it could work.

Had he felt there was any actual risk to Cora at all, he never would have done it. Not for any amount of money.

It's been brutally hard these last few days, not see-ing his daughter. Not being able to hold her, to kiss the top of her head, to smell her skin. Not being able to call and check on her and make sure she's all right.

Not knowing what the hell is going on.

Marco tells himself again that Cora is fine. He just has to hang on. It will all be over soon. They'll have Cora back *and* the money. He especially regrets how hard this is on Anne, but he tells himself that she'll be so happy to have Cora back that maybe it will give her some perspective. It has been fucking awful the last few months, dealing with his own financial problems and watching his wife slip away from him, lost in her own downward spiral.

It's all been much more difficult than expected. When Bruce Neeland hadn't called within the first twelve hours, Marco had been frantic. They'd agreed on no more than twelve hours before first contact. When he hadn't heard from Bruce by Saturday afternoon, Marco was afraid that Bruce had lost his nerve. The case had received a lot of attention. Even worse—Bruce wasn't answering the cell phone Marco was to call in an emergency. And Marco had no other way to reach him.

Marco had handed his baby over to a co-conspirator who hadn't followed the plan and whom he couldn't get hold of. He was going out of his mind with worry. *Surely Bruce wouldn't harm her?*

Marco had toyed with the idea of confessing everything to the police, telling them what he knew about Bruce Neeland, in the hopes that they might be able to track him and Cora down. But he thought the risk to Cora was too great. So he'd bided his time.

And then the onesie had arrived in the mail. The relief he'd felt when they received the onesie had been incredible. He figured Bruce must have lost his nerve about calling the house as planned, even with the untraceable, prepaid cell phone. He must have been worried about the police. So he'd found another way.

Another two days and it will all be over. Marco will take the money to the rendezvous point—one they previously picked out together—and get Cora back. And when it *is* all over, he'll call the police and tell them. He'll give them a false description of Bruce and the car he'll be driving.

If there was an easier way to raise a couple million dollars quickly, he couldn't think of it. God knows he'd tried.

Anne's parents come over Thursday morning with the money. Bundles of hundreds. Five million dollars in unmarked bills. The banks have used machines to count it all. They had to scramble to get the cash at such short notice; it was difficult. Richard makes sure they know it. It takes up a surprising amount of room. Richard has packed it all into three large gym bags.

Marco keeps a worried eye on his wife. Anne and her mother are sitting on the sofa together, Anne sheltering under her mother's protective wing. Anne looks small and vulnerable. Marco wants Anne to be strong. He needs her to be strong.

He reminds himself that she is under enormous strain. More than he is, if that's even possible. He is almost cracking from the stress of it all, and *he* knows what's going on. She doesn't. She doesn't know that they're going to get Cora back today; she has only her hope. He, on the other hand, knows that Cora will be back in their house within the next two or three hours. Soon all of this will be over.

Bruce will deposit Marco's share of the money into the offshore account as they planned. They will never have any contact with each other again. There will be nothing to link the two of them. Marco will be in the clear. He'll have his baby back, plus the cash he needs.

Suddenly Anne thrusts her mother's arm off her and stands up. "I want to come with you," she says.

Marco looks at her, startled. Her eyes are glassy, and her entire body is trembling. The queer way she's looking at him—for just a second he wonders if she has figured it out. Impossible.

"No, Anne," he says. "I'm going alone." He adds firmly, "We already talked about this. We can't be changing plans now." He needs her to stay behind.

"I can stay in the car," she says. He hugs her tight, whispers into her ear. "Shhhhh . . . it's going to be all right. I'll come back with Cora, I promise."

"You can't promise. You can't!" Her voice rises shrilly. Marco, Alice, and Richard look at her with alarm.

He holds her until she calms down, and for once her parents stand back and let him be a husband. Finally he releases her, looks into her eyes, and says, "Anne, I've got to go now. It will take me about an hour to get out there. I'll call you on my cell as soon as I have her, okay?"

Anne, calmer now, nods, her face tight with tension.

Richard goes with Marco to load the money into the car, which is parked in the garage. They take the bags through the back door, put them in the trunk of Marco's Audi, and lock it.

"Good luck," Richard says, looking tense. He adds, "Don't hand over the money until you get the baby. It's the only leverage we've got."

Marco nods and gets into the car. He looks up at Richard and says, "Remember, no police until you hear from me."

"Gotcha."

Marco doesn't trust Richard. He's afraid that Richard will call the police as soon as Marco has left. He has instructed Anne to keep Richard in her sight at all times—he whispered a reminder in her ear just now—and not to let him call the police until she hears that Marco has Cora. By the time he calls, Bruce will be long gone. But Marco is still worried. Anne doesn't look like she's functioning properly; he can't rely on her. Richard could go to the kitchen and make the call on his cell, and she might not even notice. Or Richard might just call the police in front of her once he's out of the house, Marco thinks uneasily. She wouldn't be able to stop him.

Marco pulls the car out of the garage and down the lane and begins the long drive to the rendezvous point. He's approaching the ramp for the highway when he goes cold.

He's been incredibly stupid.

Richard could already have told the police about the exchange. They could be watching the whole thing. They could all be in on it except Anne and him. Would Alice allow that? Would Richard even tell her?

Marco's hands start to sweat on the wheel. His heart is pounding as he tries to think. Richard had argued to have the police involved. They'd overruled him. When has Richard ever allowed himself to be overruled in his life? Richard wants Cora back, but he's the kind of man who hedges his bets. He'd want the possibility of recovering his money, too. Marco feels sick.

What should he do? He can't call Bruce. He has no way to do that, since Bruce isn't answering his cell. Now he's probably dragging Bruce right into a trap. Marco's shirt is already sticking to his back as he hits the highway.

EIGHTEEN

Marco tries to calm himself, breathing deeply as he drives, his knuckles white on the steering wheel.

He could take his chances and go to the exchange as planned. Maybe Richard hasn't told the police. Cora will be sitting inside the abandoned garage in an infant car seat. He will grab her, leave the money, and run.

But if Richard *has* alerted the police, then what? Then, as soon as Marco grabs Cora, drops the money, and flees, Bruce will show up for the money and the police will grab him. What if Bruce talks? Marco will go to jail for a very long time.

He could abort. He could turn around and not show up at the exchange at all and hope Bruce sends him another message through the mail. But how would he explain that to the police? How could he not show up as arranged to pick up his own kidnapped baby? He could have car trouble, he could get there too late, miss the window. Then, if Bruce got in touch again, Marco could try again and not tell Richard the details. But there was no way Richard would let Marco keep all that cash with him in the meantime. Fuck. He couldn't do anything without his father-in-law knowing about it, because Alice lets him control the money.

No, he has to get Cora today. He has to go and get her. He can't let this drag out any longer, no matter what.

With his mind spinning, a half hour has sped by. He is halfway there. He has to make a decision. He checks the time, gets off the highway at the next exit. He pulls over to the side of the road, puts his flashers on, and picks up his cell, his hands shaking. He calls Anne's cell.

She answers immediately. "Do you have her?" Anne asks anxiously.

"No, not yet, it isn't time yet," Marco says. "I want you to ask your father if he's told the police about this."

"He wouldn't do that," Anne says.

"Ask him."

Marco hears voices in the background, and then Anne comes back on the line. "He says he didn't tell anyone. He didn't tell the police. Why?"

Should he believe Richard? "Put your father on the phone," Marco says.

"What's going on?" Richard says into the cell.

"I need to be able to trust you," Marco says. "I need to know you didn't alert the police."

"I didn't. I said I wouldn't."

"Tell me the truth. If the police are watching, I'm not going. I can't take the risk that he might smell a trap and kill Cora."

"I swear, I didn't tell them. Just go get her, for Christ's sake!" Richard sounds almost as panicked as Marco feels.

Marco hangs up the phone and drives.

Richard Dries paces his daughter's living room, his heart knocking against his ribs. He glances at his wife and daughter, hunched together on the couch, and quickly looks away again. He is on edge and intensely frustrated with his son-in-law.

He has never liked Marco. And now—for Christ's sake—how could Marco even *think* about not going to the rendezvous? He could blow everything! Richard takes another worried look at his wife and daughter and keeps pacing.

He can at least understand why Marco might think Richard has called the police. From the beginning, when Marco insisted they not tell the cops, Richard had taken the opposite stand—he'd argued for telling them about the exchange, but he'd been overruled. He'd told them that five million dollars is a lot of money, even for them. He'd told them that he wasn't convinced that Cora was still alive. But he'd also said that he wouldn't tell the police, and he has not. He hadn't expected Marco to doubt him at the last minute and put everything at risk by not going to the exchange.

He'd better fucking show up. There is too much at stake here for Marco to lose his nerve.

Thirty minutes later Marco arrives at the designated spot. It's a half hour outside the city by highway, and almost another thirty minutes northwest, up a smaller highway and then off a desolate rural road. They'd chosen an abandoned farm property with an old garage at the end of the long driveway. Marco drives up to the garage and parks the car in front of it. The garage door is closed. The place appears to be deserted, but Bruce must be somewhere nearby, watching.

Cora will be in the garage. Marco feels light-headed—this nightmare is almost over.

Marco gets out of the car. He leaves the money in the trunk and walks up to the garage door. He grabs the handle. It's stiff, but he gives it a good tug. The door goes up with a loud rumble. It's dim inside, especially after coming in from the bright sunlight. He listens intently. Nothing. Maybe Cora is asleep. Then he sees an infant car seat resting on the dirt floor in the far corner with a white blanket draped over the handle. He recognizes the blanket as Cora's. He rushes over to the car seat, reaches down, and pulls off the blanket.

The seat is empty. He stands up in horror, staggering backward. He feels as though the breath has been knocked out of him. The car seat is here, her blanket is here, but Cora is not. Is this some kind of sick joke? Or a double cross? Marco's heart is pounding in his ears. He hears a noise behind him and whirls around, but he's not fast enough. He feels a sharp pain in his head and falls heavily to the floor of the garage.

When Marco comes to a few minutes later—he doesn't know how many—he rises slowly to his hands and knees, then to his feet. He's groggy and dizzy, and his head is thumping with pain. He stumbles outside. His car is still there, in front of the garage, the trunk open. He staggers over to look inside. The money— five million dollars—is gone. Of course. Marco is left behind with an empty car seat and Cora's baby blanket. No Cora. His cell phone is in the car, on the front seat, but he can't bear to call Anne.

He should call the police, but he doesn't want to do that either.

He is a fool. He gives a bellow of pain and sinks to the ground.

Anne waits in a fever of impatience. She shrugs her mother off, wringing her hands in anxiety. What is going on? What is taking so long? They should have heard from Marco twenty minutes ago. Something must be wrong.

Her parents are agitated as well. "What the hell is he doing?" Richard growls. "If he didn't go get her because he's afraid I sent the police, I'll throttle him with my own hands."

"Should we call his cell?" Anne says.

"I don't know," Richard says. "Let's give it a few more minutes."

Five minutes later no one can stand the suspense any longer. "I'm going to call him," Anne says. "He was supposed to get her half an hour ago. What if something went wrong? He would call if he could. What if they killed him! Something terrible has happened!"

Anne's mother jumps up and tries to put her arms around her daughter, but Anne pushes her away almost violently. "I'm calling him," she says, and hits Marco's number on speed dial.

Marco's cell phone rings and rings. It goes to voice mail. Anne is too stunned to do anything but stare straight ahead of her. "He's not answering." Her whole body is shaking.

"We have to call the police now," Richard says, looking stricken. "No matter what Marco said. Marco could be in trouble." He pulls out his own cell and calls Detective Rasbach from his list of contacts.

Rasbach picks up on the second ring. "Rasbach," he says.

"It's Richard Dries. My son-in-law has gone to make an exchange with the kidnappers. He was supposed to call us at least a half hour ago. And he's not answering his cell. We're afraid something has gone wrong."

"Jesus, why weren't we told about this?" Rasbach says. "Never mind. Just give me the details." Richard quickly fills him in and gives him the location of the exchange. They've kept the original ransom note. Marco had taken a photocopy to guide him.

"I'm on my way. In the meantime we'll have local police get there ASAP," Rasbach says. "We'll be in touch." Then he hangs up.

"The police are on their way out there," Anne's father tells her. "All we can do is wait."

"I'm not waiting. You take us, in your car," Anne says.

Marco is still sitting in the dirt, slumped against one of the Audi's front tires, when the police cruiser pulls up. He doesn't even lift his head. It's all over now. Cora must be dead. He has been double-crossed. Whoever has her has the money; there's no reason to keep her alive now.

How could he have been so stupid? Why had he trusted Bruce Neeland? He can't remember now why he had trusted him—his mind has shut down in his grief and fear. There's nothing to do now but confess. Anne will hate him. He is so sorry. For Cora, for Anne, what he's done to them. The two people he most loves in the world.

He had been greedy. He'd persuaded himself that it wasn't stealing if it was Anne's parents' money—Anne would inherit it all eventually anyway, but they needed some of it now. No one was supposed to get hurt. When he and Bruce had planned it, it had never occurred to Marco that Cora would be in any actual danger. It was supposed to be a victimless crime.

But now Cora is gone. He doesn't know what Bruce has done with her. And he doesn't know how to find her.

Two uniformed officers get slowly out of the police car. They walk over to where Marco is slumped against the Audi.

"Marco Conti?" one of the officers asks.

Marco doesn't respond.

"Are you alone?"

Marco ignores him. The officer pulls his radio to his mouth as his partner squats beside Marco. He asks, "Are you hurt?"

But Marco has gone into shock. He says nothing. He has obviously been weeping. The officer standing beside him puts his radio away, draws his weapon, and goes into the garage, fearing the worst. He sees the infant car seat, the white blanket thrown on the dirt floor in front of it, but no baby. He comes back out quickly.

But Marco still isn't speaking.

Soon other police cars converge, lights flashing. An ambulance arrives on the scene, and the medics treat Marco for shock.

A short time later, Detective Rasbach's car pulls up the long drive. He gets out in a rush and speaks to the officer in charge. "What happened?"

"We don't know for sure. He isn't talking. But there's an infant car seat in the garage and no sign of a baby. The trunk is open, empty."

Rasbach takes in the scene and mutters, "Jesus Christ." He follows the other officer into the garage and sees the car seat, the little blanket on the floor. His immediate reaction is to feel terribly sorry for the man sitting on the ground outside, guilty or not. He clearly expected to get his child back. If the man is a criminal, he's an amateur. Rasbach goes outside into the sunlight, squats down, and tries to look Marco in the face. But Marco won't raise his eyes.

"Marco," Rasbach says urgently. "What happened?"

But Marco won't even look at him.

Rasbach has a pretty good idea what happened anyway. It looks like Marco got out of his car, went into the garage expecting to get the baby, and the kidnapper, who never had any intention of returning the child, knocked him out and took the money, leaving Marco alone with his grief.

The baby was probably dead.

Rasbach stands up, gets out his cell, and reluctantly calls Anne on her cell. "I'm sorry," he says. "Your husband is fine, but the baby is not here."

He hears her gasp turn into hysterical sobs on the other end of the line. "Meet us at the station," he tells her.

Sometimes he hates his job.

NINETEEN

Marco is at the police station, in the same interview room as before, in the same chair. Rasbach is sitting across from him, just as he was when Marco gave his statement a few days ago, with Jennings beside him. The video camera is recording him, just like last time.

The press had somehow already gotten the news of the failed exchange. There had been a mob of reporters waiting outside the station when they brought Marco in. Cameras flashed and microphones were pushed in front of his face.

They hadn't handcuffed him. Marco was surprised that they hadn't, because in his head he had already confessed. He felt so guilty he didn't know how they couldn't see it. He thought it was a mere courtesy that they hadn't restrained him, or it was simply deemed unnecessary. After all, there was obviously no fight left in him. He was a beaten man. He was not going to run. Where could he go? Wherever he went, his guilt and grief would go with him.

They let him see Anne before they brought him

into the interview room. She and her parents were already at the station. Marco was badly shaken when he saw her. Her face showed that she had lost all hope. When she saw him, she threw her arms around him and sobbed into his neck as if he were the last thing in the world she could cling to, as if he were all she had left. They held on to each other, weeping. Two shattered people, one of them a liar.

Then they had taken him into the interview room to get his statement.

"I'm sorry," Rasbach begins. And he genuinely is.

Marco lifts his head in spite of himself.

"The car seat and blanket have gone in for forensic testing. Maybe we'll get something useful."

Marco remains silent, slumped in his chair.

Rasbach leans forward. "Marco, why don't you tell us what's going on?"

Marco regards the detective, who has always annoyed him. Looking at Rasbach, he feels his desire to confess dissolve. He sits up straighter in his chair. "I brought the money. Cora wasn't there. Someone attacked me when I was in the garage and took the money from the trunk."

Being questioned by Rasbach in this room, the feeling of playing cat and mouse, has sharpened Marco's mind. He is thinking more clearly now than he was after things went so terribly wrong an hour or so ago. Adrenaline is coursing through his system. Suddenly he's thinking about survival. He realizes that if he tells the truth, it will utterly destroy not just him but Anne as well. She could never withstand the

betrayal. He must maintain the fiction of his innocence. They have nothing on him, no proof. Rasbach
obviously has his suspicions, but that's all they are.

"Did you get a look at the man who hit you?" Rasbach asks. He is tapping his pen lightly against his
hand, a sign of impatience that Marco has not seen
before.

"No. He hit me from behind. I didn't see anything."

"Just one person?"

"I think so." Marco pauses. "I don't know."

"Can you tell me anything else? Did he say anything?" Rasbach is clearly frustrated with him.

Marco shakes his head. "No, nothing."

Rasbach pushes his chair away from the table and
stands up. He walks around the room, rubbing the
back of his neck, as if it's stiff. He turns and faces
Marco from across the room.

"It looks like another car was parked in the
weeds behind the garage, out of sight. Did you see it
or hear it?"

Marco shakes his head.

Rasbach walks back to the table, puts his hands
on it, leans forward, and looks Marco in the eye. "I
have to tell you, Marco," Rasbach says, "I think the
baby is dead."

Marco hangs his head. The tears start to come.

"And I think you're responsible."

Marco snaps his head back up. "I had nothing to
do with it!"

Rasbach says nothing. He waits.

"What makes you think *I* had anything to do with it?" Marco asks. "My baby is gone." He starts to sob. He doesn't have to fake it. His grief is all too real.

"It's the timing, Marco," Rasbach says. "You checked on the baby at twelve thirty. Everyone agrees that you did."

"So?" Marco says.

"So I have tire-track evidence that a strange car was recently in your garage. And I have a witness who saw a car going down your back lane, away from your garage, at twelve thirty-five a.m."

"But why do you think that's got anything to do with me?" Marco says. "You don't know that that car had anything to do with whoever took Cora. She could just as easily have been taken out the front door, at one o'clock." But Marco knows it hasn't done him any good, leaving the front door ajar; it hadn't fooled the detective. If only he hadn't forgotten to screw the motion-detector light back in.

Rasbach pushes himself away from the table and stands looking down at Marco. "The motion detector in the back was disabled. You were in the house at twelve thirty. A car drove away from the direction of your garage at twelve thirty-five. *With its headlights off.*"

"So what? Is that all you've got?"

"There's no physical evidence whatsoever of an intruder in the house or the backyard. If a stranger had come into your backyard to get her, we would have some tracks, something. But we don't. The only footprints in the backyard, Marco, are yours." He leans on the table again for emphasis. "I think you carried the baby out of the house to the car in the garage."

Marco says nothing.

"We know that your business is in trouble."

"I admit that! You think that's reason enough to kidnap my own baby?" Marco says desperately.

"People have kidnapped for less," the detective says.

"Well, let me tell you something," Marco says, leaning forward, looking up into Rasbach's eyes. "I love my daughter more than anything in this world. I love my wife, and I am extremely concerned for the well-being of both of them." He sits back in his chair. He thinks carefully for a moment before he adds, "And I have very wealthy in-laws who've been very generous. They would probably give us whatever money we needed if Anne asked them for it. So why the hell would I kidnap my own baby?"

Rasbach watches him, his eyes narrowing. "I will be questioning your in-laws. And your wife. And anyone who ever knew you."

"Knock yourself out," Marco says. He knows that he's not handling this well, but he can't help it. "Am I free to go?"

"Yes, you are free to go," the detective says. "For now."

"Should I get a lawyer?" Marco asks.

"That's entirely up to you," the detective says.

Detective Rasbach heads back to his own office to think. If this was a fake kidnapping, staged by Marco, he has clearly fallen in with some real criminals who've taken advantage of him. Rasbach can almost feel sorry for him. He certainly feels sorry for his distraught wife. If Marco did set this up, and has been duped, his baby is probably now dead, the money is gone, and the police suspect him of kidnapping. How he's holding it together at all is a mystery.

But the detective is troubled. There's the babysitter, a problem that's been niggling at him. And there's this commonsense question: Why would someone who could probably get money easily enough just by asking risk it all with something as stupid, as fraught with risk, as a kidnapping?

And there's that disturbing information about Anne, about her propensity for violence, that has recently come to light. The more he gets involved in this case, the more complicated it seems. Rasbach has to know the truth.

It's time to question Anne's parents.

And he will talk to Anne herself again in the morning.

Rasbach will figure it out. The truth is there. It's always there. It simply needs to be uncovered.

Anne and Marco are at home, alone. The house is empty but for the two of them and their horror and grief and dark imaginings. It would be hard to say who of the two is more damaged. Both are haunted by not knowing what has happened to their baby. They each hope desperately that she's still alive, but there is so little to sustain that hope. Each tries to pretend for the other. And Marco has additional reasons to pretend.

Anne doesn't know why she doesn't blame Marco more than she does. When it first happened, when their baby was taken, she blamed him in her heart, because he was the one who persuaded her to leave Cora at home alone. If they had taken the baby next door with them, none of this ever would have happened. She's told herself that if Cora didn't come home unharmed, she would never forgive him.

Yet here they are. She doesn't know why she clings to him, but she does. Perhaps because she has nothing else to cling to. She can't even tell if she loves him anymore. She will never forgive him for Cynthia either.

Perhaps she clings to him because no one else can share or understand her pain. Or perhaps because he, at least, believes her. He knows she didn't kill their baby. Even her mother suspected her until the onesie arrived in the mail. She's sure of it.

They go to bed and lie awake for a long time. Finally Marco gives in to a troubled sleep. But Anne is too agitated for sleep to come. Eventually she gets out of bed, goes downstairs, and roams the house, growing increasingly restless.

She begins combing the house, but she doesn't know what she's looking for and gets more and more upset. She is moving and thinking faster and faster. She's looking for something that incriminates her unfaithful husband, but she is also looking for her baby. She feels lines blurring.

Her thoughts speed up and become less rational; her mind makes fantastic leaps. It's not that things don't make sense to her when she's like this—sometimes they make *more* sense. They make sense the way dreams do. It's only when the dream is over that you see how odd it all was, how it actually didn't make sense at all.

She hasn't found any letters, or any e-mails from Cynthia on Marco's laptop, or strange women's underwear in the house. She hasn't found any receipts for hotel rooms or hidden matchbooks from bars. She's found some worrying financial information, but that doesn't interest her right now. She wants to know what's going on between Marco and Cynthia and what that has to do with Cora's disappearance. *Did Cynthia take Cora?*

The more Anne turns this over in her mind in her frenzied state, the more it seems to make sense to her. Cynthia dislikes children. Cynthia is the kind of person who would harm a child. She is cold. And she doesn't like Anne anymore. She wants to hurt her. Cynthia wants to take Anne's husband and her child away and see what that does to her, because she can.

Eventually Anne works herself into an exhausted stupor and falls asleep on the sofa in the living room.

The next morning, early, she wakes and showers before Marco realizes she's spent the night on the sofa. She pulls on black leggings and a tunic as if in a trance, filled with dread.

She feels paralyzed when she thinks of the police, of being interrogated by Rasbach again. He has no idea where their baby is, but he seems to think that they do. He asked her yesterday, after taking Marco's statement, to come in this morning. She doesn't want to go. She doesn't know why he wants to talk to her again. What's to be gained from going through the same things over and over?

From his place in the bed, propped up against the pillows, Marco watches her getting dressed, his face expressionless.

"Do I have to go?" she asks him. She would avoid it if she could. She doesn't know what her rights are. Should she refuse?

"I don't think you have to," Marco says. "I don't know. Maybe it's time we spoke to a lawyer."

"But that will look bad," Anne says worriedly. "Won't it?"

"I don't know," Marco says tonelessly. "We look bad already."

She approaches the bed, looks down at him. Seeing him like this, so plainly wretched, would break her heart if it weren't broken already. "Maybe I should speak to my parents. They could get us a good lawyer. Although it seems ridiculous to think we even need one."

"It might be a good idea," Marco says uneasily. "Like I told you last night, Rasbach still seems to suspect us. He seems to believe we staged the whole thing."

"How can he think that now—after yesterday?" Anne asks, her voice becoming agitated. "Why would he? Just because there was a car going down the lane at the same time you checked on Cora?"

"That seems to be the gist of it."

"I'll go in," Anne says finally. "He wants me there for ten o'clock."

Marco nods tiredly. "I'll come with you."

"You don't have to," Anne says, without conviction. "I could call my mother."

"Of course I'll come. You can't face that mob out there alone. Let me put some clothes on, and I'll take you," Marco says, getting out of bed.

Anne watches him walk to his dresser in his boxers. How much thinner he looks—she can see the outline of his ribs. She is grateful that he's coming to the station with her. She doesn't want to call her mother, and she doesn't think she can do this on her own. Also, she thinks it's important that she and Marco be seen together, to appear united.

There are more reporters outside their house again now after yesterday's fiasco. Anne and Marco have to fight them off to get to their cab—the police have the Audi for the time being—and there are no police officers here to help them. Finally they make it to the taxi on the street. Once inside the car, Anne quickly locks the doors. She feels trapped—all those jabbering faces crowding in on them through the windows. She recoils but stares back at them. Marco swears under his breath.

Anne looks silently out the window as the mob falls away. She can't understand how the reporters can be so cruel. Are none of them parents? Can they not imagine, for one moment, what it's like not knowing where your baby is? To lie awake at night missing your child, seeing her little body, still, dead, behind your closed eyelids?

They head downtown along the river until they reach the police station. As soon as Anne sees the building, she feels herself tensing up inside. She wants to run away. But Marco is beside her. He helps her out of the cab and into the station, his hand on her elbow.

As they wait at the front desk, Marco speaks quietly into her ear. "It's all right. They may try to rattle you, but you know we haven't done anything wrong. I'll be out here waiting for you." He gives her a small, encouraging smile. She nods at him. He rests his hands gently on her shoulders, looks into her eyes. "They might try to turn us against each other, Anne. They may say things about me, bad things."

"What bad things?"

He shrugs, averts his eyes. "I don't know. Just be careful. Don't let them get to you."

She nods, but she is more worried now, not less.

At that moment Detective Rasbach approaches them. He doesn't smile. "Thank you for coming. This way, please."

He leads Anne to a different interview room this

time, the one they've been using for Marco. They leave Marco alone in the waiting area. Anne stops at the door of the interview room and turns to look back at him. He smiles at her, a nervous smile.

She goes in.

TWENTY

Anne sits down in the seat offered to her. As she sinks into it, she can feel her knees give way. Jennings offers her a cup of coffee, but she shakes her head no, because she doesn't trust herself not to spill it. She is more anxious this time than the last time she was interviewed. She wonders about the police, why they're so suspicious of her and Marco. If anything, the police should be *less* suspicious of them after they received the onesie in the mail, and after the money had been taken. Obviously, someone else has their baby.

The detectives take their seats across from her.

"I'm so sorry," Detective Rasbach begins, "about yesterday."

She says nothing. Her mouth is dry. She clasps her hands in her lap.

"Please relax," Rasbach says gently.

She nods nervously, but she cannot relax. She doesn't trust him.

"I just have a few questions, about what happened yesterday," he tells her.

She nods again, licks her lips.

"Why didn't you call us when you got the package in the mail?" the detective asks. His tone is friendly enough.

"We thought it was too risky," Anne says. Her voice is unsteady. She clears her throat. "The note said no police." She reaches for the bottle of water that has been placed on the table for her. She fumbles with the cap. Her hand is shaking slightly as she moves the bottle to her lips.

"Is that what you thought?" Rasbach asks. "Or is that what Marco thought?"

"We both thought so."

"Why did you handle the onesie so much? Any evidence it might have offered us has been contaminated, unfortunately."

"Yes, I know, I'm sorry. I wasn't thinking. I could smell Cora on it, so I carried it around with me, to have her near me." She begins to cry. "It brought her back to me. It was like I could almost pretend she was in her crib, sleeping. That none of this ever happened."

Rasbach nods and says, "I understand. We'll run whatever tests we can on the garment and the note."

"You think she's dead, don't you?" Anne says woodenly, looking him directly in the eye.

Rasbach returns her look. "I don't know. She may still be alive. We will not stop searching for her."

Anne takes a tissue from the box on the table and presses it against her eyes.

"I've been wondering," Rasbach says, leaning back casually in his chair, "about your babysitter."

"Our babysitter? Why?" Anne asks, startled. "She didn't even come that night."

"I know. I'm just curious. Is she a good baby-sitter?"

Anne shrugs, not knowing where this is going. "She's good with Cora. She obviously likes babies—and a lot of girls don't really. They just babysit for the money." She thinks about Katerina. "She's usually reliable. You can't blame her that her grandmother died. Although—if only she hadn't, we might still have Cora."

"Let me ask you this: If someone wanted to know whether you'd recommend her, would you?" Rasbach asks.

Anne bites her lip. "No, I don't think so. She tends to fall asleep with her earbuds in, listening to music. When we get home, we have to wake her. So no, I wouldn't recommend her."

Rasbach nods, makes a note. Then he looks up and says, "Tell me about your husband."

"What about my husband?"

"What kind of man is he?"

"He's a good man," Anne says firmly, sitting up straighter in her chair. "He's loving and kind. He's smart and thoughtful and hardworking." She pauses, then says in a rush, "He's the best thing that ever happened to me, other than Cora."

"Is he a good provider?"

"Yes."

"Why do you say that?"

"Because it's true," Anne snaps.

"But isn't it also true that it was your parents who set your husband up in business? And you told me yourself that your parents paid for your house."

"Just a minute," Anne says. "My parents did not 'set my husband up in business,' as you put it. Marco has degrees in computer science and business. He started his own company, and he was very successful on his own. My parents just invested in it, later on. He was already doing very well. You can't fault Marco as a businessman." Even as she says this, Anne is faintly aware of the financial information she came across on Marco's computer the other day. She hadn't looked deeply into it at the time, and she hasn't asked Marco about it; now she wonders if she's just lied to the police.

"Do you believe your husband is honest with you?"

Anne blushes. And then hates it that she's given herself away. She takes her time answering. "Yes. I believe he is honest with me"—she falters—"most of the time."

"Most of the time? Shouldn't honesty be an 'all of the time' thing?" Rasbach asks, leaning forward slightly.

"I heard you," Anne confesses suddenly. "The night after the kidnapping. I was at the top of the stairs. I heard you accusing Marco of making out with Cynthia. She said Marco came on to her, and he denied it."

"I'm sorry, I wasn't aware that you were listening."

"I'm sorry, too. I wish I didn't know about it." She looks down at her hands in her lap, clutching the bunched-up tissue.

"Do you think he made sexual advances toward Cynthia, or do you think it was the other way around, as Marco says?"

Anne twists the tissue in her hands. "I don't know. They're both at fault." She looks up at him. "I'll never forgive either one of them," she says rashly.

"Let's go back," Rasbach prompts. "You say your husband is a good provider. Does he share with you how his business is doing?"

She shreds the tissue into small pieces. "I haven't taken a lot of interest in the business these days," Anne says. "I've been absorbed with the baby."

"He hasn't been telling you how the business is going?"

"Not recently, no."

"Don't you think that's a bit odd?" Rasbach asks.

"Not at all," Anne says, thinking as she does that it *is* odd. "I've been really busy with the baby." Her voice breaks.

"The tire tracks in your garage—they don't match your car," Rasbach says. "Someone used your garage shortly before the kidnapping. You saw the baby in her crib at midnight. Marco was in your house with the baby at twelve thirty. We have a witness who saw a car driving down the lane away from the direction of your garage at twelve thirty-five a.m. There's no evidence that anyone else was inside the house or yard. Perhaps at twelve thirty Marco took the baby out to an accomplice who was waiting in a car in your garage."

"That's ridiculous!" Anne says, her voice rising.

"Do you have any idea who that accomplice might be?" Rasbach persists.

"You're wrong," Anne says.

"Am I?"

"Yes. Marco didn't take Cora."

"Let me tell you something," Rasbach says, leaning forward. "Your husband's business is in trouble. Deep trouble."

Anne feels herself go paler. "It is?" she says.

"I'm afraid so."

"To be honest, Detective, I don't really care if the business is in trouble. Our baby is gone. What does either of us care now about money?"

"It's just that . . ." Rasbach pauses, as if changing his mind about what he's going to say. He looks at Jennings.

"What?" Anne glances nervously back and forth between the two detectives.

"It's just that I see things in your husband that you may not see," Rasbach says.

Anne does not want to take the bait. But the detective waits, letting the silence expand. She has no choice. "Like what?"

Rasbach asks, "Don't you think it's a bit manipulative of him not to be honest with you about the business?"

"No, not if I didn't show any interest. He was probably trying to protect me, because I've been depressed." Rasbach says nothing, just regards her with his sharp blue eyes. "Marco is not manipulative," Anne insists.

"What about the relationship between Marco and your parents? Marco and your father?" Rasbach says.

"I told you, they don't like each other. They tolerate each other, for me. But that's my parents' fault. No matter what Marco does, it's never good enough. I could have married anyone, and it would have been the same."

"Why do you think that is?"

"I don't know. That's just the way they are. They're overprotective and hard to please. Maybe it's because I'm an only child." She has reduced the tissue in her lap to crumbs. "Anyway, it doesn't matter about the business, not really. My parents have a lot of money. They could always help us if we needed it."

"But would they?"

"Of course they would. All I'd have to do is ask. My parents have never denied me anything. They came up with five million dollars just like that for Cora."

"Yes, they did." The detective pauses, then says, "I tried to see Dr. Lumsden, but apparently she's away."

Anne feels the blood drain from her face but forces herself to sit up straight. She knows he can't have talked to Dr. Lumsden. Even after she returns, there is no way Dr. Lumsden will talk to the detective about her. "She won't tell you anything about me," Anne says. "She can't. She's my doctor, and you know it. Why are you toying with me this way?"

"You're right. I can't get your doctor to breach doctor-patient privilege."

Anne leans back in her chair and gives the detective an annoyed look.

"Is there anything *you'd* like to tell me, though?" the detective asks.

"Why would I talk to you about my sessions with my psychiatrist? It's none of your goddamned business," Anne says bitterly. "I have mild postpartum depression like lots of other new mothers. It doesn't mean I harmed my baby. I want nothing more than to get her back."

"I can't help thinking it's possible that Marco might have had the baby taken away to cover up for you, if you killed her."

"That's crazy! Then how do you explain our getting the onesie in the mail and the ransom money being taken?"

"Marco might have faked the kidnapping, after the baby was already dead. And the empty car seat, the hit on the head—maybe that was all for show."

She gives him a disbelieving stare. "That's absurd. And I did not harm my baby, Detective."

Rasbach fiddles with his pen, watching her. "I had your mother in for an interview earlier this morning."

Anne feels the room begin to spin.

TWENTY-ONE

Rasbach watches Anne carefully, fears she might faint. He waits while she reaches for the bottle of water, waits for her color to return.

There is nothing he can do about the psychiatrist. His hands are tied. He hadn't gotten any further with the mother, but Anne is obviously afraid that she'd said something. Rasbach is pretty sure he knows what she's afraid of. "What do you think your mother told me?" Rasbach asks.

"I don't think she told you anything," Anne says sharply. "There's nothing to tell."

He considers her for a few moments. Thinks how different she is from her mother—a very composed woman, busy with her social committees and charities and much more canny than her daughter. Certainly less emotional, with a clearer head. Alice Dries had come into the interview room, smiled icily, stated her name, and then told him she had nothing to say to him. It was a very short interview.

"She didn't tell me she was coming in this morning," Anne says.

"Didn't she?"

"What did she say?" Anne asks.

"You're right, she didn't say anything," Rasbach admits.

Anne smiles for the first time in the interview, but it's a bitter smile.

"I have, however, spoken to one of your old school-mates. A Janice Foegle."

Anne goes completely still, like an animal in the wild sensing a predator. Then she stands up abruptly, her chair scraping the floor behind her, taking Rasbach and Jennings by surprise. "I have nothing more to say," she tells them.

Anne joins Marco in the lobby. Marco notices her distress, and puts his arm protectively around her. Anne can feel Rasbach's eyes on them, watching as they leave. She says nothing as she and Marco walk out of the station. Once they're on the street and hailing a cab, she says, "I think it's time we got a lawyer."

Rasbach is putting pressure on them, and it doesn't look as if he's going to let up. It has come to the point that even though they haven't been charged, they know they're being treated like suspects.

Marco is anxious about what happened in the interview between Anne and Detective Rasbach. There was panic in her eyes when she came out. Something in that interview had rattled her enough to make her want to get a lawyer as soon as possible. He tried to find out what it was, but she was vague, evasive. *What is she not telling him?* It's putting him even more on edge.

When they arrive home and have fought their way past the reporters into the house, Anne suggests they invite her parents over to discuss hiring a lawyer.

"Why do we need to have your parents over?" Marco says. "We can find a lawyer without their help."

"A good lawyer will expect a hefty retainer," Anne points out. Marco shrugs, and she calls her parents.

Richard and Alice arrive soon after. It comes as no great surprise that they've already been looking into the best lawyers money can buy.

"I'm sorry it's come to this, Anne," her father says.

They are sitting around the kitchen table, the early-afternoon sunlight slanting through the kitchen window and falling across the wooden table. Anne has made a pot of coffee.

"We think it's a good idea to get a lawyer, too," Alice says. "You can't trust the police."

Anne looks at her. "Why didn't you tell me they had you in for questioning this morning?"

"There was no need, and I didn't want to worry you," Alice says, reaching out and patting Anne's hand. "All I told them was my name, and that I had nothing to say. I'm not going to let them push me around," she says. "I was only in there for about five minutes."

"They questioned me, too," Richard says. "They didn't get anything from me either." He turns his eyes on Marco. "I mean, what can I possibly tell them?"

Marco feels a jolt of fear. He doesn't trust Richard.

But would Richard say anything to the police to stab him in the back?

Richard tells Anne, "They haven't charged you with anything, and I don't think they will—I don't see how they can. But I agree with your mother—if you're represented by a top defense lawyer, maybe they'll stop pushing you around and calling you in for questioning all the time and start focusing on who really took Cora."

Throughout this entire meeting at the kitchen table, Richard has been colder than usual to Marco. Richard barely looks at him. They have all noticed it. No one has made more careful note of it than Marco. *How stoic he's being,* Marco thinks, *about my losing their five million dollars. He hasn't mentioned it once. He doesn't have to.* But Marco knows what Richard is thinking: *My useless son-in-law screwed up again.* Marco imagines Richard sitting around in the lounge at the country club, drinking expensive liquor, telling his rich friends all about it. About what a fuckup his son-in-law is. How Richard has lost his beloved only grandchild and five million of his hard-earned dollars, all because of Marco. And what's worse, Marco knows that this time it's true.

"In fact," Richard says, "we've taken the liberty of putting one on retainer, as of this morning."

"Who?" Anne asks.

"Aubrey West."

Marco looks up, clearly unhappy. "Really?"

"He's one of the best goddamned criminal lawyers

in the country," Richard says, his voice rising a notch. "And we're paying. Do you have a problem with that?"

Anne is looking at Marco, pleading with him silently to let it go, to accept the gift.

"Maybe," Marco says.

"What's wrong with having the best lawyer we can get?" Anne asks. "Don't worry about the money, Marco."

Marco says, "It's not the expense I'm worried about. It just looks like overkill to me. Like we're guilty and we need a lawyer who's famous for big, high-profile murder cases. Doesn't that lump us in with his other clients? Make us look bad?"

There's silence around the table as they consider this. Anne looks worried. She hadn't thought of it that way.

"He gets a lot of guilty people off—so what? That's his job," Richard counters.

"What do you mean by that?" Marco says, slightly menacing. Anne looks like she's going to be sick. "Do you think *we* did this?"

"Don't be absurd," Richard says, reddening. "I'm just being practical here. You might as well avail yourself of the best lawyer you can get. The police aren't doing you any favors."

"Of course we don't think you had anything to do with Cora's disappearance," Alice says, looking at her husband instead of either of them. "But you're being vilified in the press. This lawyer may be able to put a stop to that. And I think you're being persecuted by the police, who haven't charged you and keep bringing you in under the guise of voluntary questioning—it's got to stop. It's harassment."

Richard adds, "The police haven't got anything on you, so maybe they'll start to back off. But he's there if you need him."

Anne turns to Marco. "I think we should keep him."

"Fine," Marco says. "Whatever."

Cynthia and Graham have been arguing for days. It's been a week since the fateful dinner party, and they're still arguing. Graham wants to do nothing, pretend the video doesn't exist or, better yet, destroy it. It's the safest thing to do. Yet he's troubled, because he knows the right thing to do is to go to the police with the video. But it's not legal to film people having sex without their knowledge, and that's what they've been doing. The video shows Cynthia on Marco's lap, and they're enjoying themselves. If Graham and Cynthia were charged, it would be catastrophic to his career. He's a comptroller for a very large, very conservative company. If this gets out, his career would be finished.

Cynthia isn't interested in doing what's right. What matters to her is that the video shows Marco going into his house at 12:31 a.m. the night of the kidnapping and coming out the back door of his house at 12:33 a.m., carrying the baby in his arms and into the garage. He's in the garage for about a minute, and then he comes back into view and into the Stillwells' yard. Shortly after that the soft-core porn starts.

Graham was horrified that the man had taken his own child, but he'd been indecisive, he'd dithered. He wanted to do the right thing, but he didn't want to get into trouble. And now it is too late to approach the police. They would ask why it had taken them so long. He and Cynthia would be in even deeper trouble than they would have been for simply using a hidden camera to secretly film sex acts—they could now be charged with hiding evidence in a kidnapping or obstructing the law or something. So Graham wants to pretend that the video doesn't exist. He wants to destroy it.

Cynthia has reasons of her own not to go to the police with the video. She has something on Marco, and it's got to be worth something.

She will tell Marco about the video. She is sure that he will pay her handsomely for it. No need to mention it to Graham.

It's a heartless thing to do, but what kind of man kidnaps his own child? He has it coming.

TWENTY-TWO

arco and Anne are sitting at the kitchen table, attempting breakfast. Their toast is barely touched. They are both living mostly on coffee and despair.

Marco is silently reading the newspaper. Anne is staring out the window to the backyard, seeing nothing. Some days she can't bear the newspaper and asks him how he can stand to read it. Other days she scours it from first page to last for any coverage of the kidnapping. But in the end she reads it all. She can't help it. It's a scab she can't stop picking.

It's the strangest thing, Anne finds, to read about yourself in the newspaper.

Marco gives a sudden start. "What is it?" she asks.

He doesn't answer her.

She loses interest. This is one of her hate days with the newspaper. She doesn't want to know. She gets up and tosses her cold coffee into the sink.

Marco holds his breath as he reads. The story he's reading is not about the kidnapping—but it is. He's the only one who could possibly know it's about the kidnapping, and now he's thinking furiously, trying to figure out what to do about it.

He looks at the picture in the paper. It's him. There is no doubt. Bruce Neeland, his accomplice, has been found dead—savagely murdered—in a cabin in the Catskills. The story is very short on detail, but a violent robbery is suspected. The man has had his head bashed in. If not for the photograph of the murdered man, Marco would have missed the brief news article altogether, and the valuable information it contains. The newspaper says his name is actually Derek Honig.

Marco's heart pounds as he tries to put it together. Bruce—whose real name is not Bruce at all—is dead. The article does not say when he might have been killed. That might explain why Bruce didn't get in touch when he was supposed to, why he hadn't answered his cell phone. But who killed him? And where is Cora? Marco realizes with terror that whoever killed him must have taken Cora. And whoever killed him must have the money as well. He has to tell the police. But how does Marco tell them without revealing his own terrible role in this?

He starts to sweat. He looks up at his wife, standing with her back to him at the kitchen sink. There is an inexpressible sadness in the slump of her shoulders.

He must go to the police.

Or is he being a fool? What chance is there that Cora is still alive? The bastards have the money. They must have killed her by now.

Maybe they'll ask for more money. If there's even the slightest chance that she *is* still alive, he must let Rasbach know about this. But how? How the hell can he do that without incriminating himself?

He tries to think it through. Bruce is dead—so he can't tell anyone anything. And he was the only one who knew. If they find Bruce's killer or killers, even if Bruce told them Marco was in on it, that's not proof. That's hearsay. There's no proof that Marco took her out of the crib and handed her over to Bruce in the garage.

It might even be a good thing that Bruce is dead.

He must tell Rasbach, but how? As he stares at the photograph of the dead man, it comes to him. He will tell the detective that he saw this picture in the paper and recognized the man. He'd seen him hanging around outside the house. He'd forgotten all about it until he saw the picture. They might not believe him, but it's all he can think of.

He is quite certain that no one ever saw him with Bruce. He doesn't think anyone can put them together.

He couldn't live with himself if he doesn't do everything possible to find Cora.

He will have to tell Anne first. He thinks for another minute, vacillating, and then says, "Anne."

"What?"

"Look at this."

She comes and stands over his shoulder looking down at the paper where his finger points. She studies the photo. "What about it?" she says.

"Do you recognize him?"

She looks again. "I don't think so. Who is it?"

"I'm sure I've seen him," Marco says. "Around."

"Seen him where?"

"I'm not sure, but he looks familiar. I know I've seen him recently, in our neighborhood—around our house."

Anne looks more closely. "You know, I think I *have* seen him before, but I don't know where."

Even better, Marco thinks.

Before going to the station, Marco gets on his laptop and looks for more information on Derek Honig's murder, searching all the different newspapers online. He doesn't want any surprises.

There isn't much information. The case has attracted little notice. Derek Honig had taken some time off work before his death to stay at his cabin. He'd been found by the woman who cleaned the cabin once a month. He lived alone. Divorced, no kids. Marco feels a chill, reading this. The man he'd known as Bruce had told him he had three kids of his own and knew how to take care of an infant, and Marco had believed him. His own actions now shock him. He'd handed his baby off to someone who turned out to be a total stranger, trusting him to take care of her. How could he have done it?

Anne and Marco show up at the police station unannounced. The Audi had been returned to them the previous afternoon. Marco clutches the newspaper in his hand and asks for Detective Rasbach at the front desk. He's in, even though it's Saturday.

"Do you have a minute?" Marco asks Rasbach.

"Of course," the detective says, and ushers them into the now familiar room. Jennings, right behind him, grabs another chair. The four of them sit, facing one another.

Marco places the newspaper on the table in front of Rasbach and points to the photo of the dead man.

The detective looks at the photo, skims the short article. Then he glances up from the paper and says, "Yes?"

"I recognize him," Marco says. He knows he appears nervous, even though he's trying his hardest not to. He looks the detective deliberately in the eyes. "I think I saw him around in the last couple of weeks before Cora was taken."

"Saw him where?" Rasbach asks.

"That's the thing," Marco equivocates. "I'm not sure. But the minute I saw the picture, I knew I'd seen him recently, and more than once. I think it was around our house, in our neighborhood—on our street."

Rasbach stares steadily at Marco, pursing his lips.

"Anne recognizes him, too," Marco says, nodding at his wife.

Rasbach turns his attention to Anne.

Anne nods. "I've seen him before, but I don't know where."

"You're sure?"

She nods again.

"Wait here a moment," Rasbach says, and he and Jennings leave the room.

Anne and Marco wait silently. They don't want to talk to each other with the video camera in the room. Marco has to consciously fight his urge to fidget. He wants to get up and pace around the room but forces himself to stay in his seat.

Finally Rasbach returns. "I'll go up there myself, today. If there's anything relevant to your case, I'll be in touch."

"How long do you think it'll be before we hear from you?" Marco asks.

"I don't know. I'll get back to you as soon as I can," Rasbach promises.

There's nothing Marco and Anne can do but go home and wait.

TWENTY-THREE

At home, Marco is restless. He paces the house. He gets on Anne's nerves. They are snapping at each other.

"I think I'll go to the office," he says abruptly. "I need to get my mind off things here and get back to some of my clients. Before I don't have any clients."

"Good idea," Anne agrees, wanting him out of the house. She wishes desperately that she could have a long talk with Dr. Lumsden. Lumsden had called her back quickly after the urgent message Anne had left on her voice mail, and although Dr. Lumsden had been genuinely sympathetic and supportive, the conversation had not been nearly enough. Dr. Lumsden had urged her to speak to the doctor who was covering her patients until her return. But Anne does not want to talk to a doctor she doesn't know.

Anne thinks about confronting Cynthia. She doesn't think Cynthia took her baby, not today. But she'd like to know what's going on between Cynthia and her husband. Perhaps Anne is focusing on what might be going on between her husband and Cynthia because it's not as painful as thinking about what has happened to her baby.

Anne knows Cynthia is at home. She can hear her occasionally on the other side of their shared wall. Anne knows Graham is away again—she saw him getting into a black airport limo with his bags earlier that morning, from her bedroom window. She could go over there, tell Cynthia off, and tell her to keep away from her husband. Anne stops her pacing and stares at the shared wall of the living room, trying to decide what to do. Cynthia is just on the other side of that wall.

But Anne doesn't have the nerve. She is too distraught. She's told the detective what she overheard, but she hasn't yet confronted Marco about it. And Marco hasn't said anything about it to her. They seem to have a new pattern of not speaking about difficult things. They used to share everything—well, almost everything. But since the baby, things have been different.

Her depression made her lose interest in everything. At first Marco brought her flowers, chocolates, did little things to lift her mood, but none of it worked, not really. He stopped telling her about his day, about how his business was doing. She couldn't talk about her own work, because she didn't work anymore. They didn't have much to talk about at all, except the baby. Maybe Marco was right. Maybe she should have gone back to work.

She must talk to him, must make him promise that he'll have nothing more to do with Cynthia. She is not to be trusted. Their friendship with the Still-wells is over. If Anne confronts Marco with what she knows, tells him what she overheard from the top of the stairs, he will feel terrible. He already feels terrible. She has no doubt he'll stay away from Cynthia now. There's nothing to worry about on that score.

If they survive this, she will have to talk to Marco about Cynthia, and she will have to talk to him about the business. They will have to start being more honest with each other again.

Anne needs to clean something, but the house is already spotless. It's odd, the energy she feels now, in the middle of the day, fueled by anxiety. When she still had Cora, she would drag herself through the day. Right about now she'd be praying for Cora to go down for a nap. A sob escapes from her.

She has to keep busy. She starts in the front entry-way, cleaning the antique grate that covers the air duct. The scrolled ironwork is covered in dust and has to be scrubbed by hand. She gets a bucket of warm water and a cloth and sits down on the floor by the front door, begins to clean it, getting deep into the grooves. It calms her.

As she sits there, the mail arrives, cascading through the slot in the door, landing on the floor beside her, startling her. She looks at the pile of envelopes on the floor and freezes. Probably more hate mail. She can't stand it. But what if there's something else? She puts down her wet cloth, wipes her hands dry on her jeans, and sorts through the pile. There is nothing with a typewritten address label on it like the one on the package that contained the green onesie. Anne realizes she's been holding her breath and lets herself exhale.

She doesn't open any of the letters. She would like to throw them all out, but Marco has made her promise to keep everything. He goes through all of it, every day, in case the kidnappers try again to get in touch. He doesn't share the contents with her.

Anne takes her bucket and cloth and goes upstairs to clean the grates up there. She starts in the office at the end of the hall. When she pulls off the original decorative grate to clean it more easily, she sees something small and dark inside the air duct. Startled, she looks more closely, fearing a dead mouse—or perhaps even a rat. But it's not a rat. It's a cell phone.

Anne puts her head between her knees and concentrates on not fainting. It feels like a panic attack, as if all the blood is leaving her body. There are black spots before her eyes. After a few moments, the fainting feeling dissipates and she raises her head. She looks at the cell phone inside the duct. Part of her wants to put the cover back on, go downstairs for a cup of coffee, and pretend she never saw it. But she reaches in to grab it. The phone is stuck to the side of the air duct. She tugs, firmly, and it comes away in her hand. It has been fixed to the inside wall with silver duct tape.

She stares at the cell phone. She has never seen it before. It isn't Marco's. She knows his phone. He carries it with him always. But she can't lie to herself. Someone hid this phone in their house, and it wasn't her.

Marco has a secret cell phone. Why?

Her first thought is Cynthia. *Are* they having an affair? Or is it someone else? He sometimes works long hours. She has been fat and unhappy. But until the night with Cynthia, she never thought he might actually be unfaithful. Maybe she's been completely oblivious. Maybe she's a complete fool. The wife is always the last to know, right?

The phone looks new. She turns it on. It lights up. So he's kept it charged. But now she has to draw a pattern to unlock the phone. She has no idea what it is. She doesn't even know how to unlock Marco's *regular* cell phone. She makes a few attempts, and it freezes her out after too many tries.

Think, she tells herself, but she can't. She sits numbly holding the phone, frozen in place.

There's a lot running through Detective Rasbach's mind on the drive to the crime scene in the Catskills. He thinks about the interview earlier that day with Marco and Anne Conti.

He suspects that this is Marco's way of telling him that this dead man was his accomplice—and that Marco is asking him to help him get his baby back. They both know it may be a little late for that. Marco knows that Rasbach believes he abducted Cora and that he's been outwitted. Clearly this dead man had something to do with it. He must be the mystery man who drove the car down the lane at 12:35 a.m. And what better place to hide the baby than in a remote cabin?

The baby must have been alive when she left the Contis' house, Rasbach realizes, or Marco would not have come to him now. Marco is taking a big risk, but he is plainly desperate. If what Rasbach believes is true, it puts the mother in the clear—mental-health issues aside, she must not have killed the baby.

He is very interested in seeing what he will find at the murder scene.

Meanwhile Jennings is looking for a connection between Marco and the dead man, Derek Honig. Perhaps they'll find something, however tenuous, linking the two. Rasbach doesn't think so, or Marco wouldn't have come to him. But Derek Honig is dead—maybe Marco feels it's a risk he can afford to take, on the very slight chance he can get his baby back.

Rasbach is convinced that Marco loves his daughter, that he never intended for her to get hurt. Rasbach almost feels sorry for him. But then he thinks about the baby, who is probably dead, and the mother, who is shattered, and his sympathy disappears.

"Turn here," he tells the officer driving the cruiser.

They take the highway exit and travel for some time on a lonely dirt road. At last they come to a turnoff. The cruiser bumps and sags down a rutted driveway overgrown with weeds and bushes until it comes to rest in front of a simple wooden cabin, surrounded by yellow crime-scene tape. There's another cruiser on the scene, obviously waiting for them.

The car comes to a stop, and they get out. Rasbach is happy to stretch his legs. "Detective Rasbach," he says, introducing himself to the local cop.

"Officer Watt, sir. Right this way."

Rasbach looks around, missing nothing. A glance beyond the cabin shows a small, deserted lake. There are no other cabins in view. A perfect spot to hide an infant for a few days, Rasbach thinks.

He enters the cabin. It's 1970s vintage, with ugly linoleum flooring in the kitchen, a Formica table, outdated cabinetry.

"Where was the body?" Rasbach asks.

"Over there," the officer says, jerking his head toward the main room. The room is furnished with mismatched castoffs. There is no doubt about where the body had been. The old dirty beige carpet is stained with fresh blood.

Rasbach stoops down to look. "The murder weapon?"

"We've taken it to the lab. He used a spade. Hit him over the head with it. A few times."

"Is the face still recognizable?" Rasbach asks, turning to look up at the other cop.

"Battered, but recognizable."

Rasbach stands again, considers taking Marco to the morgue to have a look. *This is what you're playing at.* "So what's the theory?"

"At first glance? We're saying a botched robbery, but between you and me, there's nothing here to take.

Of course, we don't know if there *was* something here. It's a pretty isolated spot. Drug deal gone wrong, maybe."

"Or a kidnapping."

"Or a kidnapping." The officer adds, "It looked a bit personal, the way he was struck repeatedly with the spade. I mean, he was good and dead."

"And no sign of any baby things? No diapers, bottles, anything like that?" Rasbach asks, casting his eyes around the cabin.

"No. If there was a baby here, whoever took her cleaned up pretty good."

"What did he do with his garbage?"

"We figure he burned some of it in the woodstove there, so we've been through that, and there's also a fire pit outside. But there's no garbage here at all, and nothing in the stove or the fire pit. So either our dead guy had just been to the dump or someone tidied up. There's a dump twenty miles from here, and they get the license plates, and he hadn't been there in the last week."

"So not a botched robbery. No one comes to commit a robbery, kills someone, and gets rid of all his garbage."

"No."

"Where's his car?"

"At the lab."

"What make is it?"

"It's a hybrid, a Prius V. Black."

Bingo, Rasbach thinks. He has a feeling the tires will match the prints in the Contis' garage. And no matter how thoroughly someone cleans up, if the baby was here for a couple of days, there'll be DNA evidence. It looks like they may have their first big break in the kidnapping of baby Cora.

Finally they may be getting somewhere.

TWENTY-FOUR

Marco is at his office, staring blankly out his window at the view. No one else is there. He has no staff of his own on site. Since it's Saturday, the rest of the building is quiet, too, for which he's grateful.

He thinks about the meeting he and Anne had earlier in the day with Detective Rasbach. Rasbach knows, he's sure of it. Those eyes of his seem to look right through Marco. Marco might as well have stood up and said, *This is the man I conspired with to take Cora for a couple of days and negotiate the ransom money. He's now dead. I have lost control of things. I need your help.*

They have a lawyer now. A lawyer famous for getting people acquitted—people who are guilty as hell. Marco realizes now that this is a good thing. There will be no more interviews without the lawyer present. Marco no longer cares about his reputation; it's all about staying out of jail and keeping Anne in the dark.

His cell phone rings. He looks at the display. Cynthia is calling him. That bitch. Why would she be calling? He hesitates, wondering whether to answer or let it go to voice mail, but in the end he picks it up.

"Yes?" His voice is cold. He will never forgive her for lying to the police.

"Marco," Cynthia purrs, as if the last few days had never happened, as if his child were not missing, and everything was the same as it used to be. How he wishes that were true.

"What's up?" Marco says. He wants to keep this short.

"I have something I want to talk to you about," Cynthia says, a little more businesslike. "Can you come by the house?"

"Why? Did you want to apologize?"

"Apologize?" She sounds surprised.

"For lying to the police. For telling them that I came on to you when we both know *you* came on to me."

"I'm sorry about that. I did lie," she says, with an attempt at playfulness.

"What the fuck? You're *sorry*? Do you have any idea how much trouble you've caused me?"

"Can we discuss it?" She's not playful anymore.

"Why do we need to discuss it?"

"I'll explain when you get here," Cynthia says, and abruptly hangs up the phone.

Marco sits at his desk for five full minutes, drumming his fingers on its surface, trying to decide what to do. Finally he gets up, closes the blinds, leaves his office, and locks his door. He feels uneasy about ignoring her. Cynthia is not the kind of woman you ignore. He'd better see what she has to say.

When he gets to his own neighborhood, Marco realizes that if he's going to see Cynthia, even if only for a couple of minutes, it's better that Anne not know about it. And he wants to avoid the reporters. So he'd better not park in front of the house. If he parks in the garage, he can go to Cynthia's through the back for a couple of minutes first and then go home.

He parks the Audi in his own garage and then goes through the backyard gate over to Cynthia's and knocks on the back door. He feels furtive, guilty, as if he's sneaking around on his wife. But he isn't—he just wants to see what Cynthia has to say, and then he'll get the hell out of there. He doesn't *want* to sneak around on his wife. He glances aimlessly over the patio as he waits for her to answer the door. This is where he was sitting when she crawled into his lap.

Cynthia comes to the door. She looks surprised. "I was expecting you at the *front* door," she says. It's as if she's insinuating something. But she's not as flirtatious as she usually is. He sees right away that she's not in a sexy mood. Well, neither is he.

He steps inside the kitchen. "What's this about?" Marco says. "I've got to get home."

"I think you've got a couple of minutes for this," Cynthia says, and leans back against the kitchen counter, folding her arms beneath her breasts.

"Why did you lie to the police?" Marco asks abruptly.

"It was just a *little* lie," Cynthia says.

"No it wasn't."

"I like to tell lies. Just like you."

"What do you mean?" Marco spits angrily.

"You're *living* a lie, aren't you, Marco?"

Marco starts to feel a chill. She can't know. She can't know anything. How could she? "What the hell are you talking about?" He shakes his head as if he has no idea what she's getting at.

Cynthia gives him a long, cool look. "I'm sorry to have to tell you this, Marco, but Graham has a hidden camera, in the backyard." Marco says nothing, but he feels cold all over. "And it was recording on the night you were here, the night your baby *went missing.*"

She knows, Marco thinks. *Fuck. Fuck.* He starts to sweat. He looks at her beautiful face, so ugly to him now. She is a manipulative bitch. Perhaps she's bluffing. Well, he can bluff, too.

"You had a camera on? Did you get anything on the kidnapper?" he asks, as if this is good news.

"Oh, yes," she says. "I sure did."

Marco knows he's finished. She has him on video. He can tell by her face.

"It was *you.*"

"Bullshit," Marco scoffs, trying to act as if he doesn't believe a word of it, but he knows it's no use.

"Would you like to see it?"

He would like to wring her neck. "Yes," he says.

"Come with me," she says, and turns to go upstairs.

He follows her up to her bedroom, the one she shares with Graham. He thinks how foolish she is, inviting a man who she already knows is capable of a kidnapping up to her bedroom. She doesn't appear to be afraid. She appears to be in total control. But that's what she likes—to be in control, to pull people's strings and watch them dance. She also likes a little spice, a little danger. She's obviously going to blackmail him. He wonders if he's going to let her.

A laptop lies open on the bed. She clicks some keys, and a video begins to play, with a date and time signature. Marco blinks rapidly as he watches the video. There he is fiddling with the light, going into the house. He comes out a couple minutes later with Cora in his arms, wrapped in her white blanket. It is unmistakably him. He glances around to make sure he's unobserved. He looks almost directly at the camera, but he has no idea that it's there. Then he walks quickly to the rear door of the garage and reappears about a minute later, walking back across the lawn without the baby. He'd forgotten to reset the light. Seeing it all now, after everything that's happened, Marco feels overwhelming regret, and guilt, and shame.

And anger that he's been caught. By her. She will show the police. She will show Anne. He is finished.

"Who else has seen this?" he asks. He's surprised at how normal his voice sounds to him.

She ignores his question. "Did you kill her?" Cynthia asks, almost with her old playfulness.

He is sickened by her, by her morbid, unfeeling curiosity. He doesn't answer. Does he want her to think he might be capable of killing? "Who else?" he demands, looking fiercely at her.

"No one," she lies.

"Graham?"

"No, he hasn't seen it," Cynthia says. "I told him I checked the camera but the battery had died. He didn't question it. He doesn't know anything about this." She adds, "You know Graham. He doesn't take much of an interest."

"So why are you showing this to me?" Marco asks. "Why didn't you go straight to the police?"

"Why would I do that? We're friends, aren't we?" She gives him a coy smile.

"Cut the bullshit, Cynthia."

"Fine." The smile disappears. "If you want me to keep this to myself, it's going to cost you."

"Well, that's a bit of a problem, Cynthia," Marco says, his voice very controlled, "because I don't have any money."

"Oh, come on. You must have something."

"I am stone broke," he says coldly. "Why do you think I kidnapped my own child? For fun?"

He can see the disappointment in her face as she readjusts her expectations.

"You can mortgage your house, can't you?"

"It's already mortgaged."

"Mortgage it some more."

The cold bitch. "I can't. Not without Anne knowing, obviously."

"So maybe we need to show Anne the video, too."

Marco takes a sudden step toward her. He doesn't have to play the part of a desperate man—he *is* a desperate man. He could throttle her right now if he wanted to. But she doesn't look scared, she looks excited. Her eyes glitter, and he can see her breasts rising and falling rapidly as she breathes. Perhaps it's danger she wants, more than anything else. The thrill. Perhaps she wants him to throw her onto the bed they're both standing beside. For a brief moment, he considers it. Would she not blackmail him then? Not likely.

"You're not showing that video to anybody."

She takes her time responding. She looks right in his eyes. Their faces are mere inches apart. "I would rather *not* show it to anybody, Marco. I would like this to be just between the two of us. But you've got to work with me here. You must be able to get some money."

Marco thinks furiously. He doesn't *have* any money. He doesn't know how to get any. He will have to buy time. "Look, give me some time to figure things out. You know what a shit show my life is right now."

"Things haven't exactly turned out as you planned, have they?" she says. "I presume you expected to get the baby back?"

He wants to hit her, but he stops himself.

She looks at him appraisingly. "Fine. I'll give you some time. I won't show anyone the video—for now."

"How much money are we talking about here?"

"Two hundred thousand."

It's less than he was expecting. He would have expected her to ask for more, an amount more in keeping with her flamboyant nature. But if he pays her, she'll ask for more, and more—that's the way it is with blackmailers. You never get out from under them. So the amount she's naming now is meaningless. Even if he pays her and she destroys the video in front of him, he'll never be certain there are no copies. His life is totally destroyed, on so many fronts.

"I think that's fair," she says.

"I'm leaving now. Stay away from Anne."

"I will. But if I get impatient, if I don't hear from you, I might call."

Marco pushes past her out of the bedroom and goes down the stairs and out the sliding glass kitchen doors without looking back. He's so angry he can't think straight. Angry and scared. There's proof. Proof that he took the baby. This changes everything. Anne will know. And he could go to jail for a very long time.

At that moment he doesn't see how things can get any worse. He enters his own backyard through the gate from Cynthia's patio. Anne is out there watering some plants.

Their eyes meet.

TWENTY-FIVE

Anne sees Marco come from Cynthia's back-yard, and her eyes go wide. She is shocked into perfect stillness, the watering can in her hand. Marco has been at Cynthia's. Why? There's only one reason he would be at Cynthia's. Anne asks him anyway, from across the yard. "What were you doing over there?" Her voice is cold.

Marco's got that deer-in-the-headlights look, when he's caught red-handed and doesn't know what to do. He's never been good at improvising. She almost feels sorry for him. But she can't feel sorry for him, because right now she hates him. She drops the watering can and runs past him and through the back door into the house.

He follows after her, calling desperately, "Anne! Wait!"

But she doesn't wait. She runs upstairs; she's sobbing loudly now. He follows on her heels up the stairs, pleading with her to talk to him, to let him explain.

But he has no idea how he will explain. How will

he explain why he was sneaking over to Cynthia's without revealing the existence of the video?

He expects Anne to go into their bedroom and throw herself down on the bed in tears, which is what she usually does when she's upset. Maybe she'll slam the door in his face and lock it. She's done it before. She'll come out eventually, and it will give him time to think.

But she doesn't run into their bedroom and fling herself, crying, onto their bed. She doesn't lock him out of their bedroom. Instead she runs down the hall into the office. He's right behind her. He sees her drop to her knees in front of the air-intake grate.

Oh, no. God no.

She tears the grate off, sticks her hand inside, and rips the cell phone off the side of the air duct. He feels sick. She puts the phone in her palm, holds it up to him, the tears streaming down her face. "What the hell is *this*, Marco?"

Marco freezes. He can't believe this is happening. Suddenly he has to fight the urge to laugh. It's comical, really, all of it. Cynthia's video. This. *What the hell is he going to tell her?*

"This is how you've been communicating with Cynthia, isn't it?" Anne accuses him.

He stares at her, momentarily baffled. Just in time he stops himself from saying, *Why would I use a cell phone to call Cynthia when she's right next door?* His hesitation suggests something else to her.

"Or is it someone else?"

Marco can't tell her the truth—that the hidden cell phone she now has in her hand was the only way he could communicate with his accomplice in the kidnapping of their baby. With the man who is now dead. Marco has hidden an untraceable, prepaid cell phone in the wall, to use for calling his partner in an unforgivable crime. She thinks he's been having an affair—with Cynthia or someone else. His immediate instinct is to keep her away from Cynthia. He will make something up.

"I'm so sorry," he begins. "It's not Cynthia, I swear."

She screams and throws the phone at him, hard. It clips him on the forehead and bounces to the floor. He feels a sharp pain above his right eye.

He pleads with her. "It's over, Anne. It meant nothing. It was just a few weeks," he lies, "right after Cora was born and you were so tired. . . . It was a mistake. I didn't mean to do it—it just happened." He's blurting out every excuse he can think of.

She glares at him in disgust and rage, tears smearing her face, her nose running, her hair a tangled mess. "You can sleep on the couch from now on," she says bitterly, her voice edged with pain, "until I figure out what to do." She pushes past him into their bedroom and slams the door. He hears her turn the lock.

Marco slowly picks the phone up off the floor. He touches his forehead where the phone struck him; his fingers come away bloody. Absently, he turns the cell phone on, automatically swipes the pattern to unlock the phone. There is a record of his calls—all are to one number. All unanswered.

Marco tries to find a way through his fear and confusion. Who could have known that Bruce had Cora? Had Bruce told someone else about their plan, someone who then turned on him? It seemed unlikely. Or had he been careless? Had someone seen the baby and recognized her? That also seemed unlikely.

Idly, Marco looks down at the cell phone in his hand and, with a jolt, notices the missed-calls symbol. It wasn't there the last time he looked. The ringer is turned off, of course. Who would be calling him from Bruce's phone? Bruce is dead. Marco presses REDIAL, his heart hammering behind his ribs. He hears the phone ring. Once, twice.

And then a voice he recognizes. "I was wondering when you'd call."

Anne cries herself to sleep. When she wakes, it's dark outside. She lies in bed, listening carefully for sounds in the house. She hears nothing. She wonders where Marco is. Can she even stand the sight of him? Should she kick him out of the house? She hugs her pillow close to her body and thinks.

It wouldn't look good if she kicked him out now. The press would be on them like a pack of animals. They'd look guiltier than ever. If they were innocent, why would they split? The police might arrest them. Does she even care?

In spite of everything, Anne knows Marco is a good father and loves Cora—he's in as much pain about the baby as she is. She knows he had nothing to do with Cora's disappearance, in spite of what the police have said to her and suggested with their sly questions and hypotheticals. She can't turn him out, at least for the time being, even if thinking about him with another woman makes her sick.

Anne closes her eyes and tries to remember that night. It's the first time she's tried to put herself back in that room, the night Cora went missing. She's been avoiding it. But now she sees it in her mind's eye, the last time she saw her baby. Cora was in the crib. The room was dark. Cora was on her back, her chubby arms flung up beside her head, her blond hair curling damply on her forehead in the heat. The ceiling fan swirled lazily overhead. The bedroom window was open to the night, but it was still stifling.

Anne remembers now. She stood by the crib looking down at her baby daughter's tiny fists, her bare, bent legs. It was too hot for covers. She resisted the urge to reach out and stroke the baby's forehead, afraid of waking her. She wanted to gather Cora in her arms, bury her face in the child's neck and sob, but she stopped herself. She was swamped with feelings—with love, mostly, and tenderness, but also with hopelessness, and despair, and inadequacy—and she was ashamed.

As she stood by the crib, she tried not to blame herself, but it was hard not to. It felt like her fault that she wasn't a blissed-out new mother. That she was broken. But her daughter—her daughter was perfect. Her precious little girl. It wasn't her baby's fault. None of it was her baby's fault.

She wanted to stay in Cora's room, sit in the

comfortable nursing chair, and fall asleep. But instead she'd tiptoed out of the room and returned to the party next door.

Anne can't remember anything else about that last visit at midnight. She didn't shake the baby or drop her. Not then anyway. She didn't even pick her up. She remembers very clearly that she did not pick her up or touch her when she went over briefly at midnight, because she was afraid of waking her. Because when she'd fed her at eleven, Cora had been fussy. She'd woken up, and been difficult. Anne had fed her, but then she wouldn't settle. She'd walked with her, sung to her. She might have slapped her. Yes—she slapped her baby. She feels sick with shame, remembering.

Anne had been tired and frustrated, upset about what was going on with Marco and Cynthia at the party. She was crying. She doesn't remember dropping Cora or shaking her. But she cannot remember changing the baby's outfit either. Why can't she remember? If she can't remember changing the outfit, what else can she not remember? What did she do after she slapped her?

When the police had confronted her with the pink onesie, she'd said what she thought must be true: that she'd changed the outfit. She often changed Cora's outfit at her last feeding, when she changed her diaper. She assumed she'd done the same thing then. She knows she must have. But she can't actually remember doing it.

Anne feels a chill deep in her soul. She wonders

now if perhaps she did do something to the baby during the last feeding at eleven. She slapped her, but after that she can't remember. Did she do worse than that? Did she? Did she kill her? Did Marco find her dead at twelve thirty and assume the worst—and cover up for her? Did he call someone to take Cora away? Is that why he wanted to stay longer at the party, to give the other person the time to get her? Anne tries desperately now to remember if the baby had been breathing at midnight. She can't remember. She can't be sure. She feels sick with terror and remorse.

Does she dare ask Marco? Does she want to know?

TWENTY-SIX

At the sound of his father-in-law's voice, Marco sinks to the floor. In his confusion and disbelief, he can't speak.

"Marco?" Richard asks.

"Yes." His voice sounds dead, even to his own ears.

"I know what you did."

"What I did," Marco repeats in a monotone. He is still trying to put it all together. *Why does Anne's father have Derek Honig's cell phone? Did the police find it at the murder scene and give it to him? Is this a trap?*

"Kidnapping your own child for ransom. Stealing from your wife's parents. As if we haven't given you enough already."

"What are you talking about?" Marco says desperately, trying to buy time, to work his way through this bizarre situation. He fights the panicked urge to hang up. He must deny, deny, deny. There's no proof of anything. But then he remembers there's Cynthia's video. And now there's this phone call. What exactly are the implications of this phone call? If the police found Derek's phone, if they're listening in, now that

Marco has picked up on the other end, they have all the proof they need that Marco was in collusion with Derek.

But maybe the police don't know anything about the phone. The implications of *that* are chilling. Marco feels himself go cold.

"Oh, come on, Marco," Richard says. "Man up for once in your life."

"How did you get that phone?" Marco asks. If the police didn't find the phone and give it to Richard, to trap Marco, then Richard must have gotten it from Derek. Did Richard kill Derek? "Do *you* have Cora, you son of a bitch?" Marco hisses desperately.

"No. Not yet. But I'm going to get her." His father-in-law adds bitterly, "No thanks to you."

"What? She's alive?" Marco blurts in disbelief.

"I think so."

Marco gasps. Cora, alive! Nothing else matters. All that matters is that they get their baby back. "How do you know? Are you sure?" he whispers.

"As sure as I can be, without holding her in my arms."

"How do you know?" Marco asks again, desperately.

"The kidnappers got in touch with us. They knew from the newspapers that we'd paid the first ransom. They want more. We'll pay whatever they ask. We love Cora, you know that."

"You haven't told Anne," Marco says, still trying to get his mind around this latest development.

"Obviously not. We know it's hard on her, but it's

probably for the best, until we're sure about what's going to happen."

"I see," Marco says.

"The fact is, Marco, we have to protect our girls from you," Richard says, his voice like ice. "We have to protect Cora. And we have to protect Anne. You're dangerous, Marco, with your plans and schemes."

"I'm not dangerous, you bastard," Marco says viciously. "How did you get that phone?"

Richard says coldly, "The kidnappers sent it to us, like they sent you the outfit. With a note—about you. Probably to stop us from going to the cops. But you know what? I'm glad they did. Because now we know what you did. And we can prove it, if we choose to. But all in good time. First we have to get Cora back." He lowers his voice to a hushed threat. "I'm the one in charge now, Marco. So don't you dare fuck it up. Don't tell the police. And don't tell Anne—I don't want to get her hopes up again if something goes wrong."

"All right," Marco says, his mind spinning. He will do anything to get Cora back. He doesn't know what to believe, but he wants to believe she's alive.

He must destroy the phone.

"And I don't want you talking to Alice—she doesn't want to speak to you. She's very upset about what you did."

"All right."

"I'm not done with you yet, Marco," Richard says, and abruptly disconnects the call.

Marco sits on the floor for a long time, flooded with renewed hope—and despair.

Anne gets out of bed. She walks quietly to the bedroom door and unlocks it, pulls the door back. She sticks her head out into the hall. There's a light on in the office. Has Marco been in there all this time? What is he doing?

Anne walks slowly down the hall and pushes open the office door. Marco is sitting on the floor with the cell phone in his hand. His face is awfully pale. There's a dreadful bloody mark above his eye where she clipped him with the phone. He looks up at her as she comes in. They stare at each other for a long moment, neither one sure of what to say.

Finally Anne speaks. "Are you okay, Marco?"

Marco touches the bloody bump on his forehead, realizes he has a pounding headache, and nods slightly.

He desperately wants to tell her that Cora might be alive after all. That there's hope. That her father is in charge now, and he never fails—at anything. Not like her fuckup of a husband. He wants to tell her that everything is going to be all right.

But everything *isn't* going to be all right. They may get Cora back—he hopes to God they do—but Anne's father will make sure that Marco is arrested for kidnapping. He will make sure Marco goes to jail. Marco doesn't know if Anne's fragile emotional state can survive such a shocking betrayal.

He thinks cynically for a moment about how disappointed Cynthia will be at the turn of events.

"Marco, say something," Anne says anxiously.

"I'm okay," Marco whispers. His mouth is dry. He's surprised that she's talking to him. He wonders why the change of heart. A few hours ago, she'd told him to move onto the couch while she figured out what she was going to do. He assumed that meant she was kicking him out. Now she looks almost sorry.

She comes in and sits down beside him on the floor. He suddenly feels anxious that her father might call back on the phone. How would he explain that? Furtively, he turns the phone off.

"Marco, there's something I have to say," Anne begins tentatively.

"What is it, baby?" Marco asks. He reaches up and strokes a strand of hair off her face. She doesn't pull away. The tender gesture, a reminder of happier days, makes her tears come.

She lowers her eyes and says, "You have to be honest with me, Marco."

He nods but doesn't say anything. He wonders if she suspects. He wonders what he will say if she confronts him with the truth.

"The night of the kidnapping, when you went to check on Cora the last time—" She turns to face him now, and he tenses, worried about what's coming next. "Was she alive?"

Marco starts. He didn't expect this. "Of course she was alive," he says. "Why do you ask that?" He looks at her troubled face with concern.

"Because I can't remember," Anne whispers. "When I saw her at midnight, I can't remember if she was breathing. Are you *sure* she was breathing?"

"Yes, I'm sure she was breathing," Marco says. He can't tell her he knows she was alive because he felt her little heart beating against him as he held her and carried her out of the house.

"How do you know?" she says, looking intently at him, as if trying to read his mind. "Did you actually check? Or just look at her?"

"I saw her chest moving up and down in the crib," Marco lies.

"You're sure? You wouldn't lie to me?" Anne asks anxiously.

"No, Anne, why are you asking me this? Why do you think she wasn't breathing? Because of something that stupid detective said?"

She looks down at her lap. "Because I'm not sure, when I saw her at midnight, that she was breathing. I didn't pick her up. I didn't want to wake her. I can't remember noticing if she was actually breathing."

"Is that all?"

"No." She pauses, uncertain. Finally she looks up at him and says, "When I was with her at eleven . . . it's just a blank. I can't remember it at all."

The expression on her face frightens him. Marco feels she is about to tell him something terrible, something he has somehow been waiting for, that he's been expecting all along. He doesn't want to hear it, but he can't move.

Anne whispers, "I can't remember what I did. I do that sometimes—I blank out. I do things, and then I don't remember doing them."

"What do you mean?" Marco says. His voice is strangely cold.

She looks at him, her eyes pleading. "It isn't that I forgot because of the wine. I've never told you, but when I was younger, I was ill. I thought I was past it when I met you."

"Ill how?" Marco says, startled.

She's crying now. "It's like I just check out for a bit. Then, when I come back, I don't remember anything."

He looks at her, astonished. "And you never bothered to tell me?"

"I'm sorry! I should have told you. I thought . . ." She doesn't finish her sentence. "I lied to the police about the onesie. I don't remember changing her. I just assumed I did it, but I don't actually remember any of it. My mind is . . . blank." She is becoming hysterical.

"Shhhh. . . ." Marco says. "Anne, she was fine. I'm positive."

"Because the police think I hurt her. They think I might have killed her, smothered her with a pillow or strangled her, and that you took her away to protect me!"

"That's ridiculous!" Marco says, angry now with the police for suggesting such things to her. They all know that he's the one they're after—why do they need to push her to the brink of a breakdown?

"Is it?" Anne asks, looking at him wildly. "I hit her. I was angry, and I hit her."

"What? When? When did you hit her?"

"When I fed her, at eleven o'clock. She was fussy. I . . . I kind of snapped. Sometimes . . . I would lose control . . . and slap her, when she wouldn't stop crying. When you were at work and she wouldn't stop crying."

Marco looks at her, appalled. "No, Anne, I'm sure you didn't," he says, hoping what she's told him isn't true. This is disturbing, as disturbing as her confession about having some kind of illness that makes her not know what she's doing.

"But I don't know, you see?" Anne cries. "I can't remember! I might have hurt her. Are you covering up for me, Marco? Tell me the truth!"

He takes her face between his hands and holds her still. "Anne, she was fine. She was alive and breathing at twelve thirty. This is not your fault. None of this is your fault." He takes her into his arms as she breaks down weeping.

He thinks, *This is all* my *fault.*

TWENTY-SEVEN

After Anne finally falls into a restless sleep, Marco lies awake in bed beside her for a long time, trying to figure it all out. He wishes he could discuss the entire mess with her. He misses how they used to talk, about everything, all their plans. But he can't talk to her about anything now. When he does sleep, his dreams are terrifying; he wakes at four in the morning with a start, his heart pounding and sweating all over, the sheets soaked.

This is what he knows: Richard is negotiating with the kidnappers. He and Alice are going to pay whatever it takes to get Cora back. Marco has to hope and pray that Richard will be successful where he was not. Richard has Derek's cell phone, and he was *expecting* it to be Marco on the other end. Richard—and Alice—know Marco was colluding with Derek, that he kidnapped his own child for money. Marco's first thought, that Richard had killed Derek and taken his phone, now seems absurd. How could Richard possibly have known about Derek? Was Richard capable of bashing in another man's head? Marco doesn't think so, even though he hates the bastard.

If it's true that the kidnappers sent Richard the phone, that's good. That means the police don't know about it—not yet anyway. But Richard threatened him. What had he said, exactly? Marco can't remember. He must talk to Richard and persuade him not to tell the police—or Anne—about Marco's role in the kidnapping. How will he manage that? He'll have to convince them that Anne couldn't withstand the shock, that exposing Marco as being involved in Cora's disappearance would utterly destroy her.

Anne's parents would hold it against him forever, but at least maybe he and Anne and Cora could be a family again. If they got their baby back, Anne would be happy. He could start over, work his ass off to provide for them. Maybe Richard doesn't actually want to expose him. It would embarrass them socially, hurt his reputation in the business community. Maybe all Richard wants is to have dirty secrets to hold over Marco for the rest of his life. That would be just like Richard. Marco starts to breathe a little easier.

He has to get rid of the phone. What if Anne hits REDIAL and gets her father? Then he remembers she doesn't know the pattern to open it. Still, he must get rid of it. It ties him to Cora's disappearance. He can't have the police getting their hands on it.

There's still the problem of Cynthia and her video. He has no idea what to do about that. She'll keep quiet in the short term, as long as he can convince her he'll be able to get her the money she wants.

Jesus, what a mess.

Marco gets up in the dark and moves quietly around the carpeted bedroom, careful not to wake his wife. He dresses quickly, pulling on the same jeans and T-shirt he wore the day before. He then goes down the hall to the office and removes the phone from the desk drawer where he put it last night. He turns it on and checks it one final time. Nothing. There's no need to keep the phone. If he needs to talk to Richard, he'll do it directly. The phone is the only physical evidence, besides Cynthia's video, that there is against him.

One thing at a time. He must get rid of the cell phone.

He grabs the keys to the car from the bowl by the front door. He considers leaving a note for Anne but figures he'll be home before she wakes, so he doesn't bother. He slips quietly out the back door and walks across the yard and into the garage and gets into the Audi.

It's chilly, just before dawn. He hasn't made a conscious decision about what to do with the phone, but now he finds himself driving to the lake. It's still dark. While he drives, alone on the empty highway, he thinks about Cynthia. It takes a certain kind of person to blackmail another. He wonders what else she's done. He wonders if he can get something on her that's as damning as what she has on him. Balance the scales. If he can't find something useful on her, maybe he can frame her in some way. He would need help with that. He recoils inwardly. Crime has not worked for him, and yet he seems to be digging himself in deeper and deeper.

He holds on to the idea that he may be able to get some semblance of his life back—if Cora is returned to them unharmed, if Richard keeps his secret, if he can get something on Cynthia, one way or another, to make her back off. There's no way he can pay her and keep on paying her. He can't be in her power.

But even if he can do all these things, he will never, ever have any peace of mind. He knows that. He will live for Cora, and for Anne. He will make sure he gives them as happy a life as possible. He owes them that. It doesn't matter whether he is happy or not; he has forfeited any right to happiness.

He parks the car in his favorite spot under the tree, facing the lake. He sits there for a few minutes inside the car, remembering the last time he was here. So much has happened since then. The last time he was here, just a few days ago, he was so sure he was going to get Cora back. If things had gone the way they were supposed to, he'd have his baby back now, and the money, and nobody would have known a thing.

What a fucking mess things have turned out to be.

Finally he gets out of the car. It's cool in the early morning by the lake. The sky is beginning to brighten. The cell phone is in his pocket. He starts walking down to the beach. He's going to walk to the end of the dock and throw the cell phone into the lake where no one will ever find it. That will be one thing off his plate.

He stands at the end of the dock for some time, full of regret. Then he takes the cell phone out of his pocket. He wipes the whole thing down for finger-prints with the edge of his jacket, just in case. He was a good ballplayer as a teenager. He hurls the phone as hard as he can into the lake. It lands with a loud *plop*. Ever-growing circles radiate outward from where it landed in the water. It reminds him of when he used to throw rocks in the lake as a kid. How far away that seems now.

Marco feels relieved to be rid of the phone. He turns and heads back to his car. It is quite light out now. With a start, he notices that there is another car in the lot, a car that wasn't there before. He doesn't know how long it has been there. How did he not notice the lights when it came in? Maybe the car just arrived and didn't have its headlights on.

It doesn't matter, he tells himself, although his skin crawls. It doesn't matter if someone saw him throwing something into the lake in the early morn-ing. He's too far away to be recognized.

But his car is right there, with the license number in plain view. Marco is nervous now. As he gets closer, he gets a better look at the other car. It's a police car, an unmarked police car. You can always tell them by the grille on the front. Marco feels sick. Why is there a police car here, now? Was he followed? Did the police see him throw something into the lake? Marco is sweating in the cold and can feel his heart beating in his ears. He tries to walk normally to his car, keep-ing as far away from the police car as possible without looking like he's trying to avoid it. The window rolls down. Fuck.

"Everything all right?" the officer asks, his head outside the window, getting a good look.

Marco stops, frozen in place. He doesn't recognize the officer's face—it's not Rasbach or one of his men. For one surreal moment, Marco had expected it to be Rasbach who popped his head out the open window. "Yeah, sure. Couldn't sleep," Marco says.

The officer nods, rolls up his window, and drives off.

Marco gets into the car, shaking uncontrollably. It's a few minutes before he's able to drive.

At breakfast Anne and Marco don't talk much. He is pale and distant after his experience at the lake. She is fragile, missing her baby, thinking about the day before. She still doesn't believe Marco about Cynthia. Why was he coming out of her house yesterday? If he lied about this, what else has he lied about? She doesn't trust him. But they have reached an uneasy truce. They need each other. Maybe they even still care for each other, in spite of everything.

"I need to go back to the office this morning," Marco tells her, his voice a little unsteady. He clears his throat loudly.

"It's Sunday," she says.

"I know, but I should probably go in, get caught up on some projects that are overdue." He takes another gulp of coffee.

She nods. She thinks it will do him good—he looks awful. It will take his mind off what they're dealing with, even if only for a short time. She is jealous. She doesn't have the luxury of throwing herself into work to forget, even for a moment. Everything in the house reminds her of Cora, of what they've lost. The high chair, sitting empty in the kitchen. The colorful plastic toys in the bin in the living room. The play mat she used to put Cora down on with its dangling overhead toys that the baby loved to reach for, cooing and giggling. It doesn't matter where she goes in the house, Cora is everywhere. There is no escape, no matter how temporary, for her.

Marco is worried about her, she can tell. "What will you do when I'm gone?" he asks.

She shrugs. "I don't know."

"Maybe you should leave a message with that other doctor, the one who's filling in for Dr. Lumsden. Try to make an appointment for early in the week," Marco suggests.

"Okay," Anne says listlessly.

But when Marco leaves, she doesn't call the doctor's office. She wanders around the house thinking about Cora. She imagines her dead, in a Dumpster somewhere, crawling with maggots. She imagines her in a shallow grave in the woods, dug up and gnawed on by animals. She thinks of newspaper stories she's read about lost children. She can't get the horror out of her head. She feels queasy and panicky. She looks at herself in the mirror, and her eyes are huge.

Maybe it's better that she not know what happened to her baby. But she *needs* to know. For the rest of her life, her tortured mind will supply hideous ideas that may be worse than the truth. Maybe Cora's death was quick. Anne prays that it was. But she'll probably never know for sure.

From the moment her daughter was born, Anne knew where Cora was every minute of her short life, and now she has no idea where she is. Because she is a bad mother. She is a bad, broken mother who didn't love her daughter enough. She left her alone in the house. She hit her. No wonder her daughter is gone. There is a reason for everything, and the reason her baby is gone is that Anne does not deserve her.

Now Anne is not just wandering around the house, she is moving faster and faster. Her mind is racing, thoughts stumbling over one another. She feels intense guilt about her daughter. She doesn't know whether to believe Marco when he tells her that Cora was alive at twelve thirty. She can't believe anything he says—he's a liar. She must have hurt Cora. She must have killed her own baby. There is no other possibility that makes sense.

It's a terrible possibility, a terrible burden. She must tell someone. She tried to tell Marco what she did, but he wouldn't listen. He wants to pretend it didn't happen; he wants to pretend that she's not capable of harming her own baby. She remembers the way he looked at her when she told him she hit Cora, the disbelief.

He might feel different if he'd seen her slap Cora.

He might feel different if he knew her history.

But he doesn't know, because she has never told him.

There was the incident at St. Mildred's—the one she has no memory of. She remembers only the aftermath—being in the girls' bathroom, the blood on the wall, Susan slumped on the floor as if she were dead, and everyone—Janice, Debbie, the science teacher, and the headmistress—all looking at her in horror. She'd had no idea what happened.

After that, her mother had taken her to a psychiatrist, who diagnosed a dissociative disorder. Anne remembers being in his office, frozen in her seat, her mother sitting anxiously by her side. Anne was terrified by the diagnosis, terrified and ashamed.

"I don't understand," her mother said to the doctor. "I don't understand what you're saying."

"I know," the psychiatrist said gently, "that it seems frightening, but it's not as unusual as you might think. Think of it as a coping mechanism—an imperfect one. The person disconnects from reality for a brief time." He turned to Anne; she refused to look at him. "You might feel detached from yourself, as if things are happening to someone else. You might perceive things as distorted or unreal. Or you might experience a fugue state, as you did—a brief period of amnesia."

"Is this going to happen again?" Alice asked the doctor.

"I don't know. Has it happened before?"

It had happened before, but never so shockingly.

"There have been times," Alice admitted tentatively,

"ever since she was a little girl, when she seemed to do things and not remember doing them. I . . . I thought at first she was just saying that so she wouldn't get in trouble. But then I realized she couldn't control it." She paused. "But there's never been anything like this."

The doctor clasped his hands and gazed at Anne intently, asking her mother, "Has there been any trauma in her life?"

"Trauma?" Alice echoed. "Of course not."

The doctor surveyed her skeptically. "Dissociative disorder is usually the result of some sort of repressed trauma."

"Oh, God," Alice said.

The doctor raised his eyebrows at her and waited.

"Her father," Alice said suddenly.

"Her father?"

"She watched her father die. It was horrible. She adored him."

Anne's eyes were fixed firmly on the wall in front of her; she was perfectly still.

"How did he die?" the doctor asked.

"I was out shopping. He was in the house, playing with her. He had a massive heart attack. He must have died almost instantly. She saw it. By the time I got home, it was too late. Anne was crying and pressing numbers in the phone, but she didn't know what numbers to press. Anyway, it didn't matter—no one could have saved him. She was only four years old."

The doctor nodded sympathetically. "I see," he said. He sat quietly for a moment.

Alice said, "She had nightmares for a long time. I

didn't let her talk about it—maybe that was wrong, but she would get so upset and I was trying to help. Whenever she brought it up, I tried to take her mind off it." She added, "She seemed to blame herself, for not knowing what to do. But it wasn't her fault. She was so young. And we were told that nothing could have saved him, even if the ambulance had been right there."

"That would be very difficult for any child to deal with," the doctor said. He turned to Anne, who continued to ignore him. "Stress can temporarily worsen symptoms of this disorder. I suggest you see me regularly, to try to deal with some of the anxiety you're feeling."

Anne cried in the car all the way home. When they got there, before they went into the house, her mother hugged her and said, "It's going to be all right, Anne." Anne didn't believe her. "We'll tell your father that you're seeing someone for anxiety. He doesn't need to know about this other thing. He wouldn't understand."

They didn't tell him about the incident at school. Anne's mother handled the meetings with the parents of the other three girls from St. Mildred's herself.

Since then there had been other "episodes," mostly harmless, where Anne would lose time—minutes or sometimes hours—when she wouldn't know what had happened while she was "gone." They were brought on by stress. She would find herself somewhere unexpected, have no idea how she got there, and call her mother, who would come get her. But she'd had no episodes since her first year of college. It had all happened such a long time ago; she'd thought she'd put it behind her.

But, of course, she had immediately remembered it all after the kidnapping: What if the police found out? What if Marco found out and looked at her differently? But then the onesie had arrived—and her mother no longer looked at her as if she were afraid that Anne might have killed her own child and that Marco had helped to cover it up.

Now the police know that she attacked Susan. They think she is violent. All along, Anne has been afraid that the police would believe she was guilty, whether she was or not. But there are worse things than being wrongly accused.

Anne's greatest fear now is that she *is* guilty.

Those first few days after Cora had been taken, when Anne was so sure that she'd been taken by some stranger—those had been difficult days, having to withstand the suspicion of the police, the public, and her own mother. She and Marco had borne it, because they knew they were innocent. They'd made one mistake—they'd left their baby unattended. But not abandoned.

But now, because of what happened the other night before she'd fallen asleep on the sofa, she had confused the search for signs of Marco's unfaithfulness with the search for Cora. Reality had become distorted. She remembers thinking that Cynthia had stolen her child from her.

The illness was back. When, exactly, had it returned?

She thinks she knows. It came back the night of the kidnapping, after she slapped Cora. She lost time. She doesn't know what happened.

It's almost a relief now, realizing that she did it. Better that Cora be killed quickly by her own mother, in her own bedroom, with the familiar lambs looking on, than that she be taken by some monster and molested, tortured, terrified.

Anne should call her own mother. Her mother would know what to do. But Anne doesn't want to call her mother. Her mother will try to cover it up, pretend it never happened. Like Marco. They're all trying to cover up what she's done.

She doesn't want that anymore. She must tell the police. And she must do it now, before anyone tries to stop her. She wants everything out in the open. She can't stand a minute more of the secrecy, the lies. She needs to know where her baby is, her final resting place. She needs to hold her one last time.

She glances out her bedroom window at the street. She doesn't see any reporters out there now. She dresses quickly and calls a cab to bring her to the police station.

It seems to take a long time, but finally the cab arrives. She gets into the cab quickly and settles herself in the backseat, feeling strange but determined. She needs this to end. She will tell them what happened. She killed Cora. Marco must have arranged to have her taken away and then urged them to offer ransom money afterward, to mislead the police. But now Marco will have to stop protecting her. He will have to stop lying to her. He will have to tell them where he put Cora's body, and then she will know. She must know where her baby is. She can't stand not knowing.

She can't trust anyone to tell the truth unless she goes first.

When she arrives at the police station, the officer behind the front desk looks at her with obvious concern.

"Are you all right, ma'am?" she asks.

"I'm fine," Anne says quickly. "I want to see Detective Rasbach." Her voice sounds strange to her own ears.

"He's not here. It's Sunday," the officer says. "I'll see if I can get him on the phone." She has a brief conversation on the phone, puts it down, and says, "He's on his way. He'll be here in about half an hour."

Anne waits impatiently, her mind in turmoil.

When Rasbach appears less than half an hour later, he is casually dressed, in khaki trousers and a summer shirt. He looks very different; Anne is used to him in a suit. She finds it disorienting.

"Anne," he says, looking at her closely with those eyes that miss nothing. "What can I do for you?"

"I need to talk to you," Anne says quickly.

"Where is your lawyer?" Rasbach asks. "I was informed that you would no longer talk to us without your lawyer present."

"I don't want my lawyer," Anne insists.

"Are you sure? Maybe you should call him. I can wait."

Her lawyer will just stop her from saying what she

needs to say. "No! I'm sure. I don't need a lawyer. I don't want one—and don't call my husband."

"All right, then," Rasbach says, and turns to lead her down the long hall.

Anne follows him to one of the interview rooms. She starts to talk before he's even sat down. He tells her to wait.

"For the record," Rasbach says to her, "please state your name, the date, and the fact that you've been advised to call your lawyer but have declined."

When Anne has done so, they begin.

"Why are you here today?" the detective asks her.

"I have come to confess."

TWENTY-EIGHT

Detective Rasbach observes Anne carefully. She is clearly agitated, wringing her hands. Her pupils look dilated, her face pale. He is unsure whether to proceed. She has waived her right to counsel, on videotape, but he is not confident of her mental state, whether she is capable of properly making that decision. Still, he wants to hear what she has to say. They can always disallow the confession anyway—they probably will—but he has to hear it. He wants to know.

"I killed her," Anne says. She is distressed, but she seems rational, not out of her mind. She knows who she is, where she is, and what she's doing.

"Tell me what happened, Anne," he says, sitting across from her at the table.

"I went over to check on her at eleven," Anne says. "I tried to feed her with the bottle, because I'd been drinking. But she was very fussy, she wanted the breast. She wouldn't take the bottle." She stops talking, stares at the wall over Rasbach's shoulder, as if seeing it all again as a film played on a screen behind him.

"Go on," the detective says.

"So I thought fuck it, and I put her on my breast. I felt bad about it, but she wouldn't take the bottle and she was hungry. She was crying and crying and wouldn't stop. She's never had trouble taking the bottle before—she's never refused it. How was I to know she would refuse the bottle the one night I have a few glasses of wine?"

Rasbach waits for her to continue. He doesn't want to speak and interrupt the flow of her thoughts. She seems to be almost in a kind of trance, still staring at the wall behind him.

"I didn't know what else to do. So I nursed her." She drags her eyes from the wall and looks at him. "I lied before, when I said that I remembered changing her out of the pink onesie. I don't remember. I just told you that because I assumed that's what I did, but I don't actually remember any of it."

"What *do* you remember?" Rasbach says.

"I remember nursing her, and she suckled for a bit, but she didn't have a good feed, and then she started fussing again." Anne's eyes slide to that imaginary screen again. "I held her and walked around with her a bit, singing to her, but she just cried louder. I was crying, too." She looks at him. "I slapped her." Now Anne bursts into tears. "After that I don't remember. She was wearing the pink onesie when I slapped her, I remember that, but I don't remember anything after that. I must have changed her and changed her outfit. Maybe I dropped her or shook her, I don't know. Maybe I held a pillow over her face, to stop her from crying, like you said, but she must have died somehow." She begins sobbing hysterically. "And when I went over at midnight, she was in her crib, but I didn't pick her up. I don't know if she was breathing then."

Rasbach lets her cry. Finally he says, "Anne, if you don't remember, why do you think you killed Cora?"

"Because she's gone! *Because* I don't remember. Sometimes, when I'm under stress, my mind splits off, disconnects from reality. Then I realize that I'm missing some time, that I've done something I don't remember. It's happened before."

"Tell me about it."

"You know all about it. You spoke to Janice Foegle."

"I want to hear your version. Tell me what happened."

"I don't want to." She takes several tissues from the box and wipes her eyes.

"Why not?"

"I don't want to talk about that."

Rasbach leans back in his chair and says, "Anne, I don't think you killed Cora."

"Yes you do. You said so before." She is twisting the tissues in her hands.

"I don't think so anymore. If I put this idea in your head, I'm truly sorry."

"I must have killed her. And Marco had someone take her away to protect me. So I wouldn't know what I'd done."

"Then where is she now?"

"I don't know! Marco won't tell me! I've begged him, but he won't tell me. He denies it. He doesn't want me to know that I killed my own baby. He's protecting me. It must be so hard for him. I thought if I came and told you what happened, he wouldn't have to pretend anymore, and he could tell us where he put her, and I would know, and it would all be over." She slumps in her chair, her head down.

It's true that in the beginning Rasbach suspected that something like this might have happened. That the mother might have snapped, killed the baby, and she and the husband covered it up. It could have happened. But not the way she tells it. Because if she'd killed the baby at eleven o'clock, or even at midnight, and Marco wasn't aware of it until twelve thirty, how could Derek Honig already have been waiting with a car in the lane to take the body away? No, she didn't kill the baby. It just didn't add up.

"Anne, are you sure that it was at eleven o'clock when you fed her and she was crying? Could it have been earlier? At ten, for instance?" If that were the case, Marco might have known earlier—when he checked her at ten thirty.

"No, it was eleven. I always do her final feeding at eleven, and then she usually sleeps through till about five in the morning. That was the only time I was away from the party for more than five minutes. You can ask the others."

"Yes, Marco and Cynthia agree that you were gone a long time around eleven—that you didn't get back until eleven thirty or thereabouts—and you checked on her again at midnight," Rasbach says. "Did you tell Marco you thought you might have hurt her, when you got back to the party?"

"No, I . . . I just realized last night that I must have done it!"

"But you see, Anne, that it's impossible, what you describe," Rasbach tells her gently. "How could Marco have gone over at twelve thirty not knowing the baby was dead and have someone in a car in the garage waiting to take her a couple of minutes later?"

Anne goes completely still. Her hands stop moving. She looks confused.

There's something else he needs to tell her. "It looks like the man who was murdered at the cabin— Derek Honig—is the one whose car was in your garage and who took Cora away. The tire treads are the right type, and we'll know soon if they're a match with the tracks left in your garage. We think Cora was taken to his cabin in the Catskills. Sometime later Honig was beaten to death with a spade."

Anne looks as if she's unable to take in this information.

Rasbach is worried about her. "Can I call someone to drive you home? Where's Marco?"

"He's at work."

"On a Sunday?"

She doesn't answer.

"Can I call your mother? A friend?"

"No! I'm fine. I'll get home on my own. Really, I'm fine," Anne says. She stands up abruptly. "Please don't tell anyone I was here today," she says.

"At least let me get you a cab," he insists.

Just before the cab arrives, she turns to him abruptly and says, "But . . . there would have been time, between twelve thirty and when we got home. If I'd killed her and he found her at twelve thirty and called someone. We didn't get home till almost one thirty—he didn't want to leave. You don't know for sure that the car going down the lane at twelve thirty-five was the one that had Cora in it. It could have been later."

Rasbach says, "But Marco couldn't have called anyone without our knowing about it. We have all your phone records. He didn't call anyone. If Marco had anyone take the baby away, it had to have been prearranged—planned. *Which means you didn't kill her.*"

Anne gives him a startled look, seems as if she's about to speak, but then the cab arrives and she says nothing.

Rasbach watches her go, pitying her from the bottom of his heart.

Anne returns to an empty house. She lies down on the sofa in the living room, utterly exhausted, and reviews what happened at the police station.

Rasbach had almost had her convinced that she couldn't have killed Cora. But he didn't know about the cell phone hidden in the wall. Marco *could* have called someone, at twelve thirty. She doesn't know now why she didn't say anything about the cell phone. Maybe she didn't want Rasbach to know about Marco's affair. She was too ashamed.

Either that or that man with the cabin took her away, alive, sometime after Marco checked on her at twelve thirty. She doesn't know why Detective Rasbach is so convinced that the car going down the lane at twelve thirty-five had anything to do with it.

She remembers how she used to lie here with Cora on her chest. It seems very long ago now. She would get so tired she'd need to lie down for a minute with the baby. They would snuggle together on the sofa, in the quiet part of the day, like now, and sometimes they would fall asleep together. Tears slide down her cheeks.

She hears sounds coming from the other side of the wall. Cynthia is home, moving around in her living room, playing music. Anne despises Cynthia. She hates everything about her—her childlessness, her air of superiority and power, her figure, her seductive clothing. She hates her for toying with her husband, for trying to destroy their life together. She doesn't know if she can ever forgive Cynthia for what she's done. She hates Cynthia all the more because they used to be such good friends.

Anne hates it that Cynthia lives on the other side of the wall. She suddenly realizes that they can move. They can put the house up for sale. She and Marco are infamous here anyway—the mail still piles up each day—and the house that she loved so much is now like a crypt. She feels buried alive.

They can't live here much longer, with Cynthia on the other side of the wall, within beckoning distance of Marco.

What was Marco doing coming out of Cynthia's backyard yesterday anyway, looking so guilty? He vehemently denies having an affair with her, but

Anne isn't stupid. She can't get the truth out of him, and she's tired of all the lies.

She will confront Cynthia herself. Get the truth out of her. But with Cynthia, too, how could she know what was the truth and what was a lie?

Instead she gets up and goes out the back door to the yard. She goes into the garage to get her gardening gloves. In the garage she stops and lets her eyes adjust to the light. She can smell the familiar garage smell of oil, old wood, and musty rags. She stands there and imagines what must have happened. She is so confused, by everything. If she didn't kill Cora and Marco didn't have someone take her away, then somebody, probably the man who's now dead, stole her baby from her crib and put her in his car sometime after twelve thirty while she—and Marco and Cynthia and Graham—were oblivious next door.

She's glad he's dead. She hopes he suffered.

She goes outside again and starts viciously wrenching weeds out of the lawn until her hands are blistered and her back aches.

TWENTY-NINE

Marco sits at his desk, staring out the window, seeing nothing. The door is closed. He glances down at the surface of the expensive mahogany desk, the one he chose with such care when he expanded his business and took the lease on this office.

When he looks back now on the innocence and optimism of those days, he feels sickened. He gazes with bitter eyes around his office, which so perfectly conveys the image of a successful entrepreneur. The impressive desk, the view of the city and the river out the window across from it, the high-end leather chairs—the modern art. Anne helped him decorate it; she has a good eye.

He remembers the fun they had doing it—shopping for the pieces, arranging everything. When they were done, he'd locked the door, popped open a bottle of champagne, and made love to his giggling wife on the floor.

There was pressure on him then; he had to live up to everyone's greater expectations—Anne's, her parents', his own. Perhaps if he'd married someone else, he would have been content to work his way up, building his business more slowly with grit and talent and long hours. But he had the opportunity to make things happen faster, and he took it. He was ambitious. He had that money handed to him on a silver platter, and of course he was expected to make a success of it right away. How could he not succeed, as the recipient of such a magnificent handout? There was a lot of pressure. Richard especially took a greater interest in how the business was doing, since he'd bankrolled it.

It had seemed too good to be true, and it was.

He'd gone after the big clients before he was ready. He'd made the classic rookie mistake of growing too fast. If he hadn't married Anne—no, if he hadn't accepted the wedding gift of the house and, years later, the loan of her parents' money—they might be renting an apartment somewhere, he'd have an ugly office farther away from downtown, he wouldn't be driving an Audi—but he'd be working hard and building success on his own terms. He and Anne would be happy.

Cora would be at home.

But look at how it has all turned out. He is the owner of an overextended business teetering on the edge of ruin. He is a kidnapper. A criminal. A liar. Suspected by the police. In the power of an egomaniac father-in-law who knows what he's done, and a cold-hearted blackmailer who will never stop demanding money. The business is almost bankrupt, even though he's been given so much—money for the business, connections through Richard's friends at the country club.

Alice and Richard's investment in Marco's business is lost. Like the five million dollars they'd paid for Cora. And now Richard is negotiating with the kidnappers—they'll pay even more to get Cora back. Marco has no idea how much more.

How Anne's parents must hate him. For the first time, Marco thinks about it from their point of view. He can understand their disappointment. Marco has let them all down. In the end his business has failed, spectacularly, even with all that help. Marco still believes that if he'd done it his own way, he would have been very successful—gradually. But Richard pushed him to accept contracts he couldn't deliver on. And then Marco became desperate.

When things started to go wrong, really wrong, a couple of months ago, Marco had taken to having a drink at the bar on the corner before going home to Anne, where he would feel helpless in the face of her mounting depression. It was usually fairly quiet at five o'clock, when he arrived. He'd sit at the bar, having his one drink, brooding into the amber liquid, wondering what the hell to do.

Then he'd leave and go for a walk down by the river, not wanting to head home yet. He'd sit down on a bench and stare out at the water.

One day an older man came and sat down beside him. Annoyed, Marco was about to get up, feeling that his space had been invaded. But before he could leave, the man spoke to him, in a friendly way.

"You look a bit down," he said sympathetically.

Marco was abrupt. "You could say that."

"Lose a girlfriend?" the man asked.

"I wish it were that simple," Marco had said.

"Ah, must be business troubles, then," the man said, and smiled. "They're *much* worse." He held out his hand. "Bruce Neeland," he offered.

Marco took his hand. "Marco Conti."

Marco began to look forward to running into Bruce. He found it a relief to have someone—someone who didn't really know him, who wouldn't judge him—to tell his troubles to. He couldn't tell Anne what was really going on, with her depression and her expectation of success. He hadn't told her that things were going south, and once he'd started not telling her things were going badly, he couldn't suddenly tell her just how badly things were going.

Bruce seemed to understand. He was easy to like, with a warm, open manner. He was a broker. He'd had good years, bad years. You had to be tough, ride out the bad times. "It's not always easy," Bruce said, sitting beside him in his expensive, well-cut suit.

"That's for sure," Marco agreed.

One day Marco had a little too much to drink at the bar. Later, down by the river, he told Bruce more than he meant to. It just slipped out, the problem with his in-laws. Bruce was a good listener.

"I owe them a lot of money," Marco confessed.

"They're your in-laws. They're not going to feed you to the fishes if you can't pay," Bruce said, looking out at the river.

"Maybe that would be better," Marco said sourly. Marco explained the hold his wife's parents had over him—the business, the house, even trying to turn his wife against him.

"I'd say they've got you by the short and curlies," Bruce said, pursing his lips.

"Yup." Marco took off his jacket, slung it over the back of the bench. It was summer, and the evenings were warm.

"What are you going to do?"

"I don't know."

"You could ask them for another loan, tide you over till business improves," Bruce suggested. "In for a penny, in for a pound."

"I don't think so."

Bruce looked him in the eye. "Why not? Don't be an ass. Just ask. Get yourself out of the hole. Live to fight another day. They'll want to protect their investment anyway. At least give them the option."

Marco considered. As much as he hated the idea, it made sense to come clean to Richard, to tell him the business was in trouble. He could ask him to keep it between them, not to bother Anne and Alice with it. After all, businesses failed every day. It was the economy. Things were much tougher now than when Richard started out. Of course, Richard would never see it that way. At least he would never admit it.

"Ask your father-in-law," Bruce advised. "Don't go to the bank."

Marco didn't tell Bruce, but he'd already been to the bank. He'd put a mortgage on the house a few months earlier. He'd told Anne it was to help the business expand further in a high-growth time, and she hadn't questioned it. He'd made her promise not to tell her parents. He said they had their noses in too much of Marco and Anne's business already.

"Maybe," Marco said.

He thought about it for two days. He slept poorly. Finally he decided to approach his father-in-law. It was always Richard he dealt with when it came to financial matters involving Anne's parents. Richard liked it that way. Marco screwed up his courage and called Richard and asked if they could meet for a drink. Richard seemed surprised, but he suggested the bar at the country club. Of course. He always had to be on his own fucking turf.

When Marco arrived, he was nervous and downed his drink quickly. He tried to slow down when he got close to the ice cubes.

Richard stared at him. "What's this about, Marco?" he asked.

Marco hesitated. "The business isn't doing as well as I'd like."

Richard immediately looked wary. "How bad is it?" he asked.

This is what Marco hated about his father-in-law. It was all about humiliation. He couldn't let Marco save face. He couldn't be generous.

"Pretty bad, actually," Marco said. "I've lost some clients. Some haven't paid. I'm having a bit of a cash-flow problem at the moment."

"I see," Richard said, nursing his drink.

There was a long silence. He wasn't going to offer, Marco realized. He was going to make Marco ask. Marco looked up from his drink, regarded his father-in-law's stern face. "Could you provide me another loan to get over this tough spell?" he asked. "We could structure it like a real loan. I want to pay interest on it this time."

Marco hadn't really considered the possibility that his father-in-law might refuse. He didn't think Richard would dare, because what would happen to his daughter then? It was mostly the groveling he'd been avoiding, this moment of having to ask for help, of being in Richard's power.

Richard looked back at him, his eyes cold. "No," he said.

Even then Marco misunderstood. He thought Richard was saying no to the interest. "No, really. I want to pay interest. A hundred thousand would do it."

Richard leaned forward in his seat, hulking over the little table between them. "I said *no*."

Marco felt the heat go up his neck, felt his face flush. He didn't say anything. He didn't believe Richard meant it.

"We're not giving you any more money, Marco," Richard said. "We won't *loan* you any money either. You're on your own." He settled back in his comfortable club chair. "I know a bad investment when I see one."

Marco didn't know what to say. He wasn't going to beg. When Richard made up his mind, that was it. And he'd obviously made up his mind.

"Alice and I feel the same way about this—we'd

already decided to stop giving you any more hand-outs," Richard added.

What about your daughter? Marco wanted to ask, but he couldn't find his voice. Then he realized he already knew the answer.

Richard would tell Anne about this. He'd tell his daughter what a poor choice she'd made in Marco. Richard and Alice had never liked him. They'd been waiting patiently for this day. They *wanted* Anne to leave him. To take his baby and leave him. Of course that's what they wanted.

Marco couldn't let that happen.

He stood up suddenly, bumping the little table between them at his knees. "Fine," he said. "I'll manage on my own." He turned and left the lounge, blind with rage and shame. He would tell Anne himself first. Tell her what a bastard her father really was.

It was late afternoon. Time for one more drink before he went home. He went over to his own bar for a quick one and then went for his walk. Bruce was already there, on the bench. *That* was the moment. The point at which there was no going back.

THIRTY

Y ou look like shit," Bruce said as Marco sat
down beside him on the bench.

Marco was numb. He'd screwed up his
courage to ask, but he hadn't actually considered that
Richard would say no. The business could be saved,
Marco was sure of it. There were some bad debts, clients who hadn't paid. But there was some new business he was chasing—they were just being slow about
making a decision. It could still all come right, with a
little money to tide him over. He still had his ambi-
tion. He still believed in himself. He just needed some
breathing space. He needed some cash.

"I need some money," Marco told Bruce. "Know
any loan sharks?" He was only half joking. He knew
how desperate he must seem.

But Bruce took him seriously. He turned sideways
to look at Marco. "No, I don't know any loan sharks.
And anyway, you don't want to do that," Bruce said.

"Well, I don't know what the fuck else I can do,"
Marco said, running his hand through his hair, staring angrily out at the river.

"You could declare bankruptcy, start over," Bruce said after some thought. "Lots of people do."

"I can't do that," Marco said stubbornly.

"Why not?" Bruce asked.

"Because it would kill my wife. She's . . . she's fragile right now. Post-baby. You know." Marco leaned forward, rested his elbows on his knees, and put his face in his hands.

"You have a baby?" Bruce said, sounding surprised.

"Yes," Marco said, glancing up. "A baby girl."

Bruce sat back and looked hard at Marco.

"What?" Marco said.

"Nothing," Bruce said quickly.

"No, you were going to say something," Marco said, straightening up on the bench.

Bruce was obviously turning something over in his mind. "How do your wife's parents feel about their little granddaughter?"

Marco said, "They dote on her. She's the only grandchild. I know what you're getting at. They'll give her money for her education, probably settle some money on her when she's twenty-one, but they'll tie it up in a trust so I can't get my hands on it. No help there."

"There is if you're creative about it," Bruce said, cocking his head at him.

Marco stared at him. "What do you mean?"

Bruce leaned in and lowered his voice. "Are you willing to take a little risk?"

"What are you talking about?" Marco cast about

to see if there was anyone who could overhear, but they were alone.

"They won't give *you* money, but I bet they'd pay up pretty fast to get their only grandchild back."

"What are you suggesting?" Marco whispered. But he knew.

The two men eyed each other. If Marco hadn't already had a couple of drinks, especially the miserable one he'd shared with his father-in-law, he might have given Bruce a firm no and gone home to his wife and told her the truth, as he'd planned. Declared bankruptcy and started over. They still had the house. They had each other, and Cora. But Marco had also stopped at a liquor store on his way to the river. He'd brought a bottle in a paper bag with him. Now he cracked it open, offered some to his friend, and took a long gulp straight from the bottle. The alcohol blurred things a bit, made everything seem less impossible.

Bruce lowered his voice. "You stage a kidnapping. Not a real kidnapping, a pretend kidnapping. No one gets hurt."

Marco stared at him. He leaned in closer and whispered, "How would that work? It wouldn't be pretend to the police."

"No, but if you do it right, it's the perfect crime. Your wife's parents pay, you get the baby back, it's all over in a couple of days. Once the baby comes home, the police lose interest."

Marco turned it over in his mind. The booze made it all seem a little bit less crazy.

"I don't know," Marco said nervously.

"Do you have any better ideas?" Bruce chided him, handing him the paper bag with the open bottle.

They discussed the details, hypothetically at first. He could pretend to kidnap his own child. Hand her over to Bruce, who would take her up to his cabin in the Catskills for a couple of days. He had three kids of his own, grown up now, but he knew how to take care of an infant. They would each get disposable, untraceable prepaid cell phones and communicate that way. Marco would have to hide the phone somewhere.

"I'd need about a hundred thousand," he said, looking out at the river, watching the birds circling in the sky above it.

Bruce scoffed. "Are you out of your mind?"

"What do you mean?" Marco said.

"If you're caught, the penalty is the same whether you ask for a hundred thousand or a hundred million. At least make it worth our while. No point in doing this for peanuts."

Marco and Bruce shared the bottle back and forth as Marco considered it. Richard and Alice Dries were worth about fifteen million as far as he knew. They had the money. If Marco got a million, he could save his business and pay off his mortgage, without any more help from Anne's parents. At least not directly. It would be sweet to take a couple million off that bastard Richard.

They decided on a ransom of two million. Split fifty-fifty.

"Not bad for two days' work," Bruce assured him.

Marco decided it had to be soon. If he waited

longer, he would lose his nerve. He said, "Tomorrow night we're going out—there's a dinner party next door. We'll have a babysitter, but she always falls asleep on the couch with her earbuds."

"You could go out for a smoke and sneak home and bring the baby out to me," Bruce said.

Marco thought about it. It could work. They discussed the plan in more detail.

Now if he could choose the point at which he could go back and change everything, it would be the first time he met Bruce. If only he hadn't taken that walk in the spring air down to the water, if he hadn't sat on that bench, if Bruce hadn't happened by. If only he'd gotten up and left that day when Bruce sat down and not struck up an acquaintance that had, over time, grown into a friendship. How different everything would be now.

He didn't think the police would be able to find anyone who could put Bruce and him together. Their meetings were rather sporadic, unpredictable. The only people around were people occasionally jogging or whizzing by on Rollerblades. He hadn't worried about it before, because no one was going to see Bruce again. Bruce was ready to retire—he was going to take his million and disappear.

But now Bruce is dead.

And Marco is completely fucked.

He needs to call Richard—that's the reason he came to the office, to get away from Anne so that he could have a private conversation with her father. He has to know what's going on with Cora, whether

Richard has made new arrangements with the kidnappers.

He hesitates. He can't bear the thought of any more bad news. No matter what else happens, they have to get Cora back. He has to trust that Richard can make it happen. He will deal with the rest later.

He picks up the phone and enters the number for his father-in-law. It goes directly to voice mail. *Fuck.* He leaves a brief message: "It's Marco, call me. Let me know what's happening."

He gets up and starts pacing the length of his office, like a man already locked in a cell.

Anne thinks she hears her baby crying; Cora must be just waking up from her nap. She peels off her gardening gloves and goes quickly inside and washes her hands at the kitchen sink. She can hear Cora upstairs in her crib, crying for her. "Just a minute, sweetheart," she calls. "I'll be right there." She feels happy.

Anne rushes upstairs to get her baby, humming a little. She goes into the nursery. Everything looks the same, but the crib is empty. She suddenly remembers, and it's like being violently swept out to sea. She collapses into the nursing chair.

She's not right—she knows she's not well. She should call someone. Her mother. But she doesn't. Instead she rocks herself back and forth in the chair.

She would like to blame Cynthia for all her problems, but she knows Cynthia doesn't have her baby.

Cynthia has only tried to steal her husband, the

husband that Anne herself is no longer even sure she wants. Some days she thinks Marco and Cynthia deserve each other. Anne hears Cynthia now on the other side of the wall, and all her hatred solidifies into a powerful rage. Because if they hadn't gone to Cynthia's that night, if Cynthia hadn't said no children, none of this would ever have happened. She would still have her baby.

Anne studies herself in the shattered upstairs bathroom mirror, which they still have not replaced. She looks fractured, splintered into a hundred different pieces. She hardly recognizes the person looking back at her. She washes her face, brushes her hair. She goes into the bedroom and puts on a clean shirt and new jeans. She checks: there are no reporters in front of the house. Then she walks next door and rings the doorbell.

Cynthia answers, clearly surprised at finding Anne on her doorstep.

"Can I come in?" Anne asks. Even for a day spent at home, Cynthia is nicely dressed—Capri pants, a pretty silk blouse.

Cynthia looks at her warily for a second. Then she pulls the door wide and says, "Okay."

Anne steps into the house.

"Do you want some coffee? I could put some on," Cynthia offers. "Graham's away. He's flying back late tomorrow night."

"Sure," Anne says, following her into the kitchen. Now that she's here, she wonders how to begin. She wants to learn the truth. Should she be friendly?

Accusatory? The last time she was in this house, everything was still normal. It seems like such a long time ago. Another lifetime.

In the kitchen Anne looks at the sliding glass doors that lead out to the patio and the backyard. She sees the chairs on the patio. She imagines Cynthia in Marco's lap in one of those chairs, while the dead man drives Anne's baby away. She is filled with rage, but she is careful not to show it. She has had a lot of practice feeling anger without showing it. She dissembles. Isn't that what everyone does? Everyone is faking it, all of them pretending to be something they're not. The whole world is built on lies and deceit. Cynthia is a liar, just like Anne's husband.

Anne feels dizzy suddenly and sits down at the kitchen table. Cynthia gets the coffeemaker started, then turns around and faces her, leaning back against the counter. From where Anne is seated, Cynthia looks taller and more long-legged than ever. Anne realizes that she's jealous, insanely jealous, of Cynthia. And Cynthia knows it.

Neither of them seems to want to start the conversation. It's awkward. Finally Cynthia says, "Are they making any progress with the investigation?" She wears an expression of concern as she says this, but Anne isn't fooled.

Anne looks at her and says, "I will never get my baby back." She says this calmly, as if she's talking about the weather. She feels disconnected, not rooted to anything. She realizes all at once that it was a mistake coming here. She's not strong enough to face Cynthia on her own. It was dangerous coming here. She is afraid of Cynthia. But why? What can Cynthia do to her, after what's already happened? Really, with all that Anne has lost, she should feel invincible. She has nothing left to lose. Cynthia ought to be afraid of *her*.

Then Anne understands. She is chilled to the bone. Anne is afraid of herself. She is afraid of what she might do. She needs to leave. She stands up suddenly. "I have to go," she blurts out.

"What? You just got here," Cynthia says, surprised. She looks intently at her. "Are you all right?"

Anne sinks back down into the chair, puts her head between her knees. Cynthia comes over to her and squats down beside her. She rests one of her manicured hands lightly on Anne's back. Anne is afraid she might pass out; she feels as if she's going to throw up. She breathes deeply, waiting for the feeling to pass. If she waits, and breathes, the sick feeling will pass.

"Here, have some coffee," Cynthia offers. "The caffeine will help."

Anne lifts her head and watches Cynthia pour the coffee. This woman doesn't care about her at all, but she's making her coffee, putting in cream and sugar, and bringing it over to her at the kitchen table, the way she used to. Anne takes a gulp, then another. Cynthia was right, it does make her feel better. The coffee clears her head, makes her able to think. She takes another sip and puts the cup down on the table. Cynthia has sat down across from her.

"How long have you been having an affair with my husband?" Anne asks. Her voice is matter-of-fact. There is a surprising neutrality to it, considering how angry she is. Anyone listening would think she didn't care.

Cynthia sits farther back in her chair and folds her arms across her ample breasts. "I'm not having an affair with your husband," she says, equally cool.

"Cut the bullshit," Anne says in an oddly friendly tone. "I know all about it."

Cynthia looks surprised. "What do you mean? There's nothing to know. Marco and I are not having an affair. We got a little physical on the back patio the last time you were here, but it was harmless stuff. Teenager stuff. He was drunk. We were both drunk. We got carried away. It meant nothing. It was the first and only time we've ever touched each other."

"I don't know why you both deny it. I know you're having an affair," Anne persists, looking at Cynthia over the rim of her coffee cup.

Cynthia looks at her across the table, holding her own cup with both hands. "I told you, and I told the police when they were here, that we were fooling around a bit outside. We were drunk, that's all it was. There's been nothing between Marco and me before or since. I haven't even seen him since the night of the kidnapping. You're imagining things, Anne." Her tone is patronizing.

"Don't lie to me!" Anne suddenly hisses. "I saw Marco coming out of your back door yesterday after-noon."

Cynthia stiffens.

"So don't lie to me and tell me you haven't seen him! And I know about the cell phone."

"What cell phone?" One of Cynthia's perfectly shaped eyebrows has gone up.

"Never mind," Anne says, wishing she could take this last bit back. She remembers that the cell phone might have been for someone else. It's so confusing, everything that's been happening. She can hardly keep things straight anymore. She feels as if her mind is breaking down. She was always sensitive before, but now—now her baby is gone, her husband is cheating on her, lying to her—who wouldn't lose her mind in this situation? No one could blame her. No one could blame her if she did something crazy.

Now Cynthia's expression changes. The false concern vanishes, and she regards Anne coldly. "You want to know what's going on, Anne? Are you sure you really want to know?"

Anne looks back at her, confused by her change of tone. Anne can imagine Cynthia as a schoolyard bully—the tall, beautiful girl who taunted short, plump, under-confident girls like her.

"Yes, I want to know."

"Are you sure? Because once I tell you, I'm not going to be able to take it back." Cynthia puts her cup down on the table.

"I'm stronger than you think," Anne says. There's an edge to her voice. She puts her cup down, too, leans forward over the table, and says, "I've lost my baby. What could possibly hurt me now?"

Cynthia smiles, but it's a cold, calculating smile. She sits back in her chair and looks at Anne as if she is trying to make a decision. "I don't think you have any idea what's really going on," she says.

"Then why don't you tell me?" Anne snaps.

Cynthia stands up, pushes back her chair with a scrape on the kitchen floor. "All right. Stay here. I'll only be gone for a minute."

Cynthia leaves the kitchen and goes upstairs. Anne wonders what Cynthia can possibly have to show her. She considers making a run for it. How much reality can she stand? Maybe there are pictures. Pictures of her and Marco together. Cynthia is a photographer. And Cynthia is the kind of woman to have pictures taken of herself, because she is so gorgeous and so vain. Maybe she's going to show Anne pictures of herself in bed with Marco. And the expression on Marco's face will be entirely different from the expression on his face when he's making love to Anne. She stands up. She's about to let herself out the sliding glass door when Cynthia appears in the kitchen holding a laptop.

"Losing your nerve?" she asks.

"No, I just wanted some air," Anne lies, sliding the door closed again, and turning back to the table.

Cynthia puts the laptop on the table and opens it up. They sit down and wait a couple of minutes until it boots up.

Cynthia says to her, "I'm really sorry about this, Anne, I really am."

Anne glares at her, not believing her for a second, then turns her reluctant attention to the screen. It isn't what she expected. It's a black-and-white video of Cynthia's backyard and, beyond that, Anne's own backyard. She notes the date-and-time stamp on the bottom. She goes utterly cold.

"Wait for it," Cynthia says.

She's going to see that dead man taking her child. Cynthia is that cruel. And Cynthia has had a video of it the whole time. "Why didn't you show this to the police?" Anne demands, her eyes locked on the video, waiting.

In disbelief, Anne sees Marco appear at their back door at 12:31 and twist the lightbulb on the motion detector; the light goes out. Anne feels all the blood leaving her extremities. She sees Marco go into the house. Two minutes pass. Then the back door opens. Marco is coming out of the house with Cora in his arms, wrapped in her white blanket. He glances around as if to see whether he's being observed, looks right into the camera, and then he walks quickly to the garage and lets himself in through the door. Anne's heart is banging wildly against her ribs. A minute later she sees Marco come out of the garage without the baby. It is 12:34. He walks across the lawn toward the house, where his image disappears from view briefly and then reappears on the Stillwells' back patio.

"So you see, Anne," Cynthia says into the shocked silence, "it's not about Marco and me having an affair. Marco kidnapped your baby."

Anne is stunned, horrified, and cannot answer.

Cynthia says, "You might want to ask him where she is."

THIRTY-ONE

Cynthia settles comfortably in her chair and says, "I could take this to the police, or maybe you'd prefer that I don't. You're from money, aren't you?"

Anne bolts. She pulls open the sliding door and flees, leaving Cynthia sitting alone at the table with the laptop. The image of Marco carrying Cora to their garage at 12:33 in the morning has been seared into Anne's retinas and deep into her brain. She will never get that image out of her head. *Marco took their baby.* He's been lying to her, all this time.

She doesn't know who she married.

She runs to her own house and in through the back door. She can hardly breathe. She sinks to the floor in the kitchen, leaning against the bottom cupboards, sobbing and shaking. She cries and gasps for breath and sees the same images in her head over and over again.

This changes everything. Marco took their baby. But why? Why did he do it? It can't be that Cora was already dead and he did it to protect her. Detective

Rasbach has already explained to her how that simply wasn't possible. If she'd killed Cora and Marco had discovered it at twelve thirty, he could not have had an accomplice there by 12:35. And she now knows that he took Cora out of the house at exactly 12:33. He must have arranged for someone, for the dead man, to be waiting in his car in the garage at twelve thirty, when Marco knew he would be checking on Cora. So he planned this. He *planned* it. With this man who is now dead. The man she thinks she's seen before. Where has she seen him?

Marco was behind the whole thing all along, and she knew nothing about it.

Marco abducted their baby, with this other man, who is now dead. Where is her baby now? Who took her from the man in the cabin? *What the hell happened? How could he?*

Anne sits on the kitchen floor hugging her knees, trying to figure it out. She thinks about going back to the police station and telling Detective Rasbach what she's seen. He could get the video from Cynthia. She can guess why Cynthia hadn't taken it to the police in the first place—she must be holding it over Marco. She wants to have him in her power. That's the kind of woman Cynthia is.

Why would Marco kidnap Cora? If he didn't do it to protect Anne, he did it for his own selfish reasons. The only possible reason is money. He wanted the ransom money. Her parents' money. It is an appalling realization. She knows now that the business isn't doing well. She remembers that Marco had her sign mortgage papers on the house a few months ago—to get liquid capital for further expansion plans. She thought the business was growing faster than expected, that everything was fine. But maybe he'd been lying then, too. It's all fitting together. The business going belly-up, mortgaging the house, and finally, arranging the kidnapping—*of his own child*—from her parents.

Why didn't Marco just tell her about his business troubles? They could have gone to her parents, asked for more money. Why did he do such a stupid thing? Why would he take their precious baby and hand her over to that man who was beaten to death with a shovel?

Did Marco go up to that cabin after the ransom money was taken, confront the man, and kill him in a rage? Was Marco a murderer, too? Would he have had time to get all the way out to the cabin and back without her noticing? She tries to remember what day it is, tries to review every single day that's passed since the kidnapping, but it's all a hopeless jumble in her head.

Was the cell phone part of this? She realizes that she has been wrong from the start. This is not about affairs, with Cynthia or anyone else. This is about the kidnapping. Marco kidnapped their daughter.

The man she married.

And then he sat there, in their kitchen, and told her that the dead man looked familiar.

She's suddenly afraid of her own husband. She doesn't know who he is or what he is. She is starting to understand what he's capable of.

Had he ever loved her, or had he only married her for her money?

What does she do now? Does she go to the police with what she knows? What might happen to Cora if she did?

After a long time, Anne pulls herself up off the floor. She forces herself to walk quickly upstairs to the bedroom. Trembling, she pulls out an overnight bag and starts packing.

Anne gets out of the cab at the foot of her parents' circular gravel drive. This is the house she grew up in. It is very grand. The large stone house with its lush, professionally tended gardens backs onto a wooded ravine. She pays the cabdriver and stands there for a minute with her overnight bag at her feet, looking at the house. The homes are set far apart here. Nobody will see her, unless her mother is home and happens to look out the window. She remembers vividly the day she stepped out of this house and climbed onto the back of Marco's motorcycle and decided that she was in love.

So much has happened. So much has changed.

She hates to go back to her parents. It's an admission that they were right about Marco all along. She doesn't want to believe it, but she's seen the evidence with her own eyes. She'd gone against their wishes when she'd married Marco—she'd known her own mind then, and her own heart.

Now she doesn't know anything.

There at the end of her parents' drive, from out of nowhere, Anne suddenly remembers where she saw the dead man. She trembles like a leaf in the wind, trying to make sense of this new information. Then she takes out her cell phone and calls another cab.

Marco tries Richard again, leaves another terse message on his voice mail. Richard is punishing him, keeping him out of the loop. He's going to handle it himself and not let Marco know until it's all over, when Cora is back safe and sound. If she does come back.

Even Marco admits to himself that maybe it's better this way. If anyone can pull this off, it's Richard. Richard with his bags of money and nerves of steel. Marco is exhausted, physically and emotionally. He wants nothing more than to lie down on his office couch, sleep for a few hours, and wake up to a phone call that Cora is home again, safe. But then—what happens after that?

He remembers there's an open bottle of scotch in the back of one of his filing-cabinet drawers. He stops pacing, moves over to the filing cabinet, and pulls open the drawer. The bottle is half empty. He grabs a glass, also hidden in the filing cabinet, and pours himself a stiff one. Then he resumes his pacing.

Marco can't face the possibility of never seeing Cora again. He is also terrified of being arrested and going to prison. He's sure that if he *is* arrested, the lawyer most likely to be able to get him acquitted,

Aubrey West, will no longer be acting for him. Because Anne's parents won't pay, and Marco doesn't have the money to pay for a top-notch lawyer himself.

He refills his glass from the bottle, which is now sitting open on the blotter on his expensive desk, and realizes that he's already thinking about what to do after he's arrested. Arrest now seems inevitable. Anne won't stand by him, not once she hears the truth from her own father. Why would she? She'll hate him. If *she* had done this to *him*, he would never forgive her.

Then there's Cynthia and the video.

His nose deep into his third drink, Marco for the first time considers telling the police the truth. What if he simply told Rasbach that yes, he met with Bruce—who turned out to be Derek Honig. Yes, he had business troubles. Yes, his father-in-law refused to help him out. Yes, he planned to take and hide his own baby for a couple of days to get the ransom money out of his wife's parents.

But it wasn't actually his idea. It was Derek Honig's idea.

Derek Honig was the one who suggested it. He planned it. In Marco's mind it was just a way to get a bit of an advance on his wife's inheritance. No one was supposed to die. Not his accomplice. Certainly not his baby.

Marco is a victim in this, too. Not blameless, but still a victim. He was desperate, and he fell in with someone who gave him a false name, who manipulated him into the kidnapping for his own gain. A good lawyer like Aubrey West could spin it.

Marco could come clean with Detective Rasbach. Tell him everything.

Once Cora is back home.

He would go to prison. But Cora, if she survives this, would be with her mother. Richard would no longer have anything to hold over him. And Cynthia would be shit out of luck. Maybe he could even make sure she went to jail for attempted blackmail. For a minute he imagines Cynthia in a shapeless orange jumpsuit, with unwashed hair.

He looks up from his pacing, catches his reflection in the large mirror hanging on the wall across from the window, and barely recognizes himself.

THIRTY-TWO

Marco finally returns home, once it's dark. He's had too much to drink, so he leaves the car behind and takes a cab. He arrives home disheveled, his eyes bloodshot, his body racked with tension, even with all the alcohol in it.

He lets himself in the front door. "Anne?" he calls, wondering where she is. The house is dark and feels empty. It's very quiet. He stands still, listening to the silence. Maybe she isn't here. "Anne?" His voice is louder now, worried. He walks farther into the living room.

He stops when he sees her. Anne is sitting on the sofa in the dark, utterly still. There is a large knife in her hands; Marco recognizes it as the carving knife from the wooden block on their kitchen counter. The blood drops from his heart and pools in his feet. He takes a cautious step forward and tries to see her more closely. What is she doing sitting in the dark with a knife?

"Anne?" Marco says, more quietly. She appears to be in some kind of trance. She's scaring him. "Anne, what happened?" He speaks to her the way someone might try to talk to a dangerous animal. When she doesn't answer him, he asks, in the same gentle voice, "What are you doing with the knife?"

He needs to turn on the light. He moves slowly toward the lamp on the side table.

"Don't come near me!" She holds up the knife.

Marco stops in his tracks, staring at her, at the way she's holding the knife, as if she means to use it.

"I know what you did," she says in a low, desperate voice.

Marco thinks quickly. Anne must have been talking to her father. Things must have gone horribly wrong. Marco is flooded with despair. He realizes how much he was relying on his father-in-law to save the day, to get Cora back for them. But clearly everything has fallen apart. Their baby is gone forever. And Anne's father has told her the truth.

And now this last part, this final piece—his wife has lost her mind.

"What's with the knife, Anne?" Marco asks, forcing his voice to stay calm.

"It's for protection."

"Protection from who?"

"From you."

"You don't need protection from me," Marco says to her in the dark. What has her father been telling her? What lies? He would never intentionally harm his wife or child. It's all been a terrible mistake. She has no reason to be afraid of him. *You're dangerous, Marco, with your plans and schemes.* "Have you seen your father?"

"No."

"But you've talked to him."

"No."

Marco doesn't understand. "Who have you been talking to?"

"No one."

"Why are you sitting here in the dark with a knife?" He wants to turn on the light but doesn't want to startle her.

"That's not true," Anne says, as if remembering. "I did see Cynthia."

Marco is silent. Terrified.

"She showed me the video." The look she gives him is terrible. All her pain and rage shows on her face. Her hatred.

Marco sags; he feels like his knees will give way. It's all over now. Maybe Anne wants to kill him for stealing their baby. He can't blame her. He wants to grab the knife and do it himself.

Suddenly he goes cold. He needs to see the knife. He needs to know if she's used it. But it's too dark. He can't see her well enough to see if there's blood on her or on the knife. He takes another step toward her and stops. Her eyes terrify him.

She says, "*You* kidnapped Cora. I saw it with my own eyes. You carried her out of the house wrapped in her blanket and took her to the garage. That man took her away. You planned the whole thing. You lied to me. And you kept on lying to me, all this time." Her voice is disbelieving. "And then, when he double-crossed you, you went to that cabin and beat him to death with a shovel." She's more animated now.

Marco is horrified. "No, Anne—I didn't!"

"And then you sat at the kitchen table with me and said he looked *familiar.*"

Marco feels sick. He thinks of how it must seem to her. How twisted everything has become.

Anne leans forward; she is holding the large knife tightly with both hands. "I've been living with you in this house, this whole time since Cora was taken, and all along you've been lying to me. Lying about everything." She stares at him and whispers, *"I don't know who you are."*

Marco keeps his eyes on the knife and says, desperately, "I did take her. I did take her, Anne. But it's not what you think! I don't know what Cynthia told you—she doesn't know anything about it. She's blackmailing me. She's trying to use the video to get money out of me."

Anne stares at him, her eyes huge in the dark.

"I can explain, Anne! It's not how it looks. Listen to me. I got into financial trouble. The business wasn't going well. I had some reversals. And then I met this man, this . . . Derek Honig." Marco falters. "He told me his name was Bruce Neeland. He seemed like a nice guy—we became friends. *He* suggested the kidnapping. It was all his idea. I needed the money. He said it would be fast and easy, that no one would get hurt. He planned the whole thing." Marco pauses for breath. She is staring at him, her eyes grim. Even so, it is a relief to confess, to tell her the truth.

"I took Cora out to him in the garage. He was supposed to call us within twelve hours, and we were supposed to get her back in two or three days at most. It was supposed to be so fast and easy," Marco says bitterly. "But then we didn't hear from him. I didn't know what was happening. I tried to call him with that cell phone you found—that's what it was for—but he didn't answer my calls. I didn't know what to do. I had no other way to reach him. I thought that maybe he'd lost the cell phone. Or that he'd gotten cold feet, that maybe he'd killed her and left the country." His voice has become a sob. He pauses to regain control. "I was panicking. It's been absolute hell for me, too, Anne—you've no idea."

"Don't tell me I have no idea!" Anne screams at him. "Because of you our baby is gone!"

He tries to calm her by lowering his voice. He has to tell her everything, he has to get it out. "And then when we got the onesie in the mail, I thought it was him, reaching out. That maybe something had happened to the cell and he was afraid to call me directly. I thought he was trying to get her back to us. Even when he increased the ransom to five million, I didn't think . . . I didn't think he would double-cross me. I was only worried that your parents might not pay. I thought maybe he'd upped the stakes because he felt the risk had increased." Marco stops talking for a minute, overwhelmed by reliving it all. "But then when I got there, Cora wasn't there." He breaks down, sobbing. "She was supposed to be there. I don't know what happened! Anne, I swear to you, I never meant for anyone to get hurt. Especially not Cora—or you."

He's dropped down onto his knees on the floor in front of her. She could slit his throat now if she chose. He doesn't care.

"How could you?" Anne whispers. "How could you be so stupid?" Marco lifts his head miserably and looks at her. "Why didn't you ask my father for money, if you needed it so badly?"

"I did!" Marco says wildly. "But he turned me down."

"I don't believe you. He wouldn't do that."

"Why would I lie?"

"You do nothing *but* lie, Marco."

"Ask him, then!"

They glare at each other for a moment.

Then Marco says, more quietly, "You have every reason to hate me, Anne. I hate myself for what I did. But you don't need to be afraid of me."

"Not even after you beat that man to death? With a spade?"

"I didn't!"

"Why don't you tell me everything, Marco?"

"I *have* told you everything! I did *not* kill that man in the cabin."

"Then who did?"

"If we knew that, we'd know who has Cora! Derek wouldn't have hurt Cora, I'm sure of it. He would never have hurt her—I would never have let him have her if I thought he would." But saying this, Marco is appalled at how easily he let someone else have his daughter. He'd been so desperate that he'd blinded himself to the risks.

But that was nothing to the desperation he feels now. Why would Derek harm Cora? He would have no reason to. Unless he panicked. Marco says, "He just wanted to make the exchange and get his money and disappear. Someone else must have found out he had her, then killed him and taken her. And then they cheated us." He pleads with her. "Anne, you have to believe me, I did not kill him. How could I? You know I've been here with you most of the time, or at the office. I *couldn't* have killed him."

Anne is silent, considering. Then she whispers, "I don't know what to believe."

"That's why I went to the police," Marco explains. "I told them I'd seen him hanging around the house, so they'd investigate him. I wanted to point the police in the right direction, so they could find out who killed him, to find Cora without giving myself away. But as usual they've come up empty." He adds, his voice defeated, "Although it's probably just a matter of time until they arrest me."

"They'll arrest you really fast if they see that tape," Anne mutters bitterly.

Marco looks at her. He doesn't know if she would prefer that the police arrest him or not. It's hard to read her now. "I did take Cora and hand her over to Derek. We did try to get money from your parents. But I didn't kill Derek. I couldn't kill anybody, I swear to you." He puts a tender hand on her knee. "Anne, let me have the knife."

She looks at the knife in her hands as if she doesn't know it's there.

No matter what he's done, what havoc he's wreaked, he does not want to be responsible for any more harm. Her manner is disturbing. He moves then and gently takes the knife from her hands. She doesn't resist. Relieved, he sees that the blade is clean. There is no blood on it. He studies her closely, looks at her wrists; there's no blood anywhere. She has not hurt herself. It was meant for him, to protect herself from him. He sets the knife down on the side table, gets up off the floor, and sits beside her on the sofa, facing her. He asks, "Have you heard from your father today?"

"No, but I went to my parents'," Anne says.

"I thought you said you didn't see them?"

"I didn't. I packed a bag. I was going to leave you," she says bitterly. "After I left Cynthia's, after I saw the video, I hated you for what you did." Her voice is agitated again. "And I thought you were a murderer. I was afraid of you."

"I can understand why you'd hate me, Anne. I understand that you'll never forgive me." He chokes on the words. "But you don't need to be afraid of me. I'm not a murderer."

She turns her face away, as if she can't bear to look at him. She says, "I went to my parents'. But I didn't go in."

"Why not?"

"Because I remembered where I'd seen that man before, the dead man."

"You've seen him before?" Marco asks in surprise.

She turns her head and looks at him again. "I told you."

She had, but he hadn't really believed her. At the time he'd just thought it was the power of suggestion.

"Where did you see him?"

"It was a long time ago," she whispers. "He's a friend of my father's."

THIRTY-THREE

Marco freezes. "Are you sure?"

"Yes."

She sounds strange, not like herself. Can he trust anything she says? Marco thinks rapidly. Richard and Derek Honig. The cell phone.

Was this whole thing a setup? Has Richard been controlling this nightmare from behind the scenes? *Has Richard had Cora all along?*

"I'm sure I've seen him with my father, when I was younger," Anne says. "He knows him. Why would my father know the man who took our baby, Marco? Don't you think that's strange?" She sounds like she's drifting away.

"It's strange all right," Marco says slowly. He remembers his suspicions when he'd used the secret cell phone and his father-in-law had answered. *Was this the missing link?* Honig had approached *him,* out of the blue. He had befriended Marco, listened to his troubles. He got Marco to trust him. He urged Marco to ask Richard for more money, and then Richard turned him down. What if they were in collusion and

Richard had turned down his request for more money knowing that Honig would be there, waiting to pick up the pieces? Honig had suggested the kidnapping that same day. What if this had all been carefully orchestrated by Marco's father-in-law? Marco feels ill. If so, he has been even more duped than he thought, and by the man he most dislikes in the world.

"Anne," Marco says, and then the words spill out in a rush, "Derek Honig found *me.* He befriended me. He urged me to ask your father for more money. Then, the day your father turned me down for another loan, he showed up again, *as if he knew.* It was like he knew I'd be desperate. That's when he suggested the kidnapping." Marco feels as if he's emerging from a bad dream, that things are finally starting to make sense. "What if your father is behind this, Anne?" He says urgently, "I think he got Honig to approach me, to set me up for the kidnapping. I've been played, Anne!"

"No!" Anne says stubbornly. "I can't believe it. My father would never do that. Why would he? What possible reason could he have?"

It wounds Marco that she seems to have no difficulty believing that *he* could murder a man with a spade in cold blood yet can't believe that her father would set him up. But he must remember that she's seen that damning video. That would shatter the faith of anyone. He must tell her the rest. "Anne, the cell phone, in the duct. The one Honig and I were using."

"What about it?"

"After you found it, I noticed that there were some

missed calls—someone had called from Honig's cell phone. So I called the number again. And . . . your father answered."

She looks at him in disbelief.

"Anne, he was *expecting* it to be me on the other end of the phone. He *knew* I'd taken Cora. I asked him how he got the phone. He said the kidnappers had mailed it to him, with a note, like the onesie. He said the kidnappers got in touch with him because it was in the newspapers that your parents were the ones who'd paid the ransom. He said they were asking for more money for Cora, that he was going to pay it, but he made me promise not to tell you. He said he didn't want to get your hopes up, in case it all fell apart."

"What?" Anne's face, dazed with suffering, now comes to life. "He's been in touch with the kidnappers?"

Marco nods. "He said he was going to deal with them and get her back himself, because I'd fucked it all up."

"When was this?" Anne asks breathlessly.

"Last night."

"And you didn't tell me?"

"He made me promise not to! In case things don't work out. I've been trying to reach him all day, but he won't call me back. I've been going out of my mind, not knowing what's happening. I assume he hasn't gotten her back, or we would have heard something." But now Marco sees it differently. He's been played by a master. "But, Anne—*what if your father has known where Cora is all along?*"

Anne looks like she can't take in any more. She

looks numb. Finally, her voice breaking, she asks, "But why would he do that?"

Marco knows why. "Because your parents hate me!" Marco says. "They want to destroy me, destroy our marriage, and get you and Cora back for themselves."

Anne shakes her head. "I know they don't like you—maybe they even hate you—but what you're saying . . . I can't believe it. What if he's telling the truth? What if the kidnappers are in touch with my parents and he's trying to get her back for us?" The hope in her voice is heartrending.

Marco says, "But you just said that your father knows Derek Honig. That can't be a coincidence."

There's a long pause. Then she whispers, "Did *he* kill Derek Honig with the shovel?"

"Maybe," Marco says uncertainly. "I don't know."

"What about Cora?" Anne whispers. "What's happened to her?"

Marco takes her by the shoulders and looks into her eyes, which are big and frightened. "I think your father must have her. Or he knows who does."

"What are we going to do?" Anne whispers.

"We have to think this through," Marco says. He gets up from the sofa, too anxious to sit still. "If your father does have her, or knows where she is, we have two options. We can go directly to the police or we can confront him."

Anne stares into space, as if her mind has become overwhelmed.

"Maybe we should talk to your father first, rather

than going to the police," Marco says uneasily. Marco doesn't want to go to jail.

"If we go to my father," Anne says, "I can talk to him. He'll give Cora back to me. He'll be sorry, I know he will. He just wants me to be happy."

Marco stops pacing and looks at his wife, questioning her grip on reality. If it's true that Derek Honig was a friend of her father's, then it could well be true that her father manipulated Marco into financial desperation, into kidnapping their child. Her father might have orchestrated the deception at the exchange; he might have murdered a man in cold blood. He has caused his daughter intense pain. He doesn't care if she's happy. He just wants things his way.

He is utterly ruthless. For the first time, Marco realizes what an adversary he has in his father-in-law. The man is possibly a sociopath. How many times had Richard told him that to succeed in business one had to be ruthless? Maybe that was it—maybe he was trying to teach Marco a lesson about ruthlessness.

Anne says suddenly, "Maybe my father is not part of this. Maybe Derek befriended you, and manipulated you, because he knew my father and knew he has money. But my father might not know anything about it. He might not know that Derek was the kidnapper— he might have gotten the phone and the note in the mail, like he said." She seems more lucid again.

Marco thinks about this. "It's possible." But he believes that Richard is running things behind the scenes. He feels it in his gut.

"We have to go over there," Anne says. "But you can't

just barge in and accuse him. We don't know for sure what's going on. I can tell him that I know you took Cora and that you gave her to Derek Honig. That we need his help getting her back. If my father *is* involved in this, we have to give him a way out. We have to pretend he had nothing to do with it, beg him to work with the kidnappers, to figure out how to get Cora back to us."

Marco thinks about what she's said and nods. Anne seems more like herself again, and he's relieved. Besides, she's right—Richard Dries isn't the kind of man you back into a corner. The important thing is to get Cora home again.

"And maybe my father isn't behind it at all. Maybe he really is in touch with the kidnappers," Anne says. She so obviously wants to believe that her father wouldn't do this to her.

"I doubt it."

They sit for a moment, exhausted by all that's happened, steeling themselves for what's ahead. Finally Marco says, "We'd better get going."

Anne nods. She puts a hand on his arm as they're leaving. "Promise me you won't lose your cool with my father," she says.

What can Marco do but say yes? "I promise." He adds miserably, "I owe you that."

They take a cab to Anne's parents' home, passing by increasingly stately houses until they arrive in the wealthiest suburb of the city. It's late, but they have not called first. They want the element of surprise on their side. Anne and Marco sit in the back of the taxi, saying nothing. Marco can feel Anne trembling against him; her breathing sounds fast and shallow. He takes her hand in his, to calm her. He is sweating with nerves in the hot, sticky cab; the air-conditioning doesn't seem to be working. Marco puts the window down a bit so that he can breathe.

The cab drives them up the circular gravel drive and stops at the front door. Marco pays the driver and tells him not to wait. Anne presses the bell. There are still lights on in the house. After a moment Anne's mother opens the door.

"Anne!" she says, clearly surprised. "I wasn't expecting you."

Anne pushes past her mother, and Marco follows her into the front hall.

And at once all their plans fly out the window.

"Where is she?" Anne demands. She looks wildly at her mother. Her mother seems stunned and doesn't answer. Anne starts walking rapidly through the large house, leaving Marco standing in the front hall, horrified by her behavior. Anne has lost it—he wonders how to play this now.

Anne's mother follows after her on her frantic search through the house. Marco can hear Anne calling, "Cora! Cora!"

He senses movement above and looks up. Richard is coming down the grand staircase. Their eyes meet, steel on steel. They can both hear Anne's cries: "Where is she? Where is my baby?" Her voice is becoming more and more frantic.

Suddenly Marco questions everything: Was Anne right about recognizing Derek Honig? Was Derek an associate of her father's, or has her brain supplied a detail that is simply a delusion? He found her at home in the dark, holding a knife. How reliable is anything she says? Everything he believes hinges on Richard's knowing Derek Honig. Now it's up to Marco to find out the truth.

"Let's go sit down, shall we?" Richard says, and passes him on his way to the living room.

Marco follows. His mouth is dry. He is afraid. He may not be dealing with a normal person here. Richard is quite possibly a sociopath; Marco knows he's out of his depth. He doesn't know how to handle this situation, and everything depends on how he handles it.

Marco hears Anne's footsteps; she is running now, up the elaborate staircase to the second floor. He and Richard stare at each other, listening to Anne call Cora's name as she flings back bedroom doors, running along the upstairs hall, searching.

"She won't find her," Richard says.

"Where is she, you son of a bitch?" Marco says. He has gone off script, too. None of this is going according to plan.

"Well, she's not *here*," his father-in-law says coldly. "Why don't we just wait for Anne to settle down, and we can all have a meeting."

It takes everything Marco has not to get up and go for his father-in-law's fat throat. He forces himself to sit down and to wait for what's coming.

Finally Anne bursts into the living room, her

overwrought mother right behind her. "Where is she?" Anne cries at her father. Her face is mottled and streaked with tears. She is hysterical.

"Sit down, Anne," her father says firmly.

Marco gestures for her to join him, and Anne goes and sits beside him on the large, overstuffed sofa.

"You know why we're here," Marco begins.

"Anne seems to think that Cora is here. Why would she think that?" Richard asks, feigning bewilderment. "Marco—did you tell her the kidnappers were in touch with me? I specifically asked you not to."

Marco tries to speak, but he doesn't know how to begin.

Richard cuts him off anyway. He is standing by the enormous fireplace. He turns to Anne. "I'm so sorry, Anne, but the kidnappers have let us all down—again. I'd hoped to have Cora back tonight, but they didn't show up. I brought the additional money, as arranged, but they just didn't show." He turns to Marco. "Of course, *I* didn't let them have the money anyway, the way *you* did, Marco."

Marco's anger flares—Richard can't resist the temptation to make Marco look like an incompetent fool.

"I told you not to tell her, to avoid this kind of distress," Richard says. He turns to Anne again, his eyes sympathetic. "I've done everything I can to get her back for you, Anne. I'm so sorry. But I promise you, I won't give up."

Anne sags beside him. Marco watches Richard,

the coldness he exhibited to Marco switched to warmth once he's talking to his daughter. Marco sees the flicker of uncertainty in Anne's eyes—she wants to believe her father would never hurt her.

Richard says, "I'm sorry your mother and I didn't tell you earlier, Anne, but we were afraid this might happen. We didn't want to get your hopes up again. The kidnappers got in touch with us and demanded more money. We'd pay anything to get Cora back, you know that. I went out to meet with them. But no one came." He shakes his head in evident frustration and sorrow.

"It's true," Alice says, sitting down at the other end of the sofa beside her daughter. "We're just devastated." She begins to cry, holds her arms out, and Anne sinks into her mother's embrace and begins to sob uncontrollably, her shoulders heaving.

Marco thinks, *This can't be happening.*

"The only thing left to do, I'm afraid," Richard says, "is to go to the police. With everything." He turns and looks at Marco, giving him a cold stare.

Marco stares back. "Tell them, Anne, what you know," he says.

But she looks at him from her mother's embrace as if she's already forgotten.

Desperately, Marco says, "The man who was murdered, Derek Honig. The police know that he took Cora from our place, that he took her to his cabin in the Catskills. But I'm sure you know this already."

Richard shrugs. "The police don't tell me anything."

"Anne recognized him," Marco says flatly.

Has Richard just gone a little paler? Marco can't be sure.

"So? Who was he?"

"She recognized him as a friend of *yours*. How is it, Richard, that a friend of yours had our baby?"

"He wasn't a friend of mine. I've never heard of him," Richard says smoothly. "Anne must be mistaken."

"I don't think so," Marco says.

Anne says nothing. Marco looks at her, but her eyes are turned away. Is she betraying him? Is she going to side with her father and hang him out to dry? Because she believes her father over him? Or because she is willing to sacrifice him to get her baby back? He feels the ground shifting under his feet.

"Anne," Richard says, "do you think this murdered man, the man who supposedly had Cora, was a friend of mine?"

She regards her father, sits up straighter, and says, "No."

Marco looks at her in dismay.

"That's what I thought," Richard says, eyeing Marco. "Let's review what we know," Richard says. He turns to his daughter. "I'm sorry, Anne, but this is going to be painful for you to hear." He sits down in his chair by the fireplace and takes a deep breath before beginning, as if to indicate that this has all been very difficult for him as well. "The kidnappers got in touch with us. They had our names because the newspapers figured out that we had paid the original ransom of five million. The kidnappers sent us a package. In the package were a cell phone and a note.

The note said that the cell phone was the one that the original kidnapper had been using to stay secretly in touch with the baby's father, who was in on the plan. I tried calling the only number programmed into the phone. There was no answer. But I kept it on me, and finally it rang. It was Marco."

"I know all about that," Anne says woodenly. "I know Marco took Cora and handed her over to Derek in our garage that night."

"You do?" her father says in surprise. "How do you know? Did Marco tell you?"

Marco stiffens, afraid that she's going to mention the video.

"Yes," Anne says, glancing at Marco.

"Good for you, Marco, for being man enough to tell her," Richard says. He continues. "I don't know exactly what happened, but my guess is that someone must have murdered the man in the cabin and taken Cora. And then duped Marco at the exchange. I thought all was lost, until whoever did it reached out to your mother and me." He shakes his head regretfully. "I don't know if they'll get in touch with us again. We can only hope."

Pushed to the limit, Marco loses control. "This is bullshit!" he cries. "You know what happened. You set this whole thing up! You knew my business wasn't going well. You *sent* Derek to me. You got him to suggest the kidnapping—it wasn't my idea. It was never my idea! You've been manipulating everything and everyone. Especially me. Derek pushed me to ask you for more money, and then you turned me down. You knew how desperate I was. And then right after you turned me down, there he was, in my darkest moment, with his kidnapping plan. *You* are the mastermind behind all this! Tell me, did *you* bash in Derek's head?"

Anne's mother gasps.

"Because that's what I think happened," Marco presses. "*You* killed him. *You* took Cora from the cabin, or you hired someone to do it. You know where she is. You've known all along. And you're not out one god-damned penny. Because you were behind the swindle at the exchange. You had someone show up without the baby to take the money back. But you want *me* to go to jail." Marco stops to catch his breath. "Tell me, do you even care if Cora lives or dies?"

Richard looks from Marco to Anne and says, "I think your husband is out of his mind."

THIRTY-FOUR

S how us the note," Marco demands.

"What?" Richard is momentarily caught off guard.

"The kidnappers' note, you son of a bitch," Marco says. "Show it to us! Prove to us that you're in communication with them."

"I have the phone. I didn't keep the note," Richard says, unruffled.

"Really. What did you do with the note?" Marco asks.

"I destroyed it."

"And why would you do that?" Marco asks. It's obvious to everyone in the room that he doesn't believe there is a note, that there ever was a note.

"Because it incriminated you," Richard says. "That's how I knew it would be you on the other end of the phone."

Marco laughs, but there's no humor in it. It is a hard, disbelieving laugh, bordering on rage. "You want us to believe that you destroyed the note because it incriminated me? Is it not your intention to have me arrested for kidnapping and keep me away from your daughter for good?" Marco asks.

"No, Marco, that has never been my intention," Richard says. "I don't know why you would think that. I have never done anything but help you, you know that."

"You're so full of shit, Richard. You threatened me on the phone—you know you did. You set up this whole thing to get rid of me. Why else would you do it? So—if there *was* a note, you would never have destroyed it." Marco leans forward toward Richard and says in a menacing voice, "There is no note, is there, Richard? The kidnappers aren't in touch with you, because *you* are the kidnapper. *You* have Derek's phone—you took it when you killed him, or you had your people do it. You knew where he had Cora because you arranged the whole thing. You turned on Derek—which you'd probably planned to do from the start. Tell me: What did you say you'd pay him to help you send me to jail for kidnapping?"

Marco sits back on the sofa; he sees Alice staring at him, horrified.

Richard calmly watches Marco as the younger man accuses him. Then he turns to his daughter and says, "Anne, he's making all of this up to deflect your attention from his own guilt. I had nothing to do with any of this, other than trying my best to get Cora back. And trying to protect him from the police."

"You're a liar!" Marco says in desperation. "You know where Cora is. Give her back! Look at your daughter! Look at her! Give her back her baby!"

Anne has lifted her head and is now looking from her husband to her father. Her face is anguished.

"Shall we call the police, then?" Richard challenges. "Let them sort it all out?"

Marco thinks rapidly. If Anne won't admit she knows Derek was an associate of her father's, or if she's not sure, Marco doesn't have a leg to stand on. The police already see him as their prime suspect. Richard, the respected, successful businessman, can hand him over on a silver platter. Anne and her father both know that Marco took Cora from her crib and gave her to Derek. Marco still believes Richard is behind all this. But he has nothing on Richard.

Marco is fucked.

And they still don't have Cora.

Marco believes that Richard will keep Cora hidden forever if necessary, just so that he can win.

How can Marco make Richard *think* he's won, so that he'll give Cora back?

Should Marco confess to the police? Is that what Richard wants? Perhaps once he's arrested, the "kidnappers" will miraculously get back in touch with Richard and return the baby unharmed. Because despite what Richard says in front of Anne, Marco knows Richard wants him hung out to dry for this. He wants Marco to go to jail but doesn't want to look like he's the one who turned him in.

"Fine, call the police," Marco says.

Anne starts to cry. Her mother rubs her back.

Richard reaches for his cell phone. "It's late, but

I'm sure Detective Rasbach won't mind coming out," he says.

Marco knows he is about to be arrested. He needs a lawyer. A good one. There's still some equity in the house, if Anne will agree to let him mortgage it further. But why would any woman agree to mortgage her house to defend her husband on charges of kidnapping their own child? Even if she *were* willing, her father would dissuade her.

As if reading Marco's mind, Richard says, "I need hardly tell you that we won't be paying for your defense."

They wait in tense silence for the detective to arrive. Alice, who would normally busy herself making tea for everyone, doesn't even budge from the sofa.

Marco is desolate. Richard has won, the manipulative bastard. Anne has fallen into the family fold one last time, and forever. As long as she stands by her parents, everything will work out for her. Richard will find a way to return her baby to her. He will be a hero. They'll take care of her and the baby financially while Marco rots in prison. All she has to do is sacrifice him. She has made her choice. He doesn't blame her.

At last the doorbell rings. Everyone jumps. Richard gets up to answer the door, while the others remain sitting stone-faced in the living room.

Marco decides that he will confess everything. Then, after Cora's safe return, he'll tell the police about Richard's role in all of this. They may not believe him, but surely they can investigate him. Maybe they can find a connection between Richard and Derek Honig.

But Marco is pretty sure that Richard will have covered his tracks.

Richard ushers Detective Rasbach into the living room. The detective seems to take in the situation at a glance: he looks at Anne weeping in her mother's arms at one end of the large sofa, Marco sitting at the other end. Marco knows how he must look to the detective—pale and sweating, he must look like an absolute wreck.

Richard offers the detective a chair and says, "I'm sorry, I know you don't like it when we deal with the kidnappers and don't tell you until after the fact, but we were afraid to do anything else."

Rasbach looks grim. "You say they phoned you?"

"Yes, yesterday. I made arrangements to meet them with the additional money earlier this evening, but they didn't show."

Marco watches Richard. Wonders what the hell he's doing. *Phoned him?* Either Richard is lying to the police or he's lying to Marco and Anne. When is he going to tell the detective that Marco was the one who took Cora from the house?

Rasbach reaches into his jacket and takes out his notebook. He carefully writes down everything Richard tells him. Richard says nothing about Marco. He doesn't even look at Marco. Is this all for Anne? Marco wonders. Is he showing her that he's deliberately protecting Marco, even though they know what he did? *What is Richard's game here?* Maybe Richard never had any intention of telling the police what Marco did—he just wanted to watch him twist in the wind. The absolute bastard.

Or is he waiting for Marco to throw himself on his sword? To see if he's got the guts to do it? Is this a test, one he must pass in order to get Cora back?

"Is that everything?" Rasbach says finally, standing up, flipping his notebook closed.

"I think so," Richard says. He plays the part of the concerned parent and grandparent perfectly. Smooth as glass. A practiced liar.

Richard sees the detective to the door while Marco slumps back in the sofa, exhausted and confused. If this was a test, he has just failed it.

Anne meets his eyes, for only a moment, then looks away.

Richard returns to the living room. "There, now do you believe me?" he says to Marco. "I destroyed the note to protect you. I just lied to the police. I told him the kidnappers called me—to protect you. I didn't tell them about the note and the cell phone sent to me. Both of which incriminated you. I'm not the bad guy here, Marco. You are."

Anne pulls away from her mother's embrace and stares at Marco.

"Although I don't know why I do it," Richard adds. "I don't know why you married this guy, Anne."

Marco needs to get out of here, so he can think. He doesn't know what Richard is up to. "Come on, Anne, let's go home," he says.

Anne has turned away again and doesn't look at him. "Anne?"

"I don't think she's going anywhere," Richard says.

Marco's heart sinks at the thought of going home

without Anne. Evidently Richard *doesn't* want him to go to jail. Perhaps Richard doesn't want the public humiliation of having a convicted criminal for a son-in-law. Maybe the whole time all he wanted was for Anne to know what kind of man Marco was, to separate them. It looks as though he's succeeded.

They all look at him, as if waiting for him to leave. Marco senses the hostility and reaches for his cell to call a cab. When his cab arrives, he is surprised when the three of them follow him outside, perhaps to make sure he leaves. They stand in the drive, watching him go.

Marco looks back at his wife, her father and mother on either side of her. He cannot read her expression.

Marco thinks, *She will never come home to me again. I'm all alone.*

Rasbach is uneasy on the drive back from the Drieses' mansion. He has a lot of unanswered questions. The most important one being this: Where is the missing baby? He seems no closer to a solution.

He thinks about Marco. The haunted look on his face. Marco was exhausted, spent. Not that Rasbach feels any particular sympathy for him. But he knows there's more to this than meets the eye. And he wants to find out what it is.

Rasbach has been suspicious of Richard Dries almost from the start. To his mind—perhaps it's a prejudice, stemming from Rasbach's own working-class background—nobody makes that much money without taking advantage of somebody. It's much easier to make money if you don't care who you hurt. If you have scruples, it's much harder to get rich.

As far as Rasbach's concerned, Marco doesn't fit the profile of a kidnapper. To Rasbach, Marco has always seemed like a desperate man thrown up against the wall. Someone who might do the wrong thing if pushed to it. Richard Dries, however, is a savvy businessman, a man of considerable wealth, which, rightly or wrongly, raises all sorts of red flags for Rasbach. Sometimes these people have a kind of arrogance that makes them think they're above the law.

Richard Dries is a man who bears watching.

Which is why Rasbach has put a wiretap on his phones.

He knows that the kidnappers have not phoned him. Richard is lying.

He decides to also have a couple of officers quietly watch the house.

THIRTY-FIVE

In her own bedroom—she and Richard have had separate bedrooms for years now—Alice paces back and forth on the plush carpet. She has been married to Richard for a very long time. She wouldn't have believed this of him only a couple of years ago. But now he is a man with all kinds of secrets. Horrible, unforgivable secrets, if what she's just heard is true.

She has known for some time that Richard has been seeing another woman. It wasn't the first time he'd cheated on her. But this time she knew it was different. She felt him slipping away from her, as if he already had one foot out the door. As if he were coming up with an exit plan. She'd never thought before that he would actually leave her; she didn't think he had the guts.

Because he knew that if he left her, he wouldn't get a cent. That was the beauty of the prenup. If he left her, he wouldn't get half her fortune—he wouldn't get anything. And he needed her money, because he didn't have much left of his own. Like Marco's, Richard's business had not been doing well in recent years.

He kept the unprofitable business going so people wouldn't know that he'd failed, so he could pretend to be the big businessman. She'd been pouring her own money into the company just to help him save face. She hadn't minded at first, because she loved him.

She doesn't love him anymore. Not after this.

She's known for months that this affair was more serious than the others. In the beginning she'd turned a blind eye, waiting for it to end, as the others had. After all, the physical part of their marriage had been over long ago. But as the affair continued, she became obsessed with finding out who this other woman was.

Richard was good at hiding his tracks. She couldn't trip him up. Finally she'd overcome her distaste and hired a private detective. She'd hired the most expensive one she could find, assuming, rightly, that he would be the most discreet. They met on a Friday afternoon to go over his report. She thought she'd been prepared, but what the detective had found shocked her.

The woman her husband was seeing was that woman living next door to her daughter—Cynthia Stillwell. A woman almost half his age. A friend of his daughter's. A woman he'd met at a party at his daughter's house. It was disgraceful.

Alice sat in Starbucks, staring at her veined hands clutching her purse, as the high-priced private detective with the Rolex reviewed his findings. She looked at the photos—and quickly looked away. He went over the timelines—places and dates. She paid him in cash. She felt ill.

Then she went home and decided to bide her time. She would wait for Richard to tell her he was leaving her. She didn't know what he was going to do for money, and she didn't care. She only knew that if he asked her for any, she would say no. She'd asked the private detective to keep an eye on her bank accounts, to see if Richard was siphoning money off her. She'd decided to keep the detective on retainer. But they wouldn't meet at the same Starbucks again; she'd find someplace more private. The whole experience had left her feeling dirty.

Then Cora had been taken that very night—the same day she'd met with the private investigator—and Richard's sordid affair had been thrust aside by the horror of the kidnapping. Alice had feared at first that perhaps her daughter had harmed her baby, and that she and Marco might have hidden the body to keep from being discovered. Anne had that illness, after all, and she was struggling with motherhood. She was under a lot of stress, and Alice knew that stress was a trigger for someone like Anne. Then—it had been such a relief—the onesie and the note from the kidnappers had arrived.

What a roller coaster it's been. Believing they would get Cora back that day, then losing her again. Through it all, the grief and fear for her baby grand-daughter and the concern about her daughter's fragile emotional state.

And then . . . tonight.

It wasn't until tonight that she figured it all out. She'd been shocked to hear Marco admit that he'd taken Cora himself. More shocked still to hear Marco accuse her husband of setting him up. But then, as she sat there with her arms around her shattered daughter, it all started to make an awful sense.

Richard's grand plan. The kidnapping. Setting Marco up to take the fall. Where was the five million? She was pretty sure Richard had it hidden somewhere. And then there's the second two million, which has been sitting ready in the back of the closet in the front hall, in another gym bag, waiting for the next attempt. She'd never seen the note, or the cell phone. Richard told her he'd destroyed them.

Richard was going to relieve her of seven million dollars under the guise of getting her only grandchild back from kidnappers. The son of a bitch.

So he could leave her for that appalling Cynthia.

Bad enough that he was unfaithful, that he was leaving her for a woman as young as her daughter. Bad enough that he was trying to take her money. *But how dare he hurt her daughter this way?*

And where is her granddaughter?

She reaches for her own cell phone and calls Detective Rasbach. She has things to tell him now.

She would also like to see a photograph of this man Derek Honig.

Anne spends a restless night in her old room, in her old bed. She lies awake all night, listening and thinking. On top of the aching loss of her child, she feels betrayed by everyone. Betrayed by Marco for his part in the kidnapping. Betrayed by her father for his part, even more despicable if Marco is right about him. And she's sure Marco is right, because her father denied knowing Derek Honig. If her father weren't involved in Cora's disappearance, he would have no reason to deny knowing Honig. She'd had her answer. So when he'd asked her, she'd pretended that she didn't recognize Derek, that she'd never seen him before.

She wonders how much her mother knows—or suspects.

Anne almost ruined everything last night, at the beginning. But then she got hold of herself, remembered what she had to do. She feels bad for Marco—but not that bad, given what he's done—for the way she didn't speak up last night, but she wants her child back. She is certain she has seen the dead man before, several times, at this very house, years ago. He and her father used to talk out back near the trees, late at night after she'd gone to bed. She would watch them from her window. She never saw Derek Honig with her father sitting around the pool having drinks, or with anyone else present, not even her mother. He would always arrive late, after dark, and then they'd go out back to talk, near the trees. She knew instinctively as a child not to ask her father about it, that what they were doing was secret. What sorts of things have they done together over the years, if they've kidnapped her child? What is her father capable of?

She gets up and looks out the bedroom window that faces the grounds behind the house and the woods leading into the ravine. It's been a hot night, but now there's a slight breeze coming in through the screen. It's very early—she can just see the outlines of the world outside the window.

She hears a noise from downstairs—a door closing softly. It sounds like the back door in the kitchen. Who would be going out at this early hour? Maybe her mother can't sleep either. Anne thinks about going downstairs to join her, to confront her, and see if her mother can tell her anything.

From the window she sees her father slipping away from the house and across the back lawn. He strides purposefully, as if he knows exactly where he's going. He is carrying a large gym bag.

She watches him from behind the curtain, the way she used to as a child, afraid he might turn around and catch her spying. But he doesn't turn around. He heads for the opening in the trees where the path starts. She knows that path well.

At home, Marco can't sleep either. He rattles around alone in the house, torturing himself with his thoughts. Anne has left him for good; Cynthia's video has destroyed him in Anne's eyes. She betrayed him last night, not admitting she'd seen her father with Derek Honig, but he doesn't blame her. She did what she had to do, and he understands why. Because she did what she had to do, maybe Cora will be returned to them.

Returned to Anne, not to Marco. It occurs to Marco that he may never be able to see Cora again. Anne will divorce him, of course. She will get the best lawyers, and she will get full custody. And if Marco tries to enforce his visiting rights, Richard will threaten to go to the police about his role in the kidnapping. He has forfeited any right to his child.

He is alone. He has lost the two people who matter most to him in the world, his wife and his child. Nothing else matters anymore. It hardly seems important now that he is financially ruined or that he is being blackmailed.

All he can do now is pace the house and wait for Cora to be found.

He wonders, will anyone even let him know? His exclusion from their tight family circle is complete. Maybe he will have to learn about Cora's return from the dead in the newspapers.

Anne hesitates for just a moment. There is only one reason she can think of for her father to be heading into the ravine at this hour with no one to see him, carrying a large gym bag. He is going to get Cora. Someone is going to meet with him in the ravine.

She's not sure what to do. Should she follow him? Or should she stay put and trust him to bring her baby back? But Anne is through trusting her father. She needs to know the truth.

Anne hurriedly throws on the clothes she'd worn the day before and makes her way quickly downstairs to the kitchen and out the back door. The cool, dewy air hits her and makes goose bumps come up on her arms. She starts off across the wet grass, following in her father's footsteps. She has no plan; she is operating on instinct.

She runs lightly down the wooden stairs that lead into the forested ravine, one hand on the rail, almost flying in the near dark. She once knew the way well, but it's been years since she took this path. Still, memory serves her.

It is even darker in here, in the woods. The ground underfoot is soft and damp and swallows up her footsteps. She makes little noise as she moves down the dirt path as quickly as she can after her father. It's spooky in the dark. She can't see him ahead, but she has to assume that he's sticking to the path.

Anne's heart is pounding with fear and exertion. She knows everything is coming down to this moment. She believes her father has come out here to regain possession of her child and bring her back. Suddenly she realizes that if she stumbles into the meeting, she might ruin everything. She must stay hidden. She stands still for a moment, listening, peering into the murky forest. She sees nothing but trees and shadows. She begins to move along the path again, more cautiously, but as quickly as she can, almost blindly, panting heavily with panic and exertion. She comes to a turn in the path, where another set of wooden stairs leads steeply to a residential street above. She looks up. There, ahead. She can see her father. He's alone, coming down the stairs that lead up out of the ravine and into the next street. He has a bundle in his arms. He must see her now. Can he tell it is her in the forest, in the dark?

"Daddy!" she screams.

"Anne?" he calls. "What are you doing out here? Why aren't you asleep?"

"Is that Cora?" She comes closer, breathing heavily. She's at the bottom of the stairs now; her father is halfway down, coming toward her. It's beginning to be lighter now—she can see his face.

"Yes, it's Cora!" he cries. "I got her back for you!" The bundle is not squirming; it hangs like deadweight in his arms. He walks down the stairs toward her.

She stares, appalled, at the unmoving bundle in his arms.

Then, as fast as she can, Anne runs up the steps to meet him. She stumbles, catches herself with her hands. She holds out her arms. "Give her to me!" she cries.

He hands the bundle over to her. She parts the blanket covering the baby's face, terrified of what she might find. The baby is so still. Anne looks upon the baby's face. It is Cora. She seems dead. Anne has to peer closely at her to tell if she's breathing. She *is* breathing, barely. The baby's eyes flicker behind her pale lids.

Anne lays her hand gently on Cora's chest. She can feel the tiny *thump-thump* of her heart, can feel her little chest rising and falling. She is alive, but she's not well. Anne sits down on the step and immediately puts Cora to her breast. There is still milk there.

With a bit of encouragement, the weakened baby latches on. And then she is suckling hungrily. Anne holds her baby to her breast, a moment she never thought she would have again. Tears run down her face as she looks at her nursing child.

She glances up at her father, who is still standing over her. He averts his eyes.

He tries to explain. "Someone called again, about an hour ago. Arranged another meeting, in the road on the other side of the ravine. This time a man showed up. I gave him the money, and he handed her to me. Thank God. I was just about to bring her home and wake you up." He smiles at her. "It's over, Anne, we've got her back. I got her back for you."

Anne looks down at her baby, saying nothing. She does not want to look at her father. She has Cora again. She must call Marco.

Thirty-six

Marco's stomach is churning as his cab pulls up to Anne's parents' house. He sees all the police patrol cars, the ambulance parked near the front door. He recognizes Detective Rasbach's car as well.

The cabbie says, "Hey, man, what's going on?"

Marco doesn't answer him.

Anne had called him on his cell, just a few minutes ago, and said, *I have her. She's okay. You have to come.*

Cora is alive, and Anne called him. What happens next, he has no idea.

Marco hurries up the front steps of the house he'd left just hours before and bursts into the living room. He sees Anne on the sofa, cradling their tiny daughter in her arms. A uniformed police officer is standing behind the sofa, as if protecting her. Anne's father and mother are not in the room. Marco wonders where they are, what has happened.

He rushes up to Anne and the baby and engulfs them both in a tearful embrace. Then he pulls back and looks carefully at Cora. She's thin and sickly, but she's breathing and sleeping peacefully, her fingers curled. "Thank God," Marco says, trembling, tears running down his face. "Thank God." He gazes in wonder at his daughter and gently strokes the lackluster curls on her head. He has never been happier than he is right now. He wants to hold on to this moment, to remember it forever.

"The medics have checked her over and say she's okay," Anne says, "but we should take her to the hospital and have her thoroughly examined." Anne looks drawn and tired but, he realizes, also truly happy.

"What happened? Where are your parents?" Marco asks at last, uneasily.

"They're in the kitchen," she says. But before she can say any more, Detective Rasbach joins them in the living room.

"Congratulations," the detective says.

"Thank you," Marco replies. As usual, he can't read the detective, can't tell what's going on behind those sharp, discerning eyes.

"I'm so glad your baby has been returned to you alive and well," Rasbach says. He looks directly at Marco. "I didn't like to say so before, but the odds were against it."

Marco sits nervously by Anne's side, gazing down at Cora, wondering if this happy moment is about to be snatched away from him, wondering if Rasbach is going to tell him he knows all about it. Marco wants to put that off, preferably forever, but he has to know. The tension is unbearable. "What happened?" he asks again.

"I couldn't sleep," Anne tells him. "From my bedroom window, I saw Dad going out to the ravine. He was carrying a gym bag. I thought he was going to meet the kidnappers again. I followed him into the ravine, and by the time I caught up with him, he had her. The kidnappers had called again and arranged another exchange. This time a man showed up, with Cora." She turns to the detective. "He was gone by the time I caught up with my father."

Marco waits silently. So this is how they're going to play it. He tries to work out the ramifications. Richard is to be the hero. He and Alice have paid, again, to get Cora back. Anne has just told the police this. Marco doesn't know whether she actually believes it or not.

Marco has no idea what the detective believes.

"What happens now?" Marco asks.

Rasbach looks at him. "Now, Marco, we tell the truth."

Marco feels suddenly light-headed, almost dizzy. He sees Anne look up from the baby to the detective, alert to disaster.

"What?" Marco says. He can feel the perspiration starting to prickle his skin.

Rasbach sits down in the chair across from them. Leans forward intently. "I know what you did, Marco. I know you took your baby from her crib and put her in the back of Derek Honig's car just after twelve thirty that night. I know Derek drove her to his cabin in the Catskills, where he was brutally murdered a few days later."

Marco says nothing. He knows this is what Rasbach has believed all along, but what proof does he have? Has Richard told them about the phone? Is that what he's been doing in the kitchen? *Has Anne told them about the video?* Suddenly Marco can't bear to look at his wife.

"Here's what I think, Marco," Rasbach says, speaking rather slowly, as if he understands that Marco is in so much distress that he may have trouble following. "I think you needed money. I think you set this kidnapping up with Derek Honig to get money from your wife's parents. I don't think your wife knew anything about it."

Marco shakes his head no. He must deny everything.

"After that," Rasbach says, "I'm not clear. Maybe you can help me. Did you kill Derek Honig, Marco?"

Marco starts violently. "No! Why would you think that?" He's very agitated. He wipes his sweaty hands on his pants.

"Derek betrayed you," Rasbach says calmly. "He didn't bring the baby to the exchange as planned. He took the money for himself. You knew where he was with the baby. You knew about the cabin in the woods."

"No!" Marco shouts. "I didn't know where the cabin was! He never told me!"

It is perfectly silent in the room, except for the tick of a clock on the mantelpiece.

With a sob, Marco buries his face in his hands.

Rasbach waits, lets the damning silence fill the

room. Then he says, more gently, "Marco, I don't think you meant for it to happen this way. I don't think you killed Derek Honig. I think your father-in-law, Richard Dries, killed Derek Honig."

Marco lifts his head.

"If you come clean with us, if you tell us everything you know to help us in our case against your father-in-law, we might be able to talk about a deal."

"What kind of a deal?" Marco asks. His mind is racing.

"If you help us, we might be able to offer you immunity from prosecution on the conspiracy-to-kidnap charge. I can speak to the prosecutor—I think he'll agree, under the circumstances."

Marco suddenly sees hope where there was none before. His mouth has gone dry. He can't speak. He nods instead. It seems to be good enough.

"You'll have to come down to the station," Rasbach says, "after we wrap up here." He stands up and goes back to the kitchen.

Anne remains in the living room, cradling her sleeping baby, but Marco gets up and follows Rasbach into the kitchen. He's surprised his legs work well enough to carry him there. Richard is sitting in one of the kitchen chairs, stubbornly silent. Their eyes meet; Richard's slide away. A uniformed officer nudges Richard to stand up and puts handcuffs on him. Alice watches from the background, saying nothing, her face blank.

"Richard Adam Dries," Detective Rasbach says, "you are under arrest for the murder of Derek Honig and conspiracy to kidnap Cora Conti. You have the right to remain silent. Anything you say or do can and will be used against you in a court of law. You have the right to an attorney. . . ."

Marco watches, astonished at his luck. His baby is back, safe. Richard has been found out and will get what he deserves. He, Marco, will not be prosecuted. Cynthia has nothing to hold over him now. He can feel himself breathe for the first time since this nightmare began. It's over. *It's finally over.*

Two uniformed officers lead Richard in handcuffs out through the living room and toward the front door, Rasbach and Marco and Alice following behind. Richard says nothing. He won't look at his wife, his daughter, his grandchild, or his son-in-law.

Marco, Anne, and Alice watch him go.

Marco casts a glance at his wife. They have their adored baby back. Anne knows everything now. There are no more secrets between them.

At the police station, they work out the details of Marco's deal. Marco has a new lawyer, from a top criminal firm in the city, a firm other than Aubrey West's.

Marco tells Rasbach everything. He says, "Richard framed me. He set me up. He sent Derek to me. It was all his idea. They knew I needed money."

Anne speaks up. "We thought my father was behind this. I knew he knew Derek Honig—I recognized him—he used to come to the house, years ago. But how did you know?"

Rasbach answers. "I knew he was lying. He said

the kidnappers had called him, but we have taps on his phones. We knew they hadn't called him. Then, late last night, your mother called me."

"My mother?"

"Your father has been having an affair."

"I know," Anne says. "My mother told me, this morning."

Marco says, "What does that have to do with anything?"

"Your mother-in-law hired a private detective to find out what he was up to. The detective put a GPS tracking device on Richard's car a few weeks ago. It's still there."

Marco and Anne listen closely to the detective.

"We know that Richard drove out to the cabin around the time of the murder." Marco and Anne exchange glances. Rasbach adds, addressing Anne, "Your mother recognized Honig, too, as soon as I showed her a photograph of him."

Marco says, "Richard had the cell phone, Derek's cell phone. The one we were supposed to use to stay in touch. But Derek never called me, and he never answered his cell. I noticed there were some missed calls, and when I called the number, Richard answered. He said the kidnappers sent him the phone in the mail, with a note. But I wondered if he'd killed Derek and taken it. I never believed him about the note. He said he'd destroyed it to protect me, because it implicated me."

Rasbach says, "Alice never saw the note or the cell phone. Richard said they arrived when she was out."

"Why would Richard kill Derek?" Marco asks.

"We think that Derek was supposed to return the baby when you brought the ransom money but didn't, and Richard realized he'd been double-crossed. We think Richard tracked him down to the cabin that night and killed him. That's when he saw the opportunity to make a second ransom demand for more money."

"Where was Cora after she was taken from the cabin? Who was taking care of her?" Anne asks.

"We stopped Richard's secretary's daughter in her car leaving the area just after Richard got the baby back earlier this morning. She had the baby. It turns out she's got a bit of a drug problem and needed money."

Anne gasps, horrified, her hand to her face.

Exhausted but relieved, Anne and Marco are back home at last with Cora. After going to the police station, Anne and Marco had taken Cora to the hospital, where she was checked out and given a clean bill of health. Now Marco puts together a quick meal for the two of them while Cora has another greedy feed. The press is no longer clamoring at their doorstep; their new lawyer has made it clear that Anne and Marco will not speak to them at all and has threatened legal action if they are harassed. At some point, when things settle down, they will list the house for sale.

Finally they put Cora to bed in her own crib. They have undressed her and given her a bath, studying her as carefully as they had when she was a newborn, to make sure she's all right. And it is a kind of rebirth, getting her back from the dead. Perhaps it's a new beginning for them.

Anne tells herself that children are resilient. Cora will be fine.

They stand beside the crib, looking down at their baby as she smiles and gurgles up at them. It is such a relief to see her smile; in the first few hours after they got her back, she had just suckled and cried endlessly. But now Cora is beginning to smile again. She lies on her back in the crib, the stenciled lambs and her two parents hovering over her, and playfully kicks out her legs.

"I never thought this moment would come," Anne whispers.

"Me either," Marco says, waving Cora's rattle at her. She squeals and grabs it and holds on tight.

They are quiet for a while, watching until their daughter falls asleep.

"Do you think you can ever forgive me?" Marco asks finally.

Anne thinks, *How can I ever forgive you for how selfish and weak and stupid you were?* She says, "I don't know, Marco. I have to take it one day at a time."

He nods, stung. After a moment he says, "There were never any other women, Anne, I swear it."

"I know."

THIRTY-SEVEN

Anne puts Cora back down in her crib, hoping this is the last feed of the night and that now the baby will sleep through till morning. It's late—very late—but she can still hear Cynthia moving around restlessly in the house next door.

It has been a day of shocking revelations. After her father had been taken away from the family home in handcuffs, her mother had pulled Anne aside while Marco held the sleeping baby in his arms in the living room.

"I think you should know," she said, "who your father was seeing."

"Does it matter?" Anne asked. What difference did it make who her father was seeing? She would be younger and attractive. Of course. Anne didn't care who she was; what mattered was that her father—actually, she remembers, her stepfather—had kidnapped her baby to get millions of dollars of her mother's money. Now he would go to jail for kidnapping and murder. She still couldn't believe it was all real.

"He was seeing your next-door neighbor," her mother said. "Cynthia Stillwell." Anne looked back at her mother in disbelief, still capable of being shocked by this news, in spite of everything that had happened. "He met her at your New Year's Eve party," her mother said. "I remember her flirting with him. I didn't think too much of it at the time. But the private detective found out everything. I have photographs." Her mother's face showed disgust. "Photocopies of hotel receipts."

Anne asked, "Why didn't you tell me?"

"I only found out recently," Alice explained. "Then Cora was taken, and I didn't want to upset you with it." She added, rather bitterly, "That detective was one of the best investments I ever made."

Now Anne wonders what's going through Cynthia's mind. Graham is away. She's alone next door. She must know that Richard has been arrested. It's been on the news. Does Cynthia even care what happens to Richard?

The baby is sound asleep in her crib. Marco is asleep in their bed, snoring deeply. It's the first time he's really slept in more than a week. But Anne is wide awake. And so is Cynthia, next door.

Anne slips on some sandals and lets herself out the kitchen door. She quietly walks the few steps over to Cynthia's backyard, careful not to let the gate bang shut. She crosses the patio and stands in the dark, her face a couple of inches from the glass, looking through the sliding glass door. There is a light on in the kitchen. She can see Cynthia moving around at the counter near the sink but realizes Cynthia probably can't see her. Anne watches her for a while in the darkness. Cynthia is making herself some tea. She is wearing a sexy nightgown, pale green; it's very provocative for a night spent at home alone.

Cynthia obviously has no idea Anne is there watching her.

Anne knocks lightly on the glass. She sees Cynthia jump and turn toward the sound. Anne presses her face up against the glass. She can tell Cynthia isn't sure what she should do. But then Cynthia walks over to the door and opens it a few inches.

"What do you want?" Cynthia asks coldly.

"Can I come in?" Anne asks. Her voice is neutral, even friendly.

Cynthia looks warily at her but doesn't say no, and steps back. Anne opens the door wider and comes inside, closing the door carefully behind her.

Cynthia returns to the counter and says over her shoulder, "I was just making some tea. Chamomile. Would you like some? It seems neither of us can sleep tonight."

"Sure, why not?" Anne says agreeably. She watches Cynthia busy herself making another cup of tea; she seems nervous.

"So why are you here?" Cynthia says bluntly, handing Anne the cup.

"Thank you," Anne says, settling in her old spot at the kitchen table, as if they were still friends, sitting down for some tea and a chat. She ignores Cynthia's question. She looks around the kitchen, blowing on the hot drink to cool it, as if she has nothing particular on her mind at all.

Cynthia remains standing at the counter. She's not going to pretend that they are still friends. Anne studies her over the rim of her cup. Cynthia looks tired, less attractive. For the first time, Anne can see hints of what Cynthia might look like as she ages.

"We have Cora back," Anne says blithely. "You probably heard." She cocks her head toward the common wall; she knows that Cynthia must be able to hear her baby crying through it.

"How lovely for you," Cynthia says. There is a kitchen island between them, with a wooden knife block full of knives on it. Anne has the same set at home—it was on special at the grocery store not long ago.

Anne puts her cup down on the table. "I just wanted to be clear about something."

"Clear about what?" Cynthia says.

"You won't be blackmailing us with that video."

"Oh, and why's that?" Cynthia says, as if she doesn't believe it for a moment, as if she thinks this is all just posturing.

"Because the police know what Marco did," Anne says. "I told them about your video."

"Really." Cynthia looks skeptical. She looks as if she thinks Anne is bullshitting her. "And why would you tell them that? Won't Marco go to jail? Oh, wait . . . you *want* him to go to jail." She gives Anne a superior look. "I can't say I blame you."

"Marco's not going to jail," Anne says.

"I wouldn't be so sure."

"Oh, I'm sure. Marco's not going to jail, because my father—*your lover*—has been arrested for murder and conspiracy to kidnap, as I'm sure you also probably know by now." Anne watches Cynthia's face harden. "Oh, yes, I know all about it, Cynthia. My mother had a private detective watching you two. She has photos, receipts, everything." Anne takes another sip of tea, enjoying herself. "Your secret affair isn't so secret after all."

Anne finally has the upper hand, and she likes it. She smiles at Cynthia.

"So what?" Cynthia says finally. But Anne can tell she's unnerved.

"What you might not know," Anne says, "is that Marco's cut a deal."

Anne sees something like alarm flit across Cynthia's face, and Anne comes to the reason she's here. She says, ominously, "You were in on this all along. You knew all about it."

"I knew *nothing* about it," Cynthia says scornfully, "except that your husband stole his own child."

"Oh, I think you knew. I think you were in on this with my father—we all know how much you love money." Anne says, with a trace of venom, "Maybe *you're* the one who's going to go to jail."

Cynthia's face changes. "No! I didn't know what Richard had done, not until I saw it on the news tonight. I wasn't involved. I thought Marco had done it. You can't prove anything against me. I haven't been anywhere near your baby!"

"I don't believe you," Anne says.

"I don't care what you believe—it's the truth,"

Cynthia says. She looks at Anne with narrowed eyes. "What happened to you, Anne? You used to be such fun, so interesting—and then you had a baby. Everything about you changed. Do you even realize how dull and dumpy and boring you've become? Poor Marco, I wonder how he stands it."

"Don't try to change the subject. Don't make this about me. You had to know what my father was up to. So don't lie to me." Anne's voice shakes with anger.

"You'll never be able to prove that, because it simply isn't true," Cynthia says. Then she adds, cruelly, "If I'd been involved, do you think I would have let the baby survive? It would probably have been better for Richard just to kill it at the beginning—and a lot less trouble. It would have been a pleasure to stop that brat's endless crying."

Then Cynthia looks scared—she realizes she's gone too far.

Anne's chair falls suddenly backward. Cynthia's habitual smugness is replaced by a look of blind terror; her china teacup shatters on the floor as she lets out a hideous, earsplitting scream.

Marco has been deeply asleep. But in the middle of the night, he wakes suddenly. He opens his eyes. It is very dark, but there are red lights flashing, circling around the bedroom walls. Emergency vehicle lights.

The bed is empty beside him. Anne must be up again, feeding the baby.

He is curious now. He gets up and walks over to the

bedroom window, which looks out over the street. He pushes the curtain aside and peers out. It's an ambulance. It is parked directly below him and to the left.

In front of Cynthia and Graham's house.

His whole body tenses. Now he sees the black-and-white police cars on the other side of the street, more arriving as he watches. His fingers on the curtain twitch involuntarily. His body is shot through with adrenaline.

A stretcher appears from out of the house, carried by two ambulance attendants. There must be someone on the stretcher, but he can't see for sure until the medic moves. There is no urgency about them. The medic shifts position. Marco sees that there is someone on the stretcher. But he can't tell who it is, because the face is covered.

Whoever is on the stretcher is dead.

All the blood rushes from Marco's head; he feels he might pass out. As he watches, a lock of long, jet-black hair escapes and falls down below the stretcher.

He looks back at the empty bed. *"Oh, God,"* he whispers. *"Anne, what have you done?"*

He runs out of the bedroom, glances quickly in the baby's room. Cora is asleep in her crib. Panicking now, he races down the stairs, stops dead in the darkened living room. He can see the side of his wife's head; she is sitting on the sofa in the dark, completely still. He approaches her, filled with dread. She is slumped on the sofa, staring straight ahead as if in a trance, but as she hears him approach, she turns her head.

She is holding a large carving knife in her lap.

The red, pulsing light from the emergency vehicles outside circles the living-room walls and bathes them in a lurid glow. Marco can see that the knife and her hands are dark—dark with blood. She is covered in it. There are dark splatters on her face and in her hair. He feels sick, like he might throw up.

"Anne," he whispers, his voice a broken croak. "Anne, what have you done?"

She looks back at him in the dark and says, "I don't know. I don't remember."

**Read on for a selection from
Shari Lapena's novel,**

A Stranger in the House . . .

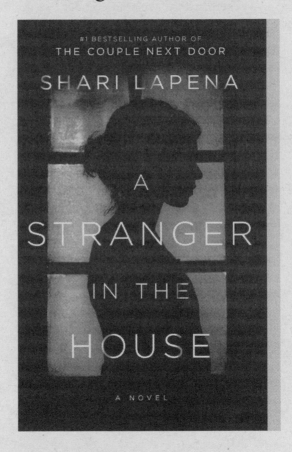

PROLOGUE

She doesn't belong here.

She bolts out the back door of the abandoned restaurant, stumbling in the dark—most of the lights are burned out, or broken—her breath coming in loud rasps. She runs like a panicked animal to where she parked the car, hardly aware of what she's doing. Somehow she gets the car door open. She buckles up without thinking, wheels the car around in a screeching two-point turn, and peels out of the parking lot, swerving recklessly onto the road without even slowing down. Something in the strip mall across the street catches her eye—but she has no time to register what she sees, because she's already at an intersection. She runs the red light, picking up speed. She can't think.

Another crossroads—she guns through it. She's driving way over the speed limit, but she doesn't care. She has to get away.

Another intersection, another red light. Cars are already crossing the other way. She doesn't stop. She bursts through it, weaving around a car in her path, leaving chaos in her wake. She hears the shriek of brakes and violent honking behind her. She's dangerously close to losing control of the car. And then she does—she has one moment of clarity, of disbelief, as she frantically pumps the brakes and the skidding car leaps the curb and plunges headfirst into a utility pole.

ONE

On this hot August night, Tom Krupp parks his car—a leased Lexus—in the driveway of his handsome two-story home. The house, complete with a two-car garage, is set behind a generous lawn and framed with beautiful old trees. To the right of the driveway, a flagstone path crosses in front of the porch, with steps leading up to a solid wooden door in the middle of the house. To the right of the front door is a large picture window the width of the living room.

The house sits on a gently curving street that ends in a cul-de-sac. The surrounding houses are all equally attractive and well maintained, and relatively similar. People who live here are successful and settled; everyone's a little bit smug.

This quiet, prosperous suburb in upstate New York, populated with mostly professional couples and their families, seems oblivious to the problems of the small city that surrounds it, oblivious to the problems of the larger world, as if the American dream has continued to live on here, smooth and unruffled.

But the untroubled setting does not match Tom's current state of mind. He cuts the lights and the engine and sits uneasily for a moment in the dark, despising himself.

Then, with a start, he notices that his wife's car is not in its usual place in the driveway. He automatically checks his watch: 9:20. He wonders if he's forgotten something. *Was she going out?* He can't remember her mentioning anything, but he's been so busy lately. *Maybe she just went out to run an errand and will be back any minute.* She's left the lights on; they give the house a welcoming glow.

He gets out of the car into the summer night—it smells of freshly mown grass—swallowing his disappointment. He wanted, rather fervently, to see his wife. He stands for a moment, his hand on the roof of the car, and looks across the street. Then he grabs his briefcase and suit jacket from the passenger seat and tiredly closes the car door. He walks along the path, up the front steps, and opens the door. Something is wrong. He holds his breath.

Tom stands completely still in the doorway, his hand resting on the knob. At first he doesn't know what's bothering him. Then he realizes what it is. The door wasn't locked. That in itself isn't unusual—most nights he comes home and opens the door and walks right in, because most nights Karen's home, waiting for him. But she's gone out with her car and forgotten to lock the door. That's very odd for his wife, who's a stickler about locking the doors. He slowly lets out his breath. *Maybe she was in a rush and forgot.*

His eyes quickly take in the living room, a serene rectangle of pale gray and white. It's perfectly quiet; there's obviously no one home. She left the lights on, so she must not have gone out for long. *Maybe she went to get some milk.* There will probably be a note for him. He tosses his keys onto the small table by the front door and heads straight for the kitchen at the back of the house. He's starving. He wonders if she's already eaten or whether she's been waiting for him.

It's obvious that she's been preparing their supper. A salad is almost finished; she has stopped slicing mid-tomato. He looks at the wooden cutting board, at the tomato and the sharp knife lying beside it. There's pasta on the granite counter, ready to be cooked, a large pot of water on the stainless steel gas stove. The stove is off and the water in the pot is cold; he dips a finger in to check. He scans the refrigerator door for a note—there's nothing written on the whiteboard for him. He frowns. He pulls his cell phone out of his pants pocket and checks to see if there's any message from her that he might have missed. Nothing. Now he's mildly annoyed. She might have told him.

Tom opens the door to the refrigerator and stands there for a minute, staring sightlessly at its contents, then grabs an imported beer and decides to start the pasta. He's sure she'll be home any minute. He looks around curiously to see what they might have run out of. They have milk, bread, pasta sauce, wine, parmesan cheese. He checks the bathroom—there's plenty of toilet paper. He can't think of anything else that might be urgent. While he waits for the water to come to a boil, he calls her cell, but she doesn't pick up.

Fifteen minutes later, the pasta is ready, but there is no sign of his wife. Tom leaves the pasta in the strainer in the sink, turns off the burner under the pot of tomato sauce, and wanders restlessly into the living room, his hunger forgotten. He looks out the large picture window across the lawn to the street beyond. *Where the hell is she?* He's starting to get anxious now. He calls her cell again and hears a faint vibration coming from behind him. He whips his head toward the sound and sees her cell phone, vibrating against the back of the sofa. *Shit. She forgot her phone. How can he reach her now?*

He starts looking around the house for clues as to where she might have gone. Upstairs, in their bedroom, he's surprised to find her bag sitting on her bedside table. He opens it with clumsy fingers, faintly guilty about going through his wife's purse. It feels private. But this is an emergency. He dumps the contents onto the middle of their neatly made bed. Her wallet is there, her change purse, lipstick, pen, a tissue packet—it's all there. *Not an errand then. Maybe she stepped out to help a friend? An emergency of some kind?* Still, she would have taken her purse with her if she was driving the car. And wouldn't she have called him by now if she could? She could borrow someone else's phone. It's not like her to be thoughtless.

Tom sits on the edge of the bed, quietly unraveling. His heart is beating too fast. Something is wrong. He thinks that maybe he should call the police. He considers how that might go. *My wife went out and I don't know where she is. She left without her phone and her purse. She forgot to lock the door. It's completely unlike her.* They probably won't take him seriously if she's been gone such a short time. He hasn't seen any sign of a struggle. Nothing is out of place.

Suddenly he gets up off the bed and rapidly searches the entire house. But he finds nothing alarming—no phone knocked off the hook, no broken window, no smear of blood on the floor. Even so, he's breathing as anxiously as if he had.

He hesitates. Perhaps the police will think they've had an argument. It won't matter if he tells them there was no argument, if he tells them they almost never argue. That theirs is an almost perfect marriage.

Instead of calling the police, he runs back into the kitchen, where Karen keeps a list of phone numbers, and starts calling her friends.

Looking at the wreckage in front of him, Officer Kirton shakes his head in resignation. People and cars. He's seen things to make his stomach empty itself on the spot. It wasn't that bad this time.

There'd been no identification on the crash victim, a woman, probably early thirties. No purse, no wallet. But the vehicle registration and insurance had been in the glove compartment. The car is registered to a Karen Krupp, at 24 Dogwood Drive. She'll have some explaining to do. And some charges to face. For now, she's been taken by ambulance to the nearest hospital.

As far as he can figure, and according to witnesses, she was traveling like a bat out of hell. She ran a red light and smashed the red Honda Civic right into a pole. It's a miracle no one else was hurt.

She was probably high, Kirton thinks. They would get a tox screen on her.

He wonders if the car was stolen. Easy enough to find out.

Thing was, she didn't look like a car thief or a druggie. She looked like a housewife. As far as he could tell through all that blood.

Tom Krupp has called the people he knows Karen sees most often. If they don't know where she might be, then he isn't waiting any longer. He's calling the police.

His hand trembles as he picks up the phone again. He feels sick with fear.

A voice comes on the line, "911. Where's your emergency?"

As soon as he opens the door and sees the cop on his doorstep, his face serious, Tom knows something very bad has happened. He is filled with a nauseating dread.

"I'm Officer Fleming," the cop says, showing his badge. "May I come in?" he asks respectfully, in a low voice.

"You got here fast," Tom says. "I just called 911 a

few minutes ago." He feels as if he might be going into shock.

"I'm not here because of a 911 call," the officer says.

Tom leads him into the living room and collapses onto the large white sofa as if his legs have given out, not looking at the officer's face. He wants to delay the moment of truth for as long as possible.

But that moment has come. He finds that he can hardly breathe.

"Put your head down," Officer Fleming says, and places his hand gently on Tom's shoulder.

Tom leans his head toward his lap, feeling like he's going to pass out. He fears that his world is coming to an end. After a moment he looks up. He has no idea what's coming next, but he knows it can't be good.

Two

The three boys—two thirteen-year-olds, and one fourteen, just beginning to sprout hair on his upper lip—are accustomed to running wild. Kids grow up fast in this part of town. They're not home late at night, hovered over computer screens doing homework or tucked in their beds. They're out looking for trouble. And it looks like they've found it.

"Yo," says one, stopping suddenly inside the door of the abandoned restaurant where they sometimes go to smoke a joint, if they have one. The other two spill around him, then stop, peering into the dark.

"What's that?"

"I think it's a dead guy."

"No shit, Sherlock."

Senses suddenly on alert, each of the boys freezes, afraid that someone else might be there. But they realize they're alone.

One of the younger boys laughs nervously in relief.

They move forward curiously, looking at the body on the floor. It's a man, sprawled on his back, with obvious gunshots to his face and chest. There's a lot of blood soaking the man's light-colored shirt. None of them is the least bit squeamish.

"I wonder if he's got anything on him," says the oldest boy.

"I doubt it," one of the boys answers.

But the fourteen-year-old slips his hand expertly into a pocket of the dead man's pants, pulling out a wallet. He rifles through it. "Looks like we got lucky," he says with a grin, holding the open wallet up for them to see. It's full of bills, but in the dark it's too hard to tell how much is there. He pulls a cell phone from the dead man's other pocket.

"Get his watch and stuff," he tells the others, as he scans the floor hopefully, looking for a gun. It would be great to find a weapon, but he doesn't see one.

One boy removes the watch. The other struggles a bit with a heavy gold ring but eventually tugs it from the corpse's finger and slips it into the pocket of his jeans. Then he feels around the man's neck to see if there's a necklace. There isn't.

"Take his belt," the older boy, obviously the leader, orders. "And his shoes, too."

They've stolen things before, although never from a dead body. They're caught up in the thrill of it, breathing rapidly. They've crossed some kind of line.

Then the older boy says, "We've got to get out of here. And you can't tell anybody."

The other two look up at the taller boy and nod silently.

"No bragging to anybody about what we did. You got that?" the bigger one says.

They nod again firmly.

"If anybody asks, we were never here. Let's go."

The three boys slip out of the abandoned restaurant quickly, taking the dead man's things with them.

Tom can tell by the cop's voice, by his facial expression, that the news is very bad. The police must break tragic news to people every day. Now it's his turn. But Tom doesn't want to know. He wants to start this whole evening over again—get out of his car, walk in the front door, and find Karen in the kitchen preparing supper. He wants to put his arms around her and breathe her in and hold her tight. He wants everything to be the way it used to be. If he hadn't gotten home so late, maybe it would be. Maybe this is his fault.

"I'm afraid there's been an accident," Officer Fleming says, his voice grave, his eyes filled with sympathy.

He knew it. Tom feels numb.

"Your wife drives a red Honda Civic?" the officer asks.

Tom doesn't respond. This can't be happening.

The officer reads off a license plate number.

"Yes," Tom says. "That's her car." His voice sounds strange, like it's coming from somewhere else. He looks at the police officer. Time seems to have slowed down. He's going to tell him now. He's going to tell him that Karen is dead.

Officer Fleming says gently, "The driver is hurt. I don't know how badly. She's in the hospital."

Tom covers his face with his hands. She's not dead!

She's hurt, but he feels a surge of desperate hope that maybe it's not that bad. Maybe it's going to be okay. He removes his hands from his face, takes a deep, shaky breath, and asks, "What the hell happened?"

"It was a single-vehicle accident," Officer Fleming says quietly. "The car went into a utility pole, head-on."

"What?" Tom asks. "How can a car go into a pole for no reason? Karen's an excellent driver. She's never had an accident. Someone else must have caused it." Tom notices the guarded expression on the officer's face. What is he not telling him?

"There was no identification on the driver," Fleming says.

"She left her purse here. And her phone." Tom rubs his hands over his face, trying to hold himself together.

Fleming tilts his head to the side. "Is everything okay between you and your wife, Mr. Krupp?"

Tom looks at him in dismay. "Yes, of course."

"You haven't had a fight, things got a bit out of hand?"

"No! I wasn't even home."

Officer Fleming sits down in the armchair across from Tom, leans forward. "The circumstances—well, there's a slight possibility that the woman driving the car, the one who had the accident, may not be your wife."

"What?" Tom says, startled. "Why? What do you mean?"

"Since there was no identification on her, we don't

actually know for sure at this point that it was your wife driving the car, just that it's her car."

Tom stares back at him, speechless.

"The accident happened in the south end of the city, at Prospect and Davis Drive," Officer Fleming says, looking at him meaningfully.

"No way," Tom says. That was one of the worst parts of the city. Karen wouldn't be caught there in broad daylight, much less be there by herself after dark.

"Do you know of any reason why your wife, Karen, would be driving recklessly—speeding and running red lights—in that part of town?"

"What? What are you saying?" Tom looks at the police officer in disbelief. "Karen wouldn't *be* in that part of town. And she *never* goes above the speed limit—she would *never* run a red light." He slumps back against the sofa. He feels relief flood through him. "It's not my wife," he says with certainty. He knows his wife, and she would never do something like that. He almost smiles. "That's someone else. Someone must have stolen her car. Thank God!"

He looks back at the police officer, who continues to observe him with deep concern. And then he realizes, the panic instantly returning. "So where's my wife?"

The new novel by
Shari Lapena

AN
UNWANTED
GUEST

*Coming Summer 2018 from
Doubleday Canada*

For Susana, María Florencia,
Juan Manuel, Jerónimo and Sofía

For Sergio, in memoriam

The author would like to thank David Blaustein, Mary Vieites, Andrés Insaurralde, Daniel Santoro, Felix Borgonovo, Jorge Remes Lenicov, Prof. Noemí Castiñeiras, Cristina Álvarez Rodríguez, Miguel Unamuno and Alfredo Carlino for his warm poem.

Design: Christian le Comte and Sophie le Comte
© Mario J. Granero, 2003
Credits: Archivo General de la Nación; Sivul Wilensky, Colección Museo del Cine 'Pablo C. Ducrós Hicken'; Instituto Nacional de Investigaciones Históricas Eva Perón; Christian le Comte y Sophie le Comte.
Hecho el depósito que previene la Ley 11.723
ISBN 987—9479—13—0
Published by Maizal Ediciones
Muñíz 438, B1640FDB, Martínez
Buenos Aires, Argentina.
E–mail: info@maizal.com
www.maizal.com
Printed in June 2005 by Morgan Internacional.

Evita

Mario J. Granero

THIS IS THE CHRONICLE OF THE LIFE and works of an exceptional figure, who transcended Argentine frontiers and triumphed over time. Idolized by the humble and destitute; hated by her enemies, neither of them will ever forget her. She did not go past history like a beautiful meteor. She was, she made and she is history. She still influences politics and the force of the symbol she embodies, has become even more important now than it was when she was alive.

* * *

There are not many personalities like Evita, who, more than 50 years after of her death, is still remembered all over the world.

Childhood

¶*Eva, her sister
and two friends
in Junin, 1930*

MARÍA EVA DUARTE WAS BORN as the forth child of a family of five, in a small town in the Province of Buenos Aires called Los Toldos, on the 7 May 1919. She spent her childhood in Junín, having very little money to make both ends meet.

She lost her father when she was seven years old. At a very young age, she became aware of social injustice. 'Until I was eleven years old, I believed that it was natural and logical' that 'there were poor people as there was grass, and that there were rich people as there were trees', as she said in her autobiography *The Reason of my Life* published in 1951.

She then realized that 'There were poor people because the rich were far too rich', and from then on, she never found it 'natural and logical' any more. As there are certain people who have a spiritual disposition to feel beauty in a way others do not, she was born with a natural disposition to feel injustice with 'a strange and painful intensity'.

¶ Thirteen-year-old Eva, in Junin.

The 'Tragic Week', an event that became a milestone in Argentine history, happened the year she was born. Despite the popular government of President Hipólito Irigoyen, social tensions found expression in violence. The working class clashed with the establishment and the result was hate, vengeance and shootings, and jail or deportation.

Eva's Life as an Actress

¶*Evita in*
'*La Pródiga*'

SINCE SHE WAS A YOUNG GIRL, María Eva Duarte had loved everything connected with the theatre. She used to declaim poetry in primary school in Junín and when she was a student at a teachers' training college, she formed part of a group that represented plays to amuse her fellow students.

Her mother Juana Ibarguren takes her to Buenos Aires in 1934 where she starts a carrer as an actress. The huge city showed her all its faces, not only the nice ones.

She studied declamation and dramatic arts at the Women's Council. When she was 17 years old, she made her debut with a short role in a play in Eva Franco's company.

Towards 1936 she was already an experienced actress, but she was not famous. She performed small roles in important casts, joined tours round the country and took part in the theatrical season in Montevideo (Uruguay). In 1937 she made a short appearance in the film *Seconds*, together with Pedro Quartucci, a famous Argentine actor.

In 1938 she also worked as an advertising model for hairdressing salons, fur shops and boutiques.

In the year 1939 Eva Perón started working in radio serials: together with Pascual Pelliciotta she led a company in Radio Pietro. That same year she got a role in the film *The Attack of the Brave*.

The following year, she acted with Luis Sandrini in *The Most Unhappy Person in Town*; and she continued performing on the radio. In 1941 she was assigned an important role in the film *A Girlfriend in Difficulties*.

Among artists, Eva Duarte was well-known for her companionship and sense of friendship. There she experienced similar injustices to those against which

she had rebelled when she was a child, in her small town in the Province of Buenos Aires. The artists' wages always depended on the whim of managers or bosses of actors' companies. Eva reflected on the possibility of creating a trade union for actors although she knew that the beginnings of such organizations are usually painful and difficult. For artists, who worked in theatres, radios and cinemas, a trade union was something belonging to a strange and distant world.

The young and beautiful actress started reading radical newspapers that apparently faced social injustice in the world, but she soon felt that they did not reflect the reality of her country.

She realized that those doctrines imported from abroad: foreign ideas and demagogy proclaimed by these papers, lead nowhere. Yet she did not fall into that sterile trap called resignation. The red flag was still stirring up meetings full of resentment but Eva was aware that this could not turn their rebellion into positive achievements.

4 June 1943, is a decisive date in Argentine history, a military coup overthrew president Ramón Castillo. In October, a certain colonel called Juan Domingo Perón accepted office as the head of the Labour State Department, an old and inoperative institution where all workers' complaints came to a dead end.

On the 29 November, this Department, impelled with unprecedented vigour, was transformed into the Secretary of Labour and Social Security with a status similar to that of a ministry.

¶*Cover of 'Guión' magazine, 1940*

Many did not understand the change; others did not pay any notice to this episode.

At that time and for the first time, Eva Duarte's economic situation started being prosperous and she rented an apartment in an elegant neighbourhood. Towards the end of 1943 the writer Francisco Javier Muñoz Azpiri began to work with her. Together they produced a radio serial about famous women. Their immediate success forced Muñoz Azpiri to write three different episodes a day for three different radio stations.

'My Wonderful Day'

¶*Luna Park*
Stadium

ON 15 JANUARY 1944, a tremendous earthquake struck the Province of San Juan.

Apart from official help, many actors from Buenos Aires started raising funds to help relieve the needs of the victims and to cooperate with the reconstruction of the city, which had been totally destroyed. Eva Duarte was among them.

A week after the catastrophe in San Juan, a festival was organized in the Luna Park in Buenos Aires to raise funds for the victims of the terrible disaster. President General Pedro Ramírez arrived at the Luna Park together with colonel Juan Domingo Perón of whom it was already spoken of in admiration. Evita met Perón on that day. It was love at first sight.

Eva's activity on the radio was extraordinary. In one of her programmes called 'Towards a Better Future' she promoted the help carried out by the Secretary of Labour and Social Security. Perón, in charge of this Secretary, spoke about his work in her programme. He explained that it was not impossible to bring capital and labour into harmony, which up to then, had seemed totally irreconcilable.

On 9 June Muñoz Azpiri, introduced by Eva to Perón, took on the Direction of Promotion in the National Information Secretary together with a handful of young intellectuals, who promoted the bloodless social revolution that had already begun. Eva Duarte worked with Perón. She knew long before anyone else, that this man was going to be a 'man of destiny'.

'My Wonderful Day'

¶Juan Domingo Perón

'I started helping Perón and I told him with my best words: if your cause, as you say, is the cause of the people, then it does not matter how far I have to go with my sacrifice, I'll be with you until the end. He accepted my offer. That was my wonderful day.'

The Parade of the Circus was being filmed at that time. Eva Duarte played an important role in it. Sometimes she was late at the set or she had to interrupt the filming because people constantly called her from the Secretary of Social Security. These incidents caused considerable problems with the film director. It became obvious that more than radio, theatre or the cinema, she was interested in social problems, and to work next to Perón.

In 1944 Eva Duarte began her trade union activity. She was chosen president of the Actors' Association.

Much had changed in the country between 1943 and 1945. Countless trade unions had benefited from Perón's social administration and there were even some executives and managers who sympathized with him. On the other hand, those who felt displaced were looking for the right moment to topple from power the man who not only was the Secretary of Labour and Social Security, but Vice–president and Minister of War as well.

Perón was accused of appointing an old friend of the Duarte's as Director of the Post Office and was forced to resign to the three positions.

¶*Letter written in Martín García*

¶Quinta San
Vicente, 1948

17 October 1945

¶*Crowd in*
Plaza de
Mayo

ON 11 OCTOBER rumour had it that a group of captains and majors wanted to kidnap Juan Perón. Together with Eva and some friends, Perón decided to resist in his apartment. Furniture was placed against the door; and provisions were bought.

At dawn 13 October, Perón was arrested. Eva insisted on accompaning him, but she was not allowed to.

During the days in which Perón was jailed in Martín García, a small island in the Río de la Plata, Eva Duarte with a group of faithful friends, visited factories and trade unions and urged the workers to rebel. She also requested her friends to try and get an *habeas corpus* for Perón, in case they would have to leave the country.

On 16 October, Eva Duarte was cowardly beaten up by a group of people who recognized her when she was getting off a taxi in Buenos Aires. 'From that day on, I believed that it must not be very difficult to die for a cause'.

18 . Evita   Without publicity, as if it were a password, the secret spread: the workers of the city of Buenos Aires, Greater Buenos Aires, and many towns around the city, decided to free Perón. He was no longer a government representative, he was the leader of a social movement, the workers had to defend him.

¶*17 October, 1954*

At dawn of 17 October the pressure of the workers could no longer be withstood and an all-out strike was called. There had never been such a strike in the country.

Workers coming from everywhere converged on the city, silently or just singing refrains. Not a single window-pane was broken. Certain newspapers tried to degrade the workers, calling them '*descamisados*', 'the shirtless'; the workers happily accepted the word and it soon became their badge of honour.

The immense crowd that congregated in the Plaza de Mayo, the main square of Buenos Aires, made the hesitant government of President Edelmiro Farrel accept that the situation had turned impossible to control. Perón was eventually freed.

¶Supporters of Perón

Perón's first phone call, from the Military Hospital, where he had been taken to, was, naturally, to Eva.

Many people regarded the 17 October 1945 as a mere episode. But Perón, after learning from Eva Duarte what had happened during the time he had been in jail, and the circumstances of his liberation, realized the magnitude of his mission, and assumed his destiny.

From that day on, the 17 October was called the 'Day of Popular Loyalty'.

The Marriage

¶ *Marriage of
Eva and Juan
Perón, 1945*

ON 22 OCTOBER, Juan Perón and María Eva Duarte got married at the registry office in Junín.

On 10 December the religious ceremony was celebrated in the church of San Francisco in La Plata, the capital city of the Province of Buenos Aires.

As he was not holding any official position at that moment, Perón stood as a candidate to the presidency of Argentina, supported by radical and nationalistic parties, by trade union leaders and by people who had been active in other political parties. The word 'Peronism' started being used in connection with the rescued leader. Sometimes Perón smiled and said that his wife was 'too much of a peronist'.

During the inland campaign, María Eva Duarte de Perón joined her voice to the voice of 'the shirtless', proclaiming the will of the people. As it was on 17 October, Eva's fervent faith reassured him of his victory. And he was not wrong.

On 24 February 1946 in free elections, guaranteed by the impartiality of the armed forces, the ticket Perón–Quijano won over the Democratic Union.

Eva was only 26 years old. She was the wife of the President of the Republic, whom she had helped to achieve victory.

She was called '*la Señora*', some did it with servility, as it is usually the case, others only because of shyness.

She was young, beautiful, intelligent, she could have eclipsed her husband, or just limit her public appearances to receive honours wearing elegant

soirée dresses that suited her as naturally as her own skin. This not even her worst enemies dared to deny.

All this would have fulfilled the aspirations of any woman. But not Eva's. It did not take María Eva Duarte de Perón long to become something outstanding: Eva Perón, an unprecedented phenomenon in the world.

On 4 June, the anniversary of the military coup that had put an end to the so–called 'terrible decade', Perón, being a general, assumed the presidency. On the way from Congress to the Pink House, Eva accompanied the presidential procession in a car.

Not many were ready to perceive what she had done to contribute to the apotheosis of 'our Colonel', as the people who had risked so much on 17 October 1945, still called him.

Eva Perón set up her offices in the Ministry of Labour and Social Security in the building of the Town Council in the streets Hipólito Irigoyen and Perú.

¶At the country house in San Vicente, 1948

Her habit of working very late, what some government officials called a 'mania', started then. There was a window in the Ministry where the lights were turned off only at dawn.

The Eva Perón Social Help Foundation

¶Children leaving for the summer resort 'Eva Perón'

¶Eva at her desk

CERTAIN STRANGE, OUTSTANDING THINGS started happening. The Charity Society, which had existed long before, used to appoint the wife of the president as its honorary president. Since the ladies of the Society did not like Eva Perón, they found an excuse for not choosing her: she was too young. With humour Eva suggested her mother.

Nobody can deny that those ladies with distinguished family names had helped the poor for many decades. But in a country so full of contradictions as Argentina was in 1946, the help had to be given in a much larger scale. The consequence was that the ladies of the Charity Society were removed and the Society was dissolved.

As a substitute, the Social Help Foundation, an unprecedented instrument of large–scale charity was created. María Eva Duarte de Perón was the head of it and she began to work with an initial contribution of 10.000 pesos.

At that time there were two opposing ideas concerning social help: the action of the ladies of the Charity Society and the idea of the wife of the president who could not understand why the general funds of the country were not spent in shoes, food, sewing machines, hospital beds or toys.

Eva Perón was aware of this and she was able to put into practice what she called 'a new conscience in motion'. Her foundation ended up raising 200 million pesos.

*¶Inauguration
of a school*

The origin of these funds never constituted a mystery. The first 3 million pesos were a present of the Stockbrokers' Association, then the Trade Employees followed, they contributed with twice as much. Charity was legalized in Argentina at that time: whenever there was a pay raise, the first month, 'went to the Foundation'. On 8 July 1948, the legal status of the Eva Perón Social Help Foundation was recognized. Her improvised organization had been institutionalised.

A day in the life of Eva Perón was long and is not easy to describe.

In the morning a hairdresser and a manicure assisted her. Meanwhile, her private secretary read out her busy agenda: audiences, meetings, receptions.

At noon, her official activity in the Government House or in the Ministry of Labour and Social Security began: she met ministers, senators, representatives, diplomats, workers and people in need. Her meetings were not always official tasks but they always had a political background.

Who had lunch at four in the afternoon in Argentina in 1946? Only Eva. She usually arrived at the restaurant of the Employee's Home called General San Martín. At six o'clock she was back at the Ministry, if she was not supposed to attend an official ceremony. Any other woman would have called that a day but two o'clock in the morning was a normal time for her to stop working.

She would often meet her husband in the same restaurant for dinner, but they were not alone. Many politicians, trade union leaders, and mainly poets, who spontaneously composed poems paying homage to her exceptional figure, accompanied them. The poets were Horacio Rega Molina, Leopoldo Marechal, José María Castiñeira de Dios, Fermín Chávez, María Granata.

In the year 1947, Mrs. Perón became aware of the necessesity of acquiring indispensable media in order not to depend on the traditional newspapers for her campaign. For a ridiculous sum of 300.000 pesos she was able to buy the young newspaper Democracia (Democracy). The idea was to have a newspaper to inform the people that a bloodless revolution was taking place and that it was for the benefit of the majority in spite of the arguments of the minority. A group of bright journalists helped her in this important mission.

The Eva Perón Social Help Foundation

¶Eva Perón Foundation

Evita . 27

Europe

¶*Arrival
from Europe,
August 1947*

IN 1947, the people of Buenos Aires were saying goodbye to María Eva Duarte de Perón in Plaza Italia. She was leaving for Europe on a special Spanish airplane: it had a bedroom, a dressing room, a living room and a dining room and it was escorted by two Argentine airplanes. She was welcomed whererever she arrived.

In Madrid an unprecedented popular apotheosis of 200.000 people awaited her. She has been the only American personality who has attracted so much attention in Madrid.

General Francisco Franco and his wife received her at the airport of Barajas. The Spanish people had not forgotten that Argentina had sent so many ships loaded with wheat, corn, meat and other products during the post war blockade.

¶Evita after a bullfight in her honor in Spain

She participated in official receptions; visited museums and churches. Apart from her official visits, she turned up in schools, working class neighbourhoods and other places that were not included in her agenda. The head of the Spanish State honoured her with the decoration of the Great Cross of Queen Isabel la Católica. In the Oriente Square in Madrid, a festival held in her honour ended at three o'clock in the morning. There she was presented with a collection of 50 regional costumes from all over Spain. During a bullfight, the Duke of Alba invited her to attend a private reception that only members of the nobility would attend. She avoided the commitment, alleging to be 'an ordinary woman'.

Eva Perón and the big delegation that accompanied her, visited Segovia, some cities in Galicia and then Seville and Granada. In the palace of El Escorial, she declared: 'What a huge orphanage this palace would make!' Then she visited Barcelona accompanied by many members of the Spanish government.

In Rome, a multitude awaited her at the airport; the Italian chancellor, Count Sforza, welcomed her. On 27 June, the Pope granted her an audience. She arrived in the Vatican wearing a long black dress, a mantilla and her Spanish decoration. Pious XII gave her a beautiful rosary as a present.

In Paris, the Minister of Foreign Affairs received her. At the airport she had lunch with the French president Vincent Auriol. When she was invited to a restaurant in the Bois de Boulogne, the people standing on the tables, cheered her. At a party organized by

Latin Americans in Paris, she wore a beautiful gold lamé dress by Dior. She did not only go to parties, she also attended the ceremony of the signing of a treaty between Argentina and France in which Argentina granted France a loan of around 151 million pesos. From Paris, she went to the Riviera to rest and then to Switzerland.

On her way back, she landed in Río de Janeiro where she was given the highest decoration of Brazil. Even there she came into contact with trade unions, as she had done during the whole trip.

When the ship entered the port of Buenos Aires, Perón met her in the presidential yacht. They embraced in front of a cheering multitude. An important morning newspaper said about Eva's trip to

¶*Leaving the Vatican Palace, June 1947*

Europe and America: 'She has done for her country much more than any of her ambassadors. All countries received her message of love and peace: misery and hunger in the world should come to an end'.

The Feminist Movement

¶*The
National
Congress
House*

IN THE FIRST MONTHS of Perón's government, Eva created the Association for Women's Suffrage. People thought that it was just another association, but it turned out to be something really important and it took her a short time to achieve success.

She explained it with incredible clarity, 'My work in the feminist movement and social help grew, my activity with the trade unions grew. Gradually, by force of circumstance rather than by my own decision'.

She had noticed that not only workers suffered from social injustice. Women were left aside in everything concerning politics. She was not a feminist, but she sought justice for that immense sector: that of mothers, women, sisters, daughters. She started organizing the feminine branch of peronism, officially called 'Feminine Peronist Party'.

On 9 September 1947, Congress passed the law. From that day on, women could vote in Argentina.

On 23 September a huge meeting was organized to celebrate the event in the Plaza de Mayo. She made a moving announcement: 'My hands tremble holding the

¶Eva visiting the social welfare warehouse

Evita . 33

laurels that proclaim our victory. My sisters, here is, summarized in tight letters and just a few articles, a long history of struggles, set backs and hopes'. While the new voters' lists were being prepared, some voices were heard criticizing the feminine vote. Not all came from male politicians.

¶Evita lecturing in Paris

It was at that time that President general Juan Domingo Perón in order to put an end to solemnities and pompous titles, chose the simple formula Juan Perón. María Eva Duarte de Perón with the same republican simplicity was then called Eva Perón. A popular revolution required a revolutionary formula.

¶Leaving the presidential residence

Her Work

¶Model for
a memorial
representing
the shirtless

In September 1949, a plot was discovered. A small group of people wanted to kill Perón. Eva's name was also included in the list. In a way, her enemies were pointing out that she had become as important as her husband. It was true, she had organized and carried out many plans and projects.

On 26 August 1948, in the Ministry of Labour and Social Security, Eva Perón solemnly proclaimed the 'Rights for the Elderly'. In July 1949, she presided over the inaugural meeting of the First National Assembly of the Feminine Peronist Movement. Some time later, the majority of the Members of Parliament accepted a request of Eva Perón's Foundation for 70 million pesos. But the executive power (Perón himself) used his right and vetoed it. Perón's wife said: 'The veto shows the President's limitless faith in the spiritual force of the Foundation'. On 14 July 1949 the 'Children's City' was inaugurated. It was called Evita City. It was a real city with a congress, a government house, castles and, mainly, games for children. The children had started calling her Evita, a diminutive of Eva. For her this diminutive tasted of glory, and she was not wrong.

All her imagination was used to achieve active charity.

She started using a sentence that everybody was going to repeat: 'In Argentina, only children have privileges'.

Encouraged by her enthusiasm, the building of the

¶*Cover of the book 'The reason of my life'*

¶*Cover of 'The rights of the labourer'*

¶Covers of
'Peronist
World'
Magazine

Trade Unions Confederation was constructed. One of her main prides was the Nurses' Training College of the Eva Perón Foundation. On 30 December she personally inaugurated the Employee's Home 'General San Martin'.

Her feverish undertaking began at that time.

Several hospitals and educational institutions were created. She inaugurated a residential home for women who had come to Buenos Aires attracted by better wages. A virtuous prelate, Monsignor Miguel de Andrea had already built a residential home for women where they were provided with accommodation and social assistance. Monsignor De Andrea had about 40 beds; Eva Peron's building was much bigger. In Burzaco, a town in the Province of Buenos Aires, and in other towns in the Provinces of Córdoba, Santa Fé and Tucumán she inaugurated homes for the elderly, they were all called Coronel Perón. In the Province of Mendoza, the Foundation built a town, Las Cuevas, which astonished the people from Chile.

In Buenos Aires, Córdoba and Mendoza homes for students were projected and some of them were built. On the avenue Paseo Colón in the City of Buenos Aires, the Ministry of Labour and Social Security was built. Today the huge building is used as the Faculty of Engineering.

People who had never been able to travel before started visiting the holiday resorts inaugurated in Ezeiza, Chapadmalal, and Río Tercero in Córdoba.

Transport facilities to tourist centres were totally overbooked. In that way, people from the north of Argentina were able to visit the beaches in Mar del Plata; the inhabitants of Buenos Aires could see the waterfalls in Iguazú and the people from the west could enjoy the thermal baths in Santiago del Estero.

In that same year, 1949, with Eva's direct intervention, the big hospital in Avellaneda, the policlinic Presidente Perón was built.

The Foundation and the Ministry of Public Health in the hands of doctor Ramón Carrillo who was sensitive to Eva's inspirations, created a series of welfare institutions: a specialized treatment hospital for children in Terma de Reyes in the Province of Jujuy, a children's hospital in the Province of Catamarca, the clinic 17 de Octubre in Lanús, the hospital Coronel Perón in San Martin, in the Province of Buenos Aires; the hospital for children in Buenos Aires; the hospital in Ramos Mejía, the clinic in Paso de los Libres in the Province of Corrientes, the clinic in Concordia in the Province of Entre Ríos, in Mendoza, San Juan, Villa Mercedes (Province of San Luis), Santiago del Estero.

She built kindergartens in San Vicente (Province of Buenos Aires), Jujuy, Catamarca, Santiago del Estero,

¶Council at the Plaza de Mayo

Tucumán, Córdoba, Salta, La Rioja, Mendoza, San Juan, Corrientes, Comodoro Rivadavia, Paraná, Gobernador Godoy (San Juan), San Luis, Granadero Baigorria (Santa Fe) and Ezeiza. The children in Argentina had to be happy.

¶Evita greeting from a train 1950

She created the Evita Children's Tournaments, which trained top athletes. All vacant lots were turned into football fields.

Perón's government opened stores that sold to lower prices than those in traditional ones. There were a hundred in the City of Buenos Aires, and more in the Province of Buenos Aires, all of them were in charge of the Foundation.

¶The train 'Shirtless' sponta- neously dec- orated by peronists

The year 1950 began with good news: on 2 January, the austere Pope Pious XII sent her a message, thanking her for the help that Argentina had sent to Italy.

Her Illness

¶*At the
Pink House's
balcony*

SUDDENLY, when nothing led to the supposition that she might be ill, Eva Perón fainted during the inauguration of the Taxi Drivers' Trade Union and Evita School.

The Minister of Education, a respected doctor, treated her and declared his doubts on the nature of her illness.

When she was operated on appendicitis as a preventive measure, the minister discovered a process that worried him.

When Eva Perón learnt about it, she reacted temperamentally because she thought that they wanted her to give up work.

When that episode was apparently overcome, she accepted an important function in the Conference of Governors of Provinces and Territories in June 1950. There she spoke to everybody, and convinced everybody. She was an unleashed revolutionary force.

But there were also some setbacks as, for instance, the railway workers' strike in January 1951. Eva Perón went from railway station to railway station exhorting the workers: 'do not let yourselves be carried away by manoeuvres against our old colonel'. The strike was eventually called off.

On 22 August a peronist congress was carried out in the avenue 9 de Julio. It had been summoned by the Confederation of Trade Unions to request Juan Perón and Eva Perón to accept the candidacies for president and vice-president. The large multitude

44 . Evita was very disappointed because Evita did not attend the meeting alleging reasons of health.

The people called for 'companion Evita' and since they insisted, she was taken to the meeting.

She was so nervous and upset that her dialogue with 'her people' was vibrant and disjointed. The people insisted that she had to accompany her husband as vice–president.

¶*Evita with a group of pilots, 1952*

She could not make up her mind and asked for four days in order to take her decision. Then she asked for another day. In the end she begged for a couple of hours at least.

What the people did not know was that the Armed Forces did not like the initiative of the Trade Unions, they did not want a woman as vice–president.

On 31 August, at 20.30, the announcement of her renouncement was made on the radio. She pointed out: 'I don't give up my work; I only reject the honour. I will continue being the humble collaborator of general Perón. All I request is that history should remember that beside the general there was a woman who spoke to him about the hopes and the needs of the people. That woman was called Evita'.

On 28 September an military coup failed.

It had been organized by the army, the navy, the air force and certain civil groups. Officially, the implications of the coup were toned down. But everybody knew that despite Eva's renouncement, certain groups did not want to have Perón as president any more.

The people gathered again in the Mayo Square and because of Evita's temperament, it was impossible for her to remain silent pretending not to see what was happening. Although she was already very ill, she made a plaintive call to her people, she asked them to gather round 'the old colonel'. Her voice, shaken with emotion, revealed an extraordinary physical effort. ¶*Evita*

Her sixth 17 October came, and she wanted to *17 October* attend the meeting one more time. The people had *1951* filled the Plaza de Mayo and during the meeting, she

was given together with some trade union leaders, the medal of 'Peronist Loyalty'.

She was crying when she spoke to the people and when she received her medal. She was too weak to stand by herself, the president had to hold her all the time.

On 2 November she was taken to the Hospital in Avellaneda. A large crowd awaited the arrival of the ambulance of the Foundation.

On the next day she was operated on by the eminent Argentine doctor Ricardo Finochietto and a famous foreign specialist.

The operation confirmed what the doctors had known from the very beginning, she had cancer.

After what she thought was a period of convalescence, she prepared to participate in a historical event to which she was intimately linked: women were going to vote for the first time in Argentina.

On Election Day, on 11 November, Eva Perón, who was still hospitalised, wanted to vote as well, so in the afternoon, the ballot box was taken to the hospital for her to put her vote.

Argentine women not only voted for the first time, but from then on, they were able to hold political positions as well. Seven women were elected for the Senate and 26 for the House of Representatives, three of them came from the territories of Chubut, Tierra del Fuego and Misiones.

In December she went out for the first time after her operation, during her short outing, she was permanently held by Perón.

On 24 January 1952, the Constituent Convention of La Pampa decided that the Province should be called Eva Perón. Congress, in an extraordinary session, agreed to call Eva Perón the Spiritual Leader of the Nation.

On 1 May, she delivered her last speech: 'I will be with my people, dead or alive'.

On 4 June, Perón assumed the second presidency. With exceptional integrity, she stood in the presidential car, the whole itinerary from Congress to the Pink House. There, while the ministers were taking their oaths, she fainted.

Her delicate health was no longer a secret. The people, deeply affected, filled the churches during the month of July, praying for her recovery. The country suffered a mood of sadness and sorrow.

The End

*¶People
paying the
respects, 1952*

ON 26 JULY 1952, at 4 p.m., she went into a coma, at 8.15 p.m., she came to and did not lose consciousness till the end.

At 8.25 p.m. a sad voice announced to the whole country that Eva Perón, 'the Spiritual Leader of the Nation' had 'entered immortality'.

Pedro Ara, a famous doctor embalmed her body.

The next morning, her corpse was taken in an ambulance of the Foundation to the round room in the first floor of the Ministry of Labour and Social Security, where it laid in state for several days. The anguish of the people was overwhelming.

During endless days and nights, they waited in over one kilometre long cues, in order to enter the funeral chapel, sometimes under heavy rain. Immense mountains of flowers surrounded the building of the Ministry. Old men and women and children fainted; nurses, doctors and soldiers served coffee and sandwiches. All official activities were adjourned.

On 1 August the coffin was transferred to the House of Parliament and from there, to the Building of the Trade Unions Confederation. A gun carriage was used; the Armed Forces and 16 workers in their work clothes escorted it.

A month after her death, the trade unions organized a night procession, headed by Perón.

The leader had assumed the presidency of the

The End

¶Headlines on 27 July 1952

Evita . 49

Foundation and he became the head of the feminine branch of his party. For some days he symbolically occupied Eva's office in the Ministry of Labour and Social Security.

Perón also decided that all the letters to the Foundation should be addressed to the name of Eva Perón, as if she were still there. The government also decided to build a monument to commemorate her.

The 17 October 1952 was the first 'Day of Popular Loyalty' without her. The doors to the balcony of the Pink House remained closed. Her recorded voice was heard; she read a chapter of 'My last will' of her unpublished book *My Message*.

One would think that after her death a cycle would be closed. But nothing the like happened, on the contrary, her charismatic force defied time.

After the military coup that overthrew Perón and his régime, her corps was taken away from the building of the Confederation of Trade Unions and during many years nobody knew where it had been placed. *The End*

Some imagined that her body had been incinerated and tossed into the sea; others thought that it had been taken and buried abroad.

The truth was that her body had been taken to Italy and buried there. In the year 1971 it was given back to Perón, who was still living in Madrid.

Her remains lie in the Cemetery of the Recoleta in Buenos Aires since 1974.

Fifty years have elapsed and Eva Perón has become a myth. Serious and objective sociological studies have been written about her life and her works. Musicals and movies have been made about her life.

Meanwhile, the grateful people who adored her in life still kindle their intact fervour. Eva Perón is now much more than politics and social conflicts.

¶Workers carrying the gun carriage

She is Argentine history, America's and the world's; although she only sought to be 'a humble woman of a big country'.

Life in Pictures

¶*Evita during a military parade, 1948 and a picture by S. Wilensky (right)*

¶Evita in a
film

56 . Evita

¶*Dressed by*
Christian
Dior, 1950

¶*Eva get-
ting ready
for a fox
hunt*

¶*Crowds cheering Eva in Santiago de Compostela*

¶*Eva's
arrival at
Milán air-
port, June
1947*

¶*Dramatic
speech on 17
October, 1951*

¶*Workers
accompany
the coffin to
the* CGT,
1952

Index

¶*Evita by*
D. Santoro